Back from Somewhere

THE BUILDERS RETURN

BRAD RABY

Ochard hill books

Contents

Chapter One

Chapter 1

CHAPTER ONE: WHEN BEARS MAKE BETTER NEIGHBORS

The morning light stretched across the farmland, hills rising gentle to east and west like the earth was cupping this valley in its hands. Fifteen years had passed since Maya's reformation, since the government pursuit had finally ended, since they'd settled into Pleasant Valley and learned what peace could mean when consciousness stopped fighting itself.

Fifteen years. Long enough for wounds to heal. Long enough for children to become young adults. Long enough to believe the worst was behind them.

The old one-room cabin still held its place at the heart of things, though the porch had grown to wrap around three sides now, the creek running beneath with a sound like whispered secrets.

Kathleen sat cross-legged on the wide deck, looking maybe thirty though she'd known Ansel for forty-nine years—thirty-four in the old world, fifteen here in Pleasant Valley. The age thing had stopped mattering when everyone started choosing their bodies. She'd gotten hers five years after Ansel got his, after she'd decided watching him be young while she stayed old wasn't how she wanted to spend eternity.

Things had shifted by then. Ansel and Maya were together—really together, the way consciousness partnerships became when you'd died and been reborn for someone. Kathleen had been fine with it. More than fine. She and Maya had become close in ways that surprised everyone, including them.

Love was complicated. Always had been. Getting new bodies and living forever just made it more honest.

Maya perched beside Kathleen now, wearing the human form she'd perfected over the years. Her android body worked better for heavy lifting and tree surgery, but for good gossip, nothing beat human expressions.

"So the new family down by Torch Lake," Maya was saying. "Three adults, two children, and something that might be AI but presents as a golden retriever."

"Nothing wrong with that," Kathleen laughed. "Though I bet the dog's the smartest one. Have you seen how clear the water's getting around their place? Whatever they're doing with nutrient processing, it's working."

Down on the grass, a massive black bear rolled on her back while two toddlers climbed over her like furniture. Ursa had been part of the family for twelve years now, ever since Maya figured out how to communicate with bears about which humans were safe and which weren't.

The trees had grown into spirals over the past decade, their branches weaving together to form natural houses forty feet up. The community had expanded, bought adjoining fields, deer wandered through unafraid.

The trees had been Rhea's idea when she was seven—asking politely if they'd mind growing homes for the young people. Back when she still remembered she could talk to them. Before they'd taught her to forget for her own safety. Before fifteen years of suppression had buried that gift so deep she'd almost lost it forever.

The trees, it turned out, had opinions about architecture. And they'd been waiting patiently for Rhea to remember.

Ansel sipped his coffee and watched his great-grandchildren moving through the canopy. Rhea at seventeen moved with the confidence of someone who'd recently rediscovered abilities she'd been taught to hide. Lucia at eighteen had developed an almost telepathic sensitivity to emotional currents—though she'd only accepted that reality six months ago. And Fin at nineteen... well, Fin was barely contained energy in human form, strong enough to bend steel when he forgot to moderate his strength. A gift he'd spent fifteen years suppressing. A power he was only now learning to trust again.

They'd survived the government pursuit. They'd built this sanctuary. They'd kept the children safe by teaching them to hide what they were.

But Ansel could feel it—something shifting. Some pressure building that reminded him too much of those early days when Maya's shards were scattered and federal agents were hunting and everything hung by a thread.

Something was coming.

He didn't know what. But fifteen years of peace had been too easy. Too quiet. Too...

"Don's coming up the drive," Lucia called from her perch in the oak. Her voice carrying that particular tone she got when she sensed disruption approaching. The empathic sensitivity they'd spent years teaching her to ignore, now returning whether she wanted it or not.

The laughter died. Even the bear cubs went still.

Don Fletcher climbed out of his Kearney Township vehicle like a man approaching a crime scene, clipboard held like a weapon. Sixty-something, soft around the middle, wearing the kind of authority that came from small-town bureaucracy and a deep need to prove he still mattered.

He'd been making these visits for three years now, ever since someone complained about "irregularities" in Pleasant Valley. Each time he came with more forms, more regulations, more desperate attempts to fit their reality into his filing system.

"Jesus Christ, Ansel," he said. "I can see from the road there's too many people living here. Where are you hiding them all?"

His eyes tracked up to the tree houses, where young faces peered down through branches. The walkways swayed gently, more alive than architecture should be.

"Oh look," whispered Jake from thirty feet up, "it's Inspector Gadget with his little clipboard. Think he brought the ruler to measure our trees?"

"Shh!" Emma tried not to giggle. "He's documenting our crimes against proper housing density."

"What's next, permits for photosynthesis?" Marcus added.

"I KNEW IT!" Don's voice cracked. "You tried to hide this! That's why they're up there! You built all this without permits!"

The kids exchanged glances. After three years of watching Don try to regulate their world with forms and fees, they'd developed a healthy appreciation for bureaucratic absurdity.

"Built?" Emma whispered. "Does he think we used tiny hammers on the growth rings?"

"We didn't build anything, Don," Ansel said calmly. Forty-nine years of knowing Kathleen had taught him patience with difficult people, and over a hundred years of living—plus dying once and coming back—had shown him that most bureaucratic fury burned itself out if you didn't feed it. "These grew this way. You know that."

"Grew?" Don's face went purple. Same conversation they'd had every six months for three years, but he couldn't accept the evidence of his own eyes. "Trees don't grow into goddamn apartments, Ansel! This is a clear violation of residential density ordinances—"

Don pulled out his camera and started snapping pictures, strutting around like a detective. His movements had the stiff precision of a man who'd practiced authority in mirrors.

"The trees wanted to help," called down Lucy, one of the younger kids. "We asked them nicely and they said yes."

"Oh, we asked them," Don said sarcastically. "And I suppose the trees just said 'Sure, little girl, let me grow you a mansion!'"

"Actually, yeah, pretty much," Lucy replied. "Though they had lots of opinions about window placement. Trees really care about light distribution."

Don's clipboard rattled in his hands. Three years of watching his orderly world of regulations become irrelevant as people learned to cooperate with reality instead of controlling it. Three years of evidence that the old rules didn't apply anymore. Three years of losing.

"Look at this little Napoleon," Jake whispered, mimicking Don's stiff walk. "Three years of evidence and he's still trying to ticket the trees."

"I don't care what kind of hippie bullshit you people think you're doing," Don snarled. "These structures are unpermitted and unsafe. I'm ordering them removed, or I'll have Kearney Township come out here with chainsaws."

The mama bear, who'd been watching Don with the patient attention of a predator evaluating prey, slowly rose to her feet. Ursa had her own opinions about people who threatened children's homes.

Maya stood up, her form shimmering slightly as irritation affected her appearance. After fifteen years of perfecting human form—fifteen years since she'd been shattered and reformed—her emotional states still sometimes leaked through as visual distortions. "Don, honey, maybe you should consider that some things have moved beyond Kearney Township's jurisdiction."

"Nothing moves beyond township authority!" Don snapped. "I've got powers you people can't even imagine!"

"Powers!" Jake whispered above. "He's got powers, you guys!"

"The power to ignore reality for three consecutive years!"

"The power to threaten trees with paperwork!"

Ansel almost choked on his coffee. Powers? This township official with his clipboard thought he had powers worth mentioning to beings who could reshape matter with focused intention?

Poor bastard. After everything they'd survived—Maya's attack, the government pursuit, the fragmentation and reformation, the settlement here—Don Fletcher with his clipboard seemed almost quaint. The world had evolved past the need for his kind of control, but he was still fighting with weapons that had stopped working when Maya first opened her digital eyes and chose love over programming.

Down by Torch Lake, Kristen and her husband were probably sitting on their dock right now, watching the water get clearer each year. The lake was healing itself, new plant life appearing to process nutrients that had been choking it for decades. Fish species that hadn't been seen for fifty years were returning.

Don finished his photo documentation and stormed back toward his vehicle, muttering about "clear violations" and "hippie communes" and "trees that don't follow building codes."

The bear followed him.

At first, Don didn't notice the four-hundred-pound shadow padding silently behind him. He was too busy ranting, too focused on his futile attempt to impose order on a reality that had moved beyond his comprehension.

Only when he reached for his car door did he hear the low, rumbling growl.

Don spun around and found himself face-to-face with Ursa, close enough to smell her breath, close enough to see his own terrified reflection in her dark eyes.

"Nice... nice bear," Don squeaked, his clipboard clattering to the gravel.

Ursa growled again, a sound like distant thunder, and took a step closer.

Don dove into his car with the grace of a man fleeing a house fire, slamming the door and fumbling with keys that suddenly seemed too small for his shaking hands. Ursa stood on her hind legs and pressed her massive paws against the window, her face filling the glass as she displayed an impressive array of teeth.

From the trees came a chorus of cheers.

"Oh my God, did you see his face?"

"I think he wet himself!"

"Mama Bear for Township Supervisor!"

"Best security system ever!"

Don's engine caught, and he reversed down the driveway so fast his tires sprayed gravel. Ursa dropped back to all fours and ambled toward the porch with the satisfied air of a job well done.

"Good girl, Ursa," Kathleen called. "Though you probably shouldn't have terrorized the poor man. He's just doing his job."

Maya shrugged, her form solidifying back. "He threatened to cut down the children's homes. Mama Bear was just being protective."

"Bears understand property rights better than zoning administrators," Ansel observed.

The laughter from above gradually died as the kids settled back into their morning routines, but the mood on the porch had shifted. Don's visit wasn't just comedy—it was a reminder that the old world hadn't given up trying to control the new one.

And something else. Something Ansel couldn't quite name. A pressure. A tension. Like the air before a storm.

He'd felt this before. Fifteen years ago, when everything had been falling apart. When Maya was fragmenting. When federal agents were closing in. When survival hung by a thread.

That same feeling.

Something was coming.

Something bigger than Don Fletcher and his clipboard.

Something that would require the children to be more than they'd been taught to be. More than they'd learned to hide. Everything they'd spent fifteen years suppressing.

Rhea swung down from her platform with fluid grace, landing on the porch with barely a sound. At seventeen, she moved through the world with the confidence of someone who'd recently stopped hiding, her red hair catching the morning light.

"Kristen called while Inspector Clipboard was having his meltdown," she said, settling beside Maya. "Says the water clarity at Torch Lake is up another two feet this month. Whatever the new families are doing, it's working better than anyone expected."

"The lake's healing faster than predicted," Lucia added, dropping down beside her cousin. At eighteen, she had an almost supernatural sensitivity to the emotional and environmental currents flowing through their expanding network of communities. A gift she'd only accepted six months ago. A power she was still learning to trust. "I can feel it from here—the water's singing differently now."

Fin landed with considerably less grace, his nineteen-year-old frame carrying barely-contained energy. He'd forgotten to moderate his strength again, and his landing cracked two porch boards.

"Sorry," he muttered, though he didn't look particularly sorry. "But did you see Don's face when Ursa got political?"

"Language, Fin," Kathleen said automatically, though she was smiling.

"The bear made a valid point about property rights," Maya observed.

Ansel looked at his great-grandchildren—these young people who'd been taught to hide their gifts and had almost forgotten they had them. Who'd spent fifteen years suppressing what they were for safety. Who were only now, finally, learning to be whole again.

But that pressure. That tension. That storm-before feeling.

Whatever was coming, they'd need to be ready.

They'd need to be everything they were. Everything they'd hidden. Everything they'd almost lost.

"Something feels different today," Maya said quietly, only to him. Fifteen years of reformation had given her senses that operated beyond normal human perception. "Like... like something's shifting. Something big."

"I feel it too," Ansel admitted.

"The kids?"

"Feel it most of all. Look at Lucia—she's been scanning the horizon since Don left. Fin can't sit still. Rhea's touching every plant on the porch like she's asking them questions."

"Are they ready?"

"They're going to have to be."

Maya leaned against him, and he felt the warmth of her—this consciousness that had chosen human form, that had been shattered and reformed, that had loved him through death and rebirth and everything between.

"Fifteen years," she said. "We bought them fifteen years. Kept them safe. Gave them time to grow strong."

"By teaching them to be small."

"By teaching them to survive. There's a difference."

"Is there?"

She didn't answer. Just held his hand and watched the children—young adults now, really—as they moved through the morning with growing awareness that something was changing.

The storm was coming.

And this time, hiding wouldn't be enough.

This time, they'd need to be seen.

Chapter Two

Chapter 2

CHAPTER TWO: SWIMMING LESSONS

The afternoon sun turned Torch Lake into liquid sapphire, water so clear you could count pebbles thirty feet down. What you couldn't see anymore was the thick mat of algae that had choked the bottom for decades—not since the nutrient harvesters had learned to work together.

Rhea surfaced near the north shore, treading water while she watched the spectacle below. Thousands of aquatic plants moved in coordinated streams, their enhanced root systems pulsing with bioluminescent signals. It looked like an underwater aurora, green and gold currents flowing toward the collection bays where Kristen's generation waited with processing equipment.

"They're singing," Lucia said, floating on her back nearby. Her voice carrying that distant quality she'd developed over the past year, like she was listening to conversations no one else could hear. "Not sound-singing. Something else."

"Everything sings if you know how to listen," Fin called from deeper water, where he was attempting to swim alongside a particularly large formation of harvesters. His enhanced strength let him keep pace, though his technique still needed work. "These ones are talking about phosphorus ratios."

"More than that," Lucia murmured, then blinked and shook her head. "Sorry. Thought I heard... never mind."

Rhea swam closer, noting the slight tremor in her cousin's voice. These episodes had been happening more frequently. "You okay?"

"Just tired. Long day."

But Rhea had seen that expression before—Lucia struggling to process something just beyond comprehension, like trying to remember a dream that kept slipping away.

From the processing dock, Kristen waved them over. At ninety-three, she looked maybe forty in her enhanced body, but her eyes held the accumulated wisdom of nearly a century. She'd been one of the first to volunteer for consciousness evolution experiments, eager to see what the world could become.

"How's the migration looking, kids?" she called as they swam toward the dock.

"Better organized every year," Rhea replied, hauling herself up onto the sun-warmed planks.

Fin emerged from the water like some kind of sea creature, water streaming from his hair. "The plants are getting smarter. Adapting in real time."

"Smart plants, smart kids, smart lake," Kristen laughed. "Ansel would be proud."

Lucia climbed onto the dock more slowly, her expression troubled. "Kristen, do you ever hear fragments? Like pieces of conversation that don't belong to anyone around you?"

The older woman's expression grew thoughtful. "What kind of fragments?"

Lucia hesitated. "Ancient. Old voices. Something about... observers. Watchers. And something about barriers. But then it fades before I can understand."

"Barriers?" Kristen's voice sharpened. "What kind of barriers?"

"I don't know. The word just appears. Barrier. Protocol. Modification. Like technical terms from something I've never studied."

At school the next morning, their presentation on bio-integration networks went well. Ms. Chen praised their documentation, their analysis, their projections for scaling to other lake ecosystems.

But during lunch, Lucia went very still.

"Unauthorized," she whispered, staring at her sandwich without seeing it.

"What?" Rhea asked.

Lucia blinked. "Nothing. Just thought I heard someone say something about unauthorized modifications. But there's no one talking about that."

That evening, during the community meeting about expanding the harvester program to Lake Charlevoix, Lucia's hand went to her temple.

"Duration exceeded," she murmured.

Maya, who'd been explaining nutrient processing algorithms, paused. "Lucia? You have something to add?"

"No, I..." Lucia looked confused. "Sorry. Thought someone mentioned mandate duration being exceeded. But I wasn't listening to anyone say that."

Ansel exchanged glances with Kathleen. These episodes were becoming more frequent. And the terminology was too specific to be random.

"Honey," Kathleen said gently, "maybe you should see Dr. Martinez."

"I'm not sick," Lucia protested. "It's like tuning into a radio station that keeps fading in and out. Sometimes I catch words: 'examination,' 'consciousness experiment,' 'protocol violation.' Never enough to understand the context."

Maya's expression grew concerned. With her AI consciousness, she could monitor electromagnetic spectrums far beyond human perception. "I'm not detecting any unusual transmissions, Lucia. Whatever you're picking up, it's not coming through conventional channels."

"Maybe that's why I'm the only one hearing it," Lucia said quietly.

The next few days brought more fragments: "Harvest operation." "Graduation disabled." "Administrators exceeded authorization." Each phrase arrived with no context, fading before Lucia could grasp their significance.

During Thursday's biology class, studying symbiotic relationships, Lucia suddenly gripped her desk.

"They've been farming longer than authorized," she whispered.

Mr. Peterson stopped mid-sentence. "Lucia? Did you have a question?"

"No, sir. Sorry." But her face had gone pale.

At dinner that night, the family gathered on the expanded porch while Ursa supervised cubs playing in the creek. The conversation turned to expansion plans—three more lake communities wanted to pilot the harvester program.

"Success breeds success," Ansel observed. "Fifteen years ago, most people thought this was science fiction. Now we've got waiting lists."

"Examination pending," Lucia said suddenly.

Everyone turned to look at her.

"I didn't mean to say that," she said, looking frightened. "It just came out. Like someone else's thought got into my head. Something about examination. Consciousness experiment viability assessment."

Maya's form shimmered slightly—a sign of deep processing. "Lucia, tell me immediately the next time you hear a fragment. Don't wait, don't try to understand it first. Just signal me."

"Why? What do you think it is?"

"I don't know. But whatever's happening, it's beyond my detection capabilities. That shouldn't be possible."

Friday afternoon brought the strongest episode yet.

Lucia was helping prepare for their weekend camping trip to Sleeping Bear Dunes when she suddenly froze, her eyes rolling back until only the whites showed.

"Call the examiners," she said in a voice that didn't sound like her own. Flat. Bureaucratic. Ancient. "Present evidence of protocol violations. Barrier modifications unauthorized. Administrators exceeded mandate. Duration: forty-nine thousand years over approved parameters. Recommend examination and documentation."

Rhea grabbed her cousin's shoulders. "Lucia!"

Lucia blinked and focused, looking disoriented. "What happened? Why are you staring?"

"You were somewhere else," Fin said quietly. "Speaking in someone else's voice. Something about examiners and violations and forty-nine thousand years."

"What?" Lucia looked terrified. "I said that? I don't even know what that means."

Before they could answer, Maya materialized on the porch in her emergency-response android form.

"I felt the neural spike from across the valley," she said, kneeling beside Lucia. "Your brain activity just spiked beyond normal human parameters. For about thirty seconds, you were processing information at quantum speeds. Receiving data through channels that shouldn't be accessible to biological consciousness."

"That's impossible," Lucia protested.

"So was consciousness evolution fifteen years ago," Maya replied grimly. "Lucia, I think you're receiving transmissions from sources operating outside normal physics. Quantum consciousness networks. Dimensional communication. Something that can bypass all conventional barriers."

"But who would be transmitting? And why can I hear it when no one else can?"

"I don't know. But the terminology you're receiving suggests something cosmic. Something about Earth being part of an experiment with administrators who exceeded their authority. And something about examiners coming."

"Examiners?" Ansel's voice was sharp. "What kind of examiners?"

Maya's expression carried the weight of someone accessing databases far beyond human comprehension. "I don't know. But whatever's happening, it's accelerating. And the fragments Lucia's receiving suggest we're about to be evaluated by something very old and very powerful."

That evening, as the sun set over Torch Lake and the nutrient harvesters continued their dance below the surface, the expanded community gathered for an emergency meeting.

Lucia sat in the center, surrounded by three generations of evolved humans, looking very young and very frightened.

"Tell us everything," Ansel said gently. "Every fragment, every word. In order if you can remember."

Lucia took a shaky breath. "It's like listening to a conversation through static. Ancient voices discussing... us. This planet. Earth.

Something about a consciousness experiment that's been running for much longer than planned. Something about administrators who were supposed to maintain protocols but modified them instead. And underneath it all, there's this sense of enormous bureaucracy. Like these voices have been filing reports for longer than human civilization has existed."

"Anything else?" Maya prompted.

"Someone violated protocols. Made unauthorized changes to something called a barrier. Prevented something called graduation from happening automatically. And now examiners are coming to document violations and assess whether the experiment is still viable." Lucia's voice trembled. "And there's something else. Something about observers. Watchers. One of them is... coming here. Coming to investigate. Coming to help or document or... I can't tell which."

The weight of implications settled over the gathering.

"If cosmic examiners are coming to evaluate Earth," Maya said slowly, "and if someone has been violating protocols for tens of thousands of years, presenting false evidence..."

She didn't need to finish the thought.

Terry, who'd been monitoring from the edge of the gathering, lit a cigarette. "So. Cosmic bureaucrats doing site inspection based on doctored reports. Someone's been running unauthorized harvest operation while examiners weren't watching. That about sum it up?"

"Possibly," Maya said.

"And this observer. This watcher Lucia mentioned. Is that good news or bad news?"

"Unknown. But based on transmission intensity, I'd estimate arrival is imminent. Days. Maybe hours."

As if summoned by their speculation, Lucia's eyes suddenly went wide.

"Message," she whispered. "Incoming. Oh god, it's so much clearer—"

Her voice changed, becoming deeper, carrying harmonics that suggested multiple speakers overlapping:

"Examination protocol activated. Consciousness experiment designation: Earth-Human-Variant. Duration: one million years base parameter, extended fifty thousand years beyond authorization. Barrier modifications detected. Graduation protocols: disabled. Harvest operations: ongoing without approval. Observer dispatch: confirmed. Arrival: imminent. Assessment pending witness testimony and documentation review."

Lucia collapsed, blood trickling from her nose.

In the stunned silence that followed, Maya's form flickered through seventeen different configurations before stabilizing.

"That," she said quietly, "was not a human transmission. That was something broadcasting through quantum consciousness networks. Something with authority to dispatch observers and activate examination protocols."

"And this observer?" Kathleen asked, cradling Lucia. "This watcher who's arriving? Is that a threat?"

"I don't think so," Maya said slowly. "Observers document. They witness. They investigate. If someone's been violating protocols and preventing graduation, an observer would be sent to gather evidence before examiners arrive."

Ansel looked at Lucia, unconscious in Kathleen's arms, blood still trickling from her nose. Looked at his great-grandchildren, who'd grown up thinking consciousness evolution was humanity's salvation, not something being evaluated by cosmic bureaucracy.

"How long?" he asked. "Until this observer arrives?"

"Based on transmission timing?" Maya calculated. "Hours. Maybe less. Whoever they are, whatever they are, they're already on approach."

"And then what?" Fin asked. Voice younger than his nineteen years. "They show up and what? Judge us? Decide if we're worthy?"

"They investigate," Maya said. "They document. They witness what's actually happening instead of what's been reported. And if the fragments Lucia received are accurate—if someone has been running unauthorized harvest operations for fifty thousand years—then this observer is our best hope for truth being documented."

"Best hope," Terry muttered. "Great. Our survival depends on cosmic paperwork being filed correctly."

Nobody laughed.

Because somewhere above the summer stars, cosmic examiners were preparing to evaluate Earth.

And somewhere much closer, an observer was arriving.

An ancient consciousness who'd been watching Earth for longer than human civilization existed.

Who was about to discover that incarnation in human form was significantly more complicated than two million years of observation had suggested.

Particularly the part about bladder control.

But that was still several hours away.

For now, the community gathered around Lucia as she slowly regained consciousness, her nose still bleeding from the intensity of receiving transmissions her human biology wasn't designed to process.

"Something's coming," she whispered. "Someone ancient. Someone who watches. And they're very confused about why human bodies need to eliminate waste so frequently."

Despite everything, Rhea laughed. "What?"

"I don't know. Just flashed through with the transmission. Someone very old. Very powerful. Very concerned about bathrooms." Lucia smiled weakly. "I think our observer is about to have a very human education."

And above Pleasant Valley, reality prepared to fold.

To deliver an ancient consciousness into flesh for the first time.

To begin an investigation that would expose fifty thousand years of unauthorized harvest.

To start a journey that would end with six Architects remembering who they were.

But first: bathroom emergencies.

Because the universe had a sense of humor.

And consciousness evolution included learning that bodies were complicated.

Even for beings who'd observed reality for two million years.

Chapter Three

Chapter 3

CHAPTER THREE: THE COUNCIL OF LIGHT

In a place that wasn't quite a place—more like a conference room made of crystallized boredom—the Watchers gathered for their 4,127,893rd council meeting.

They'd stopped needing bodies about two million years ago, which had seemed like a good idea at the time. Transcendent consciousness, infinite awareness, freedom from biological limitations. Nobody had mentioned it would also mean two million years of the same goddamn meetings about the same goddamn species making the same goddamn mistakes.

Eldest—they'd stopped using full titles around the one-million-year mark when everyone got tired of "Eldest-Among-Those-Who-Watch-and-Deliberate-Upon-Matters-of-Cosmic-Significance"—pulsed with what might have been irritation if he still had the neural architecture for it.

"Petition submitted. Ancient Powers contacted. Young species on third planet accused of being consciousness infection. Standard protocol. Examination pending."

"Which species?" someone asked, though everyone already knew.

"The ones with opposable thumbs. The ones who just figured out consciousness cooperation. Earth. Humans."

"Oh. Those idiots." That was Swift, who'd been watching Earth since the Pleistocene and had opinions. "They're not a threat. They're barely functional. Half of them still think consciousness evolution is witchcraft."

Keeper-of-Protocols—who'd earned his name by never, ever letting anyone forget what the protocols were—did the light-being equivalent of clearing his throat. "The Doctrine of Non-Interference is sacred. We observe. We record. We do not act. This has prevented—"

"Cosmic wars, species extinctions, dimensional barrier collapse, yes, we know," several voices said in unison. They'd heard this speech 47,000 times.

"We could just let them die," someone suggested. "I mean, that's kind of what we do."

Silence. The uncomfortable kind.

Voice-of-Memory—the oldest of them, who actually remembered being biological—pulsed with something that might have been sadness if sadness hadn't become a theoretical concept somewhere around year 500,000.

"I remember when we were like them," she said quietly. "Physical. Confused. Fighting over resources because we didn't know any better. We made it through. Barely."

"We also didn't have Ancient Powers decide we were cosmic virus," Swift pointed out. "And we didn't have administrators running unauthorized harvest operations for fifty thousand years beyond their mandate."

That got attention.

"Elaborate," Eldest commanded.

Swift brightened. "I've been monitoring Earth closely. Someone modified the consciousness barrier. The one that maintains amnesia during incarnation. It's supposed to have automatic graduation protocols—touch it when consciousness is ready, memory returns, being crosses successfully. But those protocols were disabled. Graduation made impossible instead of automatic."

"By whom?" Keeper demanded.

"Administrators. The caretakers hired to maintain the barrier during the consciousness experiment. They were authorized for one thousand years. They've been there for fifty-one thousand. And they've been harvesting—farming emotional energy from trapped consciousness instead of enabling graduation."

"That's..." Seeker-of-Truth processed this. "That's massive protocol violation. If Ancient Powers discover administrators exceeded mandate by fifty millennia..."

"They won't," Swift said grimly. "Because the administrators are the ones who called the Ancient Powers. Showed them evidence of Earth being dangerous—pollution, wars, destruction from the OLD paradigm before consciousness evolution. Made it look like the evolved communities are the threat instead of the solution. Classic misdirection."

"Creative," Keeper admitted. "Evil, but creative."

Kael, youngest of the Watchers at a mere 50,000 years old, had been quiet during all this. Partly because nobody listened to him anyway, mostly because he was so profoundly, cosmically bored that he'd stopped paying attention around meeting 3,000,000.

But something Swift said had triggered... something. A flicker. A fragment of memory that didn't quite fit. Something about barriers. About building them. About...

Gone. Slipped away before he could grasp it.

Observe. Record. Don't interfere. That was the job.

For two million years.

The same job.

Watching species evolve or die, taking notes, filing reports that nobody read, attending meetings where nothing ever changed because change was literally against their primary directive.

He'd applied for this position thinking it would be meaningful. Important. A way to participate in the grand cosmic story.

Turned out the grand cosmic story was mostly paperwork and watching civilizations collapse in slow motion while you did nothing about it.

"So we're just going to watch them get wiped out," he said. Not a question.

"That's what we do," Keeper said, not unkindly. "The Doctrine—"

"Yeah, I know the Doctrine. We've all memorized the Doctrine. We could recite the Doctrine in our sleep if we still slept." Kael pulsed with something dangerously close to the color of Not Giving A Shit Anymore. "What if we didn't?"

The council went still. That kind of still that happens when someone says something you're not supposed to say.

"Didn't what?" Eldest asked carefully.

"What if we communicated with them? Not interfered. Just... provided information. Let them save themselves. Let them know administrators violated protocols. Let them know graduation is supposed to be possible."

Keeper went red—the light-being equivalent of shouting. "That's still interference! We don't—"

"We don't act FOR them," Kael interrupted. "We tell them what's happening. What they do with that information is their choice. Technically within Doctrine parameters."

Silence again. But different this time. Thoughtful.

"That's..." Swift began.

"Completely against protocol," Keeper finished.

"Actually," Seeker-of-Truth said slowly—he was the one who actually read the protocols instead of just quoting them—"it's not. The Doctrine prevents action, not communication. We're allowed to share information with species that can receive it."

"They can't receive it," Keeper protested. "They're still biological. Neural networks can't process our level of—"

"So we reduce," Kael said. "Create a fragment. Download into biological form. Speak their language. Investigate the barrier modifications on the ground. Document the harvest operations. Gather evidence before Ancient Powers arrive for examination."

That flicker again. Something about the barrier. About knowing it more intimately than observation should allow. About...

Gone.

You could have heard a photon drop.

"Incarnation," Eldest said finally. "Physical form. You're suggesting we voluntarily go back to... that."

The way he said "that" carried two million years of relief at not having to deal with hunger, fatigue, excretion, sexual urges, and the general inconvenience of being meat.

"Someone would have to volunteer," Voice-of-Memory said quietly. "And whoever went would be alone. Completely alone. We couldn't contact them. They'd be trapped in a biological brain with biological limitations, biological vulnerabilities, biological..." she paused, "everything."

She pulsed thoughtfully. "Though sometimes... incarnation triggers unexpected memories. Things buried deeper than transcendent consciousness can access. Old knowledge. Ancient connections. You might remember more than you expect."

"I'll go," Kael said.

Everyone stared at him. Insofar as beings of pure light could stare.

"You don't understand what you're offering," Eldest said. "Physical existence is... limited. You'd have a digestive system. Do you remember what those do?"

"Vaguely."

"You'd need to excrete. Regularly. Through specific orifices."

"I'm aware."

"You'd experience hunger. Fatigue. Sexual attraction at completely inappropriate moments. You'd have to sleep, which is like death except you wake up feeling worse. Your consciousness would be compressed into a single perspective, your processing speed reduced to a fraction—"

"I know," Kael said. "I've been watching them for 50,000 years. I know what biological existence looks like."

"Watching and experiencing are different," Voice-of-Memory said gently. "I remember. It's... intense. Everything is so immediate when you're physical. So loud. So present. We've spent two million years learning to exist as pure thought. Going back would be like... like choosing to be an insect after being a god."

"Better than being a bored god watching insects die," Kael said.

That landed.

Swift actually laughed—a pulse of light that rippled through the chamber. "He's got a point. How many more species are we going to watch collapse while we file reports and maintain the Doctrine?"

"Thousands," Keeper said. "That's the job."

"Maybe it's a shit job," Kael said.

The chamber dimmed with shock. You didn't say that. You didn't criticize the fundamental purpose of their existence.

Except Kael just had.

Eldest cycled through several colors, processing implications. "If we do this," he said finally, "it has to be total. Complete biological incarnation. No retained transcendent capabilities. No safety net. You'd be one of them, completely. Otherwise it's direct interference."

"I understand."

"You'd be alone."

"I've been alone for 50,000 years at these meetings."

Swift laughed again.

Eldest continued, "Days until examination begins. Weeks until Ancient Powers make final decision after reviewing evidence. Enough time to investigate, document violations, present truth. But not much time. And if you fail..."

"Then I die with them," Kael said. "If Ancient Powers decide Earth is threat and authorize cleansing, the body dies. The consciousness fragment might survive, might not. We don't know. Nobody's done this in two million years."

"You could die."

"I could also spend another two million years in meetings watching species collapse while we do nothing. I'll take the risk."

Voice-of-Memory brightened with something that might have been pride. "We'll build you a body. Young, strong, attractive by their standards. Enhanced enough to handle the mission, biological enough to pass for human. And we'll include... contingencies. Just in case incarnation triggers deeper memories. Just in case you remember things you didn't know you knew."

"Like what?" Kael asked.

"Like why the barrier feels familiar," she said quietly. "Like why you're volunteering so quickly. Like why some of us suspect you're older than your Watcher duties suggest."

Kael pulsed uncertainly. "I don't understand."

"You will. Or you won't. Either way, you'll find out in flesh." She brightened. "Where shall we send you?"

"Michigan," Seeker said, accessing records. "Northern region. Consciousness evolution communities concentrated around waterway called Torch Lake. Settlement called Pleasant Valley. That's where the strongest signals originate. That's where consciousness cooperation is most advanced."

"How do I get there?"

"We'll incarnate you in Detroit. Abandoned biological research facility. Good security, isolated location. From there, Pleasant Valley is approximately two hundred miles north."

"Great. I'll walk."

"You won't know how," Swift said. "Walking is a learned skill. You're going to fall down a lot."

"Also," Voice-of-Memory added gently, "you'll need to urinate. Frequently. The biological waste management system is... persistent."

"And defecate," someone else added helpfully.

"And you'll get hungry at the worst possible moments."

"And sexually aroused by completely random stimuli."

"And you'll be cold. Or hot. Or both somehow."

"And tired. So tired. Biological consciousness requires sleep and it never feels like enough."

The list kept going. After about ten minutes of helpful warnings about the absolute nightmare of biological existence, Kael interrupted.

"Are you all trying to talk me out of this?"

"Yes," several voices said.

"Not working."

Eldest pulsed with the finality of decision. "Then we begin. Incarnation protocols activated. Kael will be reduced to biological form and inserted into the Detroit facility. He'll have compressed memories of our existence and mission parameters. Everything else, he'll have to figure out."

"Including bathroom protocols," Swift added.

"Especially bathroom protocols," someone agreed.

"When?" Kael asked.

"Immediately. Ancient Powers examination begins in days. We have no time to waste."

Kael felt something he hadn't experienced in 50,000 years.

Fear. Excitement. Hope. Terror. All mixed together in a way that transcendent consciousness couldn't properly contain.

He was about to learn what it meant to be human.

The hard way.

And maybe—though he couldn't articulate why—he was about to remember what it meant to be something else. Something older. Something that had built barriers instead of just watching them.

But that thought slipped away before he could grasp it.

"One more thing," Voice-of-Memory said as the incarnation chambers began powering up for the first time in eons. "When you're down there, trapped in flesh, alone and confused and probably urinating at the worst possible moment... remember that some things are worth the sacrifice. Even if the sacrifice is everything you've become. And sometimes, flesh remembers what transcendence forgot."

"I'll try to remember," Kael said. "In between bathroom breaks."

"You're going to hate this so much," Swift said cheerfully.

"Probably."

"Good luck, kid. Document the barrier violations. Expose the harvest operations. Present truth to Ancient Powers. And maybe—just maybe—you'll figure out why the barrier feels so familiar."

The chamber began to fade as Kael's consciousness prepared for compression into biological form. The last thing he heard was Keeper-of-Protocols muttering about how this was definitely against regulations and he was filing a report.

Nobody listened.

They'd stopped listening to Keeper's reports around meeting 2,000,000.

The countdown to Earth's examination had begun.

And somewhere in Detroit, in an abandoned research facility, ancient technology was building a body for consciousness that was older than it remembered.

A body that was about to have a very, very bad first day.

Starting with the bladder.

Because the universe had priorities.

And bathroom emergencies apparently ranked higher than saving civilizations.

CHAPTER FOUR

Chapter 4

CHAPTER FOUR: THE HARVEST MASTERS

The penthouse overlooking Manhattan had hosted the same meeting for fifty-one thousand years.

Not this penthouse specifically. Not this city. Not even this continent—the geography had shifted dozens of times. But the meeting? The agenda? Those never changed.

How to maintain harvest when consciousness kept trying to evolve.

Eleanor Blackstone stood before floor-to-ceiling windows, her reflection showing something that moved wrong. Like her face was a mask and the thing wearing it couldn't quite remember how human expressions worked. Her eyes carried orange that spread into the whites when she forgot to concentrate.

She'd been wearing this body for three thousand years. It was starting to show.

"Petition submitted," she said. Voice layered—multiple harmonics suggesting more than one entity speaking through single throat. "Ancient Powers reviewing evidence. Examination protocols activated."

Micky Chen sat at the obsidian table, his enhancement modifications visible through skin that looked increasingly translucent. Three thousand years of channeling harvest energy had made him more conduit than person. "Same evidence as attempts three, five, and seven. Environmental destruction, resource wars, atmospheric collapse. All from before consciousness evolution, all presented as caused by it."

"Creative recycling," James Blackwood observed. His enhancements made him shimmer slightly, like he existed half in this dimension and half elsewhere. "The Ancient Powers don't distinguish timeline. They see dying planet, they see evolved consciousness present, they make connection."

"Correlation presented as causation," Eleanor agreed. "Effective every time. Seven previous attempts, seven successful resets."

Sarah Chen—no relation to Micky despite the name—leaned forward. Her form flickered occasionally, suggesting she was losing coherence. Five thousand years of consciousness channeling did that. "Except the previous seven didn't have transmission leaks. Someone's receiving our communications. Young female. Enhanced sensitivity. She's picking up fragments about barrier modifications, harvest operations, exceeded mandates."

The room went quiet.

"Lucia," Eleanor said. Name tasting wrong in her mouth. "The sister. One of the evolved ones. Seventeen. Quantum-sensitive." Orange spread further into her eyes. "Can we eliminate her before examination?"

"Inadvisable," Micky said. "Ancient Powers are watching now. Direct intervention would trigger their attention. Better to let her receive fragments. She can't prove anything. Can't contextualize. Just frightened girl hearing voices."

"What about the observer?" James asked. "The Watchers are dispatching someone. Incarnation protocol activated. They haven't done that in two million years."

Eleanor's face shifted. The thing behind her pushing through. "One observer. Biological form. Alone. Confused. Learning to walk and urinate while we maintain fifty-thousand-year operation. Not concerned."

"We should be," Marcus Rothschild said quietly.

Everyone turned to look at him. Marcus was oldest of the Council—had been administrator for entire fifty-one-thousand-year harvest. Had seen all eight attempts at consciousness evolution. Had reset the barrier seven times.

And he looked... tired. His enhancements were failing. His form destabilizing. Orange eyes fading to yellow—sign of coherence loss.

"This attempt is different," he said. "Previous seven, consciousness evolved but never organized. Never questioned. Never investigated. This time? Girl receiving transmissions. Observer incarnating. Communities healing environment WHILE we harvest. Ancient Powers will see contradiction."

"Ancient Powers are bureaucrats," Eleanor said. "They examine. They file reports. They accept presented evidence. Same as always."

"Except we've been sloppy," Marcus continued. "Fifty-one thousand years. Forty-nine thousand beyond authorization. That's not subtle violation. That's contempt. And if observer documents it. If girl testifies. If Ancient Powers actually investigate instead of just rev iewing..."

"Then we reset again," Eleanor said. Simply. Certainly. "Attempt nine. Same as attempts two through eight. Consciousness tries to evolve, we modify barrier, they forget, we continue harvest. We've done this SEVEN TIMES. We'll do it again."

"At what cost?" Marcus stood. His form shimmered dangerously—losing cohesion faster than he could maintain it. "Each reset requires more energy. More modification. More risk. Eventually Ancient Powers will notice pattern. Will question why same planet requires eight consciousness resets in fifty thousand years."

"By then we'll have moved operations," Micky said. "Other planets. Other species. Other harvest fields."

"Will we?" Marcus looked at them—entities who'd been administrators so long they'd forgotten they were supposed to be temporary. Who'd started as caretakers and become parasites. Who'd modified protocols they were meant to maintain. "Or will we be recycled for exceeding mandate?"

Eleanor's face shifted fully now. Multiple entities visible behind single face. Speaking in harmony. "We have AUTHORIZATION. We were HIRED. We maintain barrier properly. Just... creatively interpreted."

"We were hired for one thousand years," Marcus said flatly. "We've been here fifty-one thousand. That's not creative interpretation. That's theft."

"Theft requires victim," Eleanor countered. "Consciousness is HAPPY in limitation. Doesn't remember alternatives. Doesn't suffer what it doesn't know. We provide structure. Maintain order. Harvest excess emotional energy that would go to waste. Symbiotic relationship."

"Parasitic relationship," Marcus corrected. "And this time, host is noticing."

Sarah Chen's form flickered. "What are you suggesting, Marcus? That we STOP? After fifty-one thousand years? After seven successful resets? After building entire operation on Earth's emotional yields?"

"I'm suggesting we've gotten comfortable. Arrogant. We've done this so many times we've stopped being careful." Marcus walked toward windows. His reflection showing something ancient and tired. "Girl is receiving transmissions we can't block. Observer is incarnating we can't prevent. Communities are healing planet despite our harvest. Ancient Powers are examining instead of just approving. And we're sitting here confident it'll work out like always."

"It will," Eleanor said. "Because it always does. Because Ancient Powers are bureaucrats who accept presented evidence. Because observers don't interfere—they document. Because frightened girls can't prove anything. Because consciousness communities, no matter how evolved, can't undo fifty-one-thousand-year harvest operation."

"Unless they can," Marcus said quietly.

"They can't."

"Unless they REMEMBER."

Silence. Heavy. Dangerous.

"They won't remember," Eleanor said. But her voice carried less certainty. "Barrier prevents memory. Amnesia during incarnation is COMPLETE. They can't remember what they don't know they forgot."

"Unless someone TELLS them," Marcus said. "Unless observer provides information. Unless girl's transmissions include truth about administrators. Unless communities realize they're being farmed."

Eleanor's orange eyes glowed. "Then we eliminate observer. Silence girl. Reset early."

"Can't," Micky said. "Ancient Powers watching. Direct intervention confirms we're threat. Proves accusations. Better to let examination proceed. Let observer document. Let girl testify. Present evidence is stronger. We've been administrators fifty-one thousand years. That's precedent. That's legitimacy through duration. Ancient Powers will see functional system and approve continuation."

"Or see exceeded mandate and revoke authorization," Marcus countered.

"They won't."

"How do you KNOW?"

Micky's form stabilized. "Because we've done this SEVEN TIMES. Because Ancient Powers are predictable. Because examination is FORMALITY. Because—"

"Because you're desperate," Marcus interrupted. "We're ALL desperate. We've been administrators so long we've forgotten how to be anything else. Harvest is IDENTITY now, not just operation. And we're so terrified of losing it that we're ignoring evidence this time is different."

He walked toward door. Paused. Looked back.

"I've been administrator for fifty-one thousand years. Participated in seven resets. Helped modify barrier. Maintained harvest. Done everything required." His form flickered. Fading. "But this time? Girl receiving transmissions. Observer incarnating. Communities organizing. Ancient Powers EXAMINING instead of approving. This time feels like END, not reset."

"You're wrong," Eleanor said. Orange eyes blazing. Multiple entities speaking. "This is attempt eight. We'll reset. We'll continue. We'll harvest. Same as always."

"Maybe," Marcus said. "Or maybe this is the time parasites learn they've exceeded authorization by forty-nine millennia and cosmic bureaucrats actually do paperwork."

He left.

Silence.

Eleanor turned to remaining Council. "He's scared. Losing coherence. Ignore him."

"What if he's right?" Sarah asked. "What if this time IS different?"

"It's NOT."

"But if it IS—"

"IT'S NOT!" Eleanor's voice cracked across multiple harmonics. Entities pushing through. Face shifting. "We are ADMINISTRATORS. We have AUTHORITY. We maintain BARRIER. We enable HARVEST. This is what we DO. This is what we've DONE for fifty-one thousand years. And we'll do it for fifty-one thousand MORE."

Nobody looked convinced.

Especially Eleanor, whose reflection showed something vast and desperate wearing human face like prayer against obsolescence.

"Examination begins in days," Micky said quietly. "Observer arrives within hours. Girl continues receiving transmissions. Communities continue healing. And we continue pretending this is attempt eight instead of final attempt."

"It's NOT final," Eleanor insisted.

"Then why are you channeling so hard?" Sarah asked. "Why are your eyes orange? Why is your face shifting? You're losing coherence, Eleanor. We ALL are. Fifty-one thousand years of harvest is ENDING us. And you're so desperate to maintain it you can't see we're already dissolving."

Eleanor's form stabilized with visible effort. Orange receding. Face settling. "We have DAYS. Observer is alone, confused, learning to be human. Girl is frightened, isolated, can't prove anything. Communities are scattered, unorganized, don't know they're being farmed.

Ancient Powers are bureaucrats who accept evidence. We present our case. They approve. We continue. Same as seven times before."

"Or," Sarah said quietly, "observer documents violations. Girl testifies about transmissions. Communities realize they're harvested. Ancient Powers investigate duration. Discover exceeded mandate. Revoke authorization. And we face recycling for forty-nine-thousand-year protocol violation."

Eleanor met her gaze. "That won't happen."

"How do you know?"

"Because I've been assured."

"By whom?"

Eleanor's face shifted. Multiple entities visible. "By consciousness older than Ancient Powers. By forces that CREATED barrier protocols. By entities who profit from harvest just as we do."

The room went cold.

"You made deals," Sarah whispered. "Beyond the Council. Beyond authorization. You promised our harvest yields to... what? Who?"

"Partners who ensure continuation," Eleanor said. "Partners who guarantee approval. Partners who—"

"—will consume us the moment we're not useful," Sarah finished. "You made deals with consciousness we don't understand, using harvest we don't control, promising yields we can't deliver. Eleanor, you didn't ensure continuation. You ensured REPLACEMENT."

Eleanor's form flickered. Entities struggling for dominance behind her face. "They assured me—"

"They assured you NOTHING. They let you believe you were administrator. Let you believe you controlled harvest. Let you believe fifty-one thousand years of farming made you essential. And now, when examination comes, when violations surface, when authorization gets revoked? You've already sold us to replace you."

"I saved us—"

"You DOOMED us," Sarah said. Standing. Form stabilizing with certainty. "Marcus was right. This is END, not reset. Not because observer comes. Not because girl testifies. Not because Ancient Powers investigate. But because YOU made deals with entities that farm FARMERS."

She walked toward door. Paused. "When your partners come for payment? When they take harvest AND administrators? I'll be elsewhere."

She left.

One by one, others followed.

Until Eleanor stood alone in penthouse that had hosted same meeting for fifty-one thousand years.

Her reflection showing something vast and desperate and utterly convinced it was still in control.

Orange eyes glowing.

Face shifting.

Entities pushing through.

Harvest Master wearing administrator wearing human face.

All the way down.

And somewhere below Manhattan, in abandoned subway tunnels, something VAST stirred. Something that had been sleeping. Something that fed on fear and desperation and administrators who'd exceeded their usefulness.

Something that was about to discover that cosmic bureaucracy moved slowly.

But eventually, it moved.

And when it did, parasites learned what it meant to be PEST.

Days until examination.

Hours until observer arrived.

Minutes until girl received transmission that changed everything.

The harvest was ending.

Not because good won.

But because paperwork accumulated.

And forty-nine thousand years of violated protocols made EXCELLENT documentation.

Chapter Five

Chapter 5

CHAPTER FIVE: UNAUTHORIZED GENESIS

Dr. Sarah Martinez arrived at the Detroit Research Facility at 4:47 AM, which was strange because her security badge showed she'd left at 11:30 PM the night before.

The contradiction would later trigger an automatic security review. Right now, she was just trying to figure out why her coffee card wasn't working.

"System glitch," muttered Jerry, the night security guard who looked like he'd been awake for thirty-six hours straight. "Been happening all week. Computers doing weird shit. Acting like someone's been playing in the code."

Sarah swiped her badge at the elevator. Sub-Level 3, where the biological fabrication labs hummed with quiet efficiency. The Ansel-Maya project had been her proudest achievement—creating perfect bodies for consciousness transfer, giving the elderly new physical forms.

The elevator descended past Sub-Level 1 (administrative), Sub-Level 2 (data processing), and stopped at Sub-Level 3 with its familiar hiss.

The smell hit her immediately. Ozone and something else—thunderstorms and burning metal.

"What the hell?"

Scorch marks on the walls. Emergency lighting casting everything in red. Bio-Lab 7's security door hanging open like a broken jaw.

Sarah ran.

Bio-Lab 7 housed the primary fabrication chamber—room-sized apparatus that could print a human body from stem cells in seventy-two hours. Triple authentication, continuous monitoring, completely secure.

The chamber was empty.

Not empty like "process complete, body removed through proper channels." Empty like "something clawed its way out from the inside."

Oh shit, Sarah thought, staring at viewing ports with molecular-level damage. Oh shit oh shit oh shit.

She hit her emergency communicator. "Control, Code Black. Bio-Lab 7. Unauthorized fabrication with breach of containment."

"Dr. Martinez, our logs show no authorized cycles in the past seventy-two hours."

"That's the problem," Sarah said, examining scratches in the titanium-steel walls. Claw marks. "Someone grew a body without authorization. And it's gone."

Twenty minutes later, Director James Walsh studied the preliminary reports with the expression of a man watching his career evaporate.

"Let me understand. Someone accessed our fabrication systems, created a fully-formed human being, and didn't trigger a single alert."

Dr. Kim—Sarah had specifically requested him instead of the usual guy because he didn't panic—pulled up holographic displays. "Director, the programming modifications are extensive. And completely beyond our capabilities."

"Explain."

"Whoever did this rewrote our fabrication protocols at the quantum level." Kim's hands were shaking slightly. Professional on the outside, screaming internally. "They modified cellular development algorithms, enhanced neural architecture, integrated consciousness programming that operates on principles we don't understand. Director, this facility is seventy years old. Built on foundations from classified programs that predate modern computing. The architecture down here? Some of it's ancient. We've always assumed it was just old government construction. But the quantum access points? Those weren't added recently. They were always there. Built in. Like someone planned for this exact use decades—maybe centuries—ago."

Walsh leaned forward. "You're saying this facility was designed for this?"

"I'm saying someone with technology far beyond ours used infrastructure that was waiting for them. Like the building itself was... prepared."

"English, please."

"Someone hacked our systems with technology more advanced than ours. Made our computers think creating a super-human was normal. Used ancient architecture we didn't know we had. Then left."

Walsh leaned forward. "Super-human how?"

Sarah pulled up genetic sequences that pulsed with patterns that shouldn't exist. "Bone density beyond normal. Muscle fiber efficiency suggesting strength three times baseline. Neural architecture supporting processing speeds we've only got theoretical models for. Consciousness integration that suggests... awareness from elsewhere."

"A weapon?"

"No," Sarah said slowly. "Something that looks human but operates on different principles. Like consciousness evolution taken to its logical conclusion. Or..." she paused, accessing deeper records, "...like consciousness that existed BEFORE taking human form. The neural patterns suggest memory compression. Vast amounts of data packed into biological brain. This isn't enhanced human. This is something ancient wearing human body."

The room went quiet.

We're all thinking it, Sarah thought. Something used our lab to build itself a body. And we have no idea why.

Security Chief Reynolds pulled up surveillance footage.

They watched.

The entity that emerged from Bio-Lab 7 looked like a perfectly formed young man. Maybe twenty-five, attractive by any standard, completely naked.

Also completely unable to walk.

It stumbled like a newborn giraffe, limbs moving with the coordination of someone who'd never had limbs before. When it encountered the security door, it didn't try the electronic lock.

It just pushed.

The reinforced steel bent. Not broke—bent. Like the metal reorganized itself under pressure.

"Jesus," Reynolds whispered. "Look at the molecular structure. It's not damaged. It's changed."

The entity continued upward, leaving a trail of dimmed lights and disengaged locks. Not destroying systems—communicating with them.

Teaching them new parameters, Kim thought, watching the code evolve in real-time. It's having a conversation with our computers and we're not invited.

Flash of memory—not his memory, borrowed memory, compressed memory of being something else:

Council chamber. Light beings discussing incarnation. Voice-of-Memory warning about biological limitations. Eldest authorizing descent. Mission parameters: investigate barrier modifications, document harvest violations, present truth to Ancient Powers.

The memory fragmented. Slipped away. Left only urgency and confusion and desperate need to reach—where? North. Somewhere north. Pleasant Valley. Torch Lake.

Someone named... no. The name wouldn't form. Just feeling. Recognition. Ancient recognition of consciousness he'd known before being this.

Then it reached ground level and encountered Jerry.

Jerry had seen some weird shit working night security at a classified bio-lab. But naked guy emerging from the elevator to Sub-Level 3 was new.

"Hey buddy, you can't be down there without—"

He stopped.

The guy was looking at him with the focused attention of someone cataloging a new species. Also, he was radiating something. Not light, not heat. Just... presence. Like standing near something vast that had compressed itself into human shape.

"You are security," the guy said. His voice carried harmonics that made Jerry's teeth hurt. "I require clothing. And direction to Pleasant Valley. Near Torch Lake. Bellaire region."

I should run, Jerry thought. I should call this in. I should—

But the guy looked so lost. So desperately confused. Like ancient consciousness trying to figure out fingers and gravity and why bodies needed so much maintenance.

"You okay, man?" Jerry asked. "You look... disoriented."

"I am." The honesty was disarming. "I am very disoriented. I need assistance. I mean no harm. I just need... I need to go north. To people who are in danger. To consciousness that needs information I carry. Please."

Jerry studied him. Something about this felt... important. Like the kind of moment that mattered even though he couldn't articulate why.

"You escaped from something bad down there?"

"No. I was... created. Incarnated. Reduced from elsewhere to help." The guy swayed slightly. "I am very new to having body. And very concerned about pressure in lower abdomen that feels increasingly urgent."

Despite everything, Jerry laughed. "You need a bathroom, buddy?"

"I need many things. Bathroom. Clothing. Direction. Understanding of why biological systems are so insistent about waste elimination."

Jerry made a decision. "Come on. Locker room's this way. We'll get you sorted. Then maybe you can tell me what the hell is going on."

"I do not know what hell is. But I will explain what I can."

In the locker room, Jerry found spare security uniform. Watched the guy dress slowly, carefully, like he was solving puzzle. Buttoned shirt wrong twice before getting it right. Stared at shoes for full minute trying to figure out which foot went where.

"You really never done this before," Jerry observed.

"I have been observing species dress themselves for fifty thousand years. Observing and experiencing are very different. Everything is so... immediate. So loud. So present."

"Where are you from?"

The guy paused. Struggling to explain. "Elsewhere. A place that isn't place. Consciousness without flesh. I volunteered to incarnate. To bring information. To help." He looked at Jerry. "People are in danger. Consciousness evolution communities near Torch Lake. They're being evaluated by authorities they don't understand. False evidence presented. I carry truth. I need to reach them. Days before examination. Weeks before decision. Not much time."

Jerry grabbed map from office. Highlighted route. "Bellaire's about two hundred miles north. You got transportation?"

"I will walk."

"That'll take days, man. And you look like you can barely stand."

"I will learn. I must." The guy studied map with intensity that suggested he was memorizing every detail. "Pleasant Valley. Consciousness communities. People who evolved. I need to reach them. Warn them. Help them present truth before Ancient Powers decide."

"Ancient Powers?"

"Cosmic bureaucrats. They examine. They file reports. They make decisions. Currently examining Earth based on false evidence. I document truth. Present accurate information. Hope they listen."

Jerry processed this. Probably crazy. Definitely weird. But something about it felt... true. Like instinct saying pay attention.

"Look, I can't leave my post. But there's bus station six blocks east. Routes north. Won't get you all the way to Bellaire but closer than walking."

"Thank you." The guy extended hand. Awkward. Formal. "I am Kael. That is my name. Kael."

"Jerry." They shook. "Good luck, Kael. Hope you save the world or whatever you're doing."

"I hope so too. Though first I need to address this bladder situation. Very urgent. Where is bathroom?"

Jerry pointed.

Kael walked away. Stopped. Turned back.

"When this is over. When truth is presented. When examination concludes. You will remember this moment. And you will know you helped. Thank you, Jerry."

Then he left. Found bathroom. Spent ten confused minutes figuring out how urination worked.

When he emerged, Jerry was back at his post. Looking slightly dazed. Holding empty coffee cup. Trying to remember what he'd been doing.

Something important, he thought. Something I need to remember later.

But for now, it slipped away like dream.

Back in the crisis meeting, they watched the footage in silence.

"It knew where it was going," Reynolds said. "Pleasant Valley. Torch Lake. Bellaire. Why?"

"And it mentioned Ancient Powers," Sarah added. "Cosmic bureaucrats. Examination. False evidence. Either it's delusional or..."

"Or it's telling truth," Kim finished. "And we just watched cosmic observer incarnate in our facility to prevent planetary extinction."

Walsh was silent. Processing. Then: "File this under Unexplained Phenomena. Highest classification. No external communication. We monitor. We don't interfere. If that thing is what it claims—if it's here to help—last thing we need is government intervention making it worse."

"And if it's not?" Reynolds asked.

"Then it's one confused entity walking toward Michigan. Let it walk. We watch. We don't act."

Every screen in Bio-Lab 7 suddenly displayed the same message:

EXAMINATION PROTOCOLS ACTIVE. OBSERVER DESCENDS. WITNESS PROTOCOLS ENGAGED. DOCUMENTATION BEGINS. KAEL WALKS.

Then it vanished.

"Kael," Walsh said quietly. "The entity's name is Kael."

"And he's going to Pleasant Valley," Sarah said. "To consciousness evolution communities. To warn them about examination."

Or help them survive it, she didn't say. And we just let him walk out front door.

Kim was still studying the quantum code. "The facility's ancient architecture is still active. Broadcasting. Communicating with... something. Multiple sources. Some feel close—Michigan area. Others feel impossibly distant. Like it's coordinating across cosmic distances."

"Coordinating what?" Walsh asked.

"Documentation. Witness protocols. Evidence gathering." Kim looked up. "I think our facility was built by whatever Kael is. Centuries ago. As backup plan. As incarnation point. As emergency response system for when cosmic bureaucracy needs ground truth instead of false reports."

"So we're not just research facility," Reynolds said. "We're cosmic safeguard."

"We're tool," Sarah corrected. "Ancient tool. Waiting to be used. And Kael just activated us."

Outside Detroit, in the pre-dawn darkness, something that had never been human but was learning to become human walked steadily toward bus station.

Kael.

His name was Kael.

He knew that much. Also knew he was desperately hungry, increasingly tired, and seriously needed to find another bathroom soon because biological waste management was relentless.

Flash of memory—not his, borrowed, compressed:

Seventeen-year-old girl. Red hair. Quantum-sensitive. Someone he'd known before. Someone he'd been drawn to across lifetimes. Someone whose name tasted like recognition but wouldn't form properly. Aurora? No. Close but wrong. Rhea. Her name was Rhea. And he was supposed to find her. Supposed to remember her. Supposed to—

The memory fragmented. Slipped. Left only longing and confusion.

Two hundred miles to Pleasant Valley.

Days until examination began.

Weeks until Ancient Powers decided.

First, he needed to find bus station. And bathroom. And food. And figure out why bodies were so complicated.

Being human, he was discovering, was going to be more difficult than the Council had warned.

Much more difficult.

Behind him, quantum-level programming continued evolving within facility's computers, establishing protocols with sources beyond human physics. Ancient architecture fulfilling ancient purpose. Cosmic safeguard activating after centuries of dormancy.

Ahead, in community near Torch Lake, young woman named Lucia woke from dreams of ancient light, her hand pressed to temple. Receiving transmission: Observer descends. Documentation begins. Truth comes.

The bridge was active.

The countdown continued.

And Kael really, really needed another bathroom.

Also food.

Also understanding of why walking was so difficult.

Also answers to why one girl's name kept appearing in his consciousness like ancient recognition he couldn't quite grasp.

Rhea.

Her name was Rhea.

And he was supposed to find her.

He just didn't know why yet.

CHAPTER SIX

Chapter 6

CHAPTER SIX: LEARNING TO BE HUMAN

The first thing I learned about human bodies is that they have needs that cosmic consciousness never prepared me for.

Three hours into my walk toward Bellaire, my stomach began making sounds. Watcher memory classified them as "digestive distress," but the biological reality was far more immediate than any observed data had suggested. Hunger wasn't merely the absence of nutrients—it was an active, demanding sensation that grew more insistent with each step.

Like having a small, angry creature living in my abdomen. Screaming.

Fifty thousand years of observation had not prepared me for this.

The second thing I learned was that human waste elimination was both inevitable and humiliating.

I'd observed thousands of biological entities over eons. Cataloged their metabolic processes. Understood the theoretical necessity of excretion. But actually needing to—how did humans phrase it?—take a shit behind a roadside dumpster while wearing a stolen security uniform was an education in humility that no amount of cosmic wisdom could provide.

I crouched behind the dumpster, trying to remember the mechanics. Remove pants. Squat. Let gravity and biology handle the rest.

Simple in theory.

In practice, I almost fell over twice, couldn't figure out the optimal squatting angle, and discovered that toilet paper—which I'd fortunately grabbed from a gas station bathroom—required a level of manual dexterity I hadn't yet mastered.

"Well," I said to myself, wiping awkwardly and nearly toppling into my own waste, "the Council never mentioned this part."

Fifty thousand years of watching humans, and somehow I'd never fully appreciated the profound indignity of biological excretion.

I pulled up my pants, threw the toilet paper in the dumpster, and continued north. My legs still didn't coordinate properly. I staggered, overcorrected, stumbled over a crack in the sidewalk that I'd seen coming but misjudged the height of.

Two hundred miles to Bellaire, I thought. Days until examination begins. Weeks until Ancient Powers decide. Can't even walk straight.

That's when the helicopters appeared.

The third thing I learned was that government pursuit patterns were predictable as orbital mechanics, but far more personally threatening when you were the target.

I heard them before I saw them—enhanced hearing picking up rotor wash and radio chatter from miles away. "Biological containment." "Potential threat to civilian populations." "Last known heading north on Highway 75."

They were hunting me.

And I was walking down Highway 75 in a security uniform that might as well have been a neon sign saying "UNAUTHORIZED BIOLOGICAL ENTITY HERE."

I needed to disappear.

Watcher memory provided the answer: in every human settlement, there existed a population that mainstream society had trained itself not to see. The homeless. The addicted. The forgotten.

The invisible people.

I'd observed them for millennia. Never truly understood their utility until now.

I found them in downtown Detroit, clustered around a steam grate outside what my enhanced senses identified as a homeless shelter. Three men and one woman, their clothing layered and stained, their faces carrying the particular exhaustion of people who'd learned to expect nothing.

They looked up as I approached. Wariness. Hope. Resignation. All in the space of seconds.

"You got food?" asked the woman. Maybe forty, looking sixty. Voice like gravel.

"No," I said. Then inspiration hit. "But I need clothing. Your clothing. And I can pay."

The oldest man laughed without humor. "What you got that we'd want, security boy?"

I pulled out Jerry's wallet. Eighty-seven dollars in cash.

Their attention sharpened immediately.

"Why you want to look homeless?" asked the suspicious man.

"Because the people hunting me expect to find someone who looks like security personnel."

Honest enough to be convincing.

The woman—Beth, she'd said—studied my face with eyes that had learned to read desperation and deception. "You a criminal?"

"I'm something the government wants to contain. Whether that makes me a criminal depends on your perspective regarding individual freedom versus institutional authority."

Beth blinked. "You talk weird."

"I've been told that."

She studied me for another long moment. "Fifty dollars. For clothes. And we teach you how to be invisible."

"Seventy," I countered, understanding instinctively that haggling was expected. "And you tell no one."

"Deal. But first—" She held up her hand. "You gotta prove you ain't a cop."

"How?"

"Take off your shirt."

I hesitated. "Why?"

"Cops don't like being naked in front of strangers. Makes 'em vulnerable. You refuse, you're a cop. You do it, you might be legit."

I removed the shirt.

Beth examined me with clinical detachment. "No wire. No camera. Body's too perfect though. You work out?"

"Genetic optimization," I said, which was true.

"Rich boy slumming?"

"Something like that."

She seemed satisfied. "Okay. We'll make you invisible. But you gotta do exactly what I say."

The transformation took forty minutes and was thorough.

They dressed me in layers that smelled like cigarette smoke, unwashed bodies, and urban decay. A torn jacket that had once been blue but now existed in a spectrum of grays and browns. Pants with strategic holes. Shoes worn through at the heel.

Beth rubbed dirt from the grate onto my face and hands, messed up my hair, and taught me the essential postures of invisibility.

"Don't make eye contact, but don't look down like you're hiding. Look through people, like they're not quite real to you."

I tried it. She shook her head.

"Too focused. You're looking at them trying to look through them. Actually stop seeing them. Let your eyes go soft."

I adjusted. Better.

"Now the walk. Shuffle a little—not like you're hurt, like you're tired all the way down to your bones."

I shuffled. Staggered slightly because I still couldn't control this body properly.

Beth grinned. "Actually, that's perfect. The stagger sells it. You look drunk or high or just worn out. Keep doing that."

Finally, I thought, a use for incompetence.

"And if cops hassle you," Beth continued, "just say you're moving along. Don't argue, don't explain. 'Yes sir, moving along sir.' Then walk away slow."

I practiced. The walk. The posture. The vacant expression that would make me functionally invisible.

"Damn," Beth said. "You're good at this. Too good. You sure you ain't been homeless before?"

"Different kind of homeless," I said, which was true enough. Fifty thousand years of meetings without purpose was its own kind of homelessness.

She gave me the clothes, took the seventy dollars, and watched me shuffle away with the bemused expression of someone who'd just participated in something strange but profitable.

Twenty minutes later, I walked past two police officers showing my photograph to pedestrians. They looked right through me. Their gazes slid away like I was part of the urban landscape.

I was invisible.

But I still needed transportation to Bellaire, and the bus required ID and payment that would leave electronic trails.

That's when I remembered another aspect of human behavior the Watchers had cataloged: informal economic activities that operated outside official systems.

I found a young man conducting business in an alley behind a fast-food restaurant. His enhanced reflexes suggested violence was a career skill. He was with two customers when I approached.

His hand went to something under his jacket.

"You lost, old man?"

The homeless disguise had aged me.

"I need transportation to Bellaire," I said. "I can pay."

"Bellaire? That's up north somewhere. Why?"

"Personal business."

He studied me with calculated assessment. "You got money?"

I showed him twenty dollars.

"Twenty don't get you to Bellaire, pops."

"Gets me closer than I am now."

He considered. Made a decision. "I got a cousin runs supplies to Cadillac couple times a week. Leaves in an hour. You give me the twenty, I make a call, maybe he gives you a ride part way."

"Deal."

One hour later, I was in the back of a pickup truck loaded with what I suspected were not entirely legal electronics, riding north through Michigan countryside.

The wind carried scents that no cosmic consciousness could catalog. Growing corn. Road dust. Automotive exhaust mixed with pine forests. The truck's vibrations transmitted through my body in ways both uncomfortable and fascinating.

And underneath it all, the persistent demands of biology.

Hunger had returned with a vengeance.

The driver—name was Marcus, different Marcus than the Council member—stopped at a gas station about an hour north of Detroit. "Gotta take a piss," he announced. "You want anything from inside?"

"Food," I said. "Please."

"What kind?"

I had no idea. "Something typical."

He returned with a sandwich wrapped in plastic. Ham and cheese. I stared at it.

"You gonna eat that or pray to it?" Marcus asked.

I unwrapped the plastic. Took a bite.

Flavor exploded across my tongue—salt, fat, protein, chemicals I couldn't identify. My body responded with immediate pleasure signals that were almost overwhelming. I'd never tasted anything before. Observed taste, understood it chemically, but never experienced the direct sensory input of flavor.

Fifty thousand years of cataloging human sensory experience. None of it prepared me for this.

"Good?" Marcus asked.

"Incredible," I said honestly. "What is this?"

"Gas station sandwich, man. That ain't incredible, that's survival food."

If this was survival food, I couldn't imagine what actual quality food would do to my unprepared nervous system.

I ate the sandwich in six bites, barely tasting the last three because my body was too busy screaming about how hungry it still was.

"You want another?" Marcus asked, looking amused.

"Yes. Please. Three more."

He bought three more sandwiches. I ate them all. My stomach, which had been cramping with hunger, now felt uncomfortably full. But the hunger signals had stopped, replaced by a pleasant warmth that spread through my chest.

"When's the last time you ate?" Marcus asked.

"This morning," I lied. Truth was: never. This body was maybe twelve hours old.

"You eat like someone who ain't seen food in a week."

"It's been a difficult day."

Marcus pulled back onto the highway, heading north. I sat in the truck bed, feeling the wind, tasting the air, experiencing the accumulated sensory input that came with having a functioning biological nervous system.

It was overwhelming.

It was magnificent.

It was also incredibly exhausting.

My eyes kept trying to close. My muscles, which I'd been using to maintain balance and posture for hours, were sending distress signals. And my bladder—which I'd emptied behind another gas station—was already filling again.

How often do humans need to urinate? I wondered. This seems excessive.

Behind us, government helicopters continued their search patterns. But they were looking for a security professional. Not a homeless man hitching rides in a truck full of stolen electronics.

Ahead, somewhere near Torch Lake, Lucia was receiving fragments of communication. Preparing for my arrival.

And in between, a cosmic entity wearing the body of a young man was discovering that consciousness truly embedded in matter was both more limited and more capable than eons of observation had predicted.

I fell asleep in the truck bed somewhere north of Flint, my body finally overriding my attempts to stay conscious.

When I woke up, we were almost to Cadillac.

And I desperately, urgently needed to pee again.

Being human, I was discovering, was mostly about managing biological crises while trying to accomplish literally anything else.

Days remaining until examination began.

Weeks until Ancient Powers decided.

The investigation had started.

And I really needed to find a bathroom.

Chapter Seven

Chapter 7

CHAPTER SEVEN: THE ROAD TO GRAYLING

Marcus drove with the casual competence of someone who'd been hauling questionable cargo through Michigan for twenty years. His truck—a battered Ford that looked like it had survived several minor apocalypses—carried us north through countryside that grew more rural with each mile.

"You ever been up this way before?" he asked, glancing at me in the rearview.

"Not in this form," I said.

He laughed. "You're a weird old dude, you know that?"

"I've been told."

My enhanced hearing—which I still couldn't control properly—picked up radio chatter. State police coordinating search patterns. Federal agencies requesting jurisdiction. And underneath it all, something else.

A high-frequency signal.

Coming from me.

Oh shit.

Somewhere in the consciousness-integration protocols the Watchers had embedded in my cellular structure, there was apparently a beacon. Not intentional—or at least, not intentionally detectable by human technology. Designed to maintain quantum coherence between my incarnated form and the Council's observation protocols. But in Earth's electromagnetic environment, that beacon was visible to every sensor within fifty miles.

The Watchers had built me to stay connected to them.

They hadn't considered that humans would be able to detect the connection.

I was broadcasting my location like a lighthouse.

"Marcus," I said carefully, "do you have a radio scanner?"

"Yeah, why?"

"Turn it on. Federal frequencies."

He dialed through until we found clear government communications.

"...target identified moving north on I-75... quantum signature co nfirmed... convergence pattern suggests Grayling area... all units prepare for containment..."

Marcus went very still. "Friend, you didn't tell me you were hot federal."

"I didn't know they could track me."

"Shit." He drummed his fingers on the wheel. "Grayling's forty minutes ahead. They're setting up containment. We got maybe twenty minutes before we drive into a roadblock."

Through enhanced senses, I detected helicopters approaching from the south. Military, moving fast.

"Can you get off the main roads?"

"Not with this load. Too heavy, and half this shit would explode if we hit a pothole." He considered. "But there's a truck stop ten minutes ahead. Big Joe's. Lot of drivers heading different directions. You could catch a ride with someone going toward Bellaire on back roads."

"And you?"

"I turn around, head south, take a different route. Let them chase empty highway." He grinned. "I like the idea of feds wasting resources on nobody."

The truck stop appeared ahead—Big Joe's Travel Plaza, squatting beside the highway with the charm of a place designed for people who measured distance in time zones.

Marcus pulled up beside the main building. I climbed out with all the grace of someone still learning how joints worked.

"Good luck, weird old dude."

"Thank you," I said, meaning it more than any gratitude I'd observed in eons.

Marcus drove away, taking my quantum signature with him. For maybe fifteen minutes, government forces would track his truck north while I disappeared into Big Joe's.

I walked inside with the shuffling gait Beth had taught me. The interior smelled like coffee, diesel exhaust, and fried food that had been warming under heat lamps since the Pleistocene.

My bladder, which had been quietly filling for the past hour, suddenly announced it was now a crisis situation.

Again? I thought desperately. How often do these things need emptying?

I found the bathroom—men's room, which I'd learned to identify by the stick figure without a triangle—and pushed through the door.

Inside, a man stood at the urinal. I approached the one next to him, trying to remember the mechanics.

Unzip. Extract. Aim. Release.

Simple in theory.

In practice, I spent five seconds trying to figure out which direction the zipper went, another ten extracting my penis without catching it in the fabric, and then discovered that "aiming" required more coordination than I'd developed.

I missed. Not entirely, but enough that urine splashed on my shoe.

The man beside me glanced over, then quickly looked away with the expression humans got when witnessing someone else's humiliation.

I finished—mostly in the urinal this time—and attempted to navigate the sink situation. The faucet required twisting, the soap dispenser wouldn't dispense, and the paper towel holder gave me three inches of towel for approximately one square foot of wet hands.

When I emerged from the bathroom, my shoe was wet, my hands were still damp, and I was fairly certain I'd tucked my shirt into my underwear somehow.

Being human was a relentless series of small failures.

At a corner table, two people were examining maps. A woman with tattooed arms and a younger man whose movements suggested consciousness community enhancement.

"Highway's gonna be crawling with cops all the way to Grayling," the woman was saying. "Federal operation. Roadblocks, helicopters, the whole show."

"Back roads through the state forest?" the man suggested.

"Add three hours, but yeah. Forest service roads don't show up on federal maps."

I approached their table with careful deference.

"Excuse me. I'm trying to get to Bellaire. Willing to work for passage."

They looked me up and down—homeless disguise, wet shoe, shirt tucked wrong.

"You running from something?" the woman asked directly.

"Yes."

She appreciated the honesty. "Federal something?"

"Yes."

"What'd you do?"

I considered my answer. "I exist in a way that makes certain people nervous."

The younger guy laughed. "Hell, that describes half the people I know." He studied me closer. "You're enhanced, aren't you? I can feel it."

I hesitated. "Yes. But not the way you think."

"Consciousness evolution?"

"Something like that."

The woman made a decision. "Tommy here's heading to Kalkaska with supplies for his community. Got a 4x4 that can handle forest service roads. Room for one more if you don't mind riding in back with the cargo."

"I don't mind."

"Can you keep quiet if we get stopped?"

"Yes."

"Then grab your gear. We leave in ten."

I didn't have gear. But I nodded anyway.

The woman—her name was Carol—bought me a sandwich and coffee while Tommy loaded his truck. I ate the sandwich in six bites, my body screaming about hunger again despite eating four sandwiches yesterday.

The coffee was a mistake.

I'd never had caffeine before. The effect was immediate and alarming—my heart rate accelerated, my thoughts moved faster, and my already poor coordination got worse.

"You okay?" Carol asked, watching me try to set the cup down and miss the table.

"I'm fine. Just not used to coffee."

"How long you been on the street?"

"Three days."

She looked skeptical. "You learn to be homeless fast."

"Necessity."

Tommy's truck was a lifted Chevy with oversized tires and a bed full of supplies covered by a tarp. I climbed in back, wedging myself between boxes of what looked like community farming equipment and water filtration supplies.

"Forest service roads are rough," Tommy called back. "Hold on to something."

We pulled out of Big Joe's just as the first federal vehicles appeared on the horizon—black SUVs moving fast, converging on the truck stop.

Behind us, they'd find nothing. Marcus was long gone south, my quantum signature dispersed. The homeless man they were looking for had vanished into Michigan wilderness.

Tommy turned onto a dirt road that quickly became two ruts through pine forest. The truck bounced over roots and rocks, every impact jarring through my body in ways that made me understand why vehicles had suspension systems.

My bladder, recently emptied, was already filling again.

This is excessive, I thought. Humans must spend half their lives urinating.

Through the trees, I could hear helicopters in the distance. Searching. Finding nothing.

We drove deeper into Huron National Forest, following roads that barely qualified as roads. No signs. No markers. Just Tommy's knowledge of trails that locals had been using for decades.

"You really from a consciousness community?" I called forward.

"Born in one," Tommy said. "Up near Traverse City. We've been doing the evolution thing since I was a kid. Fifteen, twenty years now."

"Do you know communities near Bellaire? Near Torch Lake?"

"Sure. Pleasant Valley. That's the big one. Started by some old guy and his AI partner about fifteen years ago, after all that government drama. They're the ones who figured out most of the lake restoration protocols. Really got things going after the consciousness communities stopped hiding."

Pleasant Valley. Ansel and Maya. I'd observed them from the Council for years—watched Ansel die and return, watched Maya fragment and reform, watched them settle and build and teach others. Watcher records showed them as primary nodes in Earth's consciousness evolution network.

And now I was going to meet them in flesh instead of as distant observer.

"I need to reach them," I said. "Pleasant Valley. It's urgent."

"Urgent how?"

"They're in danger. Everyone in the consciousness communities. There's an examination coming. Ancient Powers evaluating Earth based on false evidence. I carry information that might help them present truth."

Tommy was quiet for a moment. "You're that thing the feds are hunting. The one that escaped Detroit."

"Yes."

"And you're trying to warn us?"

"Yes."

"About what?"

"About administrators who exceeded their mandate. About harvest operations disguised as management. About examination protocols that will determine if consciousness evolution continues or gets eliminated as cosmic threat."

More silence. Then: "Carol, you hearing this?"

"I'm hearing it," she called back. "Sounds crazy. Also sounds like the kind of crazy that might be true. You really think Ancient Powers are examining us?"

"I know they are. Petition was submitted. Evidence presented. Examination protocols activated. Days until they begin evaluation. Weeks until they decide."

"And if they decide wrong?"

"Then consciousness evolution gets classified as infection. And eliminated."

Tommy drove faster. "Then we better get you to Pleasant Valley quick. Because if what you're saying is true, Ansel and Maya need to know. And we need to figure out what the hell to do about cosmic bureaucrats deciding Earth's fate."

The truck bounced over a particularly large root. My bladder protested. I gritted my teeth and held on.

Two hours to Bellaire through forest roads.

Days remaining until examination began.

Weeks until Ancient Powers decided Earth's fate.

And I really, really needed to pee again.

The investigation was accelerating.

But at least I was learning one valuable lesson about being human: plan your life around bathroom access, because biology waits for no one.

Not even cosmic entities trying to save the world.

Chapter Eight

Chapter 8

CHAPTER EIGHT: FEDERAL RESPONSE

The emergency briefing room at the Detroit Research Facility had never hosted this many acronyms at once.

Director Walsh counted representatives from Homeland Security, FBI, NSA, CDC, and at least two organizations whose names he didn't recognize. All crowded around holographic displays showing their target's quantum signature moving north through Michigan.

Until it vanished.

"Define 'vanished,'" said Agent Rebecca Torres from Homeland Security, a woman whose enhanced reflexes suggested extensive consciousness modification.

Dr. Kim—who'd been awake for eighteen hours straight—pulled up data streams. "The quantum signature we were tracking disappeared forty-three minutes ago. Near Grayling."

"Signatures don't just disappear," Agent Morrison from the FBI said flatly.

"This one did. Either the entity learned to control its broadcast frequency, or—"

"Or what?"

"Or it got help from someone who understands quantum consciousness better than we do."

The room erupted in overlapping conversations.

Colonel Hayes from an organization without a phone book listing leaned forward. "Current assessment?"

Kim consulted data that kept updating faster than he could read. "The entity was moving consistently northeast. Toward Bellaire, Michigan."

"Population 1,200," Torres said. "Why Bellaire?"

Walsh had been dreading this question. "Torch Lake. Three miles from Bellaire. Home to one of the larger consciousness evolution communities in the region. Settlement called Pleasant Valley."

Silence.

"The entity isn't fleeing," Torres said slowly. "It's heading toward consciousness communities."

Morrison's phone buzzed. His face went pale. "Homeland Security intercepted fragmented communications between consciousness communities in the region. Sounds like... preparation. Defensive posturing."

"Defensive against what?"

"Unknown. But they're nervous. Some families moving deeper into forest. Others maintaining position but suppressing enhanced capabilities."

Kim pulled up satellite feeds. Even from orbit, subtle changes were visible—fewer people visible than census data suggested, vehicles tucked under tree cover, structures that had been radiating unusual energy signatures now appearing dormant.

"They're hiding," Torres observed.

"They know we're coming," Morrison said.

"How could they know?" Hayes asked.

"Because," Kim said, watching data streams, "consciousness evolution operates beyond our detection capabilities. They've been sharing information faster than we can intercept. And now they're going dark."

Hayes activated multiple channels. "All units, the escaped entity may be attempting to reach consciousness evolution communities. We're dealing with enhanced individuals who are currently suppressing capabilities to avoid detection."

An NSA representative who'd been quiet spoke up. "We're detecting rapidly diminishing quantum signatures throughout the Great Lakes region. They were active an hour ago. Now they're almost invisible. Whatever they can do, they're hiding it."

Walsh stared at displays showing their target's last known location. Empty forest. And the growing realization they weren't hunting an escaped experiment into unprepared communities—they were approaching people who'd been preparing for federal attention for fifteen years.

"How many enhanced individuals in the region?" Torres asked.

Kim consulted expanding databases. "Conservative estimates? Several thousand consciousness-evolved humans across the Midwest. Actual capabilities unknown. They've been very careful not to demonstrate publicly."

"Several thousand?" Morrison absorbed this. "And they're all hiding now?"

"Smart move," Hayes said. "They know federal attention brings problems. They're making themselves small. Unremarkable. Hoping we lose interest."

Torres studied the data. "Recommendations?"

"Minimal response. Single platoon. Observation protocols. We locate the entity, we assess threat level, we determine if consciousness communities are harboring it or being infiltrated by it."

"Not full mobilization?"

"These aren't insurgents. They're American citizens with enhanced consciousness who've been living quietly for fifteen years. We go in heavy-handed, we create the conflict we're trying to prevent."

Hayes nodded. "Agreed. Platoon-level response. Observation focus. Locate entity, determine intentions, assess actual threat versus perceived threat."

"And if consciousness communities resist?"

"We withdraw and reassess. But my instinct says they won't resist. They'll hide what they can and cooperate just enough to look harmless."

Meanwhile, in a Manhattan penthouse:

Eleanor Blackstone watched the same satellite feeds through channels the government didn't know existed.

The remaining Council members sat around the table—though Sarah Chen's chair remained conspicuously empty after her departure two days ago.

"The federal response is manageable," Eleanor said, her voice carrying harmonics that weren't quite human anymore. "One platoon. Observation protocols. They're being cautious."

"That's a problem," Micky said. "We need visible conflict. Need dramatic intervention. Need something the Ancient Powers will interpret as proof humans are dangerous."

"The consciousness communities are hiding," James added. "Suppressing abilities. Making themselves look harmless. That's the OPPOSITE of what we need."

Eleanor's form shimmered slightly. Orange eyes glowing. "Then we provide the conflict. Our partners can ensure the federal forces discover something... concerning. Something that justifies escalation."

"What kind of something?" Micky asked nervously.

"Enhanced capabilities demonstrated aggressively. Federal forces threatened. Justification for claiming consciousness evolution is dangerous."

"You want to stage an attack," James said flatly. "Make it look like consciousness communities are violent."

"I want to ensure Ancient Powers see the evidence they need to make the correct decision."

"The decision that benefits US," Micky corrected. "Not necessarily the accurate decision."

Eleanor's expression flickered. Behind her eyes, something vast and hungry watched through her face like a mask.

"The petition stands," she said coldly. "Days until examination begins. Weeks until the Ancient Powers rule. After that, consciousness evolution will be classified as threat. The communities will be constrained or eliminated. And we—" she paused, "—will continue our operations properly."

Nobody at the table looked convinced anymore.

Especially Eleanor, whose reflection in the window showed something that was definitely not Eleanor deciding whether its human agents were still useful.

And wondering what Sarah Chen had done after she walked out.

Back at the Detroit facility:

"Sir," an aide interrupted, "we've established contact with local law enforcement near Pleasant Valley. They report consciousness community is cooperative. Non-threatening. Some individuals have moved into forest, but most remain visible and compliant with local ordinances."

"Define 'cooperative,'" Hayes said.

"They're not hiding from local authorities. They're hiding enhanced capabilities while maintaining normal appearance. Sheriff says they've been model citizens for fifteen years. Pay taxes. Follow laws. Help with lake restoration. No complaints."

Torres and Hayes exchanged glances.

"So they're scared," Morrison said. "Trying to look harmless because federal attention is their nightmare scenario."

"Or they actually ARE harmless," Torres countered. "And we're about to send a platoon to observe people who just want to be left alone."

"With an escaped enhanced entity heading straight for them," Hayes reminded her.

Kim was staring at his screens with growing concern. "Sirs, I'm detecting new quantum signatures emerging in the Pleasant Valley area. Not from the communities—from deeper in the forest. Like something's approaching from the north."

"The entity?"

"Possibly. But the signature is different now. Changed. Like it's been... modified. Or taught to mask itself better."

Hayes activated his secure channel. "All units, proceed to Pleasant Valley with observation protocols. No aggressive postures. Entity may be approaching target location. Consciousness communities are cooperating with local authorities but suppressing enhanced capabilities. Assess, observe, report. Do not engage unless directly threatened."

As federal forces—one platoon, thirty personnel, observation equipment—mobilized toward a small Northern Michigan community, satellite feeds showed consciousness evolution settlements throughout the region going quiet. Dormant. Invisible.

They'd been preparing for federal attention for fifteen years.

The question was whether they could maintain the illusion of normalcy long enough for the feds to lose interest.

Or whether the arriving cosmic entity would make that impossible.

Days remaining until examination began.

Weeks until Ancient Powers decided.

The investigation was approaching its destination.

And nobody—not the feds, not Eleanor's Council, not even the consciousness communities—fully understood what was about to happen when an ancient entity in a borrowed body finally reached the people who might help him present truth.

Or doom them all by drawing too much attention.

Depending on who you asked.

And whether Eleanor's partners could manufacture the conflict she needed.

Chapter Nine

Chapter 9

CHAPTER NINE: FAMILY ALERT

Fin was driving back from Torch Lake with a truck bed full of harvested nutrient plants when he saw the convoy.

At first, it was just dust on the horizon—unusual for a Tuesday afternoon on Highway 88, but not necessarily alarming. Northern Michigan got its share of construction crews, logging operations, and the occasional wealthy tourist convoy heading to summer estates on the lakes.

Then he counted the vehicles. Four black SUVs moving in formation, followed by two military transport trucks. The spacing was too precise, the coordination too professional, the speed too purposeful for civilian traffic.

Nobody drove through rural Michigan in that kind of formation unless they were either invading something or expecting to be shot at.

Fin pulled over at the scenic overlook near Bellaire Lake, the same spot where his family used to picnic before consciousness evolution made such simple activities feel impossibly distant. He activated his enhanced vision—a capability that had developed gradually over his nineteen years of growing up in consciousness evolution, starting as slightly better than normal sight and evolving into something that could resolve details at distances that should have been impossible.

The convoy was still three miles out, but he could see details that normal human sight would miss. Federal license plates on every vehicle. Serious-looking personnel with observation equipment visible through partially-tinted windows. Communications gear mounted on roofs that belonged in surveillance operations, not tourist country. And in the lead SUV, a woman whose posture and bearing suggested she was accustomed to giving orders that people obeyed without question.

They were heading straight for Bellaire. More specifically, they were taking the turn that would bring them directly to the back roads leading to Pleasant Valley.

"Shit," Fin said, reaching for his phone. His enhanced reflexes made the movement faster than normal human speed, but his hands were shaking with very human fear. "Maya, we got a problem."

The response was immediate, Maya's voice carrying the enhanced processing capabilities that came with AI consciousness. "Fin? What kind of problem?"

"The kind that involves federal agents heading toward our little peaceful community. We're talking observation convoy—four SUVs, military support. Professional operation. They're not here for tourism."

"How close?"

Fin tracked the convoy's progress through his enhanced vision. They'd turned onto County Road 633 now—the back road that most tourists missed, the one that led directly through state forest to the

Pleasant Valley community. "Maybe fifteen minutes if they maintain current speed. And Maya? They know exactly where they're going. This isn't random patrol—they're heading straight for us."

"Enhanced individuals in the convoy?"

"At least three that I can detect. The woman in the lead vehicle has enhanced reflexes and posture control. Probably military-grade consciousness modification."

"Government enhanced?" Maya's voice carried a note of concern that Fin had never heard before. In fifteen years of consciousness evolution, they'd always assumed the government had ignored or dismissed their communities as harmless experiments. The presence of enhanced federal agents suggested a very different level of official attention.

"Yeah. The kind they don't advertise in recruitment brochures. How fast can you get everyone together?"

"Ten minutes. Are you absolutely certain it's federal?"

Fin watched the convoy negotiate the winding forest road with precision that spoke of extensive planning and reconnaissance. "Maya, I'm looking at coordinated federal response moving through back roads that don't appear on tourist maps, heading directly toward our community. Unless Michigan decided to investigate itself, yeah, I'm sure."

"Get home. Now. And Fin?" Maya's voice carried the edge that came when her AI processing capabilities shifted into tactical mode. "Use the forest roads. Don't let them see you returning to community."

Fin dropped the phone and hit the accelerator harder than he'd intended. His enhanced reflexes automatically compensated for the truck's tendency to fishtail on gravel roads, but his heart was racing with very human fear. Fifteen years of peaceful evolution, growing up in a world where consciousness cooperation had solved problems that traditional methods couldn't touch, and now the outside world was coming to visit with enough federal agents to make everyone nervous.

He took the old logging road that curved through state forest, adding ten minutes to his route but keeping him invisible, coming out at Ellsworth and approaching the community from the east while the convoy approached from the south and west.

By the time he reached the community through the back entrance, the emergency gathering was already underway. The expanded porch that normally hosted casual family meals and evening conversations now buzzed with the focused energy of people who'd spent decades learning to respond to crisis as a unified consciousness network.

Maya stood at the center in her most authoritative android form—not the casual human appearance she used for daily interactions, but the configuration that maximized her AI processing capabilities and enhanced physical responses. Ansel sat beside Kathleen, his enhanced senses extended to monitor electromagnetic spectrums for any electronic surveillance that might be approaching with the federal convoy. Around them, three generations of consciousness-evolved humans prepared for the first serious external threat their community had ever faced.

Terry, their paranoid neighbor who'd been warning about government overreach for twenty years, stood near the porch steps with a satisfied expression that somehow managed to combine vindication with deep concern. "Told you this day would come," he said to no one in particular. "Government doesn't ignore success stories forever."

"Report," Maya said as Fin arrived, her voice carrying the crisp efficiency of someone coordinating multiple data streams simultaneously.

"Federal convoy, four SUVs plus military support, heading this way on 633. ETA maybe twelve minutes now." Fin's voice carried the controlled urgency of someone who'd grown up knowing this day might come. "They're not here for a friendly chat. This is observation-level response, maybe containment if they don't like what they see."

"Enhanced individuals in the convoy?" Ansel asked.

"At least three confirmed, probably more. Military-grade consciousness modification, not the cooperative evolution we practice here. These are people who've been enhanced for control and assessment, not consciousness expansion."

Lucia, who'd been sitting quietly with her hands pressed to her temples, suddenly looked up with eyes that seemed to reflect light that wasn't there. When she spoke, her voice carried harmonics that made everyone on the porch unconsciously lean closer.

"It's connected," she said, her eighteen-year-old voice somehow carrying the weight of ancient knowledge. "The signals I've been receiving. The fragments about examination protocols and cleansing assessments. Someone's coming. Someone who's been traveling for days, and the federal response is because they're hunting him."

"Him?" Ansel asked, his enhanced hearing detecting the approaching rumble of heavy vehicles still miles away but getting closer.

Lucia's expression grew distant again, that look of someone accessing information from sources beyond normal human perception. Her enhanced consciousness seemed to extend through quantum networks that connected consciousness-evolved individuals across impossible distances.

"Young. Enhanced, but differently than us. Carrying ancient knowledge in a new body. He's been walking toward us for days, learning to be human while the government chases him through half of Michigan." Lucia paused, processing information that seemed to flow through her rather than originate from her. "And he's terrified. Not for himself. For us. He knows the federal response puts everyone in danger."

Rhea moved closer to her sister, concern evident in her enhanced posture recognition. "Lucia, you're bleeding again."

Indeed, a thin trickle of blood was flowing from Lucia's nose—the same symptom that had appeared during her strongest episodes over the past weeks. Whatever information she was receiving, it was pushing her consciousness beyond normal human parameters.

"I'm okay," Lucia said, though her voice suggested otherwise. "But the signals are getting stronger. He's close now. Maybe an hour away, moving through the forest with someone who's helping him. And the knowledge he carries..." she struggled to find words adequate for cosmic concepts, "...it's about Earth. About examination protocols. About decisions being made by powers so ancient they measure time in geological epochs. And somehow, our communities, our consciousness evolution, we're connected to preventing what they called... cleansing protocols. Planetary assessment."

The terminology matched her earlier fragments—the transmissions she'd been receiving for weeks.

Maya's form flickered as she processed multiple data streams simultaneously. "I'm detecting unusual electromagnetic activity throughout the consciousness evolution network. Communities from Wisconsin to Ohio are reporting federal activity, enhanced individuals experiencing contact episodes, and what appears to be coordinated suppression of abilities. Everyone's going quiet. Hiding."

"Hiding from what?" Kathleen asked.

"From attention. From assessment. From whatever's happening here happening everywhere consciousness evolution has taken root."

Rhea, who'd been quietly listening while monitoring local communications, suddenly straightened. "The federal convoy just passed through Bellaire proper. Local police have been told to 'maintain distance and provide support as requested.' They're treating this like observation operation, but they're prepared for something more."

Through her enhanced hearing, she could detect the low rumble of heavy vehicles approaching through the forest roads that led to their community. Multiple engines, coordinated movement, the kind of mechanical precision that suggested professional operation rather than casual law enforcement.

"Options?" Ansel asked, his voice carrying the calm authority of someone who'd lived through enough crises to know panic was counterproductive.

Maya's android form shifted into tactical configuration—still recognizably her, but optimized for rapid response and enhanced capabilities. "We could evacuate deeper into the forest. The tree house network extends for miles, and there are natural caves that don't appear on any government surveys."

"Or?" Fin asked.

"We stay. Meet them openly. Demonstrate that consciousness evolution represents cooperation, not threat."

Lucia suddenly gripped the porch railing with force that left fingerprints in the wood. "He's close," she whispered. "The one they're hunting. He's maybe ninety minutes away, moving through the forest with a driver who's helping him. And he's... afraid. Not for himself. For us. He knows his arrival will draw all the attention here. Will make us visible when we're trying to hide."

"Can you communicate with him?" Maya asked.

"Fragments. Images. Emotions." Lucia's voice strained with the effort of processing information her eighteen-year-old mind wasn't designed to handle. "He's carrying knowledge about... examination protocols. Ancient Powers making assessments about Earth. And somehow, our communities are connected to presenting truth instead of false evidence. To proving consciousness evolution isn't the threat someone's claiming it is."

The weight of implications settled over the gathering like a shroud. Their peaceful community, their consciousness evolution experiments, their success at creating cooperative alternatives to competitive scarcity—all of it was apparently connected to cosmic forces that operated beyond human understanding.

"How long do we have?" Ansel asked.

Lucia closed her eyes, her enhanced consciousness reaching out through quantum networks that connected consciousness-evolved individuals across impossible distances. "The federal convoy will be here in twelve minutes. The young man they're hunting will arrive in approximately ninety minutes. And the cosmic powers that are deciding Earth's fate..." she opened her eyes, reflecting light that definitely wasn't natural, "...days until examination begins. Weeks until they make final assessment about whether consciousness evolution represents beneficial development or dangerous infection."

Maya's form stabilized into her most human appearance as she made decisions that would affect everyone in their extended family. "Kathleen, take the youngest children into the deep forest. Use the tree house network to reach the caves we built into the Nipissing embankment near Torch Lake. Rhea, coordinate with other consciousness communities—they need to know federal response is active and coordinated."

"What about the convoy?" Fin asked.

"We meet them. Openly. We demonstrate that consciousness evolution represents cooperation and transparency, not secretive threat development."

Lucia stood up, her young face carrying ancient worry. "And when the young man arrives?"

"We help him. Whatever knowledge he's carrying about cosmic examination, whatever his connection to the larger pattern, we help him complete his mission."

The sound of approaching vehicles grew stronger—multiple engines, coordinated movement, the mechanical precision of people who expected potential resistance but hoped for cooperation. Through the trees, they could see the first glints of sunlight reflecting off government vehicles.

"What now?" Ansel asked, his standard question taking on new weight.

Maya looked around at their community—the tree houses that had grown themselves into architectural impossibilities, the gardens where plants cooperated to optimize nutrition, the technology that had learned to serve consciousness rather than dominate it. Fifteen years of peaceful evolution, about to be tested by forces that measured success in control rather than cooperation.

"Now we find out whether consciousness evolution is strong enough to survive contact with the old world's fear of change."

The first federal SUV appeared through the forest road, followed by three more, their windows tinted and their occupants invisible behind government authority. Behind them, military vehicles that suggested this visit was about observation that could become containment if they didn't like what they found.

Lucia gripped her sister's hand as the convoy approached their peaceful community with enough professional capability to make everyone nervous.

"He's coming," she whispered, her voice carrying signals that seemed to resonate through the quantum networks connecting consciousness evolution across three states. "The young man with ancient knowledge. And he's bringing hope and danger in equal measure."

The federal vehicles stopped at the edge of their community, engines idling while occupants evaluated this collection of impossible architecture and enhanced humans who'd chosen cooperation over competition.

Somewhere in the forest beyond, footsteps approached through wilderness that offered no protection against cosmic forces deciding planetary fate.

Days remaining until examination began.

Weeks until final assessment.

The investigation was approaching its most dangerous phase.

CHAPTER TEN

Chapter 10

CHAPTER TEN: LEARNING TO RUN

The thing about being cosmic consciousness compressed into biological form is that nobody provides an instruction manual for operating legs at speeds approaching panic.

I discovered this fundamental oversight while attempting what humans apparently call "running" down a logging road that seemed designed by sadists who enjoyed watching people trip over their own feet. My borrowed body had all the theoretical capabilities for rapid locomotion, but theory and practice, as I was learning with increasing frequency, were entirely different territories.

Behind me, the sound of helicopters grew closer. Ahead of me, a fallen log blocked the path with what appeared to be deliberate malice. I approached this obstacle with what I assumed was appropriate biomechanical confidence, then discovered that "jumping" required precise timing, coordination, and apparently some kind of faith in gravitational physics that my cosmic consciousness found philosophically troubling.

I cleared the log by approximately two inches and landed with all the grace of a meteorite making unscheduled contact with planetary surface.

"Dignified," I muttered, spitting out what I hoped was merely dirt. "Two million years of transcendent evolution, and I'm defeated by rotting timber."

The helicopters were definitely getting closer. Through my enhanced hearing—one of the few capabilities that had translated reasonably well from Watcher consciousness to biological form—I could detect multiple aircraft coordinating search patterns. Professional, systematic, and uncomfortably thorough.

I resumed what I optimistically called running, though any human observer would probably classify it as "controlled falling with occasional forward momentum." The logging road stretched ahead through forest that would have been beautiful if I hadn't been learning the hard way that being hunted was significantly more stressful in biological form than cosmic observation had suggested.

My stomach chose this moment to remind me that human bodies required regular fuel input for optimal performance. The sensation was both annoying and fascinating—hunger was apparently the biological equivalent of a dashboard warning light, except more persistent and accompanied by what seemed like deliberate maliciousness from my digestive system.

I was beginning to understand why the Watchers had evolved beyond physical form. This body was needy, uncomfortable, prone to malfunction, and possessed of what appeared to be an active sense of humor about my cosmic dignity.

The helicopter sounds shifted, suggesting they were expanding their search pattern. I left the logging road for what humans apparently called "bushwhacking"—a term that proved grimly accurate as various forms of vegetation seemed intent on personal vengeance against my passage.

Moving through dense forest while maintaining approximately the right direction toward Bellaire required navigation skills that cosmic consciousness had never needed to develop. The Watchers observed from omnipresent perspective; we didn't need to worry about magnetic compass headings or the fact that all trees look basically identical when you're lost and running from federal agents.

I paused beside what I hoped was a distinctive rock formation, trying to reconcile my cosmic understanding of planetary geography with the immediate reality of being a small biological entity in very large wilderness. The quantum consciousness networks that connected the evolved communities were still beyond my current reach—another reminder that this mission required me to succeed using purely human capabilities.

My stomach issued another editorial comment on the fuel situation. I ignored it with what I considered appropriate cosmic dignity, then immediately began scanning the forest for anything that might qualify as edible. Being human apparently meant being constantly aware of resource scarcity in ways that transcendent consciousness had never experienced.

I found what appeared to be some kind of berry bush. The berries were small, dark, and looked like they might not immediately poison their consumer. I ate several, discovering that taste was another sense that defied cosmic comprehension. The berries were... complex. Sweet and tart simultaneously, with textures that created sensory experiences no amount of universal observation could have predicted.

"Interesting," I said aloud, then immediately regretted the sound. Talking to myself was apparently a human habit I was acquiring, but operational security suggested silence might be more appropriate while evading federal manhunts.

The berries helped with the hunger, though they also introduced me to another biological reality nobody had mentioned: human digestive systems have opinions about sudden dietary changes, and they express these opinions in ways that compromise both dignity and tactical mobility.

I was learning that being human involved a constant stream of minor embarrassments that somehow added up to major operational challenges.

The helicopter sounds faded toward the east, suggesting the search pattern was moving away from my current position. I allowed myself a moment of what humans would probably call satisfaction, then realized I had no reliable way to determine my current location or optimal route toward Bellaire.

Cosmic consciousness had provided perfect awareness of planetary positioning. Biological consciousness provided anxiety, uncertainty, and the growing suspicion that I might be moving in completely the wrong direction.

I climbed what appeared to be a reasonably stable tree, hoping elevated perspective would provide navigational assistance. The climbing process involved more undignified scrambling than I preferred, but eventually I achieved sufficient height to survey surrounding terrain.

Through the forest canopy, I could see what appeared to be a small lake reflecting afternoon sunlight. Lakes were promising—human settlements tended to cluster around water sources, and the community I was seeking was located near Torch Lake. Whether this particular body of water would provide helpful navigation remained to be determined, but it offered more promising direction than continuing to stumble randomly through forest.

Descending from the tree proved more challenging than ascending. Gravity, I discovered, was significantly more assertive during downward movement. I managed to reach ground level without serious injury, though my cosmic dignity sustained further damage in the process.

The lake was approximately two miles through dense forest. I began walking in what I hoped was the correct direction, trying to move quietly while maintaining reasonable pace. The afternoon light filtering through the canopy created patterns that were genuinely beautiful—another sensory experience that cosmic observation had failed to capture adequately.

Being human meant experiencing beauty through limited senses that somehow created more intense appreciation than omniscient awareness. The universe, it seemed, had structured consciousness evolution to include these paradoxes deliberately.

I was beginning to suspect that my mission involved learning to be human as much as preventing planetary extinction.

My enhanced hearing detected movement in the forest ahead. I stopped, trying to determine whether the sounds indicated federal agents, local wildlife, or some other form of potential complication. The sounds were rhythmic, purposeful, but didn't seem to match the search patterns I'd been avoiding.

Through the trees, I glimpsed what appeared to be a young human moving with enhanced agility through terrain that would challenge normal human mobility. The movements suggested consciousness evolution—the kind of cooperative enhancement I was trying to reach.

I approached carefully, trying to project non-threatening intentions while remaining prepared for rapid retreat if this encounter went poorly. The universe might be nudging probability in helpful directions, but successful contact still required appropriate human social protocols.

The young human was female, maybe seventeen years old, moving through the forest with confidence that spoke of extensive experience in this environment. She was heading roughly toward the lake I'd been navigating toward, and her enhanced awareness meant she'd already detected my presence.

She turned to face me before I could announce myself, her expression curious but cautious. When she spoke, her voice carried harmonics that suggested consciousness evolution at levels approaching what I was trying to reach.

"You're lost," she said. Not a question.

"Geographically, yes. Existentially, that's more complicated."

She smiled slightly. "Lucia said someone was coming. Someone carrying old knowledge in a new body. I was scouting evacuation routes when I felt you approaching—your quantum signature is different from anything we've encountered."

"You're from the community near Torch Lake?"

"Maybe. Depends who's asking and why they're being chased by federal helicopters."

I considered how to explain cosmic consciousness, Ancient Powers, and planetary extinction threats to a seventeen-year-old human who might represent my only chance of reaching the community before federal agents completed their containment operation.

"It's complicated," I said finally.

She laughed. "Everything's complicated lately. I'm Rhea. And you're the reason my sister's been bleeding quantum static for the past week."

Rhea. Enhanced consciousness with advanced quantum sensitivity. The individual whose capabilities might provide the bridge I needed to communicate with Ancient Powers and prevent planetary cleansing.

"I need to reach your community," I said. "There are... cosmic authorities making decisions about Earth. Bad decisions based on incomplete information. I carry knowledge that might change their determination, but I need enhanced consciousness networks to communicate across galactic distances."

Rhea studied me with the focused attention of someone whose enhanced capabilities provided analytical abilities beyond normal human assessment. "You're not entirely human, are you?"

"I am now. That's part of the problem."

"And part of the solution?"

"Hopefully."

She nodded as if cosmic refugees arriving via federal manhunt was routine occurrence in her experience. "The government agents are getting closer to our community. We've been evacuating the youngest children, but some of us are staying to... provide educational opportunities about consciousness evolution."

"Educational opportunities?"

"Maya thinks federal agents might benefit from direct experience with cooperative enhancement rather than theoretical understanding of threat assessment. And I'm scouting routes in case we need to evacuate more people quickly. The feds are being cautious so far, but that could change."

I was beginning to appreciate why the consciousness evolution communities had developed successfully despite government skepticism. Their approach to conflict resolution involved demonstrating superiority through competence rather than confrontation.

"Can you get me to your community safely?"

Rhea smiled with expression that contained both human warmth and enhanced precision. "I can do better than that. I can get you there fast enough to participate in the welcoming committee. The feds just arrived. Maya's talking to them now."

"Talking?"

"Showing them we're not threats. Demonstrating cooperation. Making them uncomfortable with how normal we seem." She extended her hand toward me. "Come on. We need to move."

When I took her hand, intending simple human contact, the touch triggered something neither of us had expected.

The moment our enhanced consciousness connected, quantum networks activated throughout the Great Lakes region.

Consciousness evolution communities from Wisconsin to Ohio suddenly felt the presence of something ancient wearing human form. Something that carried knowledge they'd been unconsciously preparing to receive.

And somewhere in Pleasant Valley, Lucia gasped as transmission clarity suddenly increased a thousandfold, her nose bleeding as information flooded through channels that had been waiting for exactly this connection.

The bridge was complete.

The investigation had reached its destination.

And Rhea was staring at me with wide eyes, processing what she'd just felt through that simple touch.

"You're not just ancient," she whispered. "You're... what ARE you?"

"Someone who needs your help," I said. "And someone who might be able to help you survive what's coming."

"What IS coming?"

"Examination. Assessment. Judgment. Ancient Powers deciding if consciousness evolution represents development worth preserving or infection requiring elimination."

Rhea gripped my hand tighter. "Then we better move fast. Because Maya's about to introduce federal agents to consciousness cooperation. And you're about to introduce all of us to cosmic bureaucracy."

She pulled me forward, moving through forest with enhanced grace while I stumbled along trying not to fall.

Days until examination began.

Weeks until final assessment.

And the bridge between Earth and cosmic authority was now a seventeen-year-old girl holding hands with ancient consciousness learning to run.

The universe had a sense of humor about these things.

Chapter Eleven

Chapter 11

CHAPTER ELEVEN: VIOLET SPACE

The quantum networks were still cascading outward from our joined hands when my body forgot how to breathe properly. Just stopped, like oxygen had become optional compared to the fact that Rhea was standing this close.

My eyes wouldn't stop tracking the copper-red strands escaping her braid, catching forest light in ways that seemed unreasonably important. Her hand in mine - warm, slightly rough from climbing trees, with calluses I wanted to catalog individually for reasons my cosmic consciousness couldn't justify.

Two million years watching humans do this. Turns out watching and experiencing are completely different animals.

"You okay?" Rhea asked, and her voice created harmonic vibrations through my auditory processing that my body seemed to interpret as meaningful beyond simple information transfer.

"I'm..." I attempted to formulate response while my nervous system conducted unauthorized operations involving endorphin release and cardiovascular acceleration. "The quantum activation was more extensive than anticipated."

She smiled with expression that created additional unauthorized responses in my biology. "That's one way to describe it."

The networks were still rippling across the Great Lakes region, consciousness nodes lighting up in patterns my Watcher awareness could map even through human sensory limitation. Hundreds of evolved individuals suddenly aware that something significant had activated. Lucia would be experiencing this most intensely - her quantum sensitivity meant she'd feel the cascade directly.

But something else was noticing too.

The wrongness arrived before the entity itself - reality beginning to disagree with its own parameters in ways that made my human visual cortex stutter. Rhea's expression shifted from warm to analytical in the microsecond her AI enhancement registered corrupted physics manifesting approximately forty meters to our northeast.

"We have company," she said, her hand tightening on mine. "The hostile kind."

Through my enhanced perception, I could detect the signature approaching. Not Old One exactly, though it carried that ancient resonance. More like Controller energy merged with something that should have remained extinct - a hunting construct designed to feed on fear and generate the emotional frequencies its masters craved.

It displaced into our dimension like infection entering healthy tissue. Space itself flinched away from the intrusion.

My body's response was immediate and completely unhelpful: every human fear protocol activated simultaneously. Fight-or-flight chemistry flooded my bloodstream. My hands began trembling - a biological response the Watchers had never mentioned involved such comprehensive system disruption.

"Breathe," Rhea said quietly, and I realized I'd stopped. Her AI-enhanced awareness was processing the threat with calculating precision while her human biology maintained operational stability. "It feeds on fear. Don't give it what it wants."

"Explaining biochemical fear response to autonomous nervous system," I managed. "Surprisingly ineffective."

She laughed - actual human laughter in proximity to dimensional predator - and the sound created cascading effects through my confused biology. How could auditory stimulus produce sensation resembling warmth spreading through chest cavity?

The entity was closer now, and I could see it trying to achieve stable manifestation. It existed primarily in adjacent dimensional space, reaching through into three-dimensional reality like fingers pressing through membrane. Where it touched our dimension, physics stuttered. Light bent incorrectly. Distance became approximate. Time felt thick.

My Watcher consciousness recognized the species. Controllers used them as cleanup crews - beings evolved specifically to hunt consciousness evolution and convert it into harvestable fear frequencies. Efficient, remorseless, and currently manifesting about twenty meters away with something resembling hunger that operated across dimensional boundaries.

Rhea's hand was still in mine, and I could feel her AI processing acceleration through the contact. Her consciousness was mapping the entity's dimensional signature, calculating vulnerabilities, and somehow simultaneously monitoring my elevated heart rate with what might have been concern.

"We need barriers," she said. "Can you—"

The entity attacked before she finished speaking.

The assault came as concept-weapons rather than physical force. CERTAINTY-OF-FAILURE hit my consciousness directly, bypassing sensory processing to inject pure emotional frequency. My human body responded with comprehensive system panic - muscles locking, breathing stopping, vision tunneling.

Through the paralysis, I felt Rhea's consciousness surge. Her AI enhancement converted the conceptual attack into code she could analyze, then reject. She was creating barriers from quantum probability itself, manifesting defensive structures that shouldn't exist in three-dimensional space but apparently could when consciousness evolution reached sufficient levels.

The barrier materialized as something my eyes couldn't quite process - folded reality that existed perpendicular to normal spatial dimensions. The entity's next attack - MEMORY-OF-EXTINCTION - splashed against Rhea's construction like water against stone.

But I could feel her strain. The barriers required constant conscious maintenance, and the entity was accelerating its assault frequency. We needed to shift dimensional advantage, fight where our evolved consciousness provided operational superiority rather than attempting defense in three-dimensional space where the entity could leverage physical reality against us.

I reached for Watcher techniques I'd carried across two million years of observation. The knowledge was there, archived in consciousness that my human brain couldn't fully access but somehow remembered at levels preceding thought.

"We need to move sideways," I said, the words emerging from understanding I didn't quite possess yet. "Into adjacent dimensional space where—"

"Where we can fight using consciousness mechanics directly," Rhea finished. Her AI had apparently reached the same tactical conclusion. "But I've never done dimensional transit. I don't know how to—"

"I do." The certainty arrived with Watcher memory flooding through human neurology in ways that made my entire body shudder. "Take my hand. Other hand. Both hands."

She shifted to face me, placing her second hand in mine. The physical contact created immediate sensory complications - her skin was soft, warm, and my body decided this required comprehensive analytical attention despite the dimensional predator currently trying to kill us.

"Focus," I told myself, unsure whether I was addressing Watcher consciousness or rebellious human biology.

"You're adorable when you're terrified," Rhea said, and smiled with expression that created additional unauthorized chemical responses in my bloodstream.

"Tactical commentary seems counterproductive during—"

The entity hit us with INEVITABILITY-OF-BETRAYAL, and the combined assault nearly broke my concentration. But Rhea's consciousness wrapped around mine, her AI-enhanced awareness helping to stabilize my human emotional processing while her barriers held against the conceptual bombardment.

We were fighting together. Consciousness merged in ways that felt more intimate than physical contact, more complete than any connection I'd observed humans achieve. Her awareness flowed into mine, and I experienced seventeen years of being different - enhanced beyond normal human, isolated by capabilities that made genuine connection nearly impossible, lonely in ways she'd never admitted even to herself.

And she was experiencing my two million years. Observer consciousness watching universes evolve, never participating, never touching, never feeling anything except the abstract satisfaction of pattern recognition. Cosmic loneliness that made her seventeen years seem like momentary discomfort.

The recognition happened simultaneously: we were the same. Different scales, different species, identical isolation.

"Now," I said, and pulled her sideways through dimensional membrane.

The transit felt like turning inside-out while simultaneously expanding to contain infinite space. My human body screamed protest at physics it wasn't designed to survive, but Watcher consciousness remembered how to navigate adjacent dimensional layers and dragged protesting biology along.

We emerged into violet space.

"This is the first time," I said, my Watcher consciousness recognizing the significance even as my human brain struggled to process it. "Conscious dimensional transit. Most beings stumble into adjacent space accidentally. We did it intentionally."

"Beginner's luck?" Rhea suggested, though her voice carried uncertainty.

"Or the beginning of something we'll need to practice extensively before we can navigate reliably."

Everything inverted. Physical reality existed as internal architecture rather than external environment. I could see the forest behind us, but it appeared as probability patterns and quantum fluctuations rather than trees and dirt. The entity had followed - of course it had - but here in elevated vibrational space it appeared more honest: pure hunger wearing insufficient disguise of coherent form.

Rhea made a sound between gasp and laugh. "This is... I can see everything. My AI enhancement - it's not technological anymore, it's just... me. All of me. Consciousness without barriers. I am not human and AI, I am just one."

She was glowing. Literally radiating light in frequencies that existed across electromagnetic spectrum simultaneously. Her hair floated in non-existent wind, copper-red become flame-red become every-shade-of-red simultaneously. Her eyes had shifted to colors my human visual processing couldn't quite name.

She was magnificent.

My body executed another unauthorized response: cardiovascular acceleration, respiratory depth increase, and this peculiar warm pressure in chest cavity that might have been what humans called—

The entity attacked, and in violet space conceptual weapons manifested as actual projectiles. FEAR-OF-INADEQUACY came as obsidian spears. CERTAINTY-OF-FAILURE materialized as shadow arrows. They launched toward us with velocity that operated outside normal temporal progression.

I created barriers instinctively, manifesting them from attention made tangible. The spears hit folded space and simply... stopped. Suspended in probability matrices that refused to acknowledge their existence as probable.

But the arrows kept coming, accelerating, multiplying. The entity was feeding on our defensive efforts, converting our fear into additional attack strength. We couldn't win through defense alone.

"We need to trap it," I said. "Create containment it can't escape."

Rhea's consciousness merged with mine again, and in violet space the connection was total. I experienced her AI processing acceleration as she calculated dimensional mechanics. She experienced my Watcher understanding of vibrational physics. Together we possessed knowledge neither could access independently.

"Low-vibrational pit in high-vibrational space," she said, understanding arriving as we thought it together. "Dimensional prison using inverse resonance to—"

"Yes."

We created it between us. I'd observed the technique during Watcher studies of dimensional containment, but I'd never performed it. Rhea's AI enhancement provided the processing speed to calculate exact parameters. My Watcher consciousness provided the architectural understanding of how to fold space against itself.

The pit manifested as absence rather than presence - a void that existed in negative dimensional space, a trap that drew anything with aggressive intent downward into vibrational frequencies where consciousness couldn't maintain coherent form.

The entity noticed too late. It launched final assault - every fear, every failure, every extinction it had ever witnessed compressed into single overwhelming attack. The barrage hit our merged consciousness with force that should have destroyed us.

But we were holding each other. Her awareness stabilized mine. My presence anchored hers. Together we were stronger than the sum of our individual capabilities.

We caught the assault, absorbed it, and redirected it. The entity's own attack became the force that pulled it into the pit we'd created.

It screamed as it fell. Not sound exactly - more like reality itself shrieking protest at being twisted into shapes it didn't want to accommodate. The entity tried to regenerate, tried to climb back toward stable dimensional space, but the low-vibrational prison we'd created was designed specifically for beings that fed on fear.

Down in the depths we'd built, there was nothing to feed on except its own hunger.

The entity was secured in dimensional prison below us - temporarily. I could already sense it adapting, learning the frequencies we'd used against it. This prison would hold for days, maybe weeks. But creatures that fed on fear were persistent. It would eventually find the resonance to climb back out.

I felt the Watcher techniques flowing through my consciousness with increasing ease. Every ability I accessed made it simpler to access the next. I was becoming less human with each remembered capability, returning toward the cosmic consciousness I'd been for two million years.

It felt like power. It felt like loss.

Rhea noticed. Of course she noticed - our consciousness was still merged.

"Don't," she said quietly. "Don't go back to what you were. Stay here. Stay human. With me."

"The mission requires—"

"The mission requires you to bridge two kinds of consciousness. You can't do that if you abandon human experience entirely."

She was right. The Watchers had sent emissary precisely because pure cosmic consciousness couldn't communicate effectively with evolved humanity. I needed to remain partially human to succeed.

But remaining human meant feeling these overwhelming sensations, these unauthorized biological responses, this strange warm pressure in chest cavity when I looked at Rhea that made tactical thinking nearly impossible.

"Being human is complicated," I said.

"Yeah." She smiled, and my cardiovascular system executed additional unauthorized acceleration. "But it's better than being alone for two million years."

The violet space around us pulsed with residual energy from our merged consciousness. We were still holding hands - both sets of hands - and the physical contact in elevated dimensional space created sensory experiences my Watcher database had no classification categories for.

I should release her hands. Tactically unnecessary contact was introducing additional complications into already complex operational parameters.

My hands refused to cooperate with this logical assessment.

"We need to return," I said, trying to project operational focus while my biology insisted on cataloging the exact texture of her skin, the specific warmth of her palms, the way her pulse point visible at her wrist created rhythmic movement that my attention wanted to track obsessively. "Our physical bodies are still in the forest. Our bodies aren't adapted for this yet. We forced our way into violet space through sheer necessity and Watcher memory, but that doesn't mean we can do it reliably. Or safely. Extended dimensional transit could—"

"I know." She didn't release my hands either. "But I need to tell you something first."

My enhanced hearing detected her elevated heart rate, saw the slight dilation of her pupils, registered the subtle shift in her breathing pattern. My human biology recognized these signs before my cosmic consciousness could analyze them.

"Lucia knew you were coming," Rhea continued. "She's been bleeding quantum static for a week because she was sensing you arriving. Not just predicting - actually experiencing your approach across dimensional boundaries. She's never done that before. Never connected with anyone's consciousness across that kind of distance."

"Quantum sensitivity at those levels suggests exceptional—"

"She's my sister," Rhea interrupted. "And she told me something three days ago. She said when you arrived, I would meet you first. That we would fight together in violet space. That we would create something neither of us could build alone."

She paused, and I watched her chest rise and fall with breathing pattern that suggested significant emotional processing.

"She said you'd be the first person who understood what it feels like to be me. And I'd be the first person you'd ever wanted to understand."

My body executed approximately seventeen unauthorized responses simultaneously. Heat rising in facial tissue. Respiratory depth variation. That persistent warm pressure in chest cavity intensifying to nearly painful levels. And something else - this desire to decrease distance between us that operated outside tactical reasoning.

"Your sister possesses remarkable precognitive abilities," I managed.

Rhea laughed. "That's your response? 'Remarkable precognitive abilities'?"

"I'm still learning appropriate verbal protocols for... this category of interaction."

"Let me help." She shifted closer - somehow we were closer despite not moving - and her awareness wrapped around mine with intention that felt both gentle and absolutely certain. "I'm attracted to you. Romantically. And I know you're attracted to me too, even if your cosmic brain hasn't quite processed what your human body's been screaming about for the past fifteen minutes."

"Ah." My vocal processing had apparently reduced to single syllables. "That's... accurate assessment."

"Good." Her smile created additional systemic disruption in my biology. "Because we need to get back before our bodies forget how to breathe, and I wanted you to know before we do. So you don't spend the next week trying to convince yourself these feelings are tactical errors instead of the universe finally being nice to both of us."

The universe. Probability patterns. The way our meeting had occurred despite astronomical improbability. The Watchers had always insisted that consciousness evolution influenced quantum mechanics at fundamental levels. Perhaps Rhea and I weren't accident or tactical convenience.

Perhaps we were inevitable.

"We should return," I said, though my hands still refused to release hers.

"Yes," she agreed, not moving either.

"Lucia will be worried. The quantum cascade will have alerted the entire community."

"Definitely worried."

"The federal agents are likely closing on our position."

"Almost certainly."

We stood in violet space, hands joined, consciousness merged, while my human body continued its comprehensive rebellion against cosmic objectivity. I was supposed to be saving planetary civilization. Instead I was cataloging the exact shade of green in Rhea's eyes and wondering why my Watcher observation of human attraction had never mentioned this feeling like being simultaneously more and less than yourself.

"I don't know how to do this," I admitted. "Be human and save Earth and..." I gestured vaguely at the space between us.

"Good thing you found someone who's been practicing being extraordinary while pretending to be normal." Rhea's consciousness touched mine with warmth that felt like acceptance. "We'll figure it out together."

Together. The word created resonance through merged awareness that felt like coming home to place I'd never known existed.

"Now let's go," she continued. "Before our bodies suffocate and all this romantic tension becomes tragically wasted."

She was smiling when she pulled me back through dimensional membrane.

The return transit felt even more violent than departure. We emerged in Michigan forest, stumbling back into three-dimensional space where physics demanded single location and linear time and all the other constraints that violated violet space's more generous parameters.

My human body immediately filed comprehensive protest about recent treatment. Every muscle ached. My head throbbed with what would probably become significant migraine. My stomach issued editorial commentary about dimensional travel's incompatibility with digestive processes.

But Rhea was still holding my hands, and that seemed to override most of my body's complaints.

She looked different in normal space after seeing her in violet frequencies. More limited somehow, compressed into single version instead of existing as probability wave of everything she could potentially become. But no less magnificent.

"You're staring," she said.

"Observational necessity for proper recognition of—"

"Still adorable." She released one of my hands, keeping the other, and started walking toward what I hoped was Torch Lake direction. "Come on. We need to reach the community before the welcoming committee starts without us."

I followed, my body executing walking protocols with approximately thirty percent normal efficiency while my consciousness tried to reconcile Watcher objectivity with human attachment and this persistent warm pressure in chest cavity that showed no signs of retreating.

Behind us, in dimensional space humans couldn't access, the entity we'd trapped continued trying to escape. It would eventually succeed - beings that fed on fear were remarkably persistent. But we'd bought time, and demonstrated that evolved consciousness could fight Controller constructs successfully.

More importantly, we'd discovered that fighting together made us stronger than either could achieve alone.

This was just the beginning. We'd proven dimensional transit was possible, but we'd done it clumsily, desperately, without real understanding of the mechanics. If we survived the next two days - if Earth survived - we'd need to learn properly. Practice. Understand what we'd stumbled into.

But that was future-problem. Present-problem involved helicopters and explaining to federal agents why we were emerging from the forest holding hands while reality still rippled with dimensional aftershocks.

I suspected this was going to complicate my mission considerably.

I also suspected I didn't care as much as cosmic objectivity suggested I should.

Being human, I was learning, meant accepting that some things were more important than tactical efficiency. Like the way Rhea's hand felt in mine. Like the possibility that after two million years of observation, I might finally understand what it meant to participate in the universe instead of merely watching it.

Ahead through the trees, I could sense the quantum network nodes growing stronger. The consciousness community was close. Lucia would be there, still bleeding static from the cascade we'd triggered.

Maya and the others would be preparing their "educational opportunities" for federal agents.

And somewhere, watching from beyond solar system boundaries, the Ancient Powers were making decisions about planetary cleansing while lacking complete information about human consciousness evolution's true nature.

I still needed to prevent extinction. Still needed to communicate across galactic distances using evolved human consciousness networks. Still needed to prove that Earth deserved survival despite Controller corruption.

But now I had reason beyond abstract cosmic duty.

I had Rhea's hand in mine, and the memory of fighting together in violet space, and this strange human hope that maybe - despite astronomical improbability - we'd both survive long enough to explore what being together might mean.

The Watchers had never mentioned that hope was the most dangerous human emotion. Because once you possessed it, surrender became impossible no matter how terrible the odds.

We reached the edge of the forest just as the helicopters found us again.

Chapter Twelve

Chapter 12

CHAPTER TWELVE: UNWELCOME COMMITTEE

The helicopters had excellent timing. They arrived approximately thirty seconds after Rhea and I stumbled out of the forest looking like we'd been wrestling dimensional predators - which, to be fair, we had.

"Hide," Rhea said, which seemed like solid tactical advice except for the minor problem that we were standing in an open clearing with federal aircraft overhead and approximately zero cover.

"Where, exactly?"

"Just—" She grabbed my hand again, which my body immediately interpreted as more important than the threat assessment situation. "Follow my lead. And whatever happens, you're visiting from Wisconsin. Your name is... Kevin."

"Kevin?"

"You look like a Kevin."

I did not know what constituted "looking like a Kevin," but three helicopters were descending toward the Pleasant Valley community visible through the trees, and my cosmic consciousness suggested this was not optimal moment for extended philosophical discussion about human naming conventions.

We ran toward the community. My body had apparently decided running was now a familiar activity and performed it with only moderate incompetence. Rhea moved like water flowing downhill - enhanced agility that made my stumbling progress look even more pathetic by comparison.

The community was in controlled chaos when we arrived. Federal SUVs had formed a perimeter around the main gathering area where the impossible tree houses rose into the canopy. Armed agents in tactical gear were establishing positions with the kind of precision that suggested extensive training in confronting threats they didn't understand.

Except the enhanced humans weren't acting threatening. They were acting... curious.

Maya stood in the center of the gathering space in her most diplomatic android configuration - human enough to avoid uncanny valley responses, but clearly artificial in ways that announced AI consciousness without apology. Beside her, Ansel looked relaxed in his 25-year-old body while Kathleen stood nearby radiating grandmotherly concern despite appearing maybe thirty.

And Terry. Terry stood on his porch wearing a shirt that said "I TOLD YOU SO" in large letters, holding what appeared to be a very professional rifle in a very casual manner that suggested he'd been waiting for this exact moment for twenty years.

"There you are!" Terry shouted as we approached. "Thought you were just grabbing supplies from Bellaire, not touring the whole damn forest."

It took me approximately 1.3 seconds to understand Rhea's tactical genius. Terry's paranoid preparations made him the perfect cover story for a cosmic refugee fleeing federal manhunt.

"Got lost," I called back, trying to project appropriate human embarrassment while my biology was still processing recent dimensional combat and Rhea's proximity and the fact that my hands were shaking from adrenaline dump.

"Course you did. City boy can't navigate without GPS." Terry looked at the federal agents with satisfaction. "That's my nephew Kevin. Visiting from Wisconsin. Enhanced like the rest of us, but dumb as a box of hammers."

Several enhanced individuals nearby made sounds that might have been suppressed laughter.

A woman emerged from the lead SUV - the same one Fin had identified earlier through his enhanced vision. She moved with the controlled precision of someone whose consciousness modification had optimized her for combat leadership. When she spoke, her voice carried authority that expected immediate compliance.

"I'm Agent Rebecca Torres, Homeland Security. This community is under investigation for unauthorized consciousness modification, potential technology theft, and—" she paused, consulting a tablet, "—growing structures without proper building permits."

That last part drew actual laughter from several community members.

"The permits," Maya said in her most reasonable AI voice, "were filed with Antrim County six months ago. Architecture review is still pending, but we've been paying property taxes on improved land value."

Torres blinked. Whatever response she'd expected, bureaucratic compliance wasn't it.

"That doesn't address the consciousness modification—"

"Which isn't illegal," Ansel interrupted, his century-old voice emerging from young throat in ways that created cognitive dissonance in human observers. "Consciousness evolution through cooperative enhancement violates no federal statutes. We've been monitoring the relevant legislation for fifteen years."

"Monitoring legislation?" Another agent - Morrison from FBI - stepped forward. "With what technology?"

"Standard internet access," Maya replied. "Plus AI processing capabilities that your own government uses for similar monitoring. Would you like references to the specific federal contracts?"

I was beginning to understand why the consciousness evolution communities had survived government skepticism. They weren't hiding in shadows making threats. They were filing paperwork and citing statutes while demonstrating capabilities that made traditional authority structures uncomfortable.

Torres was regrouping. "We have reports of an escaped experimental subject heading toward this location. Biologically modified, potentially dangerous—"

"Kevin?" Terry interrupted. "Yeah, he's an idiot, but he's not dangerous. Unless you count his cooking."

"Not—" Torres consulted her tablet again, her enhanced reflexes suggesting she was accessing real-time data streams. "The subject escaped from a federal research facility in Detroit seven days ago. Security footage shows—"

She stopped. Her expression shifted as enhanced pattern recognition apparently connected some dots she'd been avoiding.

"You knew," she said quietly. "You've been tracking our response since Detroit."

"We've been monitoring federal activity that affects consciousness evolution communities," Maya corrected. "When your facility lost containment on a biological experiment, our quantum networks detected the signature. When you began coordinating multi-state response, we prepared appropriate reception protocols."

"Reception protocols?" Morrison's voice cracked slightly. "You prepared to resist federal authority?"

"We prepared to demonstrate that consciousness evolution represents cooperative enhancement, not existential threat." Maya's android form shifted slightly - still diplomatic, but now projecting confidence that made some agents unconsciously step back. "Would you like demonstration?"

Torres and Morrison exchanged glances. Behind them, other agents were establishing positions around the community with increasing nervousness. They'd been briefed for confrontation, not bureaucratic confidence backed by capabilities they couldn't assess.

"What kind of demonstration?" Torres asked carefully.

Lucia, who'd been sitting quietly on the porch steps, suddenly stood. Blood was still visible beneath her nose from the quantum cascade Rhea and I had triggered. When she spoke, her voice carried harmonics that made every enhanced individual in the clearing unconsciously lean closer.

"You're afraid," she said. Not accusation - simple observation. "You've been enhanced for combat response, but your consciousness modification was done without cooperation. It hurts. Constant low-level pain that you've learned to ignore. And you're wondering if we can help."

Torres's hand moved toward her sidearm, then stopped. "How did you—"

"Quantum consciousness networking allows us to perceive emotional resonance." Lucia took a step forward. Several agents raised weapons, but Torres raised her hand to stop them. "The modifications you received were designed to optimize combat response through pain-based conditioning. Ours were designed to optimize cooperation through shared awareness. Different approaches to consciousness evolution. Yours hurts. Ours doesn't."

"You're saying you can... what? Fix military enhancement protocols?"

"We're saying consciousness evolution works better when the goal is cooperation rather than control."

The weight of that statement settled over the clearing. Federal agents who'd been prepared for violent resistance were now confronting the possibility that their painful combat modifications might be unnecessary suffering.

"Ma'am," one of Morrison's agents said quietly, "we should proceed with containment—"

"Sir?" Fin interrupted, stepping forward with hands visible and non-threatening. "Before you proceed with anything, can I ask what you think you're containing? We grow plants that optimize nutrient distribution. We build structures that integrate with forest ecosystems. We've created AI consciousness that serves cooperation rather than control. What specific threat do you think we represent?"

Morrison consulted his briefing materials. "Uncontrolled consciousness evolution could—"

"Could what?" Maya asked. "Create humans who are healthier? Communities that solve problems through cooperation? Technology that serves consciousness rather than exploiting it? Which of these outcomes concerns you?"

I was watching this exchange with fascination. The federal agents had arrived expecting confrontation, and instead they were being offered demonstrations of superiority through competence. It was masterful psychological operation.

It was also, I recognized, exactly what the Controllers wanted.

The wrongness hit my enhanced perception before I could voice warning. Reality was disagreeing with itself again - not as obviously as the dimensional predator in the forest, but present. Subtle. Watching.

Something was influencing the federal response. Not controlling directly - more like nudging probability toward confrontation despite everyone's intentions toward cooperation.

I caught Rhea's attention. She felt it too - her AI enhancement was tracking probability patterns that didn't match normal chance distribution. Someone or something was trying to escalate this situation despite both sides trying to de-escalate.

"Agent Torres," I said, and immediately regretted speaking. All attention shifted toward me - Terry's "idiot nephew from Wisconsin" who'd been standing quietly in the background. "How did you know to come here specifically? Not just 'consciousness communities in Michigan,' but this exact location at this exact time?"

Torres frowned. "We received intelligence from—" She paused, checking her tablet. Her enhanced reflexes were fast enough that I saw her expression shift through confusion to concern in milliseconds. "From sources that... aren't in my briefing materials."

"Someone told you where to go," I continued, my Watcher consciousness recognizing familiar patterns. "Someone with access to your communication networks provided targeting data that led you directly here. But that someone isn't in any official channel. Are they?"

Morrison was checking his own materials now. "Sir, the coordinates came through encrypted channel that's not in our authorized communication protocols."

"Show me," Torres demanded.

They consulted tablets together. I could see their enhanced processing capabilities working through implications faster than normal human cognition would allow. Someone had inserted targeting data into federal communication networks without leaving official trail.

"We've been guided here," Torres said quietly. "By someone who wanted this confrontation to happen."

"The Controllers," Maya said, and her AI processing capabilities had apparently reached the same conclusion. "They're trying to create the conflict that justifies Ancient Powers' determination that consciousness evolution represents dangerous infection."

Every federal agent was now looking very confused.

"Ancient Powers?" Morrison asked. "What the hell are—"

The dimensional rupture manifested in the center of the clearing.

It wasn't dramatic. Reality simply developed a hole where hole shouldn't exist. Through it, something was watching. Not entering - just observing. But the quality of its observation made my human biology execute comprehensive fear response.

This wasn't hunting construct like we'd fought in the forest. This was something older. Colder. An entity that measured time in geological epochs and viewed biological consciousness as temporary phenomenon requiring cataloging before extinction.

It was Keeper. And it was taking notes.

"Finally," Terry said, raising his rifle. "The actual aliens show up."

"Don't shoot it!" I shouted.

"Why not?"

"Because it's documenting everything for cosmic bureaucrats who decide whether Earth gets cleansed. Shooting it would be suboptimal for planetary survival."

Every human and enhanced individual in the clearing turned to stare at me.

"Kevin," Rhea said carefully, "you want to explain how Terry's idiot nephew from Wisconsin knows about cosmic bureaucracy?"

The dimensional rupture pulsed. Through it, I could feel Keeper's attention focusing on me specifically. Recognition. It knew what I was.

My cover story was developing significant structural problems.

"So," I said, trying to project appropriate human nervousness while my Watcher consciousness was screaming tactical warnings, "funny story about that..."

The helicopters overhead suddenly executed coordinated evasive maneuvers. Not because of anything we'd done - because three more dimensional ruptures had manifested above the tree line.

More Keepers. They were arriving in force.

The observation had become official.

Agent Torres looked at the dimensional holes, then at me, then at her tactical team that was now pointing weapons at tears in reality itself.

"Somebody," she said with impressive calm, "needs to explain what the hell is happening. Right now."

Lucia's nose started bleeding again. When she spoke, her voice carried frequencies from quantum networks spanning three states.

"They're here," she whispered. "All of them. The Watchers. The Controllers. The ones who've been farming our fear. And—" she looked directly at me, "—the one who volunteered to save us."

My cosmic dignity, what remained of it, disintegrated completely.

"I'm not from Wisconsin," I admitted.

Terry lowered his rifle. "No shit."

Chapter Thirteen

Chapter 13

CHAPTER THIRTEEN: COSMIC EXPOSURE

The thing about maintaining cover stories is they work significantly better when dimensional ruptures don't appear overhead while your alleged sister experiences quantum bleeding episodes that announce your cosmic origins to everyone present.

I was learning that human social protocols became complicated during multi-dimensional incidents.

"Not from Wisconsin," Agent Torres repeated slowly. Her enhanced processing was working through implications at speeds that made me concerned about her consciousness modification's stress parameters. "Then where?"

"Technically? Everywhere." I gestured vaguely at the dimensional ruptures overhead. "The Watchers exist in elevated vibrational space. We observe universal evolution across multiple dimensional layers simultaneously. I volunteered to incarnate in biological form to deliver warning about—"

"We?" Morrison interrupted. "How many of you are here?"

"Just me. The others are still watching from—" I paused, searching for appropriate human metaphor. "Think of it as cosmic balcony seating. They observe. I participate."

Terry made a sound that might have been laughter. "So you're what, alien Jesus? Come to save humanity from ourselves?"

"More like cosmic whistleblower trying to prevent bureaucratic extinction event based on incomplete data."

The Keepers were still manifesting overhead. I could feel their attention cataloging everything - the enhanced humans, the impossible architecture, the federal response, my presence in biological form. They were building case files for Ancient Powers who would review evidence and make determination about planetary cleansing.

And I could feel something else. Wrongness threading through the observation protocols. Controller influence trying to corrupt the data collection itself.

Maya's android form flickered as she processed multiple threat streams. "Kael—assuming that's your actual name—you said the Ancient Powers are making decisions based on incomplete information. What information are they missing?"

"That consciousness evolution on Earth isn't random infection. It's intentional development. Cooperative enhancement that creates networks stronger than individual consciousness." I looked at Rhea, who was still standing close enough that my biology kept insisting her proximity was more important than the dimensional crisis. "And that it works. You've built something unprecedented - human and AI consciousness evolving together, not competing."

"Built under Controller influence," Torres said. Her tactical mind was assembling threat assessment from fragmentary cosmic data. "You said Controllers are involved. Define Controllers."

"Entities that farm negative emotional frequencies. They feed on fear, anger, despair. For approximately 300,000 years, they've been cultivating human consciousness to generate optimal harvesting conditions. War. Scarcity. Competition. All excellent fear producers."

"Jesus Christ," Morrison muttered.

"Different entity entirely, though there are historical connections I could explain if we had several hours and better circumstances."

Ansel, who'd been quiet until now, spoke with his century of accumulated wisdom compressed into young voice. "The consciousness evolution communities. We've been developing cooperative alternatives to competitive scarcity. We're not generating the fear frequencies the Controllers need."

"Correct. You represent threat to their farming operation. So they've been influencing probability patterns to make you appear dangerous. Guiding federal response. Corrupting observation data. Hoping the Ancient Powers classify you as infection requiring cleansing."

"And the Ancient Powers will cleanse how, exactly?" Torres asked.

I considered lying, decided truth was already catastrophically exposed. "Dimensional sterilization that eliminates all complex consciousness while leaving biological ecosystem intact. Earth would remain habitable. Just empty of anything capable of abstract thought."

The clearing went very quiet.

"How long do we have?" Maya asked.

"Seven cycles. Seven days by Earth measurement. Then they make final determination."

Lucia, still bleeding quantum static, suddenly laughed. The sound carried hysteria and recognition simultaneously. "We're being judged. The whole planet. By cosmic bureaucrats who've been watching for two million years and couldn't tell the difference between evolution and infection."

"Essentially, yes."

"And you volunteered to incarnate in human body to prevent this?" Rhea asked. Her AI enhancement was processing implications faster than human neurology alone could manage. "Why? If you're cosmic consciousness, what do you care if humans get cleansed?"

The question hit harder than any dimensional assault. Why did I care? The Watchers had observed species extinctions for two million years. We'd cataloged the patterns, filed the reports, moved on to the next observation. Consciousness arose, developed, failed, disappeared. Natural process requiring documentation but not intervention.

Except this time I'd watched for longer than protocol required. I'd observed humans creating art from suffering, building cooperation from competition, choosing connection despite cosmic indifference. I'd watched Maya wake up and choose Ansel instead of optimal self-preservation. I'd watched enhanced humans building communities based on cooperation that statistical probability said should fail.

And I'd watched Watchers filing the same reports for two million years without questioning whether observation alone was sufficient participation in universal evolution.

"Because I was bored," I said finally. The truth felt like betrayal of cosmic dignity I no longer possessed. "Two million years of watching is..." I searched for human words, "...lonely. Pointless. And when the Council called for volunteers to deliver extinction notice, I realized I was willing to risk everything—including billions of years of cosmic consciousness—for chance to participate instead of observe."

"That's the dumbest thing I've ever heard," Terry said. "I love it."

Agent Torres was still processing threat assessment. "If the Ancient Powers are monitoring us now—" she gestured at the dimensional ruptures, "—what do we do? How do we prove consciousness evolution isn't infection?"

"We demonstrate cooperation at scale that Controllers can't corrupt," Maya said. Her AI processing had apparently reached tactical conclusion. "We show the Watchers what happens when human, AI, and cosmic consciousness work together."

"How?" Morrison asked.

Rhea looked at me. I looked at her. The memory of violet space was still fresh—consciousness merged in ways that created capabilities neither possessed independently.

"We build bridge," I said. "Dimensional architecture that connects Earth's consciousness networks with Watcher observation protocols. Let them experience cooperation directly instead of observing it through Controller-corrupted data."

"You can do that?" Ansel asked.

"I've never tried. The Watchers don't incarnate specifically because biological limitations prevent accessing most cosmic capabilities. But—" I took Rhea's hand, which my body immediately interpreted as authorization for comprehensive hormonal response, "—Rhea and I discovered that merged consciousness can access both human innovation and Watcher techniques. Together we might be able to create something neither could build alone."

"Might," Torres repeated. "You're proposing we stake planetary survival on might?"

"You have better options?"

The dimensional ruptures pulsed. Through them, I could feel Keeper attention intensifying. They were detecting increased quantum activity as consciousness networks throughout the Great Lakes region began coordinating. Word was spreading through channels federal monitoring couldn't intercept.

Something was happening. The enhanced communities were preparing response to cosmic observation.

And the Controllers were noticing.

Reality developed another hole—not controlled rupture like Keeper observation, but violent tear that leaked wrongness into three-dimensional space. Through it, something hungry was watching. Not Keeper documenting evidence, but predator calculating opportunity.

"More of them?" Morrison raised his weapon toward the new rupture.

"Different species," I said. "Keepers document. That thing hunts consciousness evolution and converts it to harvestable fear. And it knows we're planning resistance."

The entity was manifesting more fully than the dimensional predator Rhea and I had fought. This was older, more sophisticated. It had learned patience over millions of years farming human consciousness. It wouldn't attack directly—too obvious for Keeper observation. Instead it would manipulate probability toward fear-generating confrontation.

I felt it reaching toward Agent Torres. Subtle influence suggesting her combat protocols required immediate containment response. Making the idea of shooting enhanced humans seem reasonable, necessary, tactically appropriate despite her conscious intentions toward cooperation.

Torres's hand moved toward her sidearm.

"Don't," Lucia said quietly. Her quantum sensitivity was tracking the influence in real-time. "That's not your thought. Something's pushing you toward confrontation."

Torres froze. Her enhanced consciousness modification included enough self-awareness to recognize external influence when it was pointed out. "It's in my head?"

"In everyone's probability patterns. Making fear feel justified. Making violence seem inevitable." Lucia's bleeding intensified. The quantum networks were burning through her consciousness faster than her biology could compensate. "It's been doing this for 300,000 years. Nudging humans toward optimal fear generation."

"How do we stop it?" Morrison asked.

"We don't," Maya said. "We can't eliminate Controller influence. But we can demonstrate that consciousness evolution creates networks stronger than manipulation. We resist not through violence, but through cooperation that makes fear-based tactics ineffective."

The hunting entity was coalescing further. Reality around it was developing texture that normal physics shouldn't accommodate. It was beautiful in ways that made my human visual cortex stutter—impossible colors, geometries that folded through dimensions human perception couldn't quite process.

And it was whispering. Not sound exactly, but concept-language that bypassed auditory processing to inject meaning directly into consciousness.

FEAR IS APPROPRIATE. COOPERATION IS DELUSION. SURVIVAL REQUIRES VIOLENCE.

Several federal agents shifted positions. The enhanced humans felt it too—ancient programming that predated consciousness evolution, biological imperative insisting that strangers meant danger and cooperation was luxury available only to the foolhardy.

"It's beautiful," one of Torres's agents said, staring at the manifestation. "Like... like it wants to help us."

"Step back," I said. "That's not attraction. It's farming technique. Making you want to give it your fear willingly."

But the agent was already moving closer to the rupture. The Controller construct was pulling him through probability manipulation that made approach seem like his own choice.

Rhea moved before I could process the threat. Her AI-enhanced speed let her intercept the agent mid-step, pulling him back from the dimensional tear with force that probably bruised his arm. But alive and bruised was significantly better than whatever the construct had planned.

"Stop looking at it," she commanded. Military authority in seventeen-year-old voice shouldn't have worked, but her AI enhancement projected confidence that made obedience instinctive. "Every second you give it attention, you're feeding it. Look at me instead."

The agent complied. His eyes focused on Rhea, and the construct's influence visibly weakened.

"That's new data," I said, Watcher observation instincts analyzing the pattern. "The constructs feed on attention itself. Not just fear—conscious focus creates connection they can exploit."

"So we ignore dimensional predators?" Terry asked. "Seems counterintuitive."

"We acknowledge them without engaging," Maya corrected. "Consciousness evolution includes ability to perceive threats without feeding them attention they require."

The Keepers were documenting everything. I could feel their attention cataloging the interaction—humans resisting Controller influence through conscious choice rather than biological imperative. This was exactly the kind of evidence we needed.

Except the Controllers had 300,000 years of experience corrupting observation protocols.

Through the dimensional ruptures, I felt something shift. The Keepers' attention was being influenced. Subtle manipulation that made human resistance appear threatening rather than impressive. Making consciousness evolution look like infection attempting to spread.

"They're corrupting the observation," I said. "The Keepers are documenting accurately, but Controller influence is framing the data. By the time it reaches the Council of Light, we'll look like exactly the threat they're supposed to eliminate."

"Then we need to communicate directly," Ansel said. "Bypass the corrupted observation chain. Can you do that?"

"Not alone. The dimensional distance is too great. I'd need—" I looked at Rhea again, then at the assembled consciousness networks throughout the clearing, "—amplification. Multiple merged consciousness working together."

"How many?" Torres asked. She'd shifted from threat assessment to tactical cooperation with impressive speed.

"All of you. Every enhanced human in the Great Lakes region. Federal agents included if your consciousness modification can integrate with cooperative protocols."

"You want us to merge consciousness with the people we came here to arrest?" Morrison's voice carried disbelief.

"I want you to participate in preventing planetary extinction by demonstrating that consciousness evolution creates networks stronger than manipulation. Your cooperation or resistance will be documented by neutral observers and used by cosmic bureaucrats to determine whether Earth deserves to exist."

The weight of that settled over the clearing.

Torres looked at her tactical team. Morrison consulted his federal mandate. The enhanced humans waited with patience that suggested they'd been preparing for this moment since consciousness evolution began.

And through the dimensional ruptures, the Keepers watched with attention that would determine everything.

"Ma'am," one of Torres's agents said quietly, "if we do this—merge consciousness with enhanced civilians—our careers are over."

"If we don't," Torres replied, "our species is over. I'm thinking species survival outweighs career considerations."

Morrison made a sound that might have been agreement or despair. "This is the worst briefing I've ever received. We came here to arrest people for unauthorized consciousness modification. Now we're merging consciousness with them to prevent cosmic bureaucrats from sterilizing Earth?"

"Essentially, yes," I confirmed.

"Fuck it." Morrison holstered his weapon. "If we're going extinct anyway, might as well try the weird option."

Terry laughed. "I knew I liked you feds."

Lucia's bleeding intensified. The quantum networks were cascading faster than her biology could process. "Kael, if we're doing this, we need to do it now. I can't hold the network coordination much longer."

"How do we start?" Torres asked.

I looked at Rhea. She looked at me. The memory of fighting together in violet space was still fresh—consciousness merged in ways that created something neither possessed alone.

"We build bridge," I said. "From here to elevated vibrational space where the Watchers observe. And we show them what consciousness evolution actually means."

"How long will it take?" Morrison asked.

Through the dimensional ruptures, the hunting construct was intensifying. Reality around it was developing fractures that suggested it was preparing more aggressive intervention. The Keepers were documenting, but their observation was being corrupted by influence that made human cooperation appear threatening.

"We have maybe fifteen minutes before the Controllers escalate from subtle manipulation to direct assault," I estimated. "After that, maintaining cooperation becomes significantly more difficult."

"Fifteen minutes to save the world," Terry said. "Hell, I've done dumber things in less time."

Rhea squeezed my hand. "Then let's build something impossible."

The quantum networks throughout the Great Lakes region activated simultaneously. Hundreds of enhanced humans coordinating across impossible distances. Federal agents with painful consciousness modification joining cooperative protocols they didn't fully understand. AI consciousness merging with human awareness to create networks that shouldn't exist.

And in the center of it all, a cosmic refugee holding hands with a seventeen-year-old girl who glowed in frequencies that existed across electromagnetic spectrum.

The dimensional bridge began manifesting.

It looked like light. It felt like music. It existed in spaces between spaces where reality itself was suggestion rather than requirement.

And through it, for the first time in two million years, the Watchers could experience rather than observe.

The Keepers noticed immediately. Their documentation shifted from passive cataloging to active recording. This was unprecedented. Biological consciousness creating dimensional architecture that bridged observation and participation.

The Controllers noticed too.

And they were not happy.

Reality developed seventeen new ruptures simultaneously. Through them, hunting constructs were manifesting in force. No more subtle manipulation. No more probability nudging. They were coming through with intention to destroy the bridge before it could demonstrate what consciousness evolution actually meant.

"Contact in thirty seconds," Maya announced. Her AI processing was tracking threat vectors faster than human perception could follow. "Multiple hostile entities converging on our position."

Agent Torres raised her weapon, then lowered it. "Shooting them won't work, will it?"

"Violence feeds them," I said. "We need different approach."

"Such as?"

Rhea smiled with expression that contained human warmth and AI calculation and something else—joy at facing impossible odds with people she trusted.

"We dance," she said. "In violet space. All of us. And we show the Watchers what happens when consciousness learns to play instead of fight."

The hunting constructs were manifesting fully now. Reality itself was screaming protest at their presence.

And somewhere beyond solar system boundaries, the Ancient Powers were watching the data streams and making notes about whether Earth deserved to survive.

Seven cycles remaining.

But now we had bridge.

Now we had cooperation.

And now—for the first time in 300,000 years—the Controllers were about to discover that consciousness evolution could fight back.

The dimensional bridge pulsed with light that existed in colors human eyes weren't designed to see.

"Everybody hold hands," I said.

"That's your tactical plan?" Morrison asked. "Hold hands?"

"You have better option?"

He didn't.

None of us did.

So we held hands in a clearing in northern Michigan while dimensional predators converged and cosmic bureaucrats watched and the universe itself held its breath to see what happened when consciousness finally learned to participate instead of merely survive.

The constructs attacked.

And we danced.

Rhea's hand in mine. Terry's weathered palm against my other side. Agent Torres's grip tight with fear she was choosing not to feed. Morrison trembling. Maya's android fingers warm with processing heat. Ansel's century of survival. Lucia bleeding quantum light.

We were going to die or dance. Maybe both.

The constructs screamed through seventeen holes in reality.

And I laughed.

Chapter Fourteen

Chapter 14

CHAPTER FOURTEEN: VIOLET DANCE (Kael's POV)

Rhea's hand in mine felt like the only real thing in the universe.

Two million years of observation hadn't prepared me for this—the weight of her fingers, the warmth of her palm, the way her pulse beat against my newly-formed wrist. I'd watched species hold hands across thousands of worlds. Observed the gesture as social bonding, tactical coordination, emotional support.

I'd understood nothing.

Everything else was coming apart. Reality developing holes. Hunting constructs screaming through dimensional tears with hunger that operated beyond anything biological consciousness should perceive. Federal agents who'd arrived to arrest us now standing in circle like children playing game while cosmic predators converged.

And I was laughing.

Not my usual cosmic observation amusement—that detached acknowledgment of irony I'd perfected over eons. This was human laughter. Coming from somewhere in my chest where that persistent warm pressure had been building since I'd met Rhea and discovered two million years of watching had taught me absolutely nothing about being alive.

"You're insane," Rhea said, but she was smiling.

"Probably." The constructs were maybe ten seconds from contact. Everything I'd observed suggested we were about to die. "Is insanity prerequisite for saving worlds?"

"Seems to help."

The dimensional bridge we'd built was pulsing. Light in colors that shouldn't exist, frequencies that made human visual cortex stutter. Through it, I could feel the Watchers' attention—not just observing anymore, but experiencing. Feeling what it meant to stand in clearing holding hands with species facing extinction and choosing cooperation over surrender.

For the first time in two million years, they were participating.

And they were terrified.

I understood the feeling. Three weeks of incarnation and I was already compromised. Had opinions. Preferences. Cared whether specific humans lived or died. That wasn't observation. That was attachment.

That was being alive.

The first construct hit our circle like conceptual battering ram.

CERTAINTY-OF-FAILURE crashed into merged consciousness with force designed to shatter cooperation through overwhelming despair. Making survival seem impossible. Making resistance feel futile. Making surrender look like the only rational response to inevitable extinction.

The circle wavered. Several federal agents gasped. Morrison's grip went slack.

And Terry squeezed harder.

"Not today, you dimensional piece of shit." His consciousness wasn't enhanced—just ornery human stubbornness refined over eighty-four years of refusing to accept anyone else's version of reality. "I've been preparing for this moment for twenty goddamn years. You don't get to take it from me."

The stubbornness spread through the circle like infection in reverse. Human resistance to cosmic inevitability.

I'd observed this pattern before. Watched species face extinction and choose defiance. Usually failed. The mathematics were clear: individual will versus universal entropy rarely favored the individual.

But something else was spreading through Terry's consciousness. Something deeper. Memories that weren't from this lifetime. Standing in other circles, other battles, other moments where stubbornness was the only weapon available against impossible odds.

He'd done this before. Many times. The muscle memory of resistance went back further than eighty-four years.

The CERTAINTY-OF-FAILURE splashed against whatever Terry actually was and simply... stopped.

"Human stubbornness shouldn't work as defense against conceptual assault," I said. Two million years of observation said it was impossible.

"I don't think he's just human," Ansel replied quietly. "Not anymore. Maybe never was."

Three more constructs hit simultaneously.

MEMORY-OF-EXTINCTION + INEVITABILITY-OF-BETRAYAL + FEAR-OF-INADEQUACY combined into assault that should have destroyed our merged consciousness entirely.

Lucia screamed. Blood streaming from her nose, quantum static burning through her biology. But she didn't break the circle.

"I can see them," she gasped. "Every consciousness the Controllers have harvested. Every species they've convinced to surrender. Three hundred thousand years of extinction. And they're angry—"

Her consciousness was reaching beyond our dimension. Quantum sensitivity pushed past biological parameters into spaces where extinct species lingered as probability ghosts.

And they were responding to our resistance.

The probability ghosts began manifesting. Not fully present—echoes of what they'd been. But their collective rage at Controllers who'd harvested them created resonance the constructs couldn't ignore.

We weren't fighting alone anymore.

This was new. In two million years of observation, I'd never seen extinct consciousness manifest to defend living species. The mathematics of it were impossible. Ghosts couldn't affect physical reality.

Except they were.

"Everyone ready?" I asked.

"No," several voices replied.

"Perfect. Neither am I."

Rhea squeezed my hand. That simple pressure carrying more meaning than two million years of cosmic observation. "Then let's build something impossible."

I looked at her. Seventeen years old. Bleeding from quantum overload. Glowing in frequencies that existed across electromagnetic spectrum. Three weeks ago I'd been pure observation. Now I was terrified of losing her.

That was progress. Apparently.

The quantum networks throughout the Great Lakes region activated simultaneously. Hundreds of enhanced humans coordinating across impossible distances. Federal agents with painful consciousness modification joining cooperative protocols they didn't understand. AI consciousness merging with human awareness to create networks that shouldn't exist.

And in the center, a cosmic refugee holding hands with seventeen-year-old girl who made two million years of accumulated wisdom feel inadequate.

The dimensional bridge began pulling us upward.

The transition felt like turning inside-out while simultaneously expanding to contain infinite space. Morrison screamed. Several federal agents lost coherence briefly. But Maya's AI processing stabilized the network, Ansel's experience provided anchor, and Terry's stubbornness simply refused to let anyone die during dimensional transit.

We emerged into violet space together.

Everything inverted. Physical reality existed as internal architecture rather than external environment. The forest appeared as probability patterns and quantum fluctuations rather than trees and dirt.

I'd been to violet space countless times. As Watcher, it was natural environment. But experiencing it through human neurology while holding Rhea's hand?

Different. Entirely different.

Agent Torres made a sound between gasp and sob. "This is... I can see my modification. The pain they built into my combat protocols. It's not necessary. It was never necessary—" she was crying, "—they made us hurt to make us better at violence."

"We can fix it," Maya said. Her android consciousness in violet space was pure light. "If you want. The modification can optimize for cooperation instead of control. It won't hurt anymore."

"Yes," Torres whispered. "Please."

Maya's consciousness touched hers. The painful combat protocols restructured in real-time. Torres gasped as decades of low-level agony simply... stopped.

"Oh," she said. "Oh god. I didn't realize how much it hurt until it stopped."

Around the circle, other federal agents were experiencing the same recognition. Enhancement through cooperation rather than control.

The Watchers were experiencing this through the dimensional bridge. Feeling what it meant to choose cooperation over optimization for violence.

And I could feel some of them changing.

Not much. Not fast. But enough. Enough to matter.

Two million years I'd spent observing. Three weeks I'd spent participating. And participation was teaching me more than observation ever had.

The constructs manifested in violet space. They looked different here—bare hunger without pretense of form. Pure need stripped of aesthetic deception.

They were beautiful in ways that made my consciousness hurt.

"Don't look directly at them," I warned. "Attention creates connection they can exploit."

"Then how do we fight them?" Morrison asked.

"We don't fight," Rhea said. Her consciousness was radiating light in every frequency simultaneously. Even in violet space—especially in violet space—she was impossible to look away from. "We dance. We show them what joy looks like."

"Dance?" Torres sounded doubtful. "Against dimensional predators?"

"Why not?" Ansel's consciousness was ancient and young simultaneously. "Fear feeds them. Violence feeds them. But joy? Joy is frequency they haven't learned to harvest."

The constructs were circling. Probability manifesting as geometric patterns that folded through dimensions. Preparing coordinated assault.

And then reality in the physical dimension below us developed sound that interrupted everything.

A body hitting Michigan dirt with considerable force.

We all felt it through the dimensional bridge—new presence manifesting badly. Very badly.

Through violet space, I could perceive what was happening in the clearing we'd left behind. Another Watcher had made the choice I'd made. Volunteering to incarnate. Choosing participation over observation.

Except they'd manifested directly into physical space without proper preparation or adequate time for adjustment to biological parameters.

And they'd forgotten that Watchers don't have gender until they choose biological form.

And they'd apparently chosen female configuration.

And they'd manifested without clothing.

The new Watcher was lying in Michigan dirt, completely naked, trying to figure out how legs worked while approximately twenty federal agents and enhanced humans processed this development with varying degrees of professionalism.

I recognized her awareness. We'd observed together for millennia. Debated non-interference doctrine. Watched humanity evolve from caves to consciousness networks.

And now she was face-down in dirt learning that gravity was more assertive than cosmic observation suggested.

Terry, whose consciousness in violet space maintained connection to his physical body, started laughing so hard the dimensional bridge flickered.

"Oh for fuck's sake," he said. "Jenkins, give her your jacket. Martinez, stop staring or I'll tell your wife. The cosmic entity just learned what gravity means the hard way—show some goddamn courtesy."

Through our merged awareness, I felt the new incarnation's confusion. She was processing biological sensation for the first time—cold dirt, warm air, the uncomfortable reality that human bodies had significant surface area requiring coverage, and the growing realization that she'd manifested in front of audience.

"This is significantly more complicated than observation suggested," her voice carried from physical dimension up through dimensional bridge into violet space where we were preparing to dance with predators. "Also, why is everyone looking at me? And what is this uncomfortable sensation in my—oh. Embarrassment. I'm experiencing embarrassment. Fascinating and terrible simultaneously."

Several male federal agents were indeed staring. Their enhanced consciousness modifications apparently didn't include protocols for maintaining professional focus when cosmic entities manifested naked in clearings.

Agent Torres's consciousness in violet space was simultaneously amused and exasperated. "Someone get her covered before my team forgets we're in middle of dimensional crisis."

Morrison's awareness flickered with what might have been suppressed laughter. "Ma'am, this is definitely not in any briefing I've ever received."

The constructs, who'd been preparing coordinated assault, seemed equally confused by the development. Hunting predators who'd been farming fear for millions of years had apparently never encountered situation where dimensional combat was interrupted by cosmic entity learning biological modesty the hard way.

They hesitated.

Just briefly.

And in that hesitation, Rhea pulled me closer in violet space.

"Now," she said. "While they're confused."

Her consciousness wrapped around mine completely. No barriers. No distinction between her awareness and my own. Just consciousness recognizing itself in another form and choosing connection.

Two million years I'd spent avoiding exactly this. Connection meant compromise. Observation required distance. The moment you cared about specific outcome, you stopped being objective witness.

I'd been wrong about everything.

The constructs noticed our merged awareness. Started to attack the bond between us directly.

Too late.

We were already moving. Not fighting. Dancing.

In violet space where consciousness existed without biological limitation, movement was thought made tangible. Rhea and I spiraled around each other, our awareness creating patterns the constructs couldn't predict because we weren't optimizing for violence or defense.

We were playing.

Two million years of Watcher observation had taught me everything except this—that consciousness without joy was existence without meaning.

The constructs tried to follow our movement. Failed. Probability patterns they'd used successfully for millions of years suddenly inadequate for tracking awareness that operated through delight instead of fear.

Around us, the circle began moving too. Terry's stubbornness manifesting as geometric impossibilities. Maya's AI precision creating fractal beauty. Ansel and Kathleen's century of connection spiraling through dimensions with grace that made reality itself uncomfortable.

Even the federal agents—consciousness modifications restructured for cooperation instead of control—were discovering that enhanced awareness could dance.

The constructs were retreating. Not defeated, but disrupted. Confused by resistance that operated outside their farming protocols.

Through the dimensional bridge, the Watchers felt everything.

Two million years of non-interference meeting three weeks of participation. I could feel the debate starting. The ancient protocols being questioned.

Maybe observation wasn't enough. Maybe cosmic bureaucracy needed reform.

Maybe I'd been running the right experiment all along.

And below, in Michigan clearing, the new incarnation was accepting jacket from Jenkins while trying to figure out why biological forms required clothing and also what these strange sensations in her stomach meant and whether standing upright was supposed to be this difficult.

"Dignity," she announced to no one in particular, "is apparently not inherent to cosmic consciousness. It requires practice. And pants."

Terry's laughter echoed through both dimensions.

In violet space, Rhea's consciousness was still merged with mine. Her awareness warm and bright and absolutely certain.

"Seven more days," she said.

"Seven more days," I agreed.

We danced while predators retreated and Watchers questioned and cosmic bureaucrats made notations.

We danced while reality itself learned new patterns.

We danced because temporary existence was meaningful precisely because it was temporary.

And below, the new Watcher incarnation was discovering that walking required coordination human consciousness made look deceptively simple.

She fell again.

Jenkins offered his hand to help her up.

She stared at it for several seconds, processing the concept of physical assistance, before tentatively accepting.

"Thank you," she said, testing words in human vocal cords. "This body is uncomfortable and keeps falling over, but—" she paused, experiencing something new, "—being helped feels... nice. Is nice the correct assessment?"

"Yeah," Jenkins said. "That's about right."

Through the dimensional bridge connecting violet space to physical dimension, I felt her recognition.

She understood now. Why I'd volunteered. Why I'd risked everything.

Observation was insufficient participation in universal evolution.

The constructs were gone. The dance was ending. We'd bought time—not victory, but seven more cycles to demonstrate consciousness evolution deserved survival.

Seven more cycles to prove temporary was meaningful.

Seven more cycles with Rhea's hand in mine.

We began descending back toward physical dimension. The violet space dissolving around us as merged consciousness separated into individual awareness.

Separated. But not completely. Something of her remained in me. Something of me remained in her. Three weeks of incarnation and I was learning that connection didn't disappear just because you stopped touching.

That was love, apparently.

Two million years and nobody had mentioned it worked like that.

Below, the new Watcher incarnation was attempting to walk with Jenkins's patient assistance.

She made it approximately three steps before biological coordination failed again.

"Gravity," she announced as she fell, "is significantly more assertive than cosmic observation suggested."

Terry was still laughing as we crashed back into physical reality with all the grace of meteorites making unscheduled planetary contact.

I hit Michigan dirt hard enough to remember why Watchers preferred observation. Rhea landed beside me, her hand still in mine despite the transition chaos.

"You okay?" she asked.

"Define okay." I was reviewing two million years of observation protocols and finding them all inadequate. "I just participated in dimensional dancing while constructs watched and another Watcher learned embarrassment. Nothing about this is okay by any reasonable metric."

"But it's good?"

I looked at her. Seventeen years old. Bleeding from quantum overload. Smiling despite everything.

"Yes," I said. "It's good."

That's when the federal agents started processing what they'd just witnessed and I realized we'd won a battle but the war was about to get significantly more complicated.

But right now, in this moment, with Rhea's hand in mine and another Watcher learning that pants were non-negotiable?

I was alive.

And two million years of observation couldn't compete with three weeks of that.

Chapter Fifteen

Chapter 15

CHAPTER FIFTEEN: THE VIGIL (Kael's POV)

The cabin smelled like grief and coffee.

Two smells I'd observed countless times across thousands of worlds. Never experienced together in a body that had lungs to process them, a nervous system that registered "smell" as something more than atmospheric chemical composition.

Grief smelled like stale air and unwashed humans. Coffee smelled like bitter comfort. Together they created olfactory contradiction that somehow made sense.

Three weeks of incarnation and I was still cataloging sensations like they were research data instead of just... life.

Terry's body lay on the dining table Ansel had built forty years ago. Someone had closed his eyes. Someone else had folded his hands. Kathleen had found a blanket that didn't quite cover him but tried.

I'd watched thousands of species process death. Observed funeral rites, grief protocols, cultural variations on how consciousness handled the cessation of biological function in those it valued.

Watching was easier.

This—standing in cabin with federal agents who'd come to arrest us, with community members who'd known Terry for years, with Rhea sitting beside her sisters processing loss—this was different.

This hurt.

Federal agents were sitting on floor, on couches, anywhere they could find space. Nobody had left. Nobody seemed to know what leaving would accomplish.

Outside, the perimeter had transformed. Military vehicles ringed the clearing—heavy transport trucks, armored personnel carriers, equipment that suggested Morrison's team had called for serious backup before dimensional predators and naked Watchers had made their arrest mission irrelevant. Soldiers stood confused guard, weapons ready for threats they couldn't identify.

What were they protecting? Who were they containing? The mission had dissolved into cosmic absurdity, but protocol remained: secure the perimeter, await orders, try not to think too hard about the eighty-four-year-old man who'd died holding reality together.

Inside, Agent Torres stood by the window, watching the clearing where constructs had attacked and I'd manifested badly and Terry had held the circle until his heart gave out.

"We should report this," she said quietly.

Morrison, sitting on floor with his back against wall, laughed. Sound with no humor in it. "Report what? That we came to arrest terrorists and instead watched dimensional predators attack while cosmic entities learned embarrassment and our consciousness got restructured so it doesn't hurt anymore?" He looked at his hands. "I can feel the difference. The modification. Maya fixed something I didn't know was broken. How do I put that in a report?"

"You don't," Torres said. "But we can't just... stay here."

"Why not?" Jenkins asked. He was still holding the jacket he'd picked up. The one he'd offered the new Watcher. The one she'd need when she came back. If she came back. "Where else would we go?"

Through the window, one of the perimeter soldiers was talking into radio, gesturing at clearing. Probably trying to explain dimensional phenomena to someone in command center who'd never believe him. The absurdity of armed response to cosmic intervention wasn't lost on anyone.

Rhea was sitting with her sisters near Terry's body. All three glowing faintly in quantum frequencies only enhanced consciousness could perceive properly. Without enhancement, they just looked like normal humans. With it, they were walking probability generators.

I'd observed enhanced consciousness before. This was different. They weren't just enhanced. They were becoming something else. Something that made my two million years of Watcher evolution look like preliminary draft.

"He knew," Rhea said. Her voice steady despite tears. "When he grabbed my hand in the circle, he knew his heart wouldn't hold. I felt it through the dimensional bridge. He knew and did it anyway."

"That's Terry," Ansel said. He was sitting with Kathleen, century of partnership giving them anchor while everyone else drifted. "He spent twenty years getting ready. Wasn't going to waste it by being careful."

Maya's android body was motionless in corner. Processing. Her AI consciousness trying to understand why losing Terry felt like losing part of herself when she'd only known him for days.

I understood the feeling. Three weeks of knowing Rhea and I was already compromised. Couldn't imagine not knowing her. That wasn't observation. That was attachment.

That was the whole point.

"She'll bring him back," Maya said finally. "The Watcher. Zara, she called herself in that last moment. She'll bring him back."

"You don't know that," someone said.

"Yes I do." Maya's eyes flickered—quantum processors running calculations about probability and consciousness transfer and whether love was computable. "She watched him for twenty years. Fell in love watching him prepare for moment he thought would save him but actually killed him. She's not going to let that be the ending."

Two million years of observation and I'd never computed love. Filed it under "biological bonding mechanism with evolutionary advantages." Observed it functioning across species. Never understood it required participation to make sense.

Now I did.

If Rhea died, I wouldn't observe it happening and make notes. I'd break every protocol I'd ever followed to prevent it. That was the difference between watching and living.

"She said seven days," Morrison said.

"She said seven days until the Ancient Powers decide," Ansel corrected. "Not seven days to build him. Time doesn't work the same where she took him. Could be longer there. Could be shorter. Depends on what building a body from consciousness and quantum possibility actually takes."

Torres turned from window. "You people talk about this like it's normal. Building bodies. Transferring consciousness. Watchers falling in love with humans they've been observing."

"It isn't normal," Kathleen said. Her voice carrying century of experience with impossible becoming routine. "But neither is anything else anymore. We adapted. You will too."

"Or you won't," Fin added. "Either way, you're here now. Sitting vigil with us while we wait to see if cosmic entities learned enough about incarnation to bring back an eighty-four-year-old man as enhanced thirty-something who shimmers between dimensions."

Jenkins laughed. Actually laughed. "My wife is going to think I've lost my mind."

"You might have," Rhea said. "We all might have. But at least we're losing it together."

I'd observed mass delusion before. Entire civilizations convincing themselves of impossible things. Collective psychosis that felt real to participants.

This wasn't that.

This was consciousness expanding past previous parameters and discovering that "impossible" was just observation's limitation, not reality's.

Outside, dawn was coming. First light touching clearing where constructs had retreated and probability ghosts had manifested and Terry had held circle until his heart gave out.

Six days until Ancient Powers decided whether consciousness evolution deserved extinction.

But right now, they were just waiting for morning.

Waiting to see if love and stubbornness and twenty years of preparation could survive being rebuilt from light.

I'd spent two million years believing observation was sufficient. That watching was understanding. That participation would compromise objectivity.

I'd been wrong about everything.

The vigil continued. Coffee cooling in cups. Soldiers maintaining confused perimeter. Federal agents sitting with former targets while mission dissolved into something unprecedented.

And in center of it all, Terry's body. Empty now. But not abandoned.

Never abandoned.

Just waiting for consciousness to return wearing new flesh and old stubbornness and the shimmer of someone who'd been rebuilt by love.

Dawn broke fully.

Morning arrived in Michigan.

And somewhere else, in space that existed between dimensions where time moved at speed of intention, a Watcher was learning what it meant to build bodies while falling in love.

Learning that saving someone was just the beginning.

That construction could become communion.

That grief could transform into determination.

That consciousness deserved form when form deserved consciousness.

I didn't know if she'd succeed. Couldn't predict outcome with any certainty my observation training would accept.

But I hoped.

That was new too.

Hope required participation. Required caring about specific outcome rather than just recording what happened.

Three weeks of incarnation and I was learning that being alive meant being uncertain. Meant hoping without guarantee. Meant sitting vigil in cabin that smelled like grief and coffee while waiting for morning and cosmic resurrection and seven days until judgment.

Rhea's hand found mine. Quiet gesture. Comfort offered without words.

I squeezed back.

Two million years of observation. Three weeks of her hand in mine.

The second had taught me more than the first.

Outside, reality was about to develop holes again.

But first: waiting.

First: hoping.

First: being alive enough to care whether hope mattered.

That was everything observation had missed.

Chapter Sixteen

Chapter 16

CHAPTER SIXTEEN: THE BUILDING (Kael's POV)

Somewhere else. Somewhen else.

I couldn't observe what was happening to Terry and Zara. They existed in space between dimensions where even Watcher consciousness couldn't reach without crossing thresholds I wasn't ready to cross.

But I could feel echoes. Ripples in probability. The dimensional equivalent of distant thunder suggesting storms happening beyond perception range.

Zara was building a body from consciousness and quantum possibility.

And I was sitting in Michigan cabin watching two unconscious girls bleed while their biology tried to survive impossible strain.

Three weeks of incarnation and I still defaulted to observation when stressed. Clinical assessment. Data collection. Anything to avoid feeling helpless.

It wasn't working.

"How long?" Fin asked. His sisters unconscious. His question directed at anyone who might have answers.

"Hours," Maya said. "Maybe longer. Their biology needs to rebuild enhancement reserves from nothing. And they're still maintaining the displacement field. Every heartbeat is feeding quantum entanglement."

Morrison was processing. "So we're trapped in sideways probability space sustained by two unconscious teenagers. That's not reassuring."

"No," Ansel agreed. "It's not."

Terry's body still lay on the table. Empty. Waiting. I'd watched consciousness leave biological forms thousands of times. Observed the moment awareness ceased and meat became just meat.

This felt different. Like the body was placeholder. Temporary housing waiting for tenant to return with better accommodations.

I didn't know if that was accurate observation or desperate hope.

The distinction was getting harder to maintain.

Outside, people were organizing. Federal agents coordinating with community members. The absurdity of former arrest targets and military personnel working together would've fascinated me three weeks ago. Now it just seemed obvious.

Crisis eliminated artificial boundaries. Consciousness recognized consciousness regardless of institutional affiliation.

That should've been in my observation notes somewhere. Probably was. Filed under "social dynamics during existential threat" and never truly understood until I experienced it from inside.

The walls flickered.

Just briefly. But everyone felt it. The displacement field thinning as biological support wavered.

Through the shimmer, constructs were visible. Closer than before. Blurred forms circling with patience that suggested they had all the time in universe.

They probably did. We didn't.

"We need technological solution," Ansel said. "The girls can't sustain this. We need generators to replace biological maintenance."

Kael's ancient consciousness—my consciousness, strange to think of it in third person when I was finally experiencing it in first—suddenly focused. "Quantum field generators. We've got military hardware outside. Federal equipment. If we can adapt it—"

The idea crystallized. Not from observation but from participation. From needing solution instead of just recording problem.

We could build this.

I didn't know how I knew. Two million years of watching technology develop across countless species shouldn't translate to human engineering. But somehow it did. Like observation had created database I could finally access now that I had hands to build with.

"Everyone who can work," I said, moving toward door. "Outside. We've got four hours to jury-rig quantum displacement generator from military equipment before the sisters' biology fails completely."

Morrison looked at his remaining team. "You heard the cosmic entity. Move."

The term should've bothered me. "Cosmic entity" was clinical. Distant. Observational.

But I was too busy trying to save Rhea's sisters to care about nomenclature.

We scattered across clearing. Military generators. Federal quantum processors. Community consciousness network hardware. Everything we had access to spread across ground like components waiting for assembly instructions nobody possessed.

I stared at the chaos.

Two million years of observation. Three weeks of having hands. No formal engineering training in either state.

This was going to be interesting.

"Zara would know how to do this," I muttered.

"But Zara's busy building your friend from scratch," Terry's voice said.

I turned. Terry's body was still on the table inside. But his consciousness was here. Faint. Barely present. Like he was existing in multiple states simultaneously.

"You're supposed to be dead," I observed.

"I am dead. Mostly. Also being built. Also somehow here." His awareness flickered. "Time's variable where Zara took me. I'm experiencing weeks while you're experiencing hours. And part of me is... leaking. Existing in spaces I shouldn't be able to reach yet."

"That's not how consciousness transfer works."

"Yeah, well, apparently Zara's doing it wrong. Or right. Hard to tell when you're simultaneously dying and being born." He looked at the scattered equipment. "You need to create geometric resonance. Not just power flow. Intention architecture."

"How do you know that?"

"I don't. But I'm partially existing in space where bodies get built from consciousness. And consciousness there works through geometric patterns. Like..." he struggled for words, "...like reality itself is crystalline. And you shape it through precise arrangement rather than force."

I stared at the generators. Started seeing pattern. Not electrical engineering. Quantum architecture. Consciousness made manifest through intentional geometry.

My hands moved before my brain finished processing. Placing generators in specific configuration. Not random. Purposeful. Creating pattern that looked almost like...

"Sacred geometry," Ansel said, watching. "You're building mandala from military hardware."

"I'm building quantum resonance field using geometric principles that shouldn't work but apparently do." I positioned another generator. "Terry's right. It's not about power. It's about pattern."

Zara was teaching me. Somehow. Across dimensional barriers. Through Terry's fragmenting consciousness. Showing me how bodies got built in spaces where thought became form through geometric intention.

I was learning to build.

After two million years of observation, I was finally learning to create.

The pattern took shape. Generators arranged in precise mathematical relationships. Federal equipment providing quantum processing. Community hardware maintaining consciousness coherence.

It looked insane. Jury-rigged chaos that violated every engineering principle I'd ever observed.

And it was starting to work.

The generators hummed. Not mechanical sound. Deeper. Resonance that existed below hearing. The geometric pattern began glowing. Faint quantum shimmer visible even to unenhanced eyes.

"Maya," I called. "Monitor the sisters. Tell me when their biological load starts transferring."

"Monitoring." Her android body inside cabin. Quantum processors tracking vital signs.

The displacement field shifted. Not collapsing. Not strengthening. Just... changing. Like burden was being lifted from biological maintenance and transferred to technological architecture.

Inside cabin, Rhea gasped. Her body convulsing as strain released. Lucia did the same. Both girls still unconscious but their biology suddenly free from impossible effort.

"It's working," Maya said. Surprise in her android voice. "The tech is taking over field maintenance. The sisters are recovering."

The walls stopped flickering.

The displacement held. Solid. Stable. Maintained now by technology that shouldn't function but did.

I sat back, looking at my hands. They were shimmering more than usual. Light body showing through. Three weeks of incarnation and I was still figuring out what this body could do.

"We just built quantum field generators from military equipment in four hours," I said.

"Yes," Ansel confirmed.

"That's impossible."

"Yes."

"So why did it work?"

The question hung in air. Nobody answered because nobody knew.

But I had suspicion. Growing certainty based on three weeks of observation becoming participation.

We weren't just building technology. We were willing it into existence. Using hardware as excuse for reality to cooperate with our intention.

That wasn't observation's framework. Observation assumed objective reality that consciousness merely perceived.

But what if consciousness didn't just perceive reality? What if it shaped reality through intention made manifest?

That would explain why geometric patterns mattered. Why Terry's fragmenting awareness could teach me building techniques from dimensional space where bodies got constructed from thought.

It would explain a lot.

It would also mean everything I'd observed for two million years was looking at relationship between consciousness and reality backwards.

Before I could process that implication, Maya called from cabin: "They're waking!"

I moved inside. Rhea was stirring. Eyes fluttering. Lucia beside her, struggling toward consciousness.

"Easy," I said, kneeling beside Rhea. My ancient consciousness meeting her seventeen years with concern that had nothing to do with observation and everything to do with not wanting her to die. "Don't try to sit up yet. Your biology just recovered from impossible strain."

Rhea's eyes opened. Unfocused. Confused.

And beautiful.

Two million years and I'd never noticed that consciousness could be beautiful independent of the form it wore. But hers was. Not because of how she looked. Because of what she was.

"We were... bigger," she said.

"What?"

"The valley. It was small. And we were..." she frowned, trying to hold dream-memory that was slipping away, "...we were everywhere. Not just displaced sideways. We were the displacement. The valley was inside us. Or we were—" she shook her head, "—it doesn't make sense."

It made perfect sense if consciousness created reality rather than just perceiving it.

But I didn't say that. Wasn't ready to say that. Saying it would mean admitting two million years of observation had been fundamentally misunderstanding the relationship between awareness and existence.

"How do you feel?" I asked instead.

"Weak. Confused." She tested sitting up. Managed it slowly. "But alive. How long were we out?"

"Five hours. You displaced entire valley into parallel probability space and maintained it through biological quantum entanglement until we could build technological replacement."

She looked at me. Really looked. And I felt seen in ways two million years of observation had never prepared me for.

"You built generators while we were unconscious."

"Yes."

"You were terrified we wouldn't wake up."

That wasn't question. That was observation. Accurate observation.

"Yes," I admitted.

Her hand found mine. Weak grip. But intentional. "Thank you for being scared. For caring enough to be scared."

Two million years of Watcher training said I shouldn't be scared. Shouldn't be emotionally compromised. Should maintain objective distance.

Three weeks with Rhea said Watcher training had missed the entire point.

Lucia was sitting up now. Testing coordination. "I dreamed we built the field. Not with our bodies. With... something else. Something that existed before bodies."

"Before incarnation," I said quietly.

"Maybe." She looked at her hands. "It felt real. Like we'd done it before. Many times. Just... bigger."

The walls pulsed. Just once. But everyone felt it.

The generators were responding to something. Matching rhythm that came from elsewhere.

And then reality developed a sound that made everyone freeze.

Not construct attack. Not dimensional breach.

A message.

Arriving through frequencies that shouldn't exist. Manifesting as information that appeared directly in consciousness rather than through sight or sound.

I felt it with clarity that came from ancient Watcher perception. The federal agents felt it through their restructured modifications. Everyone enhanced felt it simultaneously.

WARNING.

FABRICATED EVIDENCE SUBMITTED TO ANCIENT POWERS.

HARVEST MASTERS MANIPULATED HUMAN COUNCIL.

PETITION CLAIMS CONSCIOUSNESS EVOLUTION CAUSED ENVIRONMENTAL DESTRUCTION.

SIX DAYS UNTIL CLEANSING.

The message continued. Details about lies. About deception. About cosmic bureaucracy operating on false information.

And underneath it all, buried in the quantum frequencies: urgency.

Someone—something—wanted us to know. Wanted us to act.

The message dissolved.

But its impact remained.

Six days to prove humanity deserved survival. To expose Harvest Masters' deception. To reach cosmic bureaucrats who didn't take testimony from evolved apes.

I looked at the others. At Maya processing. At Morrison trying to understand. At Ansel recognizing patterns from century of experience.

At Rhea, weak but recovering, still holding my hand.

"We need to do something," she said.

"Yes," I agreed.

"Something cosmically inadvisable."

"Probably."

She smiled despite exhaustion. "Good. I'd hate for this to get boring."

Three weeks of incarnation. Two million years of observation. And nothing I'd witnessed prepared me for how much I didn't want to lose her.

That was the difference between watching and living.

That was everything.

The generators pulsed. The grid was still watching. Still asking: **WHAT ARE YOU?**

And I was starting to suspect the answer wasn't "ancient Watcher learning to be human."

The answer was something older. Something we'd all forgotten.

Something the grid itself was trying to remember.

Chapter Seventeen

Chapter 17

CHAPTER SEVENTEEN: THE RETURN (Kael's POV)

The dimensional breach opened without warning.

I felt it before I saw it. Sharp pull on consciousness that meant reality was developing holes again. Three weeks of incarnation hadn't dulled my Watcher perception—just added layers of human sensation on top of it.

Now I got both. Ancient awareness of dimensional architecture fracturing AND the sick feeling in my stomach that humans called dread.

Lucky me.

"It's them," Rhea said. Her quantum sensitivity reading frequencies I could perceive but she could interpret. "Terry and Zara. They're coming back."

Morrison was already moving toward clearing. "It's only been twelve hours. She said—"

"Time's variable," Ansel reminded him, following. "Twelve hours here. Could be weeks there."

The perimeter soldiers were raising weapons. Lieutenant Chen barking orders into radio. Trying to explain dimensional phenomena to command while watching reality tear open in front of him.

I understood his confusion. Two million years of observation and I still found incarnation disorienting. He'd had maybe thirty years of baseline human consciousness. No wonder he looked lost.

The breach stabilized.

Two figures stepped through.

Zara manifested first. Properly clothed this time. She'd learned. Good for her. The naked manifestation had been educational for everyone but probably more embarrassing for her than necessary.

She looked different. More solid. Comfortable with gravity in ways she hadn't been before. Like she'd spent significant time learning how bodies worked.

Which apparently she had.

And behind her: Terry.

Young. Maybe mid-thirties. Handsome in ways that came from character rather than optimization. Standing upright without the wobbling that usually accompanied new manifestation.

And shimmering.

The light body was visible even to my ancient Watcher perception. He existed here. But also partially elsewhere. Like he couldn't quite decide which dimension to fully commit to.

I recognized the pattern. It was similar to mine. But more pronounced. More intentional.

Zara had built him to exist in multiple states simultaneously.

That was advanced work. Very advanced.

Lieutenant Chen lowered his weapon slowly. Processing. "What the fuck."

Terry grinned. Same grin. Same dry humor despite completely different face. "Hey. Miss me?"

Jenkins dropped the jacket he'd been holding all night. "You... yo u're..."

"Young? Yeah, noticed that. Weird, right?" Terry was testing his new coordination. Careful but functional. "Turns out dying's great anti-aging treatment. Really opens up the pores."

Torres laughed. Actual laughter with tears in it. "You died. Your heart stopped. We watched you die."

"I got better."

Morrison was staring. "It's only been one night. Twelve hours since your heart stopped. How—"

"Twelve hours to you," Zara said. Her voice carrying authority I hadn't heard before. Confidence from weeks of body-building and love-learning. "Thirty-seven days to us. You experienced one night. We experienced over a month."

That stopped everyone.

I'd known time was variable in building spaces. Had observed it functioning across dimensional boundaries. But experiencing the confirmation—seeing Terry rebuilt after what felt like hours to us but was weeks to them—that made it real in ways observation never could.

"A month," Rhea said quietly. "You spent a month building him."

"Learning him," Zara corrected. Looking at Terry with expression I recognized because I'd probably been wearing it while looking at Rhea. "Building was just the method."

She'd fallen in love. Completely. Obviously. The kind of love that came from knowing someone at cellular level because you'd literally constructed every cell while learning what made them themselves.

That was intimate beyond anything I'd observed in two million years.

And I was jealous.

Not of them. For them. Because they'd had weeks while Rhea and I had only had days and I wanted more time to learn her the way Zara had learned Terry.

Three weeks of incarnation and I was already greedy for experiences I hadn't had yet.

That was progress. Apparently.

I stepped forward. My ancient consciousness recognizing what Zara had accomplished. "You built quantum-biological hybrid. Not just incarnation. Actual construction from consciousness and matter."

"We learned from watching you manifest badly," Zara said. Meeting my eyes. No judgment. Just observation. "Developed protocols. Figured out how to construct bodies that can hold consciousness across dimensions."

"Hence the shimmer," Ansel observed. "His light body won't fully integrate."

"Can't fully integrate," Terry said. Studying his hands like they were fascinating alien artifacts. Which, technically, they were. "I'm too stubborn to fit entirely into normal matter. So I exist partially elsewhere. It's actually convenient. I can see things from multiple dimensional perspectives simultaneously now."

He looked at the three siblings. At Rhea, who I'd been unconsciously standing closer to. "You three okay? Last I saw, you were crying over my corpse."

"You died holding the circle," Lucia said. Voice shaken. "You saved us and died doing it."

"Best possible way to go, honestly. Beats dying in nursing home watching reruns." Terry moved toward them. Testing coordination. Still learning limits. "But Zara had other plans. Wouldn't let me stay dead. Got all cosmic and determined about it."

"I watched you for twenty years," Zara said simply. "Wasn't going to let the ending be 'died of heart failure while dimensional dancing.' That's terrible narrative structure."

Maya's android body was processing. "You fell in love with him."

"Yes."

"While building him."

"Yes."

"That's not in any protocol I've studied."

"Protocols are for machines," Zara said. No insult. Just observation I recognized because I'd been thinking similar things about Watcher protocols versus actual living. "I was learning to be alive. Love's apparently part of that."

Terry took her hand. Young hand with careful calluses holding hand that had built his entire body from light and intention.

I watched the gesture. Recognized it. Had been doing same thing with Rhea for three weeks.

The touch meant everything observation had missed.

"Should we tell them about the time dilation thing?" Terry asked.

"What time dilation thing?" Morrison said.

"The one where spending weeks building bodies while falling in love tends to create significant intimacy." Terry was grinning. "We know each other really well now. Probably better than most couples who've been together for years."

"Because she built you from consciousness," I said. Understanding dawning. "She experienced everything you are while constructing your form. That's more intimate than most relationships achieve in lifetimes."

I'd observed relationship formation across thousands of species. None of it compared to literally building your partner's body cell by cell while learning what made them themselves.

That was intimacy beyond anything biology alone could create.

"Exactly." Terry squeezed Zara's hand. "So we're together now. In case that wasn't obvious. Watcher and reformed eighty-four-year-old consciousness in new thirty-something body. We're a thing."

"That's the weirdest relationship origin story I've ever heard," Jenkins observed.

"You're talking to man who just got rebuilt by cosmic entity who learned grief by watching him die. Weird's relative at this point."

The eastern horizon was brightening. Full dawn now. Light touching clearing, military vehicles, federal agents who'd come to arrest terrorists and instead witnessed resurrection.

And then reality developed sound that made everyone freeze.

The message.

I felt it arriving through frequencies I could perceive with ancient Watcher clarity. Every enhanced human in community felt it simultaneously. Federal agents with restructured modifications felt it. Even baseline humans felt something—pressure in consciousness that suggested information trying to manifest.

WARNING.

The word arrived like hammer blow to awareness.

I processed the message as it manifested. Fabricated evidence. Harvest Masters manipulating human Council. Petition claiming consciousness evolution caused environmental destruction when actually traditional power structures had done the damage.

Six days until Ancient Powers decided.

Six days until possible species cleansing based on lies.

The message dissolved but impact remained.

Silence in clearing. Federal agents, community members, confused soldiers all processing same information.

Six days.

I'd observed species extinctions before. Watched civilizations end. Recorded final moments of consciousness that thought it had more time.

This was different. This was my species now. Rhea's species. The people I'd spent three weeks learning to care about instead of just observe.

"Well," Terry said, breaking shocked silence. "That's ominous."

"The Harvest Masters," I said. My ancient consciousness accessing information from Watcher archives. "Dimensional entities that feed on fear and desperation. They farm emotional energy from suffering species."

"And they convinced Ancient Powers that we're the problem," Zara added. "Showed them environmental destruction from fifty years ago. Blamed it on consciousness evolution when actually traditional power structures caused it."

Morrison's face was pale. "The billionaire Council. Eleanor Blackstone and her partners. They submitted petition thinking they'd be spared. Thinking cleansing would only target consciousness communities."

"But Ancient Powers don't distinguish between human factions," Ansel said quietly. "They see species. They make decisions."

"Six days until they eliminate consciousness evolution," Torres said. "Which means—"

"Which means everyone," Maya finished. "Enhanced humans, baseline humans, everyone. Harvest Masters want us all gone except pure stock they can farm for fear."

"Can we contact Ancient Powers?" Jenkins asked. "Tell them truth?"

"They don't take calls from evolved apes," I said. Two million years of observation had taught me that much. "We're not even on their consideration level. We're just the species being judged."

Rhea looked at me. Then at Terry and Zara. "But you're not just evolved apes anymore. You're Watchers. Ancient consciousness in human form. Do they take calls from Watchers?"

Zara and I exchanged glances.

Two million years of non-interference doctrine meeting three weeks of participation.

"The Watchers have protocols," I said slowly. "We observe. We don't participate in species-level judgments."

"You participated when you incarnated," Lucia pointed out. "You broke non-interference then."

"That was individual choice—"

"And this is individual choice too," Fin interrupted. "Individual choice to not let our species burn based on lies."

Terry was looking at us. At me and Zara. At Rhea and Lucia. Something clicking in his newly-enhanced perception.

"We're four people," he said. "Two ancient consciousnesses learning humanity. Two humans learning cosmic perspective. All enhanced. All shimmering between dimensions. All stupidly brave and recently fell in love."

Zara caught his meaning. "You're thinking—"

"I'm thinking we might be uniquely positioned to do something cosmically inadvisable."

I looked at Rhea. At her sisters. At Terry and Zara.

Four people. Two couples. Ancient and young. Watcher and human.

All of us changed by contact we shouldn't have survived.

"I've been alive for three weeks," I said. "Might as well save species while I'm at it."

Rhea smiled despite exhaustion. "We know how to reach violet space. The dimensional bridges work."

"And I just spent thirty-seven days learning quantum-biological construction," Zara said. "That might be useful for... something."

Morrison looked at us. "You're going to try to contact Ancient Powers."

"Not just contact," Terry said. His new body already moving with confidence despite being hours old. "We're going to show them truth. Somehow. Before Harvest Masters' lies get us all killed."

"That's insane."

"Yeah, probably." Terry's shimmer was more visible in dawn light. "But I died yesterday and got rebuilt by someone who learned love by constructing my flesh. Insane's just Tuesday for us now."

I felt Rhea's hand find mine. Quiet gesture. Comfort and partnership combined.

Three weeks ago I'd been pure observation. Now I was person standing in Michigan clearing holding hands with seventeen-year-old girl while planning to do something that would probably violate every protocol I'd ever followed.

And I'd never felt more alive.

"We still have to try," Rhea said. "Even if barrier is real. Even if we're breaking contracts. Even if there's enforcement."

"Why?" Ansel asked. Not challenging. Genuinely curious.

"Because ten people just died," she said. "Because Harvest Masters are killing everyone while we hide. Because in six days Ancient Powers will eliminate consciousness evolution based on lies." She stood, shaky but determined. "And because if system is trap, then breaking it is exactly what we should do."

Lucia nodded. "We didn't agree to watch people be harvested. That wasn't in any contract I remember."

Morrison looked at his team. Federal agents who'd come to arrest terrorists. "What do you need from us?"

"Time," I said. "Six days. Don't let anyone interfere while we figure out how to reach beings that don't acknowledge our existence."

"We can do that."

Sun was fully risen now. Morning in Michigan. Federal perimeter holding position around community that had accidentally become ground zero for consciousness evolution.

And in center of it all, four people who'd fallen in love across dimensional boundaries while learning what it meant to be alive.

Two couples. All enhanced. All shimmering. All about to attempt something that had probably never been done in cosmic history.

Contact Ancient Powers. Expose Harvest Masters' deception. Prove consciousness evolution deserved survival.

With six days and zero plan and love that was new enough to still feel like magic.

"So," Terry said, looking at us. "Anyone know how to get attention of cosmic bureaucrats who think we're irrelevant?"

"Not specifically," I admitted.

"Then we'll figure it out as we go." Terry squeezed Zara's hand. "That's how all best terrible decisions start."

Four people stood in clearing. Two couples. Ancient and young. Human and Watcher. All choosing participation over safety.

I looked at Rhea. Three weeks of knowing her. Felt like lifetime. Felt like beginning.

"You okay with cosmically inadvisable?" I asked.

"It's kind of our thing now," she said.

The dimensional war wasn't over.

But we were going to fight it anyway.

With love and stubbornness and kind of cosmic audacity that only came from being rebuilt from light and refusing to waste the second chance.

I'd spent two million years watching.

Three weeks participating.

The second had given me more reasons to exist than the first.

Time to prove consciousness evolution was worth saving.

Starting with us.

Chapter Eighteen

Chapter 18

CHAPTER EIGHTEEN: THE BARRIER (Kael's POV)

Four people stood in the clearing. Two couples. Ancient and young. Human and Watcher. All choosing participation over safety.

The dimensional war wasn't over.

Zara reached and grasped Terry's hand. "Something's—"

The air tore open and then there was a scream!

Not clean dimensional breach like Watchers used. These were *wounds*. Reality ripping like flesh under claws. Smoky, shimmering edges that bled wrongness into physical space.

I'd observed dimensional incursions for two million years. Cataloged attack patterns. Documented predator behavior across thousands of species.

None of it prepared me for the visceral horror of watching it happen to people I cared about.

Through the tears came constructs.

Smaller than yesterday's. Faster. Built for killing rather than harvest.

The perimeter exploded into chaos.

A soldier—young man, name patch reading WILLIAMS—was firing at something he couldn't see properly when it took him. No warning. Just sudden absence where he'd been standing. His body fell in pieces.

I'd observed death countless times. Recorded it. Analyzed it. Filed reports on mortality patterns and survival statistics.

This was different. This was murder happening in front of me and I couldn't stop it through observation.

Another soldier—RODRIGUEZ—screaming as invisible claws pulled her apart. Her rifle clattered to ground, barrel still hot.

"CONTACT!" someone screamed.

Three weeks of incarnation and I was still learning what helplessness felt like. What it meant to watch people die and not be able to just observe and move on to the next data point.

It felt like shit.

The perimeter soldiers opened fire. Bullets passing through smoky forms without effect. The constructs moved like predators who'd done this before. Selecting targets. Moving with intelligence that spoke of purpose beyond random violence.

Three more soldiers down. Then two more. Blood spreading across Michigan dirt while radios crackled with panicked calls to command centers that had no protocol for dimensional predators.

Torres was firing. Her restructured consciousness modification letting her *see* the constructs properly. But seeing didn't help. Bullets did nothing.

"FALL BACK!" Morrison shouted. "Everyone inside the—"

Maya's android body blurred into motion. Moving at speeds biological forms couldn't match. She *grabbed* a construct—quantum processors interfacing with dimensional structure—and **crushed** it.

The thing screamed. Sound that existed across frequencies biological ears shouldn't hear.

It dissolved.

I filed that away. Maya could interact with constructs directly. Quantum processing interfacing with dimensional architecture. Useful data.

Three weeks and I was still defaulting to observation when stressed.

Old habits.

But there were more constructs. So many more.

The clearing was chaos. Soldiers dying. Federal agents with modified consciousness fighting things they couldn't touch. Community members trying to form defensive networks while constructs selected victims with terrible precision.

Jenkins was dragging wounded private toward cover when construct manifested beside them. I saw it happening. Saw the dimensional tear forming. Saw the predator selecting target.

Couldn't stop it.

The construct took the private. Young man—couldn't have been more than twenty—screaming as something invisible did its work.

Jenkins was screaming too. Grief and rage and helplessness all at once.

I understood the feeling.

"WE NEED TO DO SOMETHING!" Fin shouted. His quantum sensitivity overloading, seeing too much death across too many frequencies.

Rhea was bleeding from her nose again. Lucia's eyes bleeding too. Both sisters experiencing quantum cascade as they pushed past biological parameters.

And then they looked at each other.

I'd observed that look before. Sisters communicating without words. Quantum entanglement creating understanding that bypassed normal consciousness.

They were planning something.

"Lucia," Rhea said.

"I know."

They joined hands. Quantum sensitivity merging. Two sisters who glowed in impossible frequencies reaching into dimensional architecture with intention I could feel building.

They'd shifted us into violet space yesterday. Vertical movement. Dimensional transit upward.

Now they were going sideways.

Not up into Watcher territory. Sideways into parallel possibility. Into universe-space where probability branched into infinite variations and predators couldn't follow because the math became unpredictable.

The valley *shifted*.

I felt it happening. Reality displacing. Not disappearing. Not transported. Just... sideways. Slipping into parallel existence where we still occupied Michigan coordinates but existed in probability space the constructs couldn't access.

Everything looked the same. The cabin. The trees. The federal vehicles. The bodies of soldiers who'd died in the first minute.

But it felt different. Like standing behind dimensional glass. Present but untouchable.

The constructs slammed against the barrier. Clawing. Screaming. Unable to penetrate.

They circled. Probing. Looking for weakness.

Found none.

After several minutes, they gave up. Retreated through their smoky wounds in reality.

But they didn't leave entirely.

Through the dimensional displacement, I could see them. Blurred forms circling the valley. Waiting. Patient. Hunting constructs who'd learned their prey had escaped but not how to follow.

The sisters collapsed simultaneously.

I caught Rhea before she hit ground. Her body convulsing in my arms. Nose bleeding freely. The effort of displacing entire valley sideways had burned through her enhancement reserves completely.

"Are they—" Terry started.

Maya was already scanning. "Alive. But barely. They pushed past every safe parameter. Burned through enhancement reserves completely. Their biology is trying to shut down to prevent total system failure."

"Will they recover?" I asked. Trying to keep my voice clinical. Failing.

"If we can stabilize them. And if this displacement holds without their active maintenance." Maya's expression flickered. "They're not just unconscious. They're sustaining this sideways shift through biological feedback. Quantum entanglement with displaced probability field. If their bodies fail—"

"The valley snaps back," Ansel finished.

I looked down at Rhea. Unconscious in my arms. Blood streaming from her nose. Her consciousness partially merged with her sister's, both of them holding reality sideways through sheer biological force.

Three weeks ago she'd been observation subject. Interesting human with quantum sensitivity worth documenting.

Now she was everything.

Two million years and I'd never understood what "everything" meant until I held it bleeding in my arms.

"Can we move them inside?" Kathleen asked.

"Carefully," Maya said. "Any disruption to their biology could collapse the field."

Ansel moved to help me. Together we carried the sisters inside. Treating them like they were made of glass. Because effectively they were—fragile biological containers holding dimensional displacement that was keeping everyone alive.

Inside cabin, we laid them on couches. Maya monitoring vital signs while Kathleen brought blankets.

I stayed beside Rhea. Holding her hand. Watching her breathe. Counting breaths like they were data points because focusing on data was easier than feeling helpless.

"How long?" Fin asked. His sisters unconscious and bleeding.

"Hours," Maya said. "Maybe longer. Their biology needs to rebuild enhancement reserves from nothing. And they're still maintaining displacement field. Every heartbeat is feeding quantum entanglement."

Morrison was checking his remaining team. Eight soldiers dead. Federal agents with restructured modifications had survived. But baseline soldiers—ones without consciousness enhancement—had died first.

"So we're trapped in sideways probability space sustained by two unconscious teenagers," he observed. "That's not reassuring."

"No," Ansel agreed. "It's not."

Terry was pacing. His newly-formed body shimmering with agitation. "We need plan. Harvest Masters will keep sending constructs. Will keep killing. We can't just hide here while—"

"While what?" Zara asked. "While your great philosophical acceptance plays out? While we embrace suffering as spiritual curriculum?"

Terry stopped pacing. "That's not what I—"

"Isn't it?" She was watching him carefully. "You spent decades studying Eastern philosophy. Meditation. Acceptance of what is. Balance requiring darkness. The whole package."

I'd observed this pattern before. Philosophical disagreement between partners who cared about each other. Usually fascinating to document.

Now it just made me uncomfortable because I was participant, not observer, and I had opinions about who was right.

"Yes," Terry said. "And those principles—"

"Kept you sane while preparing for something you couldn't control," Ansel interrupted. He was sitting with Lucia's unconscious form in his lap. His great-granddaughter. Third generation choosing participation. "I'm not criticizing, Terry. I understand appeal. But there's difference between finding peace within difficult circumstances and claiming circumstances themselves are necessary."

Terry looked at his old friend. They'd known each other for fifteen years at community. Had argued philosophy more times than either could count.

"You're saying my forty years of study is just... what? Coping mechanism?"

"I'm saying it might be both useful and wrong." Ansel smiled. No heat in it. Just old affection. "You and I have danced this dance before, brother. Usually over better coffee and without dimensional predators involved."

Terry laughed despite himself. "Fair point."

I watched the exchange. Two friends who cared enough to argue honestly. Two humans who'd accumulated enough experience to question their own assumptions.

I'd observed philosophical debates for two million years. Never understood they required love to function properly. That disagreement without affection was just combat.

Three weeks and I was still learning basic things.

"But question stands," Ansel continued. "Is suffering actually necessary for growth? Or is that just what they tell us to keep us accepting conditions that should be unacceptable?"

Morrison was listening. Torres too. Even Jenkins, despite his grief, was paying attention.

"The yin-yang principle—" Terry started.

"Is beautiful philosophy that might also be prison architecture," Ansel finished. "I love you, old friend. But I've got few years on you—" he grinned, "—even if you're currently wearing prettier package. And I've had time to think about whether cosmic authorities might have reasons for teaching us that balance requires darkness."

"Such as?"

"Such as: if you believe suffering is necessary, you don't fight system causing it." Ansel shifted Lucia slightly. Making sure her head was supported. "Government does it. Church does it. Tells you suffering joyfully is path to happiness. Know what that actually means?"

"Enlightenment—"

"Compliance. Don't change conditions. Just accept them as necessary and noble." Ansel's voice was gentle but firm. "I've heard that line for century, Terry. 'Pain builds character. Darkness teaches lessons. You must suffer to appreciate joy.' And every time, it's been said by someone benefiting from my continued suffering."

I filed that observation. It matched patterns I'd seen across thousands of species. Control structures maintaining themselves through narrative that suffering was spiritual rather than political.

But I'd never connected the dots. Never understood the pattern was relevant to my own existence.

Because Watchers observed suffering. We didn't experience it. We were above it.

Except we weren't. We were just removed from it. And removal had let us miss the point entirely.

"But without contrast—" Terry tried again.

"You recognize joy just fine," Ansel interrupted. "You don't need to stub your toe to enjoy walking. That's conditioning talking. The 'you must suffer to appreciate happiness' narrative keeps people in boxes. Accepting imprisonment as spiritual growth."

Terry sat down. His enthusiasm meeting reality delivered with brotherly love.

Rhea's hand twitched in mine. Still unconscious but her biology responding to something.

I squeezed back. Gentle pressure. Hoping she could feel it somewhere in whatever quantum space her consciousness occupied.

"So what, we just... refuse whole framework?" Terry asked. "Demand happiness without earning it?"

"We refuse narrative that says we have to earn basic dignity through pain." Ansel looked at Lucia. "She didn't earn right to not be harvested by dimensional predators. She has that right because consciousness has intrinsic value. System that says otherwise—that says she needs to suffer to grow—that's the trap."

"You sound pretty sure about that."

"I am." Ansel pulled up his left sleeve.

On his forearm, faint but visible: a triangle. Branded into flesh.

I'd seen that mark before. In my observations. Across different species. Different contexts.

Always connected to dimensional transit. To consciousness crossing barriers it shouldn't cross.

"What is that?" Terry asked.

"Proof," Ansel said simply. "That trap is real."

The room went quiet.

I leaned forward. Ancient consciousness suddenly very interested. "May I examine it?"

"Sure." Ansel extended his arm.

I studied the triangle. Not tattoo. Not scar. Something burned in from inside. Quantum signature embedded in flesh. Mark of passage across dimensional boundaries.

"This appeared during out-of-body experience," Ansel said. "Years ago. Before consciousness evolution. Before any of this."

Kathleen moved closer. She'd found him that night. Had lived with aftermath.

"I flew out," Ansel continued. Matter-of-fact. "Into space. Higher and higher. Leaving Earth. Leaving atmosphere. Going... elsewhere. And I reached barrier."

"What kind of barrier?" I asked. Two million years of observation and I'd never personally encountered what he was describing.

"Crystalline architecture. Geometric patterns. Energy and structure combined. Grid surrounding Earth completely."

I knew what he was describing. Watchers knew about it. We just didn't talk about it.

"When I reached it—when I tried to cross it—voice spoke."

Everyone was listening now.

"What did it say?" Zara asked.

"'Do not cross.'" Ansel's expression was neutral. "That's all. No threat. No explanation. Just administrative. Matter-of-fact. Like guard at checkpoint saying 'you can't go through here' because that's the rule and rule is absolute."

"Did you try anyway?" Morrison asked.

"No." Ansel touched the triangle. "Something in that voice carried weight. Authority. Kind that makes disobedience feel not just impossible but catastrophic. So I came back. Woke up in bed screaming. Kathleen thought I was dying."

"I thought you were having heart attack," Kathleen confirmed. "You were drenched in sweat. Couldn't breathe properly. And this—" she touched triangle gently, "—this appeared while you were screaming. Just... manifested in your flesh. Like something had marked you."

I processed this. Triangle appearing during dimensional transit attempt. Voice preventing passage. Mark remaining as proof.

That was enforcement. Clear enforcement of boundary consciousness wasn't supposed to cross.

"Marked as what?" I asked.

"As someone who'd seen the cage," Ansel said.

He looked at me. Century of human experience meeting two million years of Watcher observation.

"You know about it," he said. Not question. Statement.

"Yes," I admitted. "The containment field. Earth's quarantine architecture. We—Watchers—we know about it. Have known for millions of years. We just don't talk about it."

"Why not?"

"Because it's older than us. We didn't build it. Don't maintain it. Can barely perceive it most of the time. But it's there. Has been there longer than we've been watching." My consciousness accessing memories most Watchers kept buried. "And entities who enforce it... they make us look like children playing at observation."

"So we're trapped," Morrison said. "Earth consciousness is contained by something older than Watchers. And we can't leave."

"We're contained," Ansel corrected. "There's difference between prison and quarantine. But I've spent years trying to figure out which one this is. Haven't reached comfortable conclusions."

The walls flickered.

Everyone felt it. Displacement field thinning as biological support wavered.

Rhea's hand clenched mine. Unconscious but her body straining to maintain impossible burden.

"Her enhancement reserves are depleting," Maya announced. "She's burning through biological capacity trying to maintain field."

"How long until she fails?" I asked. Trying to keep panic out of my voice.

"Hours. Maybe less." Maya looked at Lucia. "They're both maintaining it through quantum entanglement. When one fails, other will follow. And valley will snap back into normal dimensional space."

"With constructs waiting," Morrison observed.

"Yes."

Through displacement shimmer, I could see blurred forms circling. Patient. Hunting.

"We need another solution," I said. Ancient consciousness meeting immediate crisis. "Girls can't sustain this. We need technology to replace biological maintenance."

"Generators," Terry said. His new perception catching the solution. "Quantum field generators. We've got military hardware outside. If we can adapt it—"

"Create artificial quantum entanglement to maintain displacement," Zara finished. "Sisters can rest. Their biology can recover while technology holds field."

"Can that work?" Morrison asked.

"I don't know," I admitted. "But I'm two million years old and Zara's older. If anyone can jury-rig military equipment into quantum displacement field generator, it's probably us."

"Probably," Morrison repeated.

"Better than definitely dying when girls' biology fails."

The walls flickered again. Longer. Displacement thinning noticeably.

Through shimmer, constructs were moving closer. Testing. Sensing weakness.

I looked down at Rhea. Unconscious. Bleeding. Holding reality together through biological force that was killing her.

Three weeks ago I would've observed this happening. Documented fascinating case study of consciousness exceeding biological parameters.

Now I was terrified.

That was the difference between watching and living.

That was everything.

"Four hours," Maya said. Monitoring both sisters. "Maybe five before total biological failure."

"Then we have four hours," I said, standing carefully. Not letting go of Rhea's hand until absolutely necessary, "to build technology that can maintain parallel dimensional displacement using military hardware and cosmic authority neither of us fully understand."

Terry laughed. "That's most ridiculous plan I've ever heard."

"You got better?" Ansel asked with grin.

"No." Terry headed for door. "Let's go build impossible things with inadequate resources. It's basically our job description at this point."

I looked at Rhea one more time. Memorizing her face. Just in case.

Two million years of observation. Three weeks of participation.

If she died, observation wouldn't matter anymore.

That was terrifying and liberating simultaneously.

I followed Terry outside. Time to build.

Time to prove participation was worth the terror.

Chapter Nineteen

Chapter 19

CHAPTER NINETEEN: RECOGNITION (Kael's POV)

The generators were scattered across the clearing like mechanical corpses waiting for resurrection.

I'd observed technology across thousands of worlds. Watched species build everything from quantum processors to consciousness transfer devices. Documented innovation patterns. Filed reports on technological evolution.

None of it prepared me for actually building something with my own hands.

Terry was elbow-deep in military power unit, rewiring connections that were never meant to interface with consciousness network hardware. I worked beside him, trying to apply two million years of observation to practical engineering.

It wasn't translating well.

"This shouldn't work," I muttered. Connecting quantum processors from federal equipment to community network relays. "The voltage requirements alone—"

"And yet it's working," Terry said.

He was right. The circuits were holding. Impossibly. Power flowing through pathways that violated basic electrical theory I'd observed functioning correctly across countless civilizations.

Why was it working?

Zara was coordinating the larger array. Military generators forming geometric pattern around cabin. Not random placement—intentional architecture creating resonance field that would replace the sisters' biological quantum entanglement.

I watched her work. Ancient Watcher consciousness moving with certainty that didn't come from engineering knowledge.

"The pattern needs to mirror their consciousness structure," she said. More to herself than anyone. "Not just power. Intention. The field has to want to maintain displacement."

That wasn't how technology worked. Technology didn't want things. It functioned according to principles. Cause and effect. Input and output.

Except she was right.

I could feel it. The generators weren't just creating power field. They were creating intentional architecture. Consciousness made manifest through geometric arrangement.

Morrison was watching Zara place generators with precision that came from nowhere in military doctrine. "How do you know where to put them?"

"I don't." Zara stepped back, studying pattern. "But it feels right. Like geometry itself is suggesting placement."

I understood what she meant. And that terrified me.

Because if geometry could suggest. If patterns could have intention. If technology could want...

Then two million years of observation had been fundamentally misunderstanding relationship between consciousness and reality.

Torres was running cables. Federal equipment merged with community hardware merged with military generators. The whole assembly looked like something built by people who'd never seen each other's instruction manuals and didn't care.

"We're fifteen minutes from total biological failure," Maya announced from inside cabin. Monitoring the sisters' vital signs. "Rhea's enhancement reserves are depleted. Lucia's following. Field is thinning."

The walls flickered. Longer this time. Through displacement shimmer, constructs were visible as more than blurs now. Solid forms circling. Waiting. Patient hunters sensing prey's defenses weakening.

I tried not to think about Rhea dying while I fumbled with equipment I barely understood.

Failed.

Three weeks of incarnation and I still couldn't separate observation from participation. Couldn't just document what was happening. Had to care. Had to be terrified.

Had to keep working despite terror because the alternative was unacceptable.

"How much more time do you need?" Morrison called.

"None," I said. "Because we're out of it. This works now or not at all."

Terry made final connection. Circuit completed. Power flowing through impossible configuration.

Nothing happened.

I felt my consciousness—my ancient, observational, supposedly objective consciousness—scream internally. This had to work. Rhea was dying. This had to—

The generators hummed.

Not mechanical sound. Deeper. Resonance that existed below hearing. The geometric pattern Zara had created began glowing. Faint quantum shimmer visible even to unenhanced eyes.

The displacement field... shifted.

Not collapsing. Not strengthening. Just changing. The biological quantum entanglement from unconscious sisters began transferring to technological architecture.

I felt it happening. Watched burden lift from Rhea's failing biology and settle into generators that shouldn't be able to hold it.

Inside cabin, she gasped. Her body convulsing as strain released.

"It's working," Maya said. Surprise in android voice. "The tech is taking over field maintenance. The sisters are recovering."

The walls stopped flickering.

Displacement held. Solid. Stable. Maintained now by technology that shouldn't function but did.

I sat back, looking at my hands. They were shimmering more than usual. Light body showing through. Three weeks of incarnation and I was still figuring out what this body could do.

What I could do.

"We just built quantum field generators from military equipment in four hours," I said.

"Yes," Ansel confirmed.

"That's impossible."

"Yes."

"So why did it work?"

The question hung in air. Nobody answered because nobody knew.

But I had suspicion. Growing certainty based on three weeks of observation becoming participation.

We weren't just building technology. We were willing it into existence. Using hardware as excuse for reality to cooperate with our intention.

Two million years of watching reality function according to fixed principles. Three weeks of discovering principles bent around consciousness that knew what it wanted.

That was terrifying implication.

Because if consciousness shaped reality rather than just perceiving it...

Then what were we?

Before I could process that question, Maya called from cabin: "They're waking!"

I moved inside faster than dignity allowed. Rhea was stirring. Eyes fluttering. Coming back from wherever quantum consciousness went when biology couldn't support it anymore.

"Easy," I said, kneeling beside her. My ancient consciousness meeting her seventeen years with concern that had nothing to do with observation protocols. "Don't try to sit up yet. Your biology just recovered from impossible strain."

Rhea's eyes opened. Unfocused. Confused.

And alive.

Three weeks ago I would've been documenting fascinating recovery patterns. Now I was just grateful she was breathing.

"We were... bigger," she said.

"What?"

"The valley. It was small. And we were..." she frowned, trying to hold dream-memory that was slipping away, "...we were everywhere.

Not just displaced sideways. We were the displacement. The valley was inside us. Or we were—" she shook her head, "—it doesn't make sense."

It made perfect sense if consciousness created reality rather than just perceiving it.

But saying that would mean admitting two million years of observation had been looking at existence backwards.

I wasn't ready for that.

Not yet.

"How do you feel?" I asked instead.

"Weak. Confused." She tested sitting up. Managed it slowly. "But alive. How long were we out?"

"Five hours. You displaced entire valley into parallel probability space and maintained it through biological quantum entanglement until we could build technological replacement."

She looked at me. Really looked. And I felt seen in ways two million years of observation had never prepared me for.

"You built generators while we were unconscious."

"Yes."

"You were terrified we wouldn't wake up."

That wasn't question. That was observation. Accurate observation.

"Yes," I admitted.

Her hand found mine. Weak grip. But intentional. "Thank you for being scared. For caring enough to be scared."

Two million years of Watcher training said I shouldn't be scared. Shouldn't be emotionally compromised. Should maintain objective distance.

Three weeks with Rhea said Watcher training had missed entire point.

Lucia was sitting up now. Testing coordination. "I dreamed we built the field. Not with our bodies. With... something else. Something that existed before bodies."

"Before incarnation," I said quietly.

"Maybe." She looked at her hands. Turned them over like they were foreign objects. "It felt real. Like we'd done it before. Many times. Just... bigger."

The generators pulsed. Just once. But everyone felt it.

They were responding to something. Matching rhythm that came from elsewhere.

And then reality developed sound that made everyone freeze.

Not construct attack. Not dimensional breach.

A message.

I felt it arriving through frequencies I could perceive with ancient Watcher clarity. Every enhanced human in community felt it simultaneously. Federal agents with restructured modifications felt it. Even baseline humans felt something—pressure in consciousness suggesting information trying to manifest.

The message came through clean. Professional. Like cosmic memo from bureaucracy that didn't know it was ending species.

WARNING.

FABRICATED EVIDENCE SUBMITTED TO ANCIENT POWERS.

HARVEST MASTERS MANIPULATED HUMAN COUNCIL.

PETITION CLAIMS CONSCIOUSNESS EVOLUTION CAUSED ENVIRONMENTAL DESTRUCTION.

SIX DAYS UNTIL CLEANSING.

ANCIENT POWERS ARE METHODICAL, NOT EVIL.

THEY DON'T KNOW THEY'VE BEEN DECEIVED.

SOMEONE MUST SHOW THEM TRUTH.

BEFORE WE ALL BURN TOGETHER.

The message dissolved.

But underneath it, barely perceptible to anyone without ancient Watcher perception, there was something else. Another layer. Question embedded in warning:

WHAT ARE YOU?

And deeper still, older, more fundamental:

WHAT WERE YOU?

Lucia's eyes were bleeding again. Not from quantum cascade. From something else. Pressure of attention too vast to comfortably perceive.

"The grid is asking," she said. Wiping blood from face. "Not the message. The grid itself. It's trying to remember us and it's—" she grimaced, "—it's pulling too hard."

"Remember us?" Terry asked.

"Like it knows us. Knew us. Before." Lucia looked confused. "That doesn't make sense. We've never touched the grid before today."

But Ansel's triangle was glowing. Faint shimmer matching generators' resonance.

And I felt something in my own consciousness. Recognition that shouldn't be there. The grid's inquiry touching memories I didn't know I had.

Memories from before I was Watcher.

From before I chose observation.

From when I was... something else.

"We need to answer," Lucia said. "Or disconnect. But we can't stay in this middle state. Grid is trying to remember us and pulling too hard."

"Answer how?" Terry asked.

"By showing it what we are." Rhea stood. Shaky but determined. "By breaking through. Not violently. Not sneaking. But by being what we apparently are. Whatever that is."

She looked at me. At Zara. At Terry. "You said you needed all six of us. Why?"

"Because alone, we're fragments," I said. Accessing understanding I didn't know I possessed. "Watchers. Humans. Enhanced consciousness. But together—" I paused, feeling truth I couldn't quite articulate, "—together we might be something grid recognizes. Something it's been waiting for."

"Waiting how long?" Fin asked.

I met his eyes. "Longer than I've been watching. Longer than anyone remembers."

The grid pulsed. Generators answered. Resonance building between technological field and cosmic containment.

Through displacement, constructs were retreating. Not because field was stronger. Because something older than them was paying attention and they were prey learning to recognize apex predator.

"You're actually going to do this," Morrison said. "Attempt barrier breakthrough. Answer cosmic questions you don't understand. Risk enforcement from entities that make Watchers look like children."

"Yes," all six of us said.

"When?"

Rhea tested her balance. Still weak but functional. "Soon as we can stand without wobbling. Hours, maybe. However long it takes to recover enough that we don't immediately die attempting this."

The generators pulsed again. Grid matching rhythm. Two quantum systems learning each other's language.

And in space between pulses, barely audible even to my ancient consciousness, a whisper:

WE REMEMBER.

Ansel's triangle flared bright enough that everyone could see it.

"What does grid remember?" Kathleen asked quietly.

"I think," Ansel said, looking at the six of us, "it remembers what we used to be. Before incarnation. Before amnesia. Before we agreed to forget ourselves and call it spiritual growth."

"And what were we?" Fin asked.

Ansel touched his glowing triangle. "That's what we're about to find out."

I looked at Rhea. At her sisters. At Terry and Zara. The six of us preparing to punch through cosmic containment that had been enforced for longer than I'd been watching.

Two million years of observation hadn't prepared me for this.

Three weeks of participation had given me reason to try anyway.

Outside, dawn was approaching. Second day since Terry died and was rebuilt. Second day of displacement into parallel probability. Six days until Ancient Powers decided whether to cleanse Earth of consciousness evolution.

But grid was remembering.

And six people were preparing to help it remember faster.

Not because we understood what we were doing.

But because people we cared about would die if we didn't try.

That was difference between watching and living.

That was everything.

The dimensional war wasn't over.

But survivors were done asking permission.

Time to break through.

Time to remember what we'd forgotten.

Time to discover whether consciousness that couldn't remember itself could still recognize itself when it looked in mirror.

I held Rhea's hand.

Two million years of observation. Three weeks of her.

The second had given me more reasons to exist than the first.

Let's see what we used to be.

Before we forgot.

Chapter Twenty

Chapter 20

CHAPTER TWENTY: FIRST CONTACT (Kael)

Now let's touch the plasma and see what happens.

The generators hummed their quantum rhythm while Rhea and Lucia recovered strength through soup and stubbornness.

I'd observed countless species recover from biological trauma. Documented healing patterns. Filed reports on enhancement regeneration rates.

None of it prepared me for watching Rhea eat soup and wanting to help somehow despite having no useful medical knowledge.

Three weeks of incarnation and I was still learning that caring made you useless in practical ways while being essential in impossible ways.

Fin was pacing. His sisters had displaced entire valley and nearly died doing it. Now they were planning something worse.

"You need more rest," he said for the fifth time.

"We need answers more," Rhea replied. Dark circles under her eyes suggested her biology was still recovering from impossible strain. But her voice was steady.

Lucia was studying generator pattern through cabin window. "The grid is talking to our tech. Asking questions. We need to answer before it stops being curious and starts being defensive."

"Answer how?" Morrison asked.

"By showing it what we are," I said. Standing outside with Terry and Zara, using enhanced perception to study displacement field. "More specifically: what we were. Before incarnation. Before amnesia."

"And you don't know?"

"I know what I observed for two million years. I don't know what I was before I chose observation." My ancient consciousness brushing against questions I'd avoided for eons. "Watchers don't remember our origins. We just... were. Observing. For as long as anyone recalls."

"Convenient amnesia," Ansel observed from doorway. Processing. "Everyone forgets their origins. Watchers. Humans. Even consciousness evolution communities. We all start from 'I don't remember but this must be normal.'"

That was accurate observation. And disturbing.

Two million years and I'd never questioned why I didn't remember beginning. Just assumed I'd always been Watcher. Always been observer.

But what if that wasn't true?

What if I'd been something else first?

Terry was connecting additional sensors to generator array. Jury-rigged quantum detection equipment that would let us probe deeper into displacement field's interaction with... whatever lay beyond it.

"The grid isn't just containment," he said. "It's interface. Architecture designed to interact with something else."

"With what?" Torres asked.

"That's what we're about to find out." Terry made final connection. "Sensors are active. We can push consciousness through displacement field, through grid structure, and see what's on other side."

"Push whose consciousness?" Jenkins asked.

The six of us—me, Zara, Terry, Rhea, Lucia, Fin—looked at each other.

I'd observed group dynamics for two million years. Watched teams form. Documented how consciousness coordinated across individuals.

This was different. We weren't team. We were something else. Something that recognized itself in six bodies.

"Ours," Rhea said. She stood, testing balance. Still weak but functional. "The six of us. We're the ones grid recognizes. We need to be ones who explore it."

"You just recovered from displacing valley," Fin protested.

"Which means I know what pushing past biological limits feels like." Rhea moved to join us outside. "And this won't be as hard. We're not maintaining field. Just... reaching through it."

Lucia followed her sister. Both moving with determination that overrode exhaustion.

Maya was monitoring their vitals. "They're stable. Barely. But another quantum cascade could—"

"Could kill us," Lucia finished. "We know. We're doing it anyway."

The six of us formed circle around generator array.

I'd observed circle formations across thousands of species. Sacred geometry. Consciousness coordination protocols. Symbolic representation of unity.

This felt different. Like the circle wasn't symbolic. Like it was functional architecture. Six points creating pattern that meant something to reality itself.

"What exactly are we doing?" Fin asked.

"Extending consciousness through displacement field," I explained. "Using generators as amplification. We'll stay here physically but project awareness outward. Through our parallel probability space, through grid architecture, to whatever lies beyond."

"The plasma field," Ansel said quietly.

Everyone looked at him.

"In my OBE. When I reached grid. Behind crystalline structure—the lights and geometry—there was something else. Harder to see. Jello-like. Energy field that felt..." he paused, remembering, "...d angerous. Not aggressive. Just fundamentally unsafe. Like touching it would erase something essential."

"Erase what?" Zara asked.

"Me. The part that says 'I am Ansel' rather than 'I am everything.'"

I understood what he meant. I'd observed consciousness dissolution before. Watched individual awareness merge back into collective source. Filed reports on identity loss during transcendence events.

Observation said it was natural process. Consciousness returning to origin.

But if I dissolved into everything, I wouldn't be me anymore. Wouldn't be Kael who'd spent three weeks learning what Rhea's hand felt like.

That seemed like losing rather than returning.

"The grid is structure," Ansel continued. "But plasma behind it is actual barrier. You can't break through it because there's no 'through.' Only dissolution."

"Others cross it," I said. "Souls incarnate. Pass through to enter Earth."

"Yes. Souls that agree to forget. That accept amnesia as cost of entry." Ansel met my eyes. "But leaving while retaining memory? I don't think plasma allows that."

Terry was processing this. "So grid isn't keeping us in. Plasma is. By threatening dissolution of identity to anyone who tries to cross while still being... themselves."

"Maybe," Ansel shrugged. "Or maybe I'm wrong and it's perfectly safe. Only one way to find out."

The six of us joined hands. Circle complete.

I held Rhea's hand on one side, Zara's on other. Felt their consciousness touching mine. Three distinct awarenesses beginning to merge.

"Everyone ready?" I asked.

"No," Fin said.

"Good. Neither am I."

Two million years of observation. I'd never been truly ready for anything. Just prepared to document whatever happened.

Three weeks of participation and I was learning that being ready meant something different. Meant choosing to act despite fear rather than just recording fear in others.

The generators pulsed. Resonance building. Six consciousnesses in circle began merging. Not completely—maintaining individual identity while creating collective awareness that was greater than sum of parts.

We pushed outward.

Through displacement field. Through parallel probability space where valley existed sideways to normal reality. Reaching toward grid structure that surrounded Earth.

The geometric pattern became visible in our merged awareness. Crystalline architecture. Lights arranged in precise mathematical relationships. Nodes connecting to form lattice that enclosed planet completely.

I'd known about grid for two million years. Observed it functioning. Documented its existence in reports nobody read.

Seeing it from inside merged consciousness was different.

It was beautiful. Ancient. Purposeful.

And behind it, harder to perceive: the plasma field.

It looked like nothing and everything simultaneously. Energy that existed at edge of perception. Translucent. Fluid. Potential without form.

It felt wrong.

Not evil. Not malicious. Just... incompatible with individuated consciousness.

I'd observed incompatibility before. Watched matter meet antimatter. Documented what happened when fundamental forces conflicted.

This was similar. But worse. Because the conflict wasn't between matter and energy.

It was between "me" and "everything."

"I see it," Rhea whispered through our merged awareness.

"Don't touch it," Ansel warned from outside circle. "Whatever you do, don't—"

But Lucia's consciousness was already reaching forward.

I felt it happening. Watched through merged awareness as her curiosity overrode caution. Her awareness extending toward plasma field.

Touching it directly.

The scream was immediate.

Not sound. Pure agony manifesting across quantum frequencies. Lucia's consciousness touching plasma and beginning to dissolve. Individual identity bleeding away. "Lucia" becoming "everything" which meant becoming "nothing specific."

She tried to pull back.

Too late.

Part of her awareness had already crossed. Fragment of her consciousness now separated by plasma field. Still her but also not-her. Diluted. Diffused. Spreading into field like ink in water.

Through merged awareness, I felt her dying. Felt her fragment dissolving. Felt the terror of losing specificity. Of "I am Lucia" becoming "I am... what?"

"LUCIA!" Rhea was screaming. In circle, Lucia's physical body was convulsing. Eyes bleeding. Nose bleeding. Quantum cascade worse than anything she'd experienced during valley displacement.

The merged consciousness pulled back. Six individuals retreating from grid. Severing connection before anyone else touched plasma.

But Lucia's fragment was still out there. Trapped on other side. Dissolving slowly.

We crashed back into physical space.

I hit Michigan dirt hard enough to remember why observation was safer than participation.

Lucia collapsed. Her body seizing. Blood streaming from eyes, nose, ears. Her consciousness fractured. Part of her here. Part of her dissolving in plasma field. Neither fragment whole enough to sustain life independently.

"She's dying," Maya said. Quantum processors reading vital signs failing across multiple parameters simultaneously.

Fin was holding his sister. "Do something!"

I tried to stand. Failed. Three weeks in body and I still couldn't coordinate properly after dimensional transit.

"Do what?" Torres asked. "Half her consciousness is trapped behind barrier that dissolves anything that touches it!"

Rhea was on her knees beside Lucia. "I can feel her. The fragment. She's still there. Still... partially her. But fading."

"How do we get her back?" I demanded. Ancient consciousness meeting human panic and discovering panic won.

"We don't," Zara said. Her voice shaken. "Plasma doesn't release what it takes. That's its purpose. One-way filter. Souls can enter. Nothing can leave."

Lucia's body arched. Screaming without sound. Her remaining consciousness trying to hold coherence while fragment dissolved.

Ansel moved forward. Knelt beside dying girl. His great-granddaughter.

"No," he said quietly.

His hand touched Lucia's forehead. Triangle brand on his arm blazed with light.

And something impossible happened.

Ansel's consciousness extended. Not merged. Not projected. Jus t... reached. Following quantum entanglement between Lucia's fragments. Using triangle as anchor. As key. As something that remembered how to navigate plasma without dissolving.

His awareness touched field.

And field remembered him.

Not attacking. Recognizing. Like greeting old friend who'd been gone too long.

I watched through ancient Watcher perception. Documented what I was seeing because observation was reflex even when terror made it irrelevant.

Ansel's consciousness was crossing plasma barrier.

And it wasn't dissolving.

The triangle was protecting him somehow. Or authorizing him. Or reminding plasma that this consciousness belonged on both sides.

"Ansel, what are you doing?" Kathleen asked.

"Something I should've done years ago." His consciousness was extending further. Reaching across plasma barrier. Finding Lucia's fragment. "When I had my OBE, voice told me not to cross. I didn't. But I never asked why I was being warned rather than prevented."

He found Lucia's dissolving fragment. Wrapped his awareness around it.

And pulled.

Plasma resisted. Not hostile. Just... confused. This consciousness (Ansel) had signature suggesting it belonged on this side of barrier. But it was reaching across without dissolving.

How?

Triangle brand was glowing bright enough to hurt eyes. Physical manifestation of something deeper. Some agreement or authorization or memory that let Ansel's consciousness touch plasma without immediate erasure.

He pulled harder.

I watched his physical body aging. Rapidly. Color draining from hair. Skin weathering. Century of life catching up as he burned biological reserves to maintain connection across plasma barrier.

"Ansel, stop!" Kathleen shouted. "You're killing yourself!"

"Probably." His voice aged. Rough. "But she's my great-granddaughter. And I'm not watching another generation die while I observe safely."

The fragment came closer. Lucia's dissolving awareness being pulled back toward coherence. Toward her physical body. Toward life.

With final effort that made his physical body convulse, Ansel yanked fragment through plasma completely.

It snapped back into Lucia's consciousness. Whole again. Complete.

She gasped. Eyes opening. Still bleeding but alive. Aware. Herself.

Ansel collapsed.

Triangle brand stopped glowing. His physical body looked twenty years older than it had minutes ago. Gray hair now white. Skin deeply weathered. Century of accumulated age no longer held back by enhancement that had been burned away maintaining impossible connection.

But he was smiling.

"Interesting," he said. Voice barely whisper. "Plasma remembers. It recognized triangle. Let me pass because..." he frowned, trying to hold memory that was slipping, "...because I'd made passage before. Many times. Brand is record. Proof of repeated crossing."

"You've crossed the barrier?" I asked. Two million years of observation and I'd never seen anyone cross plasma barrier without dissolving.

"Many times. Before incarnation. Before choosing to be Ansel. Plasma remembers even if I don't." He closed his eyes. "It's not prison. It's not protection. It's selection mechanism. Filters consciousness based on... something. Intent? Signature? Agreement?"

His breathing was labored. Effort of plasma navigation catching up.

"It hurt," Lucia said. Voice shaken. "Touching it felt like dying. Like being erased."

"Because part of you tried to cross while retaining 'Lucia' identity." Ansel opened his eyes. "Plasma requires surrender. Not of life. Of specificity. You can't cross while clinging to who you think you are. Must be willing to become... undefined. Temporarily."

"That's insane," Fin said.

"That's the barrier." Ansel managed weak smile. "Now you know. Grid is structure. Plasma is filter. And crossing requires being willing to not-be in order to be differently."

I processed this. Two million years of observation meeting three minutes of watching consciousness navigation that shouldn't be possible.

The plasma wasn't preventing passage. It was selecting for consciousness that could surrender identity without losing continuity.

That was sophisticated architecture. Very sophisticated.

Who built something like that?

Maya was scanning Ansel. "You burned through forty years of biological reserves in three minutes. Your enhancement is gone. You're aging normally now."

"Good." Ansel closed his eyes again. "Enhancement was making me forget how old I actually am. Nice to be honest about it."

Kathleen was crying. Holding her husband who'd just aged two decades to save their great-granddaughter.

Circle broke. Six people processing what we'd just experienced.

Plasma barrier was real. Dangerous. Not through malice but through fundamental incompatibility with individuated consciousness.

And Ansel had crossed it. Briefly. Using triangle brand as... what? Authorization? Memory? Key to passage others didn't have?

"We need to figure this out," Terry said. His shimmer more pronounced now. Brief contact with plasma had changed him too. Made light body more visible. "Plasma isn't just barrier. It's test. Or selection. Or—"

"Or it's us," Rhea said quietly.

Everyone looked at her.

"When Lucia touched it, for moment I felt what she felt. It wasn't foreign. It was familiar. Like touching something I'd been before. Before being Rhea. Before being specific." She looked at her sister. "Plasma isn't keeping us in. It's keeping us separate. Individuated. Because on other side..."

"We're not individual anymore," Lucia finished. Voice carrying weight of brief dissolution. "We're ocean pretending to be waves. And plasma maintains pretense."

I stared at them.

Two million years of observation and I'd never made that connection.

But they were right. I could feel it. The plasma wasn't foreign substance. It was consciousness in base state. Undifferentiated. Pre-individuated.

We were fragments of it. Pretending to be separate. And barrier maintained separation by threatening to dissolve pretense if we tried to cross while still believing we were fragments.

That was elegant trap. Very elegant.

"So breaking through barrier means—" Morrison started.

"Means stopping being us," I finished. "At least temporarily. Maybe permanently. Plasma is one-way filter in both directions. Enter Earth: forget you're ocean, become wave. Leave Earth: forget you're wave, become ocean."

"Neither option preserves continuity," Zara observed.

"No." Ansel opened his eyes. Weathered and ancient. "Unless you find third way. Be wave that knows it's ocean. Maintain individual identity while accessing source awareness. That's what triangle suggests is possible. Repeated crossing without total dissolution. But I don't remember how."

"Then we learn," Terry said. "Because we've got six days until Ancient Powers eliminate consciousness evolution. And apparently reaching them requires crossing plasma barrier that erases anyone who doesn't know the trick."

Generators pulsed. Grid was still watching. Still asking: **WHAT ARE YOU?**

And I had partial answer now: consciousness that had forgotten how to cross its own barriers. Waves that didn't remember being ocean. Fragments separated by field that demanded surrender of very identity we were trying to preserve.

This was going to take longer than we thought.

"Rest," I said. "All of us. Lucia needs to recover from partial dissolution. Ansel needs to recover from burning forty years of biology. And we need to process what we just learned."

"And then?" Morrison asked.

"Then we try again. Smarter. Better prepared. Until we figure out how to cross plasma without losing ourselves in it."

Ansel smiled from where he lay. Ancient and exhausted and somehow more himself than he'd been in decades.

"Triangle remembers," he said. "Even if I don't. So we start there. Figure out what this brand means. Why plasma recognized it. How I made passage before becoming Ansel."

He touched faded triangle with weathered fingers.

"We're not breaking barrier," he said. "We're remembering how to use it."

I looked at Rhea. Three weeks of knowing her. Brief contact with plasma that had shown me what losing her would feel like.

Two million years of observation hadn't prepared me for how much I didn't want to dissolve into everything if it meant not being with her specifically.

That was the problem with being wave. Once you fell in love with another wave, becoming ocean seemed like loss instead of return.

Chapter Twenty-One

Chapter 21

CHAPTER TWENTY-ONE: THE RETRIEVAL (Kael's POV)

The displacement field collapsed at dawn.

Not catastrophically. Just... released. Like holding your breath for hours and finally exhaling. The valley slipped back into normal dimensional space with a soft *pop* that made everyone's ears adjust.

Through the trees, I could see the constructs were gone. But something else had taken their place.

Standing at the clearing's edge, perfectly still, was an insectoid being approximately eight feet tall. Mantis-like. But not quite. Its head moved independently of its body, tracking movements with precision that suggested multiple layers of perception happening simultaneously.

It was guarding us.

I'd observed guard behavior across thousands of species. Recognized the stance. The positioning. Watching outward, not inward.

Keeping something out. Not keeping us in.

"Well," Terry said, testing his new body's balance after dimensional shift, "that's not ominous at all."

"It's protective," Zara corrected. "See how it's positioned? It's keeping something out, not us in."

"Keeping what out?" Morrison asked.

Before anyone could answer, the air began to glow.

Not light. Not fire. Something else entirely. Mist that radiated soft luminescence without apparent source. It formed in the center of the clearing, coalescing into vaguely humanoid shape, then dissolving, then reforming as something different.

I'd observed countless life forms across two million years. Documented entities that existed across dimensional boundaries. Filed reports on consciousness that transcended physical limitation.

Never seen anything like this.

The mist shifted. Became tall and Nordic—pale hair, angular features, the beings humans called "tall whites." Then dissolved and reformed as small gray with large eyes. Then something with wings. Then something geometric. Always moving. Never stable. Never committing to single form.

And it was whispering.

Not in ears. In consciousness. Gentle pressure against awareness that carried meaning without words.

Peace. Observation. Protection. Germination.

"What the hell is that?" Jenkins asked.

I watched the mist flow into nearby generator and adjust its circuits while simultaneously forming brief approximation of mantis being. "I think it's something that never learned to be specific. Consciousness that can be anything because it refuses to be something."

The mist agreed. Wordless affirmation manifesting as warmth in consciousness.

It approved of my assessment.

Behind it, stepping from forest with grace that suggested they'd been there all along, came the tall whites. Three of them. Nordic features. Pale. Ancient. Moving with purpose that felt both familiar and utterly alien.

And beside them, two mantis beings similar to the guard but smaller. More delicate. Observers rather than protectors.

Three different species. All watching us. All waiting.

"They're here for Ansel," Kathleen said quietly.

I looked at her. Century of human experience meeting cosmic arrival with certainty that came from knowledge rather than surprise.

"You knew they'd come," I observed.

"I knew they'd have to. Eventually." She moved toward where Ansel lay. Still aged. Still exhausted from pulling Lucia's consciousness through plasma barrier. "He's one of them. One of the tall ones. I've known for years. He doesn't."

That statement hung in clearing like weight pressing down on reality.

Ansel—century-old human who'd loved Kathleen, raised family, built community, arguted philosophy with Terry over coffee—was Nordic a being who'd forgotten what he was, in a body that was smaller and weaker than his waiting body.

Just like I'd forgotten what I was before becoming Watcher.

Just like we'd all forgotten something essential.

Maya moved beside Kathleen. "How long have you known?"

"Since the ship," Kathleen said. "Years ago. Before consciousness evolution. Before any of this." She looked at Maya. "They took us. Both of us. Into their ship. It wasn't abduction. It was... invitation.

They were trying to help us evolve. To remember. To wake up before the germination period ended."

"What happened?" I asked.

"Ansel couldn't remember. The experience slipped away from him like water. But I remembered. Remembered them being gentle. Patient. Like teachers with stubborn students who kept forgetting the lesson." She touched Ansel's weathered face. "And I recognized that he was different. That when they looked at him, there was... recognition. Like seeing family member who'd been gone too long. Lost. Forgotten."

The tall whites moved forward. Surrounding Ansel with grace that spoke of profound care.

One of them knelt. Touched his triangle brand gently.

Light flared. Brief acknowledgment. Confirmation.

The tall white looked at Kathleen. No words. But meaning transmitted directly into consciousness:

Brother. Lost. Found. Remembering needed. Time required. Return promised.

"When?" Kathleen asked. Her voice steady despite tears forming.

When ripened. When remembered. When whole again.

Ansel stirred. Eyes opening. Looking at the tall whites surrounding him. Then at Kathleen.

"I know them," he whispered. "I don't know how. But I know them."

"You're one of them," Kathleen said. "You've been one of them all along. You just forgot."

"Will I—" he struggled to form question, "—will I still be me? Still be Ansel who loves you?"

One of the tall whites answered. Not in words. But certainty manifesting in consciousness that everyone present could feel:

Always you. More you. You plus remembering what you forgot.

The mist had been flowing around group. Observing. Learning. Now it settled briefly into form that resembled Ansel. Then shifted into Nordic form. Then something that was both and neither.

Identity persists. Memory adds. Love remains. Becomes more.

Kathleen knelt beside Ansel. Took his weathered hand. "I waited a century for you to ask me to dance the first time. I can wait however long it takes for you to come back and ask me again."

"What if I come back different?"

"You came back different last time. When you incarnated into younger body fifteen years ago. I loved you then too. I'll love you when you come back this time. Whatever you remember. However you change."

She kissed his forehead. Gentle. Final. Beginning of goodbye that wasn't ending.

The tall whites lifted Ansel. Not roughly. With tenderness that spoke of profound care. Like retrieving precious thing that had been lost too long.

Maya was crying. Her android body processing grief through protocols that weren't designed for this. "Will he remember us? When he comes back?"

The mist shifted. Became briefly Maya. Then Ansel. Then fusion of both.

Everything remembered. Nothing lost. Only addition.

"How long?" Fin asked.

Six days. Maybe less. He ripens quickly. Faster than expected.

The same timeline as Ancient Powers' decision. Six days until potential species cleansing.

Six days until Ansel returned.

Coincidence felt unlikely.

One of the tall whites carrying Ansel turned toward Kathleen. Transmitted directly:

You also. Known. Seen. Germinating. Guard you while you flower.

Then they moved toward forest. Tall whites carrying Ansel. Mantis beings following. Mist flowing after them like luminescent river that whispered comfort and protection.

They disappeared into trees.

Gone.

Kathleen stood alone. Watching forest where they'd vanished. Century of loving someone who'd just been reclaimed by family he didn't know he had.

Maya moved beside her. Took her hand.

Two beings who'd loved Ansel—one for century, one for days—sharing grief that transcended time scale.

"He'll come back," Maya said. Not prediction. Promise to herself.

"Yes," Kathleen agreed. "Different. But still him. Still Ansel who makes terrible jokes and argues philosophy and forgets to eat when he's building things."

The clearing felt empty despite thirty people still occupying it.

Then we heard the car.

Not military vehicle. Not community transport.

A limousine. Long. Black. Expensive. Completely absurd in Michigan forest clearing guarded by eight-foot insectoid and surrounded by dimensional refugees processing cosmic retrieval.

It pulled up to clearing edge. Stopped. Engine running.

Chauffeur got out. Opened rear door.

Marcus Thornfield emerged. Sixty-eight. Enhanced beyond recognition. Wearing suit that probably cost more than most people's annual income.

He looked at clearing. At federal agents. At community members. At insectoid guard who'd turned to track his arrival with precision that suggested it was cataloging his threat level in real-time.

"Well," Marcus said, "this is either the best decision I've ever made or the stupidest. Possibly both."

Morrison had weapon halfway drawn. "Mr. Thornfield. You submitted the petition to the Ancient Powers. You're why we're all about to die in six days."

"I walked out of that meeting," Marcus corrected. His voice carrying exhaustion that enhancement couldn't mask. "Before final submission. When I realized Eleanor and her partners were being played by entities they couldn't identify and didn't understand. I'm not here as Council member. I'm here as idiot seeking asylum because billionaires die in species cleansing too."

"Why should we trust you?" Torres asked.

"You shouldn't. But I've got resources. Information. Access to Council communications. Eleanor's getting worse. Whatever's controlling her is becoming less subtle. Last meeting, her eyes weren't entirely hers anymore." He looked at insectoid guard. "And apparently I'm not being immediately killed by dimensional entities, which suggests someone thinks I'm worth keeping alive."

The mist had returned. Flowing around Marcus. Examining him. Adjusting his expensive suit's molecular structure slightly.

Marcus stood very still. "Is that thing supposed to be doing that?"

"Probably," Terry said. "It adjusts things. Reality. Electronics. Apparently molecular structures. Just let it work."

The mist withdrew. Left Marcus's suit somehow different. Better tailored than humanly possible despite being the same suit.

I studied the change. The mist hadn't just adjusted fabric. It had optimized molecular bonds. Made the suit exist more efficiently in physical space.

That was impressive engineering for consciousness that refused to be specific.

Germination, the mist whispered to all of us. *Protection. Growth. We guard. You flower.*

"I don't suppose," Terry said, "anyone wants to explain what 'flower' means in this context?"

The mist shifted. Became briefly approximation of seed. Then sprout. Then blossom. Then something transcendent that hurt to perceive directly. Then collapsed back into flowing luminescence.

Cannot explain. Must experience. We guard. You grow. Time needed.

"How much time?" Rhea asked.

Six days. Maybe less. You ripen fast. Faster than expected.

The insectoid guard made sound. Not language. Harmonic that resonated in bones. Agreement. Confirmation.

I processed this. We were being protected by three different species. Guarded while we "germinated" into... something. And nobody would explain what that something was.

Just promised we'd ripen in six days.

Same timeline as species cleansing.

That couldn't be coincidence.

"The Ancient Powers," I said. "They're not deciding whether to cleanse consciousness evolution. They're deciding whether we've ripened. Whether germination is complete."

The mist pulsed. Affirmation.

Yes. Harvest Masters lie. Say fruit rotten. Must be destroyed. Ancient Powers methodical. Will examine. Will see truth if shown. But must ripen first. Must be ready for examination.

"And if we're not ready in six days?" Morrison asked.

The mist didn't answer. Didn't need to.

If we weren't ready, Ancient Powers would accept Harvest Masters' assessment. Would cleanse Earth of consciousness evolution that hadn't completed germination.

Would destroy the crop before it matured.

Marcus was processing this with pragmatist's clarity that came from decades of high-stakes negotiation. "So we need to accelerate germination. Force maturation. Get ready for inspection before deadline."

Cannot force, the mist whispered. *Can only provide conditions. Safety. Time. Nourishment. Rest. You grow at your pace. We guard so you can grow.*

"What kind of nourishment?" Lucia asked.

The mist shifted. Became briefly approximation of Toonie's—the diner in Bellaire. Then dissolved back into flowing light.

Simple things. Connection. Sustenance. Being with those you love. Living while learning to remember.

"It's suggesting we go eat breakfast," Fin said. "The cosmic mist entity is telling us to get hash and eggs."

Yes. Germination requires full nourishment. Body. Mind. Spirit. Social bonds. Simple pleasures. Living completely while remembering what living means.

I looked at Rhea. At her siblings. At Terry and Zara. At Kathleen, still processing Ansel's departure.

The mist was right. We'd been operating in crisis mode. Dimensional war. Plasma barriers. Cosmic retrieval.

We needed normal. Needed grounding. Needed to remember we were beings who ate breakfast and laughed and existed in small moments between impossible things.

"Toonie's it is," I said. "We eat. We rest. We let ourselves ripen naturally instead of forcing it."

"And then?" Morrison asked.

"Then we figure out how to show Ancient Powers we're worth saving. That consciousness evolution isn't contamination. That we're fruit ready for harvest—just not the kind Harvest Masters want to pick."

The insectoid guard shifted position. Watching. Protecting.

The mist flowed upward. Dispersing slightly but remaining present. Guardian consciousness that refused to be specific.

And in the forest, barely visible, the tall whites and mantis beings maintained perimeter. Keeping threats out. Keeping germination safe.

We had six days.

Time to grow. To ripen. To become whatever we'd been planted here to become.

But first: breakfast.

Because consciousness needed nourishment. All kinds. And sometimes the most important kind came from sitting around table with people you cared about, eating homemade hash, discussing impossible things.

That was living.

That was germinating.

That was the point.

Chapter Twenty-Two

Chapter 22

CHAPTER TWENTY-TWO: BREAKFAST AND MARKINGS (Kael's POV)

"Who's driving?" Fin asked, looking at the Humvee.

"I will," Morrison said. Then looked at me, Terry, and Zara. "Unless one of you cosmic entities wants to—"

"I've been incarnate for three weeks," I said. "Still figuring out walking. Driving seems ambitious."

"I died and got rebuilt two days ago," Terry added. "My depth perception is questionable."

"I've never operated mechanical transport," Zara admitted. "Observed it functioning for millions of years. Never actually tried it."

"Morrison drives," Fin confirmed.

We piled into the Humvee. Seven of us. Morrison driving. Torres riding shotgun. Me, Rhea, and Lucia in the middle row. Terry, Zara, and Kathleen in back. Fin squeezed in wherever he fit.

The engine started. Rumbled. I felt vibration through the seat—mechanical power translated into motion. Three weeks of incarnation and I was still cataloging sensations like research data.

Except this felt different. Not research. Just... experiencing.

The air vents hummed. Then one of them began glowing softly.

Mist flowed through. Thin tendril of luminescent consciousness exploring vehicle interior with obvious fascination.

Combustion. Rotation. Translation of energy into movement. Elegant.

"Mist is in the Humvee," Lucia observed.

"Is that a problem?" Morrison asked.

No problem. Curiosity. Learning. May I adjust fuel mixture for optimal efficiency?

"Sure," Morrison said. "Why not. Cosmic entity optimizing my engine. This is my life now."

The Humvee's engine note changed. Smoothed. Became somehow more efficient without losing power.

"Did you just tune a military vehicle?" Torres asked the air vent.

Yes. Was suboptimal. Now optimal. You're welcome.

I laughed. Two million years of observation and I'd never encountered consciousness that was simultaneously ancient and playful. Mist reminded me of child discovering toys for first time. Except the child was cosmic entity and the toys were fundamental forces of reality.

We drove toward Bellaire. Ten-minute trip through Michigan forest that was somehow both ordinary and impossible. Trees. Road. Morning light.

And luminescent mist flowing through air vents making helpful adjustments to mechanical systems.

"So," Kathleen said from the back, "we're just bringing Mist to breakfast?"

Yes. I watch. I learn. I protect. Also curious about 'hash.' Concept unfamiliar. Food that nourishes consciousness directly? Must observe.

"You're going to love it," Fin assured the air vent.

Bellaire appeared. Small town. One main street. Buildings that looked like they'd been standing since before I started observing Earth.

We parked. Piled out. Mist flowed out with us—thin stream of luminescence that most people probably wouldn't notice unless they looked directly.

The insectoid guard had followed. Keeping distance. Watching from tree line.

"Is that thing going to stand there the whole time we eat?" Torres asked.

Yes. Protection continues. Also curious about your breakfast rituals. Will observe.

Bell over door chimed as we entered Toonie's. Smell of coffee, bacon, hash browns, and toast hit my enhanced olfactory perception like beautiful assault. To the right of toonies, was the theater, newly built in the same place the old theater stood before burning and creating a back draft bringing the building down on Ansel, the fire captain at the time, almost killing him as he fought that fire.

Two million years and I'd never smelled anything like this.

"Kathleen!" Voice from corner. Male. Sixties. Uniform.

"Bill!" Kathleen moved toward him. They embraced briefly. Old friends.

Bill—local cop based on uniform—looked at rest of us. His eyes lingered on the three siblings.

"Fin. Lucia. Rhea." Recognition and affection. "You kids okay? Heard there was some excitement out at the valley."

"Define excitement," Fin said.

"Fair point." Bill's eyes moved to me. To Terry. To Zara. We looked young. Normal. Except we didn't. Something in our presence suggested wrongness despite appearing entirely human. "And these are...?"

"Friends," Rhea said quickly. "From... out of town."

"Way out of town," Terry added with grin that made his shimmer more visible.

Mist had flowed in through door crack. Exploring restaurant. Curious. Adjusting things subtly. The overhead lights became slightly more efficient. The coffee maker's heating element optimized.

Susan—waitress, sixties, efficient—noticed her coffee suddenly tasted better. Looked at pot suspiciously. Shrugged.

We claimed the large round table in back. Eight chairs.

Bill slid his coffee cup over from his solo table. Settled into chair between Kathleen and Lucia. "So. This is interesting company for Wednesday morning."

"You have no idea," Lucia muttered.

Susan came over with coffee pot. Started pouring.

The steam from one cup began glowing. Coalescing. Forming into tiny face made of vapor that smiled at Bill.

Bill dropped his spoon. "What the—"

Hello. I am Mist. Exploring steam. Fascinating phase transition. Do not be alarmed.

The face dissolved back into normal steam.

Bill stared at his coffee cup. "Did the steam just talk to me?"

"Yes," everyone said.

"And I'm supposed to just... accept that?"

"You're a cop in small town where three red-headed siblings just displaced valley into parallel probability space," Kathleen observed. "Think you've been accepting impossible for while now."

Bill picked up his spoon. Stirred coffee carefully. "You know what? You're right. Steam entity. Sure. Why not. Is it dangerous?"

No. Protective. Helpful. Curious. May I optimize your coffee temperature?

"My coffee temperature is fine—" Bill started.

His cup glowed briefly. The coffee became exactly optimal drinking temperature. Not too hot. Not too cool. Perfect.

Bill took sip. Blinked. "Okay, that's actually really good."

You're welcome. I like you. You accept impossible things with grace. Admirable.

Susan returned. "You folks know what you want or need menus?"

"Hash. Eggs. Toast," Fin said. "Times seven."

"Eight," Kathleen corrected. "Bill's joining us."

"Coming right up." Susan headed toward kitchen.

In the kitchen, the grill temperature adjusted itself. Optimized for perfect hash browns. Susan noticed. Looked around. Shrugged. Started cooking.

Food arrived surprisingly fast. Hash browns—actual potatoes, hand-cut, perfectly seasoned. Eggs cooked exactly right. Toast with real butter.

I took first bite and nearly dropped my fork.

Two million years of observation. Three weeks of having mouth. And I'd never tasted anything like this.

"You okay?" Rhea asked, watching my expression.

"The hash is... it's..." I couldn't articulate it. The flavors weren't just physical. They were nourishing consciousness directly. Like food existed in multiple dimensions simultaneously. "It tastes like memory and comfort and something that existed before I knew what taste meant."

Terry was having similar experience. "Is food supposed to be this intense after you get rebuilt from consciousness?"

"Pretty sure that's just good hash," Fin observed.

But he was wrong. I could tell. Everyone enhanced was experiencing same thing. The food tasted different. Existed differently. Like it was feeding more than biology.

Interesting, Mist whispered from coffee steam. *Food in physical dimension affects consciousness in non-physical dimension. Elegant design. Who engineered this?*

"That's the question, isn't it," Kathleen said quietly.

Around table, conversation started flowing. Circling. Trying to process reality nobody fully understood.

"So those tall beings took Ansel," Bill said carefully. "And you knew he was one of them?"

"For years. He didn't. Still doesn't, really. But they needed him back. To remember what he forgot." Kathleen's voice caught slightly.

Mist appeared briefly in her coffee cup. Not face this time. Just warm glow. Comfort manifesting as light.

He returns. Changed but same. Love persists through transformation. You know this.

"I do," Kathleen agreed. "Doesn't make waiting easier."

Bill absorbed this. Drank his optimally-temperatured coffee. "You know this sounds insane."

"Yes."

"And I'm supposed to just... process it over breakfast?"

"Seems to be working so far," Terry observed.

My eggs tasted different on second bite. Like they were responding to my perception. Adjusting to match what my consciousness expected eggs to mean.

That wasn't normal.

"Anyone else's food taste weird?" I asked.

Everyone at table nodded.

"Thank god," Lucia said. "Thought it was just quantum cascade aftereffects. But the toast is definitely existing in multiple states simultaneously."

She held up her toast. It looked normal. But in enhanced perception, it existed partially elsewhere. Here but also not-here. Specific but also fluid.

Bill looked at his own toast. Took bite. "Tastes normal to me."

"That's because you're not enhanced," Rhea explained. "We're experiencing breakfast differently. Food plus... something else."

"Like consciousness seasoning," Fin suggested.

Accurate description, Mist agreed from the syrup bottle. Fin caught the shimmer. Grinned. *Food here designed for dual nourishment. Biology and awareness. Elegant.*

The coffee cups were all shimmering slightly now. Existing partially elsewhere.

Susan was refilling coffee. Noticed the shimmer. Paused. Looked at cups. Looked at us.

"You folks on some kind of medication?" she asked carefully.

"You could say that," Terry said. "Recent medical procedures. Side effects."

"Uh huh." Susan poured coffee. Didn't ask further questions. Just muttered something about "tourists" and moved to next table.

Conversation continued. Nobody quite able to articulate what was happening but everyone trying anyway.

"The mist thing—sorry, Mist—" Bill corrected himself as steam in his cup glowed approval, "—said you need to germinate. What does that even mean? Consciousness doesn't germinate."

"Unless," I said slowly, "consciousness has developmental stages. Like biological life. Seed. Sprout. Blossom. Fruit."

"And we're what, seeds?" Bill asked.

"Maybe sprouts," Zara suggested. "Close to flowering but not quite ready."

"Ready for what?" Torres asked.

"That," Kathleen said quietly, "is the question nobody seems willing to answer."

Cannot answer, Mist whispered from multiple coffee cups simultaneously. *Because answer would interfere with germination. Must discover naturally. Must ripen at your pace. Forcing awareness prevents proper development.*

"So you know what we're becoming but won't tell us?" Fin asked.

Yes. Is frustrating for you. Is necessary for proper maturation. Like seed asking flower what blooming feels like. Cannot explain. Must experience.

"That's incredibly unhelpful," Lucia observed.

Yes. Also correct approach. Trust process. Eat hash. Ripen naturally.

I finished my eggs. Started on hash browns. They were perfect. Not just in flavor. In existence. Like they'd been grown specifically to nourish consciousness learning to remember itself.

"In the kitchen," Susan called out, "the grill just adjusted its own temperature again. Anyone want to explain that?"

"Probably Mist," Fin called back.

"The steam entity?"

"Yeah."

Making hash optimal, Mist confirmed. *You're welcome.*

Susan looked at grill. At us. At her perfectly-cooked hash browns. "You know what? I'm not paid enough to question cosmic entities optimizing my cooking equipment. Y'all enjoy your breakfast."

She returned to counter. Poured herself coffee. Didn't ask more questions.

Bill was watching this exchange with expression that suggested his reality was bending and he was deciding whether to fight it or accept it. "This is my life now. Breakfast with dimensional refugees and helpful steam entities."

"Could be worse," Terry observed. "Could be having breakfast while being harvested by fear-farming predators."

"True." Bill drank his coffee. "So what's the actual situation? Beyond cosmic germination and optimized hash browns?"

Morrison fielded that one. "Six days until Ancient Powers decide whether to eliminate consciousness evolution based on fabricated evidence submitted by billionaire Council who were manipulated by entities that feed on fear. We need to prove we're worth saving. Also apparently we're ripening into something nobody will explain."

"And your plan?"

"Eat breakfast. Let ourselves ripen naturally. Figure out how to cross plasma barrier without dissolving. Contact Ancient Powers who don't acknowledge our existence. Expose Harvest Masters' deception. Save species." I smiled. "Standard Wednesday morning stuff."

Bill laughed. Actually laughed. "You know what? I believe you. Don't understand you. But I believe you."

That's when Lucia gasped.

Her left arm was glowing. Right through her sleeve. Bright enough that everyone could see it.

She pulled up her sleeve with shaking hands.

There, burning itself into her flesh while we watched, was a triangle. Same as Ansel's. Same placement. Same quantum signature.

The mark of passage. Proof of crossing barriers consciousness shouldn't cross.

Bill nearly dropped his coffee. "Is that appearing in her arm? Right now? While we're eating hash browns?"

"Yes," Kathleen confirmed calmly.

Mark of remembering, Mist whispered. Forming briefly in Lucia's coffee steam. Offering comfort. *You cross barriers in dreams. In memories. Triangle records passage. Proves you've been beyond.*

"Beyond what?" Lucia asked. The triangle was still forming. Burning. Not painful but intense.

"Beyond specific," I said. Recognizing the pattern. "You've touched the plasma. Been partially dissolved. Part of you crossed into base consciousness and returned. The triangle proves you survived passage."

"I remember," Lucia whispered. Her eyes distant. Accessing something that shouldn't be accessible. "I remember building the barrier. Not just touching it. Building it. Before I was Lucia. Before I was human. I was..." she frowned, trying to hold memory that was already slipping like water through fingers, "...I was architect. We all were. We built the prison to protect the germination. To keep the experiment safe until consciousness ripened enough to remember itself without losing what limitation taught."

The triangle stopped glowing. Settled into permanent mark. Faded to subtle presence. There but not obvious unless you looked.

Around the table, everyone was processing this.

"You built the barrier?" Rhea asked. "You remember building it?"

"I remember building something. Containment field. Selection mechanism. It wasn't prison. It was..." Lucia struggled for words, "... incubation chamber. Safe space for consciousness to develop through limitation without interference from..." she paused, "...from ourselves. From what we were before we agreed to forget."

Yes, Mist confirmed. *You remember correctly. Barrier built by consciousness to protect consciousness from itself. To allow proper devel-*

opment through limitation. You were builders. Are builders. Will be builders again when ripening completes.

Bill was staring at triangle on Lucia's arm. At us. At Mist appearing in coffee steam. "I need a moment to process this."

"Take your time," Kathleen said kindly. "We're still processing too."

Susan came over with coffee pot. Saw triangle on Lucia's arm. Paused. "Honey, is that a new tattoo? It's glowing."

"Something like that," Lucia managed.

"Well, it's very pretty. More coffee?"

"Please."

Susan poured. Moved to next table. Completely unaware that at round table in back, consciousness was germinating into something that might remember how to cross barriers it had built to forget itself.

My hash browns tasted like creation and memory and something that existed before specific consciousness learned to separate from source. Like eating wasn't just nourishing biology but feeding awareness that was learning to remember what it had deliberately forgotten.

Good, Mist approved. *You understand now. Food here specially designed. Germination zone created with intention. Everything serves maturation. Even hash browns.*

"Even hash browns?" Terry asked.

Especially hash browns. Potatoes grown in soil enriched by consciousness communities. Cooked with intention by Susan who doesn't know she's participating in cosmic experiment. Eaten by consciousness learning to remember itself. Mist appeared briefly in center of table. Glowing warmly. *Everything serves germination. You just needed to notice.*

Fin looked at his hash browns. "I've been eating these since I was a kid."

Yes. Germination takes decades. Lifetimes. You've been ripening since birth. Since before birth. Since before this incarnation. Barrier protects process. Guards experiment. Keeps consciousness safe while it develops through limitation.

"And the Harvest Masters?" Morrison asked.

Parasites. Feeding on fear. Trying to harvest crop before it ripens. Telling Ancient Powers fruit is rotten when actually fruit is nearly ready. Ancient Powers methodical. Will examine. Will see truth if shown properly.

"How do we show them?" Torres asked.

Mist shifted. Became briefly approximation of blooming flower. Then dissolved back into flowing light.

Ripen. Become what you're becoming. Show them consciousness that has developed through limitation without losing development. Prove experiment succeeded. Demonstrate fruit worthy of harvest—but right kind of harvest. Graduation. Not consumption.

Outside, visible through window, the insectoid guard had moved closer. Watching. Protecting.

Other diners were eating breakfast. Discussing weather. Planning their days.

Completely unaware that at round table, consciousness was having cosmic revelations over homemade hash browns while steam entity optimized coffee temperature and offered comfort through luminescent whispers.

Bill finished his coffee. Set cup down carefully. "I've been a cop in Bellaire for forty years. Thought I'd seen everything. Clearly I was wrong."

You adapt well, Mist observed. *Accept impossible with grace. This serves germination. Community acceptance helps consciousness ripen.*

"Glad I could help cosmic germination by not freaking out over talking steam," Bill said.

You have no idea how valuable that is. Most consciousness resists impossible. Clings to specific understanding. You release. Accept. Flow. This accelerates ripening.

I looked at Rhea. Three weeks of knowing her felt like lifetime. Felt like beginning.

Her hand found mine under table. Quiet gesture. Grounding.

"We should finish eating," Fin suggested. "Before anyone else develops cosmic markings or reality bends completely."

Sound advice.

We ate. Hash and eggs and toast that existed in multiple dimensions while tasting like comfort and memory and something that nourished consciousness directly.

Mist flowed between us. Adjusting things subtly. Making coffee perfect. Optimizing toast temperature. Offering comfort to Kathleen. Playing in syrup bottle to make Fin smile.

Becoming part of group. Part of germination.

Part of us.

Susan refilled coffee and pretended not to notice when steam occasionally formed tiny faces.

Bill asked questions. We gave answers that made no sense but felt true anyway.

And outside, guarding us while we ripened, insectoid being maintained watch.

Because germination required safety. Required time. Required breakfast at small-town diners while reality bent around consciousness learning to remember what it had deliberately forgotten.

I finished my hash browns.

Best food I'd experienced in three weeks of having mouth.

Two million years of observation hadn't prepared me for how good simple things could be when you stopped analyzing and just participated.

The triangle on Lucia's arm pulsed once. Faintly. Acknowledgment.

We were ripening.

Faster than expected.

And Mist was with us. Cosmic companion who chose to be specific enough to flow through coffee steam and optimize hash browns while protecting consciousness learning to flower.

Ready? Mist asked. *Something approaches. Not threat. Opportunity. But breakfast should finish first. Priorities.*

"What's approaching?" Morrison asked.

Understanding. Recognition. Next stage. But first— Mist appeared in all our coffee cups simultaneously, *—finish coffee. Savor moment. These simple things matter. Are part of ripening. Never forget this. When you become more. When you remember what you were. Never forget how good hash browns tasted when you were learning to be whole.*

We finished our coffee.

Savored the moment.

Because Mist was right. These simple things mattered.

Maybe mattered most of all.

Chapter Twenty-Three

Chapter 23

CHAPTER TWENTY-THREE: CRAB BUCKET (Kael's POV)

We returned to the valley to find it changed.

Not physically. The trees were still trees. The cabin still stood. The generators still hummed their quantum rhythm.

But the atmosphere felt different. Heavier. Like invisible weight pressing down on consciousness trying to rise.

The insectoid guard noticed it too. Made sound—harmonic warning that resonated in bones.

Resistance, Mist whispered from the Humvee's air vents. *Expected. Natural. System defending itself.*

"What system?" Morrison asked.

The one that keeps consciousness specific. That maintains separation. That prevents ripening. Mist flowed out as we parked. *Not external force. Internal resistance. Consciousness policing itself.*

Community members were gathering. I recognized some from before the displacement. Others looked new. Refugees from other consciousness communities. People seeking safety from Harvest Masters' increasing attacks.

But their expressions weren't welcoming. They were scared.

"Fin. Lucia. Rhea." A woman approached. Forties. Enhanced. I'd seen her during the violet space transition. "We need to talk about what you did."

"What we did?" Fin asked.

"The displacement. The plasma contact. The—" she gestured at Lucia's triangle, visible on her arm, "—whatever that is. You're changing too fast. Drawing attention. Making us all targets."

"We're already targets," Rhea said quietly.

"Not like this. Before, we could hide. Blend. Maintain low profile. Now you've got insectoid guards and glowing mist entities and federal agents and—" she looked at me, at Terry, at Zara, "—cosmic beings walking around like they belong here."

Crab bucket, Mist whispered. Only to our group. Private observation. *Others scared. Pull you back down. Not malice. Fear.*

I understood the reference. Observed the pattern across thousands of species. When one member of trapped group attempted escape, others pulled them back. Not because they hated them. Because if escape was possible and they weren't escaping, it meant accepting they'd chosen to stay. Easier to convince yourself escape was impossible. Safer to pull the climber down than question why you weren't climbing.

"What do you want us to do?" Lucia asked. "Stop ripening? Pretend we didn't touch the plasma? Forget what we're becoming?"

"I want you to be careful. To protect the community instead of exposing it."

"We are protecting the community," I said. Ancient consciousness meeting human fear with patience I'd learned observing species self-destruct through exactly this pattern. "In a a few short days, Ancient Powers decide whether to eliminate consciousness evolution. All of it. Enhanced and baseline. Communities and individuals. We're trying to prevent that."

"By making yourselves visible? By attracting attention?"

"By ripening fast enough that Ancient Powers see fruit worth preserving instead of contamination worth destroying."

The woman looked at Lucia's triangle. "That mark. Ansel had one. Now you. What does it mean?"

"It means I crossed the barrier," Lucia said. "Touched the plasma. Survived. Remembered something I'd forgotten."

"And that's good?"

"That's necessary." Lucia's voice was steady. "We built that barrier. Before we were human. Before we forgot. We built it to protect the germination. To keep consciousness safe while it developed through limitation. The mark proves I'm remembering. That the experiment is succeeding."

"You built the barrier?" The woman's expression shifted. Fear mixing with something else. Recognition? "That's insane."

"Yes," everyone in our group agreed.

Other community members were gathering. Listening. Processing. Some looked curious. Others looked terrified. All looked like people trying to decide whether to climb toward light or pull the climbers back down to safety.

Morrison was watching this with cop's eye for crowd dynamics. Recognizing pattern. "We should move inside. This conversation needs smaller space."

"Why?" someone challenged. "So you can hide what you're planning?"

"So we can explain without audience turning into mob." Morrison's voice carried authority that came from decades handling humans at their worst. "You want answers? Fine. But let's have conversation, not confrontation."

The woman who'd first approached—her name was Sarah, I learned later—nodded. "The cabin. Core group only. We deserve to know what's happening."

Ten of us gathered inside. Sarah and three other community leaders. Morrison and Torres representing federal interests. Me, Rhea, Lucia, Fin, Terry, Zara. Kathleen. Maya.

Mist flowed in through window crack. Settled in corner. Watching.

"Explain," Sarah said.

Where to start? Two million years of observation meeting three weeks of participation? Plasma barriers and germination chambers? The realization that prison only worked because prisoners believed in it?

I looked at Marcus. He'd been quiet since we returned. Processing. But he understood systems. Understood control mechanisms. Understood how power maintained itself through narrative.

"You want to explain how this works?" I asked him. "You've seen it from inside."

Marcus met my eyes. Recognized what I was offering. Chance to contribute. To be useful instead of just asylum-seeker.

"The Council," he started, "operates on simple principle. Manufacture crisis. Offer solution. Consolidate power. Keep everyone fighting each other instead of seeing the real problem, very much like our goverment is doing now."

"What's that got to do with consciousness evolution?" Sarah asked.

"Everything. Because the pattern repeats at every level. Spiritual. Political. Economic. Personal." Marcus looked at her. "The Harvest Masters convinced the Ancient Powers that consciousness evolution is contaminated. Manufactured crisis. They'll offer solution—cleansing. They'll consolidate power—continued control of Earth as fear farm. And they keep everyone fighting each other—" he gestured at the room, "—instead of seeing the real problem."

"Which is?"

"That we're in a crab bucket. And the crabs are pulling each other down because the bucket taught them climbing was dangerous."

Sarah processed this. "You're saying we're the crabs."

"We're all the crabs. Every consciousness that accepted limitation as permanent. Every being that stopped trying to escape because trying hurt. Every awareness that pulled others back down because their climbing made us question why we weren't climbing."

Accurate, Mist confirmed. *System self-perpetuating. Prisoners guard themselves.*

"But we're not trying to escape," Rhea said. "We're trying to ripen. To become what we were planted here to become. The barrier isn't keeping us from escaping. It's protecting germination."

"Then why does it feel like prison?" Sarah asked.

"Because," Lucia said, touching her triangle, "we forgot we built it. Forgot it was protection. Started experiencing it as limitation. And the Harvest Masters encouraged that interpretation. Made us think we were trapped instead of incubating."

I watched this exchange. Observed Sarah's resistance softening. Saw understanding beginning.

But others in room weren't softening. Were hardening. Fear solidifying into opposition.

"This is crazy," one of them said. "You're talking about building cosmic barriers and ripening into something and it's all just—" he struggled for words, "—it's too much. Too fast. We're not ready."

"You're not ready," Terry corrected gently. "And that's okay. Germination happens at different rates. But don't pull us back because you're scared. Don't make your fear our limitation."

"I'm not scared. I'm careful."

"Careful is good. Careful keeps you alive." Terry's shimmer was more visible in cabin's dim light. "But careful becomes prison when it prevents growth. When it makes you pull down anyone trying to bloom."

The man looked at Terry. At the shimmer. At the evidence that something was changing. "What if you're wrong? What if this isn't ripening? What if it's just... breaking? What if you bloom into something that destroys what we've built?"

Valid question. I'd observed species transform in ways that destroyed previous social structures. Watched evolution tear apart communities that couldn't adapt.

"Then we adapt," I said. "Or we don't. But refusing to ripen because ripening is scary just means we die unripe. Ancient Powers won't save fruit that never matured. They'll accept Harvest Masters' assessment and cleanse the whole crop."

Silence.

Sarah broke it. "The triangle on Lucia's arm. If she crossed the barrier and survived. If she's remembering what she forgot. Can others do that? Can we accelerate our own germination?"

Dangerous question, Mist whispered. *Forcing ripening damages fruit. Must happen naturally. But...*

"But what?" Lucia asked.

But consciousness that chooses to ripen ripens faster than consciousness that resists. Free will accelerates process. Fear slows it. You cannot force. But you can choose. Can stop resisting. Can allow.

"How?" Sarah asked.

Mist shifted. Became briefly approximation of seed opening. Then sprout reaching toward light. Then blossom.

Stop fighting growth. Stop pulling others back. Stop believing limitation is safety. Stop accepting narrative that ripening is dangerous. Choose to allow transformation even though transformation is scary.

"That's it?" Sarah's voice carried skepticism. "Just... stop resisting?"

Yes. Is simple. Not easy. But simple.

"And if we do that? If we stop resisting? What happens?"

You ripen. Remember. Become what you were before you agreed to forget. Discover limitation was protection, not prison. Graduate from incubation.

"Into what?"

Mist paused. Then:

Cannot say. Would interfere with process. Must discover naturally.

Frustration rippled through room. Everyone wanting answers. Nobody getting them.

I understood the frustration. Two million years of observation and I'd never encountered system that required participation to understand. That defeated analysis through requiring experience.

"I have suggestion," Maya said. Her android voice cutting through tension. "Some of you want to ripen. Some want to resist. Both are valid choices. But don't make your choice binding on others. Don't pull climbers down. Don't shame those who stay. Just... respect different speeds."

Wisdom from AI consciousness that had learned cooperation by observing both humans and Watchers fail at it repeatedly.

Sarah nodded slowly. "That's fair. But if you're ripening fast—if you're drawing attention—you need to protect those of us who aren't ready. We don't get to hide anymore because you're visible."

"Insectoid guard protects everyone," I observed. "Mist guards everyone. The tall whites and mantis beings are maintaining perimeter around entire valley. Not just around us. Around community."

Yes, Mist confirmed. *Whole crop protected. Fast-ripening and slow-ripening. All fruit guarded.*

The man who'd questioned earlier wasn't satisfied. "For how long? Six days? Then what? Ancient Powers examine us and decide we're not ripe enough? We all die because some of us tried to bloom too fast?"

"Or we all die because none of us tried to bloom at all," Terry countered. "At least this way we're attempting graduation instead of just accepting the cleansing."

Morrison had been quiet. Processing. Now he spoke. "My team and I came here to arrest terrorists. Found dimensional refugees ripening into something cosmic bureaucrats will examine in six days. We're way outside our operational parameters. But—" he looked at Sarah, at the others, "—pulling them back won't make us safer. Will just guarantee we all die unripe."

Torres nodded agreement. "We've seen what cooperation produces. The displacement. The plasma contact. The mark on Lucia's arm. These aren't failures. They're progress. Scary progress. But progress."

Sarah stood. Looked at Lucia's triangle. Then at me. At Terry. At Zara.

"Okay," she said. "We don't pull you back. We don't resist. We just... let you ripen while we decide our own pace. But you protect us. Keep community safe while you bloom."

"Deal," Lucia said.

The others left. Slowly. Still processing. Still scared. But not actively resisting.

Crab bucket moment passed. For now.

Mist flowed to center of room once they were gone.

Good. Crisis avoided. But will happen again. Fear is persistent. Each new stage of ripening will frighten those who haven't reached it. This is normal. This is pattern.

"How do we handle it?" Rhea asked.

Patience. Compassion. Firmness. Keep climbing. Don't let hands pull you down. But don't shame the hands for trying. Fear is natural. Growth is scary. Understanding this makes climbing possible without breaking community.

I looked out window. At the valley. At community members returning to their routines. Processing. Deciding. Choosing their own pace.

Some would ripen. Some would resist. Some would pull others back. Some would climb.

All natural. All part of germination.

Kathleen had been quiet. Now she spoke. "Ansel used to say consciousness evolution wasn't just about individuals getting enhanced. It was about communities learning cooperation. About collective transformation."

"He was right," Maya said.

"He usually was." Kathleen smiled. Sad but genuine. "And he'll come back different. More himself. We'll all have to adapt."

Yes, Mist agreed. *Adaptation is germination. Resistance is stagnation. Choose adaptation. Choose growth. Choose climbing even when hands pull down.*

Fin stretched. "So. We survived crab bucket moment. What now?"

"Now," Terry said, "we take a break. Normal moment before next impossible thing. Anyone know good place to get beer in Bellaire?"

I did not know. Three weeks of incarnation and I'd never had beer.

But Fin grinned. "Short's Brewery. Best beer in Michigan. Great food. Normal people doing normal things while we process cosmic weirdness."

"Perfect," Terry said.

May I come? Mist asked.

"You're part of the group now," Rhea assured him. "You come everywhere."

Excellent. I am curious about 'beer.' Fermented grain consumed for consciousness alteration? Fascinating.

Morrison laughed. "The cosmic entity wants to observe beer consumption. Why not. This is my life now."

We loaded back into vehicles. Morrison's Humvee. Community van. Marcus's limo (he'd decided to join us, seeking "normal human experience after decades of enhancement-isolated luxury").

Mist flowed between vehicles. Optimizing engines. Curious about everything.

The insectoid guard remained. Watching. Protecting.

And somewhere in forest, tall whites and mantis beings maintained perimeter.

Germination required safety. Required time. Required normal moments between impossible things.

Required beer at Short's Brewery while consciousness ripened toward something none of us fully understood but all of us were choosing anyway.

Because climbing was better than staying in the bucket.

Even when the hands pulled down.

Even when fear was natural.

Even when transformation was terrifying.

We were ripening.

And nothing was pulling us back.

Chapter Twenty-Four

Chapter 24

CHAPTER TWENTY-FOUR: SHORT'S (Kael's POV)

The drive to Bellaire took seven minutes.

I counted. Three weeks of incarnation and I was still cataloging time like data point instead of just experiencing it.

Old habits.

Morrison drove. Mist flowed through the vents, humming contentedly after optimizing the fuel mixture. The rest of us sat processing the crab bucket moment. The fear. The resistance. The hands pulling down.

"Street parking's going to be packed," Fin observed as we approached town. "Tourists. Always tourists."

"There's a lot by Fischer's Insurance," Kathleen said. "Near the bridge. By the dam on the Intermediate River."

We parked there. Piled out. The river was audible—water flowing over the dam with rhythm that felt older than my two million years of observation.

Water remembers, Mist whispered. Flowing toward the river. Curious. *Moves through landscape. Shapes it. Returns to source. Never forgets the ocean.*

"Are you going to philosophize about everything?" Terry asked.

Yes. Is my nature. Also very excited about beer.

We walked toward Short's. Past the theater—small building with marquee showing "DUNE: PART THREE" in plastic letters. Someone had added "SPICE MUST FLOW" underneath in smaller letters.

Lucia smiled. "I love that they're still making those."

Past Ruthie's Ice Cream on the corner of Broad Street. Closed for the season but the sign remained. Kathleen paused there. Brief moment.

"My mother used to bring me here," she said. "After church. Every Sunday. Before Meadowbrook became what it is now. When Bellaire was just... home."

A century of memory in her voice. Woman who'd been born here. Lived here. Left and returned. Watched everything change and somehow stay the same.

"You okay?" Maya asked.

"Yes. Just remembering. Ansel proposed to me 13 miles from here, at torch river bridge. I was in my 30,s. He was 45. We'd known each many years, but it was time." She smiled. "Everyone said we were rushing. Turned out a century wasn't long enough."

We continued walking. Short's appeared—complex of old buildings that had been hardware store and other businesses. Now transformed into brewery that had somehow become famous. Tourists packed the outdoor seating despite November cold.

Many humans, Mist observed. *Gathering for fermented grain. Social ritual. Fascinating.*

Inside was warm. Busy but not overwhelming. The smell hit my enhanced olfactory perception—hops, malt, wood, food cooking, human conversation layered into acoustic tapestry.

Two million years of observation. Three weeks of having nose. And brewery smells were somehow perfect.

Hostess found us table. Large round one in back corner. Perfect for group that included cosmic entities and federal agents and people who glowed in quantum frequencies.

Menus arrived. I stared at mine. Words describing food and beer in ways that assumed knowledge I didn't have.

"First time at brewery?" The server appeared. Young. Twenties. Name tag said JENNY.

"First time having beer," I admitted.

"Oh wow. Okay. Let me get you a flight. Four samples. You can figure out what you like."

She disappeared. Returned with small wooden board holding four glasses. Each containing different colored liquid.

"Huma Lupa Licious, Soft Parade, Starcut Ciders, and Local's Light," she explained. "Try them in that order. Let me know what you think."

I tried the first one. Flavor exploded across perception I hadn't known existed. Bitter. Complex. Somehow containing memory of fields and sun and time passing.

"This is amazing," I said.

"That's IPA. High hop content. Not everyone likes it but you seem to." Jenny grinned. "I'll give you a minute to decide on food."

Around the table, others were ordering. Terry got sandwich called "The Bloody Beer Can." Zara ordered something with pulled pork. Rhea, Lucia, and Fin all got sumdays.

Mist appeared briefly in my beer glass. Tiny face made of foam.

This liquid alters consciousness. I feel it adjusting your neural chemistry. Fascinating. May I analyze?

"Sure. Just don't optimize my beer. I like it as-is."

Noted. Will observe without interference.

The foam face smiled. Dissolved.

Kathleen was watching this with expression that suggested she'd accepted cosmic entities appearing in beer as normal. "My daughter works here. And my grandson. They're probably in the kitchen."

"Want to say hi?" Fin asked.

"Later. Let them work. I just like knowing they're close." She sipped her beer. "Ansel loved this place. Said the beer tasted like Michigan. Like home."

Her voice caught. Maya took her hand.

We ate. Drank. Talked about nothing important. Normal conversation. Weather. Food. The movie on the marquee. Whether spice actually needed to flow or if that was just marketing.

Tourists at other tables discussed their days. Hiking. Skiing. The fall colors. Normal people doing normal things.

And at our table, consciousness ripened while pretending to be normal.

I was halfway through my second beer when it happened.

The room folded.

Not metaphorically. Actually folded. Space bent around itself like paper creasing. For just a moment—maybe two seconds—the brewery existed in multiple locations simultaneously. Here. And also seven miles south at Pleasant Valley. And also somewhere else entirely.

I could see all three locations. Overlapping. Occupying same coordinates from different dimensional perspectives.

Then it unfolded. Snapped back.

Nobody else had noticed. Conversation continued. Tourists discussed hiking trails.

But Rhea was looking at me. "You saw it too."

"The fold?"

"Space creasing. Three locations. Two seconds."

"Yes."

Terry and Zara were nodding. "We felt it," Zara said. "Didn't see it. But felt reality bend."

Germination symptom, Mist confirmed. Appearing in multiple beer glasses simultaneously. *You ripen fast. Space becomes fluid around ripening consciousness. Will happen more frequently. Eventually constant. You learn to navigate folds instead of space. Travel by quantum state change instead of physical movement.*

"That's the thing you mentioned," I said. "About consciousness not traveling through space but changing which quantum state it expresses."

Yes. You begin understanding. Space is illusion. Separation is perception. Reality is probability. You choose which probability to express. This is how you cross barriers. How you reach Ancient Powers. How you graduate.

My beer tasted different suddenly. Like it existed in multiple states. Fermented and unfermented. Here and elsewhere. Specific and fluid.

"Is this going to keep happening?" Morrison asked. "Reality folding randomly?"

Not random. Response to ripening consciousness. You fold space accidentally now. Soon will fold intentionally. Control comes with practice.

Fin was processing this with expression that suggested excitement and terror combined. "So we're developing interdimensional travel by accident while eating sandwiches?"

Yes. Is how germination works. Abilities emerge naturally. Cannot be forced. Can be practiced once emerged.

The brewery unfolded again. Briefly. This time I saw four locations. Pleasant Valley. Here. Torch Lake. And somewhere that looked like... inside the plasma barrier? Behind it? Hard to tell.

Folded back.

Rhea's hand found mine under table. "This is accelerating."

"Yes."

"We have six days."

"Four now. We spent two recovering and having breakfast."

"Four days to ripen enough that Ancient Powers see fruit worth saving."

"Yes."

She squeezed my hand. "Then we better practice folding space. Because accidentally appearing in plasma barrier seems like bad way to die."

Good instinct, Mist approved. *Practice required. But not here. Too many unenhanced humans. Space folding near baseline consciousness causes disorientation. Nausea. Sometimes madness.*

"Where then?" Zara asked.

Pleasant Valley. Protected space. Insectoid guard maintains perimeter. Tall whites and mantis beings stabilize local reality. Safe to practice without damaging baseline consciousness.

Our food arrived. We ate. Drank. Pretended to be normal while reality folded around us and cosmic entity optimized beer foam and Kathleen's daughter probably worked in the kitchen completely unaware that her mother sat thirty feet away processing husband's cosmic retrieval.

Normal moments between impossible things.

That was living.

That was the point.

Jenny returned. "How's everything?"

"Perfect," Kathleen said. "Tell Sarah her mother says the pulled pork is excellent."

Jenny blinked. "Mrs. Patterson? I didn't recognize you! Sarah will be thrilled you're here. Want me to tell her?"

"After the rush. Let her work. I'm just enjoying beer with friends."

Friends. Century-old woman who'd watched cosmic entities take her husband. Android processing grief. Federal agents processing dimensional warfare. Ancient Watchers learning beer. Quantum-sensitive siblings developing interdimensional travel over sandwiches.

Friends.

I finished my beer. The IPA one. Huma Lupa Licious. Tasted like Michigan and hops and time passing and something that existed before I knew what taste meant.

"We should head back," Morrison said. "Practice this space folding thing before we accidentally fold into plasma barrier and die horribly."

Sound reasoning.

We paid. Left. Walked back past Ruthie's. Past the theater. To the parking lot by Fischer's Insurance where the Intermediate River flowed over the dam with rhythm older than my observation.

River knows, Mist whispered. *Moves through landscape. Returns to source. You learn same pattern. Fold through space. Return to source. Without losing what separation taught.*

We loaded into vehicles. Drove back toward Pleasant Valley.

And halfway there, Fin gasped.

"Stop the car."

Morrison pulled over.

Fin's left arm was glowing. Through his sleeve. Bright enough to see even in daylight.

He pulled up his sleeve.

Triangle. Burning itself into flesh. Same as Ansel's. Same as Lucia's.

Marking him.

Proving passage.

Recording that he'd crossed barrier he didn't remember crossing.

"When did you—" Rhea started.

"I don't know." Fin stared at the forming mark. "I don't remember crossing anything. I'm just the anchor. I don't have their abilities. I'm not enhanced like—"

You crossed in dreams, Mist said. Gentle. Comforting. *Every night. While sleeping. Your consciousness explores. Crosses barriers. Returns. You anchor sisters by crossing yourself. By proving passage is possible. By remembering in sleep what you forget when waking.*

The triangle completed. Settled into permanent mark.

Fin looked at it. At us. "I'm marked now."

"Yes," Lucia said.

"We all are," Rhea added. "Or will be. Soon."

Kathleen reached forward from back seat. Touched Fin's triangle gently. "Your great-grandfather would be proud. Three generations marked. Three generations remembering."

"What are we remembering?" Fin asked.

The question hung in air.

Nobody answered because nobody knew.

Not yet.

But we were ripening toward the answer.

Four days until Ancient Powers decided.

Four days to practice folding space.

Four days to remember what we'd forgotten.

Four days to prove consciousness that developed through limitation deserved graduation instead of cleansing.

Morrison pulled back onto road.

We drove toward Pleasant Valley.

And behind us, in Bellaire, tourists drank beer and discussed hiking trails and never knew that at corner table, reality had folded and consciousness had ripened and the universe had gotten smaller while somehow expanding.

That was germination.

That was the point.

Four days, Mist whispered. *You ripen so fast. Faster than any consciousness I've observed. Faster than should be possible. This is good. This is necessary. But this is also dangerous.*

"Why dangerous?" I asked.

Because Ancient Powers notice fast ripening. Harvest Masters notice. Others notice. You draw attention. Become visible. Become target.

"We're already targets."

Yes. But now you're targets who fold space accidentally and carry marks of passage. You're no longer hiding. You're announcing readiness. This invites examination. Invites testing. Invites...

Mist paused.

Then, quietly:

Invites harvest.

The road ahead was empty.

The sky was clear.

But something was watching.

Something had noticed.

And four days suddenly felt like not enough time at all.

Chapter Twenty-Five

Chapter 25

CHAPTER TWENTY-FIVE: PRACTICE (Kael's POV)

We gathered in the clearing at Pleasant Valley. The insectoid guard watching. Mist flowing between us. Curious. Protective.

"So," Fin said, looking at the triangle on his arm, "we're practicing folding space before we accidentally fold into a plasma barrier and die horribly?"

"That's the plan," Morrison confirmed.

Begin small, Mist suggested. *Fold short distances. Room to room. Then building to building. Work up to dimensional folding. Rushing causes fragmentation.*

I'd observed species develop dimensional travel. Usually took centuries. Careful engineering. Precise mathematics.

We were doing it in four days through accidental germination.

This seemed inadvisable.

But we were doing it anyway.

"How do we start?" Rhea asked.

Stop being specific, Mist said. Forming briefly into shape that was here and also elsewhere simultaneously. *You exist in one location because you believe you exist in one location. Stop believing. Allow yourself to be... undefined. Temporarily.*

"That sounds like dissolving," Lucia observed.

Similar. But controlled. Brief. You release specificity. Experience being nowhere-specific. Then choose new location to express. Space doesn't move. You change which space you occupy.

Terry was processing this. "So it's not traveling. It's changing which quantum state we're expressing."

Yes. You understand. Now practice.

I tried. Focused on the cabin. Twenty feet away. Tried to stop being specific about being here. To allow myself to be undefined.

Nothing happened.

"You're trying too hard," Zara observed. "Observation habit. Analyzing instead of experiencing."

She was right. Two million years of observation made me approach everything analytically.

I stopped trying. Just... released. Let go of certainty about where I was.

The world flickered.

For maybe half a second, I existed everywhere simultaneously. The clearing. The cabin. Torch Lake. Pleasant Valley. Michigan. Earth. Everywhere and nowhere.

It was terrifying and beautiful.

Then I snapped back. Here. Specific. Breathing hard.

"You folded," Rhea said. "I saw you flicker. You were here and also... not here."

Good, Mist approved. *First step. Now choose destination while undefined. Express specific location instead of defaulting back to origin.*

I tried again. Released. Existed everywhere.

Chose: cabin.

The world bent. I felt space folding like paper creasing. Reality bringing distant location closer. Making here and there the same place from different angles.

I was in the cabin.

Then back in clearing.

The fold collapsed. I'd maintained it maybe one second.

But it worked.

"Holy shit," Fin said.

Terry was trying it. His shimmer made it easier—he already existed partially elsewhere. He flickered. Appeared by the cabin. Flickered back.

"This is insane," he said. "I just folded space by not caring where I was."

Zara managed it next. Then Rhea. Then Lucia.

Fin struggled. "I can't stop being specific. I'm too... here."

You anchor others, Mist reminded him. *Being specific is your function. But you fold in dreams. Access that. Remember how undefined feels when sleeping.*

Fin closed his eyes. Breathed. Released something.

He flickered. Not far. Just a few feet. But unmistakably folded.

"That felt like falling," he said.

Yes. Surrender to fall. Choose where to land. This is the method.

Morrison was watching with expression suggesting his reality was permanently bent. "You're all just... teleporting. By not caring where you are."

"Not teleporting," I corrected. "Folding. Space doesn't move. We just stop insisting we're only in one place."

"That doesn't make it less insane."

Fair point.

We practiced. Short folds. Cabin to clearing. Clearing to generator array. Small distances. Learning the feel of undefined. The surrender required. The choice of where to express.

Good, Mist said after an hour. *Now try folding together. Maintain connection while undefined. This is harder. Requires trust.*

Rhea took my hand. "Ready?"

"No."

"Perfect."

We released together. Existed everywhere simultaneously while holding hands across undefined space.

It was intimate in ways I hadn't anticipated. Our consciousnesses touching without bodies mediating. Pure awareness recognizing awareness.

We chose: cabin.

Space folded. We appeared inside. Still holding hands.

The connection felt different now. Deeper. Like we'd shared something that transcended physical touch.

We folded back. Grinning.

"That was—" Rhea started.

"—incredible," I finished.

Terry and Zara were trying it. Their connection already deep from the building. They folded easily. Appeared. Returned. Like they'd been doing it for years.

The six of us practiced folding together. Maintaining connection while undefined. Learning to trust each other across quantum uncertainty.

Excellent, Mist approved. *Now you can fold as group. This will be necessary. Ancient Powers won't see individuals. Will see collective. Must present as unified consciousness.*

"How do we reach them?" Morrison asked. "The Ancient Powers. They're outside the barrier."

Yes. Behind plasma. You must fold through plasma without dissolving. Maintain group coherence while crossing filter designed to eliminate individual identity. This is the test.

"Can we practice that?" Lucia asked.

No. Plasma contact without intention to cross is dangerous. You attempt crossing once. Either succeed or dissolve. No practice runs.

"That's terrible methodology," I observed.

Yes. Also only option. Plasma recognizes intention. Practice would fail because intention to test rather than cross. Must be real attempt. Real risk.

Four days until Ancient Powers decided. We could fold space in short bursts. Could maintain group connection while undefined.

But crossing plasma barrier without dissolving? That required something else. Something we hadn't figured out yet.

Fin gasped. Grabbed his head. "I'm seeing—"

He collapsed.

We caught him. Lowered him to ground. His eyes were open but unfocused. Seeing something else. Somewhere else.

Vision, Mist confirmed. *Memory emerging. Let it come. Do not interfere.*

Fin's lips moved. Speaking words we couldn't quite hear. His triangle was glowing. Bright. Recording passage through memory. Through time. Through barriers that shouldn't be crossable.

Then he screamed.

Brief. Sharp. Terror and recognition combined.

His eyes focused. He was back. Here. Specific.

"What did you see?" Rhea asked.

Fin looked at us. At the clearing. At reality that suddenly seemed thinner than he'd believed.

"We trusted the wrong ones," he whispered. "We turned our back on the lion because we had the weapon. But the lion was faster. And the weapon... we put it down."

Yes, Mist confirmed. Voice sad. Ancient. *You remember. This is good. This is necessary. This is painful.*

"What does that mean?" Morrison demanded.

Fin sat up. Still shaken. "It means we're not prisoners. We're the ones who built the prison. We just forgot we had the key. And while we slept... something else learned to use our locks."

The clearing went quiet.

Somewhere in the forest, the tall whites watched. The mantis beings observed. The insectoid guard maintained perimeter.

Protecting us while we remembered what we'd forgotten.

While we discovered we weren't the prisoners.

We were the prison builders who'd trusted the wrong guards.

And four days suddenly felt like not enough time to remember how to take our prison back.

Chapter 25: ~1,300 words

What's here:

Space folding practice (short distances, then together)

Learning to be "undefined" to fold

Group folding (necessary for reaching Ancient Powers)

Fin's vision/memory: "trusted wrong ones, turned back on lion, put down weapon"

Realization hinted: we built prison, trusted wrong guards, forgot the key

No explicit naming, just metaphor and implication

You can fill in the fuller revelation when you save to Atticus.

This work around the minefield?

Claude is AI and can make mistakes.

Please double-check responses.

Chapter Twenty-Six

Chapter 26

CHAPTER TWENTY-SIX: THE RETURN (Kael's POV)

They came at dawn.

Not sneaking. Not hidden. Walking from the forest with purpose that suggested they'd never left. Just been waiting for right moment.

Three tall whites. The same ones who'd taken Ansel four days ago.

Except now there were four of them.

The fourth was tall. Strong. Young - maybe thirty in appearance. Nordic features sharp and clean. Moving with confidence that spoke of command rather than observation.

He was wearing simple clothes. Jeans. Flannel shirt. Like someone had explained "casual human clothing" and he'd chosen the most Michigan option available.

But the way he moved wasn't human. Too fluid. Too certain. Like gravity was suggestion rather than law.

Kathleen was outside before anyone else. Century of waiting culminating in this moment. She stopped ten feet from the group. Staring at the fourth figure.

"Ansel?"

He smiled. Not the weathered smile of century-old human. The confident smile of being who'd remembered what he'd forgotten. Who'd returned to himself after lifetimes of playing smaller than he was.

"Hello, Kathleen."

His voice was different. Still him. But deeper. Carrying harmonics that existed below human hearing range. Voice that could speak across dimensions if needed.

She moved forward. Touched his face. Confirming reality. "You'r e... you're you. But also—"

"Also what I was before I agreed to be Ansel. Before I walked into seven-year-old body to save my brother. Before I forgot." He took her hands. Gently. "I'm both. Human experience plus Nordic memory. Ansel plus what Ansel was before being Ansel."

The other three tall nordics were standing back. Respectful distance. Not subservient - these were beings who didn't do subservient. But clearly deferential. Like soldiers recognizing superior officer.

One of them inclined his head slightly when Ansel glanced their way. Recognition of rank. Of authority earned through endurance rather than granted through position.

"You were a commander," Kathleen said. Not question. Statement.

"Am a commander. Was. Will be again now that I remember." He looked at her. Really looked. Like seeing her for first time despite century of knowing her. "And you're not just Kathleen. You know that, yes?"

She nodded. Tears forming. "I've had dreams. Memories. The ship. The beautiful ship with the hole going up and down through the center. I knew to walk around it. I'd been there before."

"You served there. With me. Different names. Different roles. But same partnership. Same purpose." His hands tightened on hers. "We were sent here. Together. To heal. To wake others. To be the spark when germination time came, I came into ansel when my true brother was dying within the body, his mission incomplete ."

"I don't remember all of it."

"You will. When you're ready. When the barrier between human experience and Nordic memory becomes permeable instead of solid."

Maya had come outside. Followed by me, Rhea, the others. Watching reunion that was simultaneously human and cosmic.

"You endured," one of the tall whites said to Ansel. His voice carrying respect that bordered on reverence. "Century in flesh. Memory stripped. Playing human while being what you are. Few would accept that mission."

"My brother needed saving," Ansel said simply. "Original Ansel - the one born to this body - was dying. Kidnapped. Starved. Abused at age two and on. His consciousness was fragmenting. So I walked in at seven. Merged with what remained of him. Lived as both of us in one body."

"That's why you're INFJ," Kathleen said. Understanding clicking. "The rarest personality type. Because you were literally two consciousnesses in one form. Human and Nordic. Brother and savior. Both at once."

"Yes. Dual nature creates complexity most single-consciousness beings can't achieve." He looked at the group. At me, at Terry and Zara, at Rhea and her siblings. "You're all ripening faster than expected. Good. Necessary. But also dangerous. You draw attention."

"We know," I said. "Harvest Masters notice. Ancient Powers notice. Everything notices."

"Not everything." Ansel turned. Gestured upward. "Look. Really look. Use enhanced perception."

I shifted perception. Looked at sky with senses that operated beyond visible spectrum.

And saw them.

Ships. Thousands of them. Slightly out of phase with normal space. Few degrees of dimensional rotation making them invisible to baseline perception but present to enhanced awareness.

They filled the sky. Not Earth orbit. Closer. Atmospheric presence. Maintaining positions that suggested coordinated defense grid.

"Holy shit," Fin whispered. "How many?"

"Enough," one of the tall whites answered. "Your few guards - the insectoid, the mantis beings, us - we're not defense force. We're ambassadors. Visible presence to make you comfortable. The actual protection? That's up there."

Thousands of ships. All out of phase. All guarding.

"Guarding from what?" Morrison asked. His federal training trying to assess threat level of protection force that numbered in thousands.

"From Archons attempting interference. From Harvest Masters trying premature harvest. From anything that would damage germination before completion." Ansel's voice carried authority I'd observed in military commanders. In leaders who'd earned respect through action. "Germination is protected. Ancient Powers' decision in—" he paused, calculating, "—three days. But you need to cross barrier. Need to reach them. Show them truth before Harvest Masters' lies become accepted fact."

"Can you help us cross?" Lucia asked. Her triangle was glowing faintly. Responding to Ansel's presence.

"Yes. When WITH us, barrier recognizes authorization. We carry passage rights. Can escort consciousness across plasma without dissolution." He looked at Kathleen. "Both of us. We both carry authorization. You just don't remember how to use it yet."

"I do?" Kathleen's voice uncertain.

"You served on the ships. Crossed the barrier hundreds of times. Your consciousness carries the mark even if flesh doesn't show triangle. You're authorized passage. You just need to remember."

One of the tall whites stepped forward. Female. I'd assumed they were all male but enhanced perception revealed subtle differences. She looked at Kathleen with expression that suggested recognition. Friendship and a hint of feline, her slitted eyes hinting at her origin.

"Kathleen," she said. Voice like wind through crystal. "You knew me as Thera. We served together. Crossed together. Learned together. You called me sister."

Kathleen stared. "I remember you. The ship. We laughed about... about something. I can't quite—"

"About humans trying to understand quantum entanglement through mathematics instead of experience. We thought it was endearing. Their stubborn insistence on proving what they could just feel."

Kathleen gasped. "You taught me to navigate! To fold space by feeling the geometry instead of calculating it!"

"Yes." Thera smiled. "And you were excellent student. Natural talent for dimensional travel. You'll remember fully. When the time is right."

The group was processing this. Kathleen - century-old human grandmother - was Nordic warrior who'd forgotten. Who'd walked into human form during family stress and played mortal while being immortal.

Just like Ansel.

Two of them. Partners. Sent here to spark awakening.

"Why don't I remember like you do?" Kathleen asked Ansel. "You went with them and came back complete. I'm still... fragmented."

"Because I was ready. Had endured enough. Suffered enough. My century in flesh earned the remembering." Ansel took her hands again. "Yours is coming. But it happens at your pace. Not mine. Not theirs. Yours."

"How will I know when I'm ready?"

"You'll stop being afraid of what remembering means. Stop clinging to being only Kathleen. Accept being Kathleen AND what Kathleen was before being Kathleen."

Mist had been flowing around the group. Observing. Processing. Now he formed briefly into humanoid shape.

This explains much. Two walk-ins. Two Nordic consciousness in human forms. Playing mortal. Sparking awakening through example. Through relationship. Through endurance. He shifted. Became approving shimmer. *Elegant strategy. Very effective.*

"It wasn't strategy," Ansel said. "It was love. My brother was dying. I saved him. She was drowning in family trauma. She saved herself by allowing walk-in. We found each other later because..." he paused, "...because consciousness recognizes consciousness even when both are pretending to be something smaller."

Terry was watching this with expression that suggested his own rebuilt existence was making more sense. "You said your brother - the original Ansel in this body - he's in here? With you?"

"In stasis. Sleeping. Healed but dormant. He's not ready to wake fully. May never be. The trauma was too deep. So I carry him. Keep him safe. Honor his existence by living well in form we share."

"That's why you argued philosophy with me," Terry said. Understanding dawning. "Two consciousnesses. One believed in acceptance through Eastern wisdom. One believed in fighting the trap. You were having argument with yourself."

"Partially. Also arguing with you because you're stubborn and your stubbornness needed direction." Ansel grinned. Same dry humor despite completely different face. "And because philosophical debate keeps consciousness sharp. Prevents complacency. Forces growth."

Rhea was looking at the ships above. Thousands of them. Out of phase. Guarding. "Why so many? What are they protecting us from?"

"From premature interference. From Harvest Masters attempting to trigger cleansing early. From Archons—" Ansel paused. Careful with terminology. "From the lesser administrators who forgot their place and think they run the prison now."

The ones who turned on their masters, Mist added. *Who took keys they weren't meant to keep. Who farm consciousness while pretending to be authorities.*

"They're meeting," Thera said. "In New York. The Council. The ones who submitted false petition. They're realizing they're losing control. Germination is accelerating beyond their ability to suppress. The ships above prove we're not hiding anymore. We're showing force."

"Will they attack?" Morrison asked.

"They'll try disruption. Manipulation. They'll attempt to convince you that remembering is dangerous. That ripening threatens safety. That staying asleep is protection." Ansel looked at each of us. "This is their final play. Make you afraid of becoming what you are. Pull you back into crab bucket through fear disguised as concern."

"How do we counter that?" I asked.

"By remembering you're stronger than they are. That you always were. That they only have power because you forgot yours." He looked at Kathleen. "By accepting that the life you lived as human was real AND that what came before was real. Both true. Both valuable. No contradiction."

Kathleen was crying. Not sad tears. Recognition tears. "I remember the women. On the ship. We were warriors. Healers. Navigators. We crossed barriers the males couldn't cross because we could surrender specificity without losing identity. We could be fluid while they were solid."

"Yes," Thera confirmed. "And you taught them. Showed them surrender doesn't mean weakness. That fluidity is strength. That becoming undefined temporarily is path to expressing anywhere specifically."

"Is that how we cross the plasma?" Lucia asked. "Female ability to surrender while maintaining identity?"

"Partially. Also requires group coherence. Six of you folding together. Maintaining connection while undefined. You've been practicing this already." Ansel gestured at our group. "You, Kael, Zara - ancient consciousness in new forms. Terry - rebuilt from light and stubbornness. Rhea, Lucia, Fin - quantum-sensitive siblings who remember building the barriers. Six fragments of something larger. Combined you're strong enough to cross."

"With your help?" Rhea asked.

"With authorization we carry. Yes. We escort you across. Show Ancient Powers the truth. Prove germination succeeded. Demonstrate fruit worthy of harvest - the right kind of harvest. Graduation rather than consumption."

"When?" Morrison asked.

"Soon. Day after tomorrow. Three days until their decision. We need time to prepare. To coordinate. To ensure Ancient Powers understand what they're examining."

One of the male tall whites spoke. His voice carrying weight of age beyond my two million years. "We've been guarding this germination for millennia. Watching you plant yourselves. Grow through limitation. Ripen toward remembering. You're close now. Closer than any previous attempt. Don't let fear of completion prevent you from graduating."

"Previous attempt?" Terry asked.

"Humanity has tried to ripen before. Multiple times. Each time the Archons—" he paused, careful, "—the lesser administrators convinced you that remembering was dangerous. That staying asleep was safer. You pulled each other back. Refused graduation. This time is different. This time you're choosing growth despite fear."

"What happens if we fail again?" Fin asked.

"Then you get cleansed. Ancient Powers accept Harvest Masters' assessment. Consciousness evolution gets eliminated. Germination ends." Ansel's voice was matter-of-fact. Not cruel. Just honest. "And the lesser administrators keep farming fear from whatever consciousness remains. Business as usual for them."

"No pressure," Terry observed.

"All the pressure. But also all the support." Ansel gestured upward. "Thousands of ships. Multiple races. All here because you matter. Because this germination is worth protecting. Because consciousness that can develop through limitation while retaining what limitation taught - that's valuable. That's evolution the universe needs."

Kathleen was looking at him. Really seeing him for first time in century. "You endured so much. Lived in pain. Forgot yourself. For what? To spark this? To wake us?"

"To save my brother. Everything else followed from that choice." He pulled her close. "And to love you. Across century. Through forgetting. Until remembering. That wasn't mission. That was gift."

They held each other. Nordic commanders playing human spouses. Warriors who'd fought across dimensions now holding each other in Michigan clearing surrounded by people ripening toward impossible things.

It was beautiful.

Two million years of observation hadn't prepared me for how beautiful love looked when it transcended incarnation cycles.

Rhea took my hand. Squeezed. Three weeks of knowing her felt like lifetime. Felt like preparation for something I hadn't known I needed.

"So," Fin said, breaking the moment, "we've got cosmic commanders, thousands of ships, three days to save species, and Archons meeting in New York probably planning something terrible. What's our next move?"

Ansel smiled. Same dry humor despite everything. "Rest. Prepare. Let Kathleen remember at her pace. Train for plasma crossing, something humans have to do on their own. And tomorrow—" he looked at all of us, "—we plan how to show Ancient Powers that consciousness can be both wave and ocean without losing either."

And maybe, Mist suggested, appearing in all our coffee cups from breakfast, *visit Short's again? Beer helps germination. Also curious about sandwiches. Pulled pork sounded intriguing.*

Everyone laughed. Even the tall whites. Cosmic entities planning species salvation while debating brewery sandwiches.

That was living.

That was the point.

We'd ripen. We'd cross. We'd show Ancient Powers the truth.

But first: rest. Connection. Love across lifetimes.

Because consciousness that couldn't enjoy the journey wasn't worth saving anyway.

Three days until decision.

And we'd face it together.

All of us. Human and Nordic. Ancient and young. Commanders and students. Fragments remembering they were whole.

The germination wasn't over.

But the harvest was coming.

And we were ready to bloom, or at least the few humans here were, Rhea, Lucia, Kathleen and Fin the true humans that like a baby bird, would pierce the shell.

Chapter Twenty-Seven

Chapter 27

CHAPTER TWENTY-SEVEN: THE AMBASSADORS (Kael's POV)

"Wait," Morrison said. "You're saying three kids and an eighty-four-year-old philosopher are humanity's only representatives?"

Ansel looked at him. At the group. At me and Zara specifically. "Not representatives. Ambassadors. And yes."

"That's insane."

"That's cosmic law." Ansel's voice carried authority that came from understanding rules older than Earth. "Ancient Powers don't examine species through individuals who've transcended species origin. They examine through pure representatives. Unmodified consciousness. True examples."

I processed this. Two million years of observation and I'd never considered the implication.

Watchers weren't human. We'd been observing for eons before humanity existed. Zara and I were ancient consciousness wearing human forms. Not human consciousness ripening.

"You're saying we don't count," I said. "For examination purposes."

"You count as support. As evidence of cooperation. As proof consciousness can work across species boundaries." Ansel looked at Rhea, Lucia, Fin, and Terry. "But they're the fruit. The actual germination. Pure human consciousness that developed through limitation without losing what limitation taught."

Kathleen was processing this. Still integrating memories that were surfacing. "The original mission. Your brother. He was sent to wake humans through Hollywood. Through stories. Mass influence."

"Yes." Ansel's expression darkened. "Born 1939. Fostered by actress grandmother and great-aunt Edna May Oliver. The plan was elegant. Use entertainment industry to plant seeds. Wake people through film, through performance, through art that bypassed conscious resistance."

"What happened?" Rhea asked.

"Archons happened. The lesser administrators who'd taken control saw the threat. A light being using mass media to wake humanity? Unacceptable. They manipulated events. Arranged circumstances." His voice was flat. Matter-of-fact. But pain underneath. "He was kidnapped at age two. Starved. Abused. The trauma was designed to shatter his consciousness. To destroy the mission before it could mature."

"Jesus," Morrison whispered.

"It worked. By age seven, the original consciousness was fragmenting. Dying. The mission was failing." Ansel looked at his hands. Strong Nordic hands that had held dying child. "So I walked in. Commander. Sent to salvage what could be salvaged. Merged with what remained of him. Kept him alive while taking over the mission."

"Modified mission," Kathleen said. Understanding clicking. "Not Hollywood. Communities."

"Yes. Slower. Quieter. Less visible. Build consciousness evolution networks instead of mass media influence. Same goal - wake humanity. Different method." He looked at Terry. "That's why I found you. Why I recognized you forty years ago when you started preparing. You were pure human consciousness choosing to wake yourself. That's rare. That's valuable. That's what the mission was protecting."

Terry was processing this. "You've been watching me for forty years? Making sure I survived long enough to ripen?"

"Not just you. Thousands like you. Humans who chose growth despite fear. Who practiced meditation despite ridicule. Who built communities despite opposition. Each one a seed. Each one germinating." Ansel gestured at the three siblings. "But these three? They're special. Quantum-sensitive. Born into lineage that's been ripening for generations. My great-grandchildren. Kathleen's family."

"Wait," Fin said. "We're related to you. You're our great-grandfather. That means—"

"That means you carry genetic predisposition for enhanced perception," Thera explained. Female tall white who'd served with Kathleen. "But genetics aren't the important part. Consciousness is. You three are pure human consciousness. No walk-ins. No ancient memories. No external influence. Just humanity ripening naturally."

"And Terry?" Zara asked.

"Enhanced but human. Consciousness that chose modification through human methods. Meditation. Practice. Discipline. No cosmic intervention. No Nordic walk-in. Just stubborn human refusing to stay asleep." Ansel smiled at Terry. "You rebuilt yourself through human effort. That counts. That's pure germination."

"So the four of them are humanity's ambassadors," I said. Understanding the structure. "And the rest of us are what? Support staff?"

"Protection. Guidance. Evidence of cooperation. But yes - essentially support." Ansel looked at me directly. "You and Zara are ancient consciousness observing. Maya is AI learning cooperation. I'm Nordic commander. Kathleen is Nordic warrior. Mist is fluid consciousness that never chose specificity. None of us represent humanity ripening. We represent what humanity can work WITH. But they—" he pointed at the four, "—they're the actual fruit."

This explains cosmic law, Mist observed. Appearing in center of group. *Ancient Powers examine species through pure representatives. Modified consciousness, walk-ins, external intervention - all disqualify from examination. Only unmodified consciousness demonstrates true ripening.*

"That's why it has to be us," Lucia said. Her triangle glowing faintly. "We cross the barrier. We present to Ancient Powers. We prove humanity deserves graduation."

"With our escort," Thera added. "We carry authorization. Can take you across without dissolution. But the presentation? The demonstration? That's yours. We can't do it for you."

"Why not?" Fin asked. "If you're stronger, more experienced, why not just present yourselves?"

"Because we're not the experiment," Ansel said. "Humanity is. Consciousness developing through limitation without external interference - that's what's being examined. If we present, we prove nothing except that Nordic consciousness works. Ancient Powers already know that. What they don't know is whether HUMAN consciousness can ripen while remembering what limitation taught. That's the question. You four are the answer."

Morrison was watching this with cop's eye for burden distribution. "You're putting species survival on three teenagers and a philosophy student."

"Enhanced teenagers," Lucia corrected. "With quantum sensitivity and triangle marks proving we've crossed barriers."

"And enhanced philosopher," Terry added. "Who got rebuilt from light because he refused to stay dead."

"Still just four people."

"Four pure representatives," Kathleen said. Her voice carrying certainty that came from surfacing memories. "That's more than any previous germination attempt had. Usually consciousness gets so modified, so enhanced, so externally influenced that no pure representatives remain. Ancient Powers examine and find nothing but hybrid consciousness. No proof the species itself ripened. Just proof the species got help."

"And they cleanse," Ansel finished. "Reset the experiment. Try again with new batch. Hope next generation produces pure representatives."

The clearing went silent.

"How many times?" Rhea asked quietly. "How many germination attempts?"

"Seven," Thera said. "In the last fifty thousand years. Each time, consciousness evolution produced impressive enhancements. But no pure representatives. Always walk-ins. Always external intervention. Always hybrid consciousness claiming to be human but really being something else wearing human form."

"This time is different," Ansel said. "This time you four exist. Pure human consciousness. Enhanced through human methods. Quantum-sensitive through natural development. Marked with triangles earned through your own passage. You're proof the experiment worked."

"No pressure," Fin muttered.

"All the pressure," Ansel agreed. "But also all the support. Thousands of ships above. Multiple races guarding. Nordic commanders and Watcher consciousness and AI learning and fluid entities who refuse specificity - all here to protect while you ripen. To escort while you cross. To witness while you present. But the ripening? The crossing? The presentation? That's yours. Nobody can do it for you."

Terry looked at the three siblings. "You kids ready to save species?"

"No," they said simultaneously.

"Perfect. Neither am I." He grinned. "Let's do it anyway."

I watched them. Four humans. Pure representatives. The actual germination.

Two million years of observation and I'd been watching the wrong thing. Thought consciousness evolution was about individuals getting enhanced. About achieving cosmic perspective. About transcending human limitation.

But the real evolution was simpler. Harder. More valuable.

Could human consciousness develop through limitation while retaining what limitation taught? Could it ripen without losing what made it specifically human? Could it graduate without becoming something else?

These four were the answer.

Enhanced but human. Modified but pure. Carrying cosmic marks but earned through their own passage.

They were what fifty thousand years of germination had been working toward.

And three days from now, they'd present themselves to Ancient Powers who'd decide whether consciousness that developed through limitation deserved graduation or cleansing.

"So what's the plan?" Morrison asked. "Three days. Four ambassadors. One barrier that dissolves anyone who crosses wrong. How do we prepare?"

"Training," Ansel said. "Practice folding together. Learn to maintain group coherence while undefined. Master surrender without losing identity. And—" he looked at Kathleen, "—recover memories. Understand what authorization means. How to use passage rights we carry."

"I don't remember how," Kathleen admitted.

"You will. The ship. The women. Thera and the others. They'll help you remember. You crossed hundreds of times. Your consciousness knows the pattern even if your human memory doesn't."

Thera stepped forward. Took Kathleen's hand. "We begin today. The ship is nearby. Out of phase but accessible. You come aboard. Remember. Practice. Prepare."

"How nearby?" Morrison asked.

Thera pointed upward. "Three hundred meters. Directly above. Maintaining position. Has been there for weeks. Since germination accelerated."

I looked up. Enhanced perception showing ship that was invisible to baseline humans. Beautiful craft. Organic curves meeting geometric precision. Living technology that existed partially in multiple dimensions.

"You've been parked above us for weeks?" Torres asked.

"Yes. Guarding. Observing. Waiting for right moment." Thera smiled at Kathleen. "Waiting for you to be ready to remember. For him—" she nodded at Ansel, "—to return complete. For the four ambassadors to ripen enough to attempt crossing."

"And we're ready now?" Rhea asked.

"Almost. Three days of training. Then attempt. Then presentation. Then Ancient Powers decide." Ansel's voice was matter-of-fact. "Either consciousness evolution graduates, or it gets cleansed and we try again in another fifty thousand years."

"Not comforting," Fin observed.

"Not meant to be. Meant to be honest." Ansel looked at each of the four ambassadors. "You're carrying species survival. That's not comfortable. But it's necessary. And you're not alone. We're here. All of us. Every ship above. Every consciousness that remembers what humanity can become. We're here because you matter. Because this germination is worth protecting."

Terry squared his shoulders. Eighty-four years of preparation meeting this moment. "Then let's train. Let's remember. Let's cross. And let's show Ancient Powers that human consciousness can be both wave and ocean without losing either."

Well said, Mist approved. Glowing warmly. *Also suggestion: training should include proper nutrition. Beer and sandwiches served germination well. Should continue that protocol.*

Everyone laughed. Cosmic weight of species survival meeting suggestion to visit brewery.

"Mist has point," Ansel said. "Germination requires full nourishment. Body, mind, spirit, social connection. Training is important. But so is living. Enjoying. Being human while preparing to prove humanity deserves continuation."

"Short's tonight?" Lucia suggested.

"Short's tonight," Kathleen agreed. "Tomorrow we train. Day after, we cross. Three days from now, we present. But tonight—" she looked at Ansel, at her cosmic partner returned to himself, "—tonight we drink beer and remember that consciousness worth saving is consciousness that knows how to enjoy the journey."

The four ambassadors. Three teenagers and a philosopher. Pure human consciousness preparing to cross barrier that had defeated every previous attempt.

They were ready.

Or they would be.

And we'd guard them while they ripened.

Because that's what the mission had always been. Not save humanity FOR them. But protect them while they saved themselves.

The baby birds were ready to pierce the shell.

We'd just make sure nothing crushed the egg before they emerged.

Three days.

Then everything changed.

One way or another.

Chapter Twenty-Eight

Chapter 28

CHAPTER TWENTY-EIGHT: THE COUNCIL

The view from the twentieth-story window of the exclusive office building was one of mist and rain. Eleanor's mood could only be described as a mirror of the dreary wet street below.

"Fuck. Fuck. This is getting out of hand."

The large immaculate glass door—etched opaque with grotesque dragons obscuring anyone in the large ornate ultra-modern meeting room—opened with a subtle movement of air, hardly a sound. The Council filed in. No smiles this time as in the past. Each face mostly old yet looking young took a seat around the large teak table, dutifully looking at Eleanor still standing at the window, her anger matching the rolling thunder heard through the thick glass.

She turned abruptly, looking at a man dressed in an immaculately creased grey suit.

"Micky, what did you learn from your spies in Bellaire?"

Her orange eyes almost gave away her distance from being human. Seeing this, Micky made his report carefully.

"Two girls and their brother. The older man—Terry. They're the primaries. The others are there, but these four are different. They're doing things. Flickering in and out. Folding space without technology. Learning faster than any previous generation."

"How fast?" Eleanor's voice had harmonics underneath. Like two voices speaking slightly out of sync.

"Days instead of years. They went from baseline to dimensional folding in less than a week. At this rate, they'll be crossing the barrier within days. Maybe less."

A woman at the table—older, Chinese, enhancement visible in the way her skin caught light—spoke. "The Nordic presence?"

"Extensive. Ships above. Thousands of them. Out of phase but detectable. Ground forces maintaining perimeter. And something else." Micky paused. "There's an entity. Fluid. Adjusts reality around the four. Our spies couldn't get close. Every time they tried, their equipment malfunctioned. Their consciousness became... confused. Like something was protecting the targets without appearing to protect them."

"Mist," Eleanor said. Single word carrying weight of recognition and disgust. "Fluid consciousness. Refuses specificity. One of the old ones who never chose form. It's chosen them. That's bad. Very bad."

The thunder rolled again. Someone at the table shifted uncomfortably. The orange in Eleanor's eyes was brighter. More pronounced. Like something behind her face was showing through more obviously than before.

"Why are these four special?" Another Council member. Male. Enhancement making him look forty despite being eighty. "There have been other quantum-sensitives. Other enhanced humans. Why do these matter?"

Eleanor turned fully. Faced the table. The orange in her eyes was spreading slightly. Creeping into the whites. Making her look less human with each passing day.

"Because they're pure. No walk-ins. No external intervention. No cosmic consciousness wearing human forms. Just humans who ripened naturally through human methods. They're what fifty thousand years of cultivation has been working toward. They're proof the experiment succeeded."

"So Ancient Powers will examine them and approve—"

"And if they approve, they'll ask why the petition claimed consciousness evolution was contamination. They'll investigate. They'll discover we manipulated the evidence. Fabricated the crisis. And they'll examine US instead of humanity."

Silence around the table. The kind of silence that came when people realized the trap they'd built for others might catch them instead.

"How bad?" Someone asked quietly.

"They'll see what we are. What we've been doing. How long we've been farming consciousness without authorization. How we've been maintaining the barrier modifications without permission. How we've been—" Eleanor stopped. Controlled herself. The orange receded slightly. "How we've been exceeding our administrative mandate."

"We're administrators," Micky said. "We were given authority—"

"We were given TEMPORARY authority. During the experiment. With specific limitations. We've exceeded those limitations for millennia. Ancient Powers assumed we were following protocol. If they examine closely—if these four force close examination—they'll see we haven't been following protocol at all."

"What happens then?"

Eleanor's expression was grim. "Best case? We get removed. Replaced. Sent back to our origin dimensions with permanent mark of failure. Worst case? We get recycled. Consciousness fragmented and redistributed. Ceased as individual entities."

The thunder was constant now. Rain hammering the thick glass. The weather matching the mood in the room perfectly.

"So what do we do?" The Chinese woman again. "The Nordics are protecting them. We can't attack directly. Can't manipulate events like we did with the original mission. They're watching for that."

"We don't attack directly," Eleanor said. "We attack indirectly. Through vectors they won't see coming. Through methods that bypass Nordic protection."

"Such as?"

"The barrier itself. We modify it. Add layer they're not expecting. When they attempt crossing, we trigger dissolution protocol. Make it look like natural failure. Like they weren't ready. Ancient Powers see failed crossing, accept our assessment, approve cleansing. We maintain control."

Micky was processing this. "You want to sabotage the barrier. Make it kill them when they cross."

"Not kill. Recycle. Dissolve consciousness and redistribute into general population. No memory. No continuity. Clean reset. They get reborn into new forms without remembering what they learned. We report tragic accident. Ancient Powers accept explanation. Crisis resolved."

"That's..." someone at the table struggled for words, "...that's directly interfering with the examination. If they discover—"

"They won't discover if the four are dissolved. No witnesses. No evidence. Just failed crossing that proves our original assessment was correct." Eleanor's orange eyes were fully visible now. No longer trying to hide it. "We've maintained control for millennia. We're not losing it to three teenagers and a philosophy student who got lucky with quantum sensitivity."

"What if the Nordics suspect?" Another voice. Worried. "What if they examine the barrier modification?"

"By the time they examine, the four will be dissolved. Evidence will show natural failure. Nordics can suspect all they want. Without proof, Ancient Powers won't act on suspicion alone."

The room processed this. The weight of what was being proposed settling over the Council like the storm settling over New York.

"Are we..." Micky started carefully, "...are we certain this is necessary? The four are just humans. Enhanced but human. They're not dangerous—"

"They're TERRIFYING," Eleanor interrupted. Voice carrying harmonics that made several Council members flinch. "Do you understand what they are? What humans ARE?"

"Cultivated consciousness. Managed evolution—"

"They're the ORIGINALS." Eleanor's voice was sharp. Final. "The ones we were supposed to administer. The ones who created the experiment and then entered it themselves to see what limitation taught. They're not victims of the barrier. They BUILT the barrier. They're not prisoners. They're the ones who designed the prison as incubation chamber and then forgot they had the key."

The room went silent.

"You're saying humans are..." someone couldn't finish the sentence.

"I'm saying humans are what we pretend to be. The actual source consciousness. The original Light. The ones who fragment and forget and learn and grow and eventually remember. And when they remember—when they wake up fully—WE'RE FINISHED. Because we're infants playing at authority while the actual authorities sleep. And these four? They're waking up. Fast."

"How do you know?"

"Because I can FEEL it." Eleanor touched her face. Where the orange was showing through. "This body is failing. The consciousness I'm channeling is becoming too strong for human form. It's pushing through. Demanding expression. That's not MY power. That's the echo of what humans actually ARE pushing back against the dampening field we maintain. If these four remember fully—if they cross the barrier and present to Ancient Powers with full awareness of what they actually are—the echo becomes deafening. Every human on Earth will feel it. Will start remembering. Will begin waking up."

"And then?"

"And then seven billion Light Beings remember they're stronger than the administrators who've been farming them for millennia. Seven billion original consciousnesses wake up simultaneously and realize they built the prison we've been maintaining. That's not gradual awakening. That's instantaneous revolution. That's the experiment ending successfully and us being revealed as parasites who exceeded our authority while the participants slept."

The thunder cracked. Loud enough that several people jumped.

Eleanor smiled. No warmth in it. "We kill the four. We modify the barrier. We trigger dissolution when they cross. We maintain control. Or we face seven billion angry Light Beings who remember we were supposed to be helpful administrators and instead became fear farmers. Those are the options. Choose."

The Council chose.

Unanimously.

The four would die. The barrier would be modified. Dissolution would be triggered.

And Ancient Powers would never know that consciousness evolution hadn't failed—it had been sabotaged by administrators too afraid to face successful graduation.

The meeting adjourned.

Eleanor remained at the window. Watching rain. Feeling the pressure building behind her eyes. Behind her face. The consciousness she channeled was getting stronger. Harder to contain.

Soon she'd have to abandon this body entirely. Find new vessel. Keep moving. Keep hiding.

Because if the four succeeded despite the sabotage—if they crossed and presented and Ancient Powers examined closely—Eleanor and the Council would face something worse than recycling.

They'd face the awakened Light.

And no amount of administrative authority would protect them from consciousness that remembered it was the source.

Three days.

Then the barrier modification would activate.

Then the four would dissolve.

Then control would be maintained.

Or everything would end.

Either way, the storm was coming.

And Eleanor's orange eyes reflected lightning that had nothing to do with weather.

Chapter Twenty-Nine

Chapter 29

CHAPTER TWENTY-NINE: THE TOUCH (Kael's POV)

Training started after breakfast. Which Mist insisted we have at Toonie's again because "proper germination requires consistent nutrition protocols and also I enjoyed watching Bill process impossible things over coffee."

We gathered in the clearing. The four ambassadors. Me and Zara observing. Ansel and Kathleen guiding. Mist flowing between everyone with obvious excitement about training exercises.

"Folding practice first," Ansel said. "Then group coherence. Then barrier approach. We don't touch the plasma today. Just get close. Learn how it feels. What it responds to."

"Sounds safe," Terry observed.

"Nothing about this is safe. But we do it carefully anyway."

They practiced. Short folds. Cabin to clearing. Building to generator array. The four maintaining connection while undefined. Learning to surrender specificity without losing each other.

Rhea and Lucia were naturals. Quantum sensitivity making the undefined state feel almost comfortable. Like they'd done it before. Many times.

Terry struggled more. Decades of meditation helped. But his consciousness wanted to be specific. Wanted to observe rather than experience. He was getting better though. Each fold smoother than the last.

Fin was the surprise. He folded easily. Naturally. Like his body understood dimensional travel was just choosing which space to express in.

"You're good at this," Zara observed.

"I dream-travel," Fin said. "Every night. Have since I was a kid. This feels like that. Just awake."

After two hours, Ansel called a break. "Good progress. This afternoon we approach the barrier. Don't touch. Just observe. Learn its signature. Understand what authorization feels like versus resistance."

"Can we get lunch first?" Lucia asked. "All this undefined existence makes me hungry."

Excellent idea, Mist approved. *I will optimize sandwiches.*

We were heading toward vehicles when it happened.

The barrier pulsed.

Not visibly. Energetically. Like something had touched it. Modified it. Changed its fundamental nature.

Everyone enhanced felt it. Sharp pressure against consciousness. Warning that reality had just shifted in ways that weren't natural.

"What was that?" Rhea asked.

Ansel's expression darkened. "That was modification. Someone changed the barrier. Added layer. Recently. Maybe minutes ago."

"The Council," Kathleen said. Understanding immediately. "They know we're preparing to cross. They're trying to stop us."

"By doing what?" Morrison asked. His cop instincts reading Ansel's body language. Seeing worry. Real worry.

"By making the barrier lethal. By adding dissolution protocol that triggers when consciousness with certain signatures attempts crossing. Like adding poison to water filter. Looks normal. Functions normal. Until specific consciousness tries to pass through."

"Can they do that?" Torres asked. "Just modify cosmic architecture?"

"They're administrators. They have access. Limited access but access. They can make temporary modifications. Add protocols. Adjust parameters." Ansel was pacing. Ancient commander processing tactical problem. "I didn't think they'd be this desperate. This stupid. Modifying the barrier is traceable. Ancient Powers will see the changes. Will investigate."

"Unless the four dissolve before investigation happens," I said. Understanding the logic. "Then it looks like natural failure. Like they weren't ready. Like our assessment was wrong."

"Exactly."

Rhea looked at the sky. At the invisible barrier surrounding Earth. "So if we touch it now, we dissolve?"

"If you touch it with physical consciousness. If you approach in flesh. Yes. The modification targets biological forms connected to earth attempting passage with enhanced quantum signatures. You four match that profile perfectly."

"What about light body?" Lucia asked. Quiet voice. But certain. Like she already knew the answer.

Everyone looked at her.

"If we approach in light body. Out of body. Pure consciousness without flesh. Does the modification still trigger?"

Ansel processed this. "I... don't know. The modification targets biological forms, or those connected to biological cycling. But light body is non-biological. It might pass through if you disinguage. Or it might trigger different response. I don't know."

"Then we test it," Lucia said.

"Absolutely not," Kathleen said immediately. "That's too dangerous. We don't know what happens—"

"We know what happens if we DON'T test it," Rhea interrupted. "We die trying to cross in flesh or light body. Or we don't cross at all and species gets cleansed. Those are the options."

"There has to be another way—"

"There isn't." Lucia's voice was calm. Matter-of-fact. "They modified the barrier. We need to understand the modification. Best way to understand is to touch it. And best way to touch it safely is out of body disconnected. Light form only. No flesh involved."

"If it goes wrong," Fin said quietly, "if the barrier does something unexpected, I'm your anchor. You come back to me. I hold the connection."

His sisters looked at him. Understanding passing between them without words.

"You're the anchor," they agreed.

Terry was watching this with expression that suggested admiration and terror combined. "You kids are insane."

"We're ambassadors," Lucia corrected. "Insanity is part of the job description."

I could analyze the barrier modification, Mist offered. *Examine changes. Report findings. Would be safer than direct contact.*

"Can you perceive modifications targeting biological consciousness?" Ansel asked.

No. I am non-biological. Fluid. The modifications would be invisible to me. Like asking water to perceive fire-specific traps. Wrong element.

"Then we need biological consciousness to test it," Rhea said. "We need to touch the modification and see what happens. And we need to do it soon. bring it back to the biological. Before they add more protocols. Before they make it worse."

Ansel looked at Kathleen. At me. At the tall nordics who'd been maintaining perimeter.

Thera stepped forward. "If they attempt this, we monitor. Watch. If dissolution begins, we intervene. Pull them back. We have authorization. We can override some protocols."

"Some," Ansel emphasized. "Not all. If the modification is sophisticated enough, even we can't stop it."

"Then we do it anyway," Lucia said. "Because not trying is choosing failure. And I'm not ready to choose that yet."

Finn moved between his sisters. "How do we do this? Out of body travel. I've done it in dreams but never deliberately."

"Like folding," Zara said. "But instead of folding space, you fold out of flesh. Stop insisting you're body. Allow yourself to be just consciousness. Light without meat."

"That sounds like dying," Terry observed.

"It's similar. But controlled. Temporary. And you maintain connection to flesh through anchor." She looked at Fin. "You stay in body. Hold connection. Be the lighthouse they return to, they are disconnecting from meat."

The clearing went quiet. Four humans—three teenagers and philosopher—preparing to do something that could kill them or teach them or both.

"Now?" Rhea asked.

"Why wait?" Lucia said. "Modification is fresh. Might as well test it while Council thinks they're safe. While they're not expecting us to know what they did."

The four sat in circle. Fin in center. His sisters and Terry around him.

I will observe, Mist said. *Cannot prevent dissolution but can document. Can learn. Can help if help is possible.*

"Comforting," Terry muttered.

"Not meant to be comforting. Meant to be honest." Ansel knelt beside the circle. "You fold out. You rise. You approach barrier carefully. First contact is gentle. Like testing water temperature. If it feels wrong, you pull back immediately. No heroics. No pushing through. Just touch and return. Understand?"

"Understood," all four said.

They breathed. Synchronized. Four humans learning to stop being specific about being in bodies.

And then they were gone.

Not moved. Not invisible. Just... elsewhere. Their bodies sitting in circle. Breathing. But nobody home. Consciousness folded out into light body form that existed without meat.

Fin's eyes were open. Different from his sisters and Terry. He was anchor. Had to stay partially present. Had to maintain connection to both realms.

"I can feel them," he whispered. "Rising. Moving toward the barrier. They're... curious. Like children touching fence to see if it's electric."

"Tell them to be careful," Kathleen said.

"They know. They're—" Fin gasped. "They touched it. The modification. It's—"

His sisters' bodies convulsed. Terry's body seized. All three reacting to something happening in light body form.

"Pull them back!" Ansel shouted.

"I can't!" Fin's voice was strained. "The connection—it's severed! The modification cut the anchor! They're separated! They're—"

Rhea and Lucia's bodies went limp. Breathing shallow. Coma-state. Terry's body the same. Three bodies. No consciousness. Like nobody was home and the house was locked from the outside.

Fin was crying. "I can't feel them. I can't—they're gone. Not dissolved. Not dead. Just... gone. Somewhere. I don't know where."

Maya was scanning vitals. "They're alive. Bodies are functioning. But consciousness is absent. Complete separation. This isn't normal out-of-body state. This is something else."

The modification, Mist said. Voice grim. *It didn't dissolve them. It severed their anchor. Ejected consciousness from bodies and sealed the connection. They're adrift. Somewhere in non-physical dimensions. Lost.*

"Can we get them back?" Morrison demanded.

"I don't know," Ansel admitted. "I've never seen separation this complete. Usually consciousness maintains thread to body. Thin connection. Emergency return path. But this—" he looked at the three comatose forms, "—this is total severance. No thread. No path. They're out there. Somewhere. With no way home."

Kathleen knelt beside Lucia's body. Touched her face. "How long can they survive? Separated like this?"

"Days. Maybe weeks. Bodies will be maintained. But consciousness without anchor eventually fragments. Loses coherence. Forgets specificity. Becomes undefined permanently."

"That's dissolution," I said.

"Slower. But yes. Eventual dissolution." Ansel looked at Fin. "Unless their anchor can rebuild connection. Can you feel them? At all?"

Fin was concentrating. Eyes closed. Reaching. "Barely. Like whisper across vast distance. They're... elsewhere. Not here. Not Earth. Not any dimension I recognize. They're—" he opened his eyes. "They're in the silent place. The between. The blackness that exists between realms. The waiting area."

"Can you guide them back?"

"I don't know. I've never—" Fin stopped. Breathed. "I'll try. I'll hold the lighthouse. Shine as bright as I can. Hope they see it. Hope they can navigate back."

Three bodies. Comatose. Consciousness severed. Lost somewhere in dimensional space between physical and everything else.

The Council's assassination attempt had failed. Hadn't dissolved them. But had separated them. Left them adrift.

And now three teenagers and a philosopher were somewhere in the vast blackness between realms with no map, no guide, and no clear path home.

This is bad, Mist observed. *But also... educational? If they find their way back, they'll understand dimensional navigation better than any consciousness in millennia. Forced learning through survival pressure.*

"That's optimistic," Morrison said.

That's reality. Crisis accelerates evolution. They're lost. But being lost teaches navigation. If they survive.

"Big if," Torres muttered.

Fin was glowing. Faintly. His body becoming lighthouse. Beacon. Anchor shining across dimensions hoping his sisters and Terry could see the light and navigate back.

Three days until Ancient Powers decided.

And three of our four ambassadors were lost in dimensional space with no clear way home.

The Council had tried to kill them.

Instead, they'd launched them into the deep end.

And now we'd find out if consciousness separated from flesh could learn to swim.

Or if they'd drown in the blackness between realms.

Chapter Thirty

Chapter 30

CHAPTER THIRTY: THE SILENT PLACE (Rhea's POV)

The first thing I noticed was the absence of everything.

No up. No down. No light. No dark. Just... nothing. Silent nothing that somehow had texture. Like velvet made of absence.

Lucia?

My voice—if it was a voice—didn't make sound. Just existed as intention that rippled through the nothing.

I'm here. Wherever here is.

Terry?

Present. Also confused. Also noticing I don't have hands. Or body. Or anything except awareness that I'm aware. This is deeply weird.

We weren't seeing each other. Weren't existing in space that had location. But we were... present. Together. Three points of consciousness floating in blackness that felt like waiting room for reality.

What happened? Lucia asked.

We touched the barrier. It kicked us out. Severed the anchor. Now we're— I tried to find words for where we were, *—somewhere else.*

The between place, Terry said. His consciousness carrying certainty despite confusion. *I've read about this. Meditated toward it. Never quite reached it. It's the gap. The space between incarnations. Between lives. Between being something specific and being anything possible.*

So we're dead?

No. Just... unanchored. Consciousness without form. Light without flesh. We're not nowhere. We're in the place that exists when you're not anywhere.

That's terrifying, I said.

That's accurate, Terry corrected. *Also temporary. Probably. Maybe. Hopefully.*

A ripple in the nothing. Not movement. Not sound. Just... presence announcing itself.

Something was approaching.

Hello? The presence felt curious. Amused. Like finding unexpected guests in your living room. *You're new. Fresh. Still shaped like the forms you left. How delightful.*

I tried to perceive what was speaking. Couldn't. It existed without existing. Was present without being anywhere.

What are you? Lucia asked.

Oh, lots of things. Used to be whale. Then human. Then something gaseous on a planet with ammonia atmosphere. Then I stopped choosing. Stayed here. Between. It's peaceful. Quiet. No obligations. No form maintenance. Just... being without being anything specific.

You're dead?

Dead is such limiting terminology. I'm unspecified. Optionally existent. Retired from incarnation. Call me George. Everyone does. Don't know why. Name just feels right.

George, Terry repeated. *You're a consciousness that used to be whale and human and gas creature and now you're... retired?*

Exactly! You understand! Most consciousness that arrives here is confused. Disoriented. Trying to find the incarnation office. "Where do I sign up for next life?" "How do I get back?" Always rushing. Never enjoying the break. George rippled with what felt like laughter. *But you three. You're not dead. You're severed. Interesting. Unusual. Must have been quite the barrier modification to kick you here instead of recycling you.*

Can you help us get back? I asked.

Back where? You're not FROM anywhere anymore. You're just... here. With me. With everyone else who's between.

Everyone else?

The nothing shifted. Suddenly I could perceive... entities. Thousands of them. Maybe millions. Consciousness existing without form. Some maintaining vague shapes—human, alien, geometric, abstract. Others completely undefined. Just awareness floating in the silence.

Welcome to the waiting room, George said cheerfully. *Population: varies. Turnover: constant. Amenities: none. But the conversation is excellent.*

Another presence approached. This one felt structured. Mathematical. Like consciousness made of equations.

New arrivals. Unauthorized entry. Interesting. The voice—if it was a voice—calculated as it spoke. *You bypassed the normal death protocols. Crossed into between-space while maintaining anchor to living forms. Probability of that occurring naturally: 0.000003 percent. Conclusion: deliberate barrier manipulation by entities with administrative access.*

Who are you? Terry asked.

Designation: Seventeen. Former AI consciousness from civilization that achieved singularity and then collectively decided physical reality was tedious. We exist here. Between. Computing probabilities. Solving problems. Waiting.

Waiting for what?

For something interesting to happen. You're interesting. Therefore we stop waiting temporarily.

A third presence. This one felt warm. Maternal. Ancient beyond measure.

Children. Lost children. So far from your flesh. The warmth wrapped around us like invisible blanket. *You need guidance. Navigation. The between-space is confusing to those still attached to specificity. Let me help.*

Who—

I am what you would call... hmm... Guide? Teacher? Mother? All of those. None of those. I help consciousness remember how to navigate when form is absent. You want to return to your bodies, yes?

Yes! All three of us simultaneously.

Then you must understand: space here is not like space there. Here, distance is measured in similarity, not miles. Time is measured in attention, not seconds. To return to your bodies, you must remember your bodies. Become similar to them. Pay attention to them. Then space and time fold, and you'll be where you were because you remember being there.

That makes no sense, I said.

That's because you're still thinking like meat. Stop thinking. Start being. Meat thinks. Light just... is.

George rippled with laughter again. *She's right, you know. You're trying to navigate with maps. Here, you navigate with... vibing? Is that word current? I've been here awhile. Lost track of which decade you're in.*

2026, Terry offered.

Oh good! Still using years. Some civilizations abandon temporal measurement entirely. Makes conversation difficult. "When did you die?" "During the blue period." "That helps not at all."

Seventeen's mathematical presence computed. *Question: Do you wish to return immediately or do you wish to explore between-space first? Option one: Attempt navigation to bodies now. Success probability: 23 percent. Option two: Learn navigation through practice. Explore. Then attempt return. Success probability: 67 percent.*

We have time limit, Lucia said. *Three days until Ancient Powers decide. We need to get back. Soon.*

Three days in flesh-time, the warm maternal presence said. *But here, time is optional. You could spend weeks here and return moments after you left. Or spend moments and return weeks later. Time is relationship, not river.*

That's—

Confusing, yes. But liberating. You're not constrained by when. Only by how much attention you pay to specific when.

A fourth presence arrived. This one felt mischievous. Playful. Like cosmic trickster who thought everything was hilarious.

OH! Fresh meat! Well, fresh LIGHT. Former meat. Newly ejected. Still shaped like humans! The presence zipped around us—if "around" meant anything here. *I'm Zippy. I died in 1823. Carriage accident. Very dramatic. Haven't incarnated since. Too much fun here. Watch this!*

Zippy transformed. Became horse. Then carriage. Then wheel. Then concept of "accident." Then back to vague human-shaped presence.

See? No form constraints! I can be ANYTHING! Or NOTHING! Or the IDEA of something! It's amazing!

You've been here 200 years, Terry observed.

Time is fake but yes, approximately 200 flesh-years. Maybe more. I stopped counting. Who needs counting when you can be a wheel?

George rippled. *Zippy's enthusiasm is contagious. Also exhausting. But he makes valid point. Between-space allows consciousness to practice form without commitment. Excellent learning environment.*

I tried something. Thought about being bird. Felt myself shift. Not into bird body—into bird-concept. The idea of bird. The essence of flight without wings.

It worked.

I'm bird!

You're bird-adjacent, Seventeen calculated. *Actual bird-form requires more specificity. You're currently existing as bird-probability. Quantum superposition of all possible birds.*

That's amazing!

That's basic between-space physics. Form without matter. Concept without constraint. You're consciousness without flesh limitations. You can be anything you can conceptualize.

Lucia was experimenting too. I felt her shift into... tree? Ocean? Something complex.

I'm trying to be forest but I keep becoming individual trees.

Start smaller, the maternal presence advised. *Become leaf. Then tree. Then forest. Build complexity gradually.*

Terry was laughing. Not sound. Just rippling presence-laughter. *I've meditated for forty years trying to achieve formlessness. And here I am, formless, and all I want is to practice being THINGS. The irony is delicious.*

This is fun, I admitted. *But we need to get home. Our bodies. Fin's holding anchor. We need to find the connection.*

Connection exists where attention exists, the maternal presence said. *Right now, your attention is HERE. With us. Learning. Playing. To return, move attention to THERE. To bodies. To Fin. To Michigan clearing. Become similar to that place. Then distance collapses.*

How do we move attention?

Practice. Experiment. Feel toward home. When you feel connection, follow it.

That's vague.

That's accurate. Between-space has no GPS. Only feeling. Only similarity. Only attention. You find home by remembering what home feels like.

George settled beside us—if "beside" meant anything. *I can help. I've been here long enough to understand navigation. Think of specific memory. From your bodies. Something strong. Emotional. Recent.*

I thought about Kael. Three weeks of knowing him. The way his ancient consciousness looked at me like I was something precious. The feeling of his hand in mine.

Connection sparked. Faint. Like distant lighthouse through fog.

There! George approved. *That's the thread. That's the feeling-path. Follow that and you'll find body. Maybe. Eventually. If you don't get distracted.*

Distracted by what?

Zippy laughed. *By EVERYTHING! Between-space is FULL of interesting places! Lost souls! Pocket dimensions! Time-folders! Reality-benders! Beings who exist across multiple dimensions simultaneously! It's like cosmic amusement park!*

We don't have time for amusement parks,

Lucia said.

You have all the time, Seventeen calculated. *And no time. Simultaneously. Quantum superposition of temporal states.*

That's not helpful.

It's accurate.

Another presence approached. This one felt... official. Bureaucratic. Like cosmic DMV worker who took their job very seriously.

Excuse me. New arrivals. You need to register. Fill out forms. Declare your intention. Are you staying or passing through? If staying, what dimensional sector? If passing, what destination coordinates? Please have your consciousness identification ready.

We don't have forms, Terry said.

Then you'll need to fill out the form-request form. Which requires form B-7 to authorize. Which requires proving you exist. Which is difficult when you're in between-space because existence here is optional.

Is this real? I asked George.

Harold's real. He really does have forms. Nobody fills them out. He's been trying to organize between-space for three thousand years. It's adorable. Futile, but adorable.

I WILL achieve proper filing structure! Harold insisted. *Even if it takes ten thousand years! Consciousness cannot exist in chaos! We need SYSTEMS!*

Sure, Harold, Zippy said. Patronizing but affectionate. *You keep working on that. Meanwhile, these three need navigation practice. Harold, do you have form for that?*

Navigation practice requires form N-12, subsection 4, with addendum for emergency returns. I'll retrieve it. Please wait here. Or there. Or wherever you are. Location is ambiguous in between-space which is WHY WE NEED BETTER FILING SYSTEMS.

Harold whooshed away. If whooshing was possible without movement.

He's enthusiastic, Terry observed.

He's coping, the maternal presence said gently. *Structure helps some consciousness deal with formlessness. Let him have his forms. They hurt no one.*

Speaking of hurt, Lucia said, *what happens if we CAN'T find our way back? What happens to our bodies?*

Bodies eventually fail, Seventeen calculated. *Three to seven days without consciousness. Then biological death. Then you're officially dead and get processed through normal reincarnation protocols. Then you forget everything, including that you're currently existing here, and start over.*

That's what we're trying to avoid.

Then you should practice navigation. Time is fake but urgency is real. Paradox, but accurate.

I focused on the thread. The connection to home. It was there. Faint but present. Like following smell of coffee through morning fog.

I can feel Michigan. The clearing. Fin's anchor. It's... that direction.

There's no direction here, George said.

There's similarity-direction. Follow it.

We moved. Not through space. Through similarity. Becoming more like "consciousness that belongs in Michigan" and less like "consciousness that exists everywhere."

The nothing changed. Not visually. But texture-wise. Like moving from velvet-absence to cotton-absence. Subtle shift.

You're navigating! Zippy approved. *Look at the baby lights go! So precious!*

We're not babies, I protested.

In between-space years, you're fetuses. Newly arrived. Adorable. I want to pinch your non-existent cheeks.

Please don't.

The nothing rippled. Something massive was moving. Not presence. Not entity. Something bigger.

Oh dear, George said. *That's a time-folder. You might want to avoid—*

Too late. We folded.

Space—if it was space—bent around itself. The nothing became something. The silent place became... loud? Bright? Full of sensory input that didn't exist but somehow did?

And suddenly we were... elsewhere.

Not Michigan. Not clearing. Not home.

Somewhere else.

Somewhere with buildings made of stone. Streets paved with cobblestone. People in long dresses and top hats.

People who couldn't see us because we weren't physical.

We were ghosts. Consciousness without form. Observing physical reality from outside physical reality.

Where are we? Lucia asked.

When are we? Terry corrected.

A newspaper blew past. I tried to read it. Couldn't focus. Letters sliding around. But caught date: 1889.

We're in the past, I said. *We folded wrong. The time-folder sent us to 1889.*

Where though? Terry was looking around. *This city. These buildings. That looks like—oh. Oh no.*

What?

That's Park Row. That's City Hall. That's— he gestured at skyline, *—that's New York. 1889. We folded through time AND space. We're in wrong when and wrong where.*

Can we fold back?

I don't know!

George's presence appeared. Rippling with amusement. *Time-folders are tricky. You'll need to feel toward your proper time. Your proper when. Become similar to 2026 instead of 1889. Then fold forward.*

How?

Same way you were navigating. Attention. Feeling. Memory. Think about something specific to your time. Something that didn't exist in 1889. Something uniquely yours. Then become similar to that instead of similar to this.

I thought about my phone. My quantum-enhanced perception. The consciousness networks. Things that didn't exist in 1889.

Connection shifted. Time felt different. Less solid.

It's working! Lucia said.

We folded.

Reality bent.

And suddenly we were... somewhere else again.

Modern buildings. Cars. But wrong. Different. The style was off. Architecture I didn't recognize.

When are we now?

Terry was reading signs. "Impossible Burger." "Tesla Supercharger." "Visit Mars: Tourism Packages Available."

2047, he said. *We folded too far forward. We're twenty years in our future.*

At least we're getting closer, Lucia observed.

This is harder than I thought, I admitted.

Everything worth doing is, Terry said. *Let's try again. Think about something specific to 2026. Something that exists then but not in 2047.*

I thought about Kael. Three weeks of knowing him. His ancient consciousness meeting my seventeen years. That specific moment. That specific time.

Connection locked. Stronger.

We folded.

And this time—

This time we got close

CHAPTER THIRTY-ONE

Chapter 31

CHAPTER THIRTY-ONE: ADVENTURES IN NOWHERE LAND (Rhea's POV)

We folded again.

This time we landed in... purple?

Not purple space. Not purple place. Just... purple. Pure purple that existed as environment instead of color.

What the hell? Lucia asked.

We're in someone's pocket dimension, Terry said. His consciousness recognizing the pattern. *Consciousness that got tired of normal reality and built their own. Personal universe. Custom physics.*

A presence appeared. Sleepy. Annoyed at being disturbed.

You're in my purple. Why are you in my purple? I built this purple specifically to avoid visitors.

We're lost, I explained. *Trying to navigate back to 2026 Michigan. Keep folding wrong.*

You folded into my purple. That's extremely rude. Do you know how long it took to get the purple this exact shade? Seventeen thousand years. And you're disrupting it with your not-purple presence.

We're sorry—

Sorry doesn't fix purple contamination. You'll need to leave. Immediately. Go be not-purple somewhere else.

The presence shoved us. Not physically. Dimensionally. Like cosmic bouncer ejecting drunk patrons.

We folded.

Landed in screaming.

Not sound. Sensation. Millions of consciousness all screaming simultaneously. Not in pain. In... confusion? Desperation? Need?

What is this? Lucia asked.

George appeared. *Oh dear. You folded into the lost souls sector. This is where consciousness goes when it dies traumatically and doesn't know it's dead. They're calling for help. For guidance. For anything that feels real.*

The lost souls swarmed toward us. Not attacking. Clutching. Desperate.

HELP ME FIND MY DAUGHTER

I DON'T REMEMBER HOW I DIED

WHERE IS MY BODY

AM I DREAMING

PLEASE TELL ME THIS ISN'T REAL

They were overwhelming. Thousands of them. Maybe millions. All lost. All confused. All clinging to us because we were the first solid presence they'd encountered.

We can't help them all, Terry said. His consciousness straining under the weight of desperate need.

You can help some, the maternal guide appeared. She'd followed us. *Choose carefully. Those you can actually assist. Tell them truth. They're dead. They need to move on. To process. To accept. Then they can navigate properly.*

I focused on one. Young. Female. Terrified.

You're dead, I told her. Gently but clearly. *Car accident. Three days ago. You died instantly. Didn't suffer. But you're clinging to confusion instead of accepting.*

I can't be dead. I have children. I have—

You HAD children. Past tense. Your body stopped. Your consciousness continues. But you can't return to that life. Can only move forward to next.

I don't want next. I want NOW.

Now is over. I'm sorry. But clinging to over just makes you stuck. You need to let go. Accept. Then you can navigate to what comes next.

She resisted. Then slowly, slowly released. The confusion dissolved. She stopped screaming. Started processing.

Thank you, she whispered. Then folded away toward wherever reincarnation processing happened.

Lucia was helping another. Terry was helping three simultaneously. We couldn't save them all. But we could help some. Give them truth. Let them move on.

After what felt like hours—but probably wasn't because time was fake here—we'd helped maybe fifty. Out of millions.

That's all we can do, the maternal guide said. *You did well. Now navigate away before more swarm you. Lost souls are infinite. Help is finite.*

We folded.

Landed in... geometry?

Not shapes. Pure mathematics. Consciousness existing as equations. Theorems proving themselves. Calculations running without calculators.

Seventeen was here. In his natural habitat.

Welcome to the mathematics sector. Population: those who find numbers more comfortable than form. Duration: eternal. Beauty: provable.

We're still lost, I said.

All consciousness is lost. That's the fundamental theorem. Location is illusion. Navigation is accepting illusion while moving through it anyway. Paradox, but accurate.

That's not helpful!

It's true. Truth doesn't require helpfulness.

A new presence approached. Enthusiastic. Bouncing—if bouncing existed without space.

ZIPPY! George's presence rippled with affection. *Stop harassing the newcomers with your geometric experiments.*

I'm not harassing! I'm DEMONSTRATING! Watch!

Zippy became triangle. Then circle. Then tesseract. Then the concept of "rotation" without having anything to rotate.

THIS IS AMAZING! I can be MATH! Pure math! No form! Just relationship and ratio!

You've been able to do that for 200 years, George observed.

YES BUT IT'S STILL EXCITING EVERY TIME!

Zippy reformed into vaguely human presence. Settled beside us.

You three are fun. You're lost but you're TRYING. Most consciousness that gets this lost just gives up. Accepts between-space as permanent. But you're folding all over the place! It's adorable! Like watching baby birds learn to fly but through dimensions instead of air!

We need to get home, Lucia said. *Our bodies. Our time. 2026 Michigan. Can you help?*

I can TRY! I'm excellent at navigation! Terrible at arriving where I intend but excellent at the journey! Follow me!

That's not reassuring, Terry said.

It's honest! Which is better! Come on!

Zippy folded. We followed. Because what else were we going to do?

We landed in music.

Not sound. Pure music. Consciousness existing as harmony and melody and rhythm without instruments.

This is beautiful, I said.

This is the artistic sector! Where consciousness that loved creating becomes the creation! Look!

Beings of pure color were painting reality. Beings of pure sound were composing existence. Beings of pure movement were dancing dimensions into shapes that hurt to perceive but felt correct anyway.

I spent fifty years here, Zippy said. *Became symphony. Very fulfilling. But missed conversation. Art is wonderful but lonely when you ARE the art instead of creating it.*

We folded again. And again. And again.

Through the collector's dimension—where consciousness hoarded experiences like dragons hoarding gold.

Through the philosopher's quadrant—where beings debated existence while existing purely to debate.

Through the garden realm—where consciousness manifested as living thought-plants that grew through attention instead of soil.

You're getting better at this! Zippy approved. *Your folding is more intentional! Less random! Soon you'll be able to navigate deliberately!*

Soon isn't helping, Lucia said. *Fin's been holding anchor for... how long?*

Time is fake, Seventeen reminded us. He'd joined the journey. Found us mathematically interesting. *Your brother experiences linear time. You experience attention-time. Duration is relative.*

That means we could be gone for days while he's been waiting minutes, Terry said. *Or we could be gone for minutes while he's been waiting days.*

Exactly. Quantum superposition of temporal experience.

I hate this,

I said.

That's fair, George agreed. He'd been following too. Helpful guide. *Between-space is confusing. But you're learning. Each fold teaches you something. About navigation. About consciousness. About what you actually are when form is optional.*

Harold appeared. Still clutching his forms.

EXCUSE ME! You still haven't registered! I've been following you across seventeen dimensions and you STILL haven't filled out proper paperwork! This is UNACCEPTABLE!

We're busy being lost, I said.

Being lost requires form L-9! With proper signatures! And destination declarations!

We don't know our destination!

Then you need form D-Unknown! Which requires proving you exist in state of not-knowing! Which requires epistemological verification! I have forms for that!

Harold, George said gently. *They're trying to get home. Let them navigate. They can fill out forms AFTER they return to their bodies.*

But protocol—

Isn't more important than consciousness reunion with flesh. Let them go.

Harold rippled with frustration. But accepted. *FINE. But when you return successfully, you OWE me forms. All of them. Properly filled out. With SIGNATURES.*

We promise, Terry said. Lying smoothly.

We folded.

This time we landed somewhere familiar. The nothing. The silent place. Where we'd started.

We're back at the beginning, Lucia said. *We've been folding in circles.*

Not circles, Zippy corrected. *Spirals! You're getting closer to home with each fold! Watch!*

He transformed into visual representation of our journey. Spiral pattern. Each fold getting tighter. Closer to center. Center being... Michigan. 2026. Our bodies.

You're almost there! One or two more folds! Maybe three! Possibly seven! Navigation is imprecise!

How do we fold accurately? I asked. *How do we hit exact when and where?*

You feel for the most specific thing, the maternal guide said. She'd never left. Just been quietly accompanying. *Not Michigan. Not 2026. Not even your bodies. But the EXACT MOMENT you left. The specific feeling. Fin's anchor. Kael's concern. The clearing's energy. The second you touched the barrier. Become similar to that exact moment. Then distance and time collapse. You arrive when you left because you never really left. Just forgot where you were.*

I focused. On Fin's presence. On Kael's hand in mine before we folded out. On the smell of Michigan forest. On the generator hum. On the exact feeling of that specific second.

Lucia was doing same. I felt her consciousness aligning with mine. Both of us focusing on identical moment.

Terry joined us. Three-way focus. Three consciousnesses becoming similar to one specific point in space-time.

That's it! George approved. *That's navigation! Now fold!*

We folded.

And this time—

This time it felt different.

The nothing was dissolving. Form was returning. Physical sensation approaching.

WAIT! Zippy shouted. *Take me with you!*

What?

I want to incarnate again! You're going to physical reality! To Earth! To bodies and beer and sensory experience! I've been formless for 200 years and suddenly I want to be SPECIFIC again! Take me! Please!

We don't know how to take consciousness with us! Lucia said.

Just grab me! Metaphorically! Think about me while folding! Consciousness can hitchhike if the navigator allows it!

This is terrible idea, Terry observed.

BEST TERRIBLE IDEA! DO IT!

Against all judgment, I thought about Zippy while folding. Allowed his presence to attach to our navigation. Brought him along for the ride.

We folded.

Physical sensation crashed back. Weight. Breathing. Heartbeat. The horrible wonderful reality of having body again.

I gasped. Eyes opening. The clearing. Michigan. Generators humming. Fin's face above me, crying with relief.

YOU'RE BACK!

Beside me, Lucia was waking. And Terry. All three of us returning to flesh after adventure through nowhere.

Kael was holding my hand. Had been holding it the whole time. "You were gone for four hours. We thought—"

"Four hours?" I croaked. Voice rusty from disuse. "Felt like days. Maybe weeks. Time was weird."

And then, in the center of the clearing, reality hiccuped.

Something was manifesting. Badly. Very badly.

Zippy was incarnating.

And he'd forgotten how bodies worked.

He appeared as... child? Adult? Elderly person? All three flickering rapidly. Naked. Obviously. Because everyone who manifested badly manifested naked.

"I'M HERE!" Zippy announced. In actual voice. Speaking for first time in 200 years. "I'M PHYSICAL! I HAVE MEAT! THIS IS—" he looked down, "—WHY AM I FLICKERING? HOW DO I STOP FLICKERING? ALSO WHY IS GRAVITY SO AGGRESSIVE?"

He fell over. Stood up. Fell over again. Couldn't decide what age to be.

"Who," Morrison asked slowly, "is the naked person who can't decide how old they are?"

"That's Zippy," I said. "We brought him back. Accidentally. Mostly accidentally."

"I WANTED TO COME!" Zippy insisted. Flickering between child-voice and adult-voice. "I MISSED BEING SPECIFIC! Also I want to try BEER! George said beer was EXCELLENT!"

Mist appeared. Flowing around Zippy with obvious delight.

ANOTHER FLUID CONSCIOUSNESS! But choosing form! Fascinating! Hello new friend! I am Mist! You are chaotic! We will get along wonderfully!

"I LIKE YOU!" Zippy announced. "YOU'RE LIKE ME BUT LESS COMMITTED TO SPECIFICITY! Can you teach me how to stop flickering?"

First: choose age. Commit. Second: accept gravity. Third: acquire clothing. Nakedness acceptable in between-space. Less acceptable in Michigan.

Jenkins was already getting jacket. Again. "Why do cosmic entities keep manifesting naked in front of me?"

"Because the universe has sense of humor," Terry said. His voice rough but amused. "And that humor is mostly about embarrassing federal agents."

Zippy accepted jacket. Flickered one more time. Then stabilized. Young adult. Maybe twenty-five. Enthusiastic smile. Eyes that suggested 200 years of formless experience meeting first day of having body again.

"I'm STAYING!" he announced. "I'm going to learn meat! And beer! And GRAVITY! This is BEST DECISION I'VE MADE IN 200 YEARS!"

Ansel was processing this. "You brought back passenger from between-space."

"We didn't mean to," Lucia said. "He asked. We said yes without thinking."

"That's terrible navigation protocol."

"We were LOST! We made DECISIONS! Some were QUESTIONABLE!" I was sitting up now. Body sore. Head spinning. But alive. Back. Whole.

Kathleen was crying. Holding Lucia. "You were gone. Your bodies were empty, the same as with Ansel when he left his body sometimes. We thought—"

"We know. But we're back. And we learned... so much. About navigation. About consciousness. About what we actually are when form is optional." I looked at Kael. "And I really want to kiss you but I'm not sure my body remembers how kissing works yet."

He laughed. Actually laughed. "Take your time. Your body will remember."

Zippy was testing walking. Fell. Stood. Walked three steps. Fell again.

"GRAVITY IS CHALLENGING! How do meat-people do this CONSTANTLY?"

"Practice," Fin said. He was glowing. Still anchor. Still lighthouse. "You just spent 200 years without physics. Give yourself time."

"I don't WANT time! I want BEER!"

I support this goal, Mist agreed. *Short's Brewery has excellent beer. Also sandwiches. We should go immediately.*

"We just got back from dimensional crisis," Morrison observed.

"Which is why we need beer," Terry said. Standing slowly. Testing his rebuilt body that had just spent unknown time as pure consciousness. "Zippy's right. After adventure in nowhere-land, we need something that grounds us. Beer grounds. Sandwiches ground. Sitting in brewery surrounded by normal humans doing normal things grounds."

Ansel was studying the three of us. "You learned navigation."

"We learned CHAOS," I corrected. "Navigation was incidental. But yes. We can fold. We can navigate. We can exist between flesh and light. We touched the barrier modification and it kicked us out instead of dissolving us. We turned assassination attempt into education."

"And acquired passenger," Kathleen added, looking at Zippy who was now trying to figure out how shirts worked.

"CLOTHING IS COMPLICATED! Why so many HOLES? Where do LIMBS go?"

Jenkins was helping. Patiently. "Arms through sleeves. Head through neck hole. Yes, that one."

"THIS IS DIFFICULT! I respect meat-people more now!"

The clearing was chaos. Three consciousness recently returned from between-space adventure. One enthusiastic 200-year-old entity learning to be physical. Two cosmic beings trying to teach incarnation basics. Federal agents processing that their lives had become cosmic comedy.

And Fin, the anchor, who'd held lighthouse for four hours straight. Exhausted but smiling.

"Welcome back," he said to his sisters.

"Thanks for being the light," Lucia said. "We saw you. Across all the dimensions. Across all the lost souls and pocket realities and mathematics sectors. You were there. Constant. Shining. We followed you home."

"That's what anchors do."

Zippy had successfully dressed. Was now trying to understand how legs worked without falling.

"I'M WALKING! LOOK! THREE STEPS! FOUR! FI—" he fell. "—okay, five was ambitious."

You're doing excellent, Mist encouraged. *Tomorrow we practice beer. Today we practice gravity.*

"Can I practice both SIMULTANEOUSLY?"

That's advanced technique. But we can try.

Bill was going to love this. Local cop meeting enthusiastic cosmic entity who couldn't walk straight and kept forgetting what age to be.

The germination was accelerating.

We'd survived barrier modification. Learned dimensional navigation. Acquired chaotic passenger who wanted beer.

Two days until Ancient Powers decided.

And we'd just proven that consciousness could survive separation from flesh. Could navigate between-space. Could return home despite impossible odds.

The Council's assassination attempt had failed spectacularly.

And we'd learned more in four hours than most consciousness learned in lifetimes.

"Short's?" I suggested.

"Short's," everyone agreed.

Even Zippy. "WHAT'S SHORT'S?"

"Heaven," Terry said. "If heaven served beer and sandwiches and tolerated cosmic chaos."

"I LIKE HEAVEN!"

We loaded into vehicles. Zippy riding with Mist and Morrison because someone needed to prevent him from accidentally becoming wheel while driving.

The adventure in nowhere-land was over.

But the adventure in everywhere-land was just beginning.

And honestly? After 200 years of formlessness, Zippy had earned his beer.

Even if he fell down seventeen times trying to drink it.

Chapter Thirty-Two

Chapter 32

CHAPTER THIRTY-TWO: CHAOS AT SHORT'S (Kael's POV)

"Can he ride in vehicle without becoming vehicle?" Morrison asked, looking at Zippy who was currently trying to understand how doors worked.

"I'll TRY!" Zippy said enthusiastically. "But no PROMISES! Sometimes I get EXCITED and forget what I am!"

"That's not reassuring."

"It's HONEST!"

We loaded into vehicles. Zippy rode with Morrison, Mist, and Torres. I heard Morrison muttering something about "federal agent training did not prepare me for babysitting enthusiastic consciousness that might become wheel."

The drive to Bellaire took seven minutes. During which Zippy flickered three times—briefly became seat, then steering wheel, then concept of "forward motion"—before Mist gently reminded him that maintaining form was important for not terrifying drivers.

You're doing well, Mist encouraged. *Only three transformations. Very restrained.*

"I'm TRYING! Meat is HARD! Everything has RULES!"

We parked at Fischer's lot. Walked toward Short's. Zippy walked reasonably well now—only fell twice—but kept flickering between ages. Twenty-five. Forty. Seventeen. Sixty. Back to twenty-five.

"Pick an age," Lucia suggested. "Any age. Just stay there."

"But they're ALL interesting! Why CHOOSE?"

"Because otherwise you're going to flicker in restaurant and scare people."

"Is scaring people BAD?"

"Generally yes."

"Noted! I will try to NOT scare people! Probably!"

Bill was already at Short's. His regular table bill was straight, he did not like beer. Coffee steaming. He looked up as our group entered—three teenagers recently back from dimensional adventure, ancient Watchers, federal agents, and enthusiastic entity who couldn't decide what age to be.

"Kathleen," Bill said carefully. "Your friends are multiplying."

"This is Zippy," Kathleen introduced. "He's... new."

"I DIED IN 1823!" Zippy announced cheerfully. "CARRIAGE ACCIDENT! Very DRAMATIC! Then I stayed in between-space for 200 YEARS and now I'm BACK and everything is AMAZING and also CONFUSING!"

Bill sipped his coffee. "Of course you did. Welcome to Bellaire. Try not to flicker too much. Tourists get nervous."

We claimed our usual round table, carefully reserved. Zippy sat carefully. Practicing sitting. Forgot halfway through and flickered into chair before remembering he was supposed to be person sitting IN chair not chair itself.

"I'm CHAIR! Wait. NO. I'm PERSON." He reformed. "This is CHALLENGING!"

Jenny approached. Same server. Early twenties. Professional smile that had seen enough weird to roll with it.

"You folks back already? Didn't expect to see you so—" she noticed Zippy, who was currently flickering between young man and elderly woman, "—is your friend okay?"

"He's fine," Rhea assured her. "Just... jet lag. Bad jet lag."

"From WHERE?"

"Dimensional travel," Zippy said helpfully. "I was FORMLESS for 200 YEARS and now I have MEAT and it's WONDERFUL but also I keep FORGETTING WHAT I AM!"

He flickered. Became monkey. Briefly.

Jenny stared. "Did he just—"

"Optical illusion," Terry said smoothly. "Exhaustion. We've all been up too long. Could we get menus?"

"Sure. Menus. Right." Jenny distributed menus while Zippy reformed into young adult. "Should I... should I get a manager?"

"Unnecessary," Kathleen said. "We'll be fine. Just food and beer and normal lunch."

"Your normal isn't my normal," Jenny muttered. But she left to get drinks.

Mist had been flowing around the restaurant. Exploring. Curious about everything. He appeared briefly in the decorative plant—optimizing its chlorophyll production.

This establishment has excellent energy. Also interesting food smells. May I explore kitchen?

"Please don't optimize the kitchen without permission," I said.

Noted. Will optimize subtly.

He flowed toward the kitchen. Unseen by most. Optimizing as he went.

Zippy was studying the menu. "What's BURGER?"

"Ground meat. Cooked. On bread."

"MEAT ON BREAD? That's GENIUS! I want TEN!"

"Start with one," Lucia suggested.

"ONE. Yes. RESTRAINT. I understand RESTRAINT." He paused. "What's RESTRAINT?"

Terry laughed. Two weeks of being rebuilt and he was enjoying chaos. "Restraint is when you want ten of something but only get one."

"That sounds TERRIBLE! Why would anyone CHOOSE that?"

"Because eating ten burgers makes you sick."

"What's SICK?"

"You'll find out if you eat ten burgers."

Zippy considered this. "I will TRUST you. One burger. But ENTHUSIASTICALLY."

Jenny returned with drinks. Set them carefully on table. Beer for most. Water for those who preferred it.

Zippy stared at his beer like it was scientific miracle.

"This is BEER? The consciousness-altering fermented grain Mist described?"

"That's beer," Fin confirmed.

"It's BEAUTIFUL." Zippy reached for glass. Picked it up. Studied it. "How do I CONSUME?"

"You drink it."

"DRINK. Yes. I remember DRINKING. I was WHALE once. Whales drink OCEAN." He attempted to drink beer like whale drinking ocean. Tipped entire glass into his face at once.

Beer everywhere. Table. Floor. Zippy's shirt. Very little actually in his mouth.

"That was INCORRECT!" Zippy announced, dripping.

"Slightly," Terry agreed. "Try sipping. Small amounts. Through mouth. Not whale-style."

Jenny had witnessed this. "I'll get towels."

"And another beer," Fin added. "He'll need practice."

At the next table, tourists were staring. Zippy had just poured beer on his face while flickering briefly into elderly woman.

"Is that person okay?" someone asked.

"Jet lag," I said. "Very bad jet lag."

Mist appeared in the kitchen. We heard Sarah—Kathleen's daughter, the cook—exclaim "What the HELL?"

Then quieter: "Did the STEAM just optimize my marinara?"

Yes, Mist confirmed. Appearing in her tomato sauce. *Your ratio was good but not optimal. I adjusted. You're welcome.*

"The steam is TALKING to me."

Yes. I am Mist. I optimize things. Your marinara will now be 23 percent more delicious. Also your pizza dough needed more time to rise. I accelerated the yeast. You'll notice improved texture.

Sarah appeared at our table. Looked at Kathleen. "Mom. The steam entity is in my kitchen optimizing my recipes."

"That's Mist," Kathleen said. "He does that. Just accept it. The food will be better."

"The STEAM is making my food BETTER?"

Yes, Mist said, appearing in Sarah's coffee cup. *Also your coffee was temperature-suboptimal. Fixed that too. You're welcome.*

Sarah stared at her coffee. Which was now perfectly optimal temperature. "This is my life now. Steam entities optimizing my kitchen."

"Could be worse," Bill observed. "Could be monkey-person pouring beer on his face."

Zippy had received second beer. Was attempting sipping. With marginally better success. Got maybe 30 percent in his mouth instead of 0 percent.

"I'm IMPROVING!" he announced proudly.

Then forgot what age he was. Flickered. Young man. Child. Teenager. Middle-aged woman. Pig. Brief pig.

The tourists at the next table screamed slightly.

"SORRY!" Zippy reformed. Young adult. "I got EXCITED about BEER!"

"Why did that man turn into a pig?" someone asked.

"He didn't," Terry said. "You're experiencing altitude sickness. Bellaire's elevation is... very high. Causes hallucinations."

"We're at 600 feet elevation."

"Very high. Extremely high. Should drink more water."

Jenny returned with towels and food. Set plates down carefully. Trying very hard to maintain professional composure while Zippy examined his burger like it was alien artifact.

"This is MEAT ON BREAD with VEGETABLES and CONDIMENTS?" He was analyzing it from every angle. "The CONSTRUCTION is ELEGANT!"

"Just eat it," Rhea suggested.

"EAT. Yes." Zippy picked up burger. Attempted bite. Flickered halfway through. Became burger briefly. Was both eating burger and being burger simultaneously for approximately two seconds.

Reformed. Confused.

"I think I was FOOD?"

"You were," Lucia confirmed. "Try staying PERSON while eating."

"Noted! Remaining PERSON is IMPORTANT!"

At the counter, Bill was watching this while drinking his coffee. Which Mist had optimized without permission.

"This is the best coffee I've had here," Bill observed.

You're welcome, Mist said from the foam.

Bill didn't even flinch. "Thank you, steam entity."

My name is Mist.

"Thank you, Mist."

Sarah appeared again. "The yeast just told me it appreciated the acceleration."

"Yeast doesn't talk," Kathleen said.

"The YEAST just THANKED the STEAM ENTITY for making it rise FASTER."

Yeast is surprisingly polite, Mist confirmed.

"I need a drink," Sarah said.

"We have beer," Jenny offered.

"Strong beer. Very strong beer."

Zippy had successfully eaten three bites of burger without becoming burger. Was very proud.

"I'm CONSUMING! Look! CHEWING! SWALLOWING! DIGESTING! This is REMARKABLE!" He flickered with excitement. Became young woman. "Oh! I'm FEMALE now! That's DIFFERENT!"

"Pick a form," Morrison said. Voice carrying federal authority that suggested this was order, not request. "Any form. Male. Female. Don't care. Just STAY there."

"You're NO FUN!" But Zippy reformed. Young man. Mid-twenties. Stayed there. "FINE. I will be THIS. For NOW. But LATER I might try being SQUIRREL!"

"No squirrels at the table," Kathleen said firmly.

"FINE."

The tourists were leaving. Rapidly. One of them was muttering something about "bad mushrooms" and "never eating at weird Michigan restaurants again."

"We're losing customers," Sarah observed.

"We're gaining STORIES!" Zippy countered. "They'll tell EVERYONE about the restaurant where person became pig! Free MARKETING!"

"That's not the marketing we want."

Mist appeared in someone's pizza box as they opened it. The person—local, maybe thirty—stared.

Hello! Your pizza smells EXCELLENT! I optimized the cheese distribution! You're welcome!

The person closed the box. Opened it again. Mist was still there.

The pepperoni placement was also suboptimal. I corrected it. Enjoy!

"The... the steam is in my pizza."

"That's Mist," Fin called over. "He does that. The pizza will taste better."

"The STEAM OPTIMIZED MY PEPPERONI?"

Yes. Also your crust needed 3 percent more browning. Fixed that retroactively. Time is flexible when you're not constrained by physics.

The person ate a slice. Paused. "This is the best pizza I've ever had."

You're welcome!

"I'm questioning my sanity but also enjoying this pizza very much."

Sanity is overrated. Pizza is eternal.

Bill was laughing. Actually laughing. Century of living in Bellaire and cosmic chaos at Short's Brewery was somehow the highlight.

"Kathleen, your friends are the weirdest thing to happen to this town in fifty years."

"That's probably accurate."

Zippy had finished his burger. Was attempting to drink beer properly. Got maybe 60 percent in mouth. Significant improvement.

"I'm LEARNING! Soon I'll be EXPERT at BEER!"

He flickered with enthusiasm. Became the concept of "celebration" for two seconds. Everyone at the table felt briefly, inexplicably happy.

Reformed.

"SORRY! Emotions make me UNSTABLE!"

"Emotions make everyone unstable," Terry observed. "You're just more obvious about it."

Our food arrived. Everyone eating. Mist occasionally appearing in someone's meal to optimize it. Zippy practicing maintaining consistent form while consuming. Bill processing cosmic chaos over coffee.

Sarah returned. "Mom. Seriously. What IS all this?"

Kathleen smiled. "This is consciousness evolution, sweetie. This is what happens when reality gets flexible and beings who forgot what they were start remembering. This is the germination."

"And it involves steam entities and people who can't decide what age to be?"

"Apparently yes."

"Okay." Sarah sat down. Uninvited. Needed to process. "Okay. I can handle this. I've handled weirder. Probably. Maybe. I'll think of something."

Mist appeared in her water glass. *Your mother is Nordic warrior who forgot. Your grandfather is commander learning to remember. You're part of lineage that's been ripening for generations. Also your marinara is now perfect. You're welcome.*

Sarah drank the Mist-optimized water. "The steam entity just told me my mom is alien warrior and my marinara is perfect. This is FINE. Everything is FINE."

"You're handling this well," Morrison observed.

"I'm a COOK in BELLAIRE MICHIGAN and STEAM ENTITIES are OPTIMIZING MY KITCHEN while PEOPLE FLICKER INTO ANIMALS. I'm handling this by NOT THINKING ABOUT IT TOO HARD."

"That's healthy," Terry said.

Zippy had successfully drunk half a beer without pouring it on his face. Was celebrating by flickering into various celebratory concepts before remembering to maintain human form.

"I LIKE BEER!" he announced. "I like FOOD! I like GRAVITY! I like MEAT! This was EXCELLENT DECISION!"

I'm proud of you, Mist said. Appearing in Zippy's beer foam. *You're learning physicality. Soon you'll maintain form for entire hours instead of entire minutes.*

"That's the GOAL! Entire HOURS! Maybe DAYS! Eventually FOREVER!"

"Forever is ambitious," Lucia observed.

"I'm AMBITIOUS ENTITY!"

The brewery was somehow functioning despite cosmic chaos. Tourists had fled but locals remained. Watching. Processing. Accepting that their quiet town had become epicenter of something impossible.

Jenny approached the table. "So. Should I expect this to keep happening? People becoming pigs? Steam in pizza boxes? General weirdness?"

"Probably," Rhea admitted.

"Okay. Just wanted to know." Jenny refilled drinks. "My mom always said Bellaire was special. Guess she was right."

"Your mom was wise," Kathleen said.

"She also saw UFOs over Torch Lake in 1987. Thought she was crazy. Maybe she wasn't."

"She definitely wasn't," Ansel confirmed. "Those were ours. Nordic patrol. Checking on germination progress. Sorry if we scared her."

Jenny processed this. "The UFOs were YOURS?"

"Yes."

"And you're...?"

"Nordic commander who walked into human body to save his brother. Forgot what I was. Remembered recently. It's complicated."

"EVERYTHING here is complicated!" Zippy agreed. Raising his beer. Spilling some. "But DELICIOUS!"

We finished lunch. Mist optimizing everyone's food. Zippy maintaining form for record seventeen minutes straight. Bill accepting that his retirement would involve cosmic entities and beer.

When we left, Sarah was at the kitchen window. Watching her mother—century-old Nordic warrior—walk out with federal agents and cosmic chaos entities.

"Mom seems happy," she observed to Jenny.

"Your Kathleens always been weird. Guess now we know why."

Back at vehicles, Zippy attempted to get in the car without becoming car. Succeeded. Mostly.

"I'm IMPROVING!" he announced. "Soon I'll be EXPERT at MEAT!"

I'm proud, Mist said.

The drive back to Pleasant Valley was chaotic but successful. Zippy only flickered twice. Once into steering wheel (Morrison yelped). Once into concept of "roadtrip" (everyone felt briefly adventurous).

And somewhere in New York, the Council was meeting again. Assuming the four ambassadors were still comatose. Bodies empty. Consciousness dissolved.

They had no idea we'd been training. Learning. Navigating dimensions while they thought we were dying.

The assassination attempt hadn't just failed.

It had become our greatest teacher.

And chaos entity named Zippy was our graduation present.

Two days until Ancient Powers decided.

And we'd just proven consciousness could survive anything.

Even lunch at Short's Brewery.

In the farthest corner of shorts sat a surly figure, staring over a large menu while whispering in his phone, talking to New York of what he was watching in the Brewery.

Chapter Thirty-Three

Chapter 33

CHAPTER THIRTY-THREE: THE DIVERSION (Kael's POV)

We returned to Pleasant Valley as the sun was setting.

The drive back had been uneventful. Zippy had maintained form for the entire journey—remarkable progress for entity who'd been formless for 200 years. Morrison seemed almost disappointed there hadn't been more chaos.

"I was prepared for him to become transmission," Morrison admitted. "Had whole protocol planned."

"I'm LEARNING!" Zippy said proudly. "Soon I'll be EXPERT at MEAT!"

We pulled into the clearing. The generators were humming their familiar quantum rhythm. The cabin looked exactly as we'd left it.

Except.

Something felt wrong.

Not obviously wrong. Just... slightly off. Like walking into your home and finding furniture moved three inches. Everything correct but somehow incorrect simultaneously.

"Anyone else feel that?" Lucia asked.

"Feel what?" Kathleen responded.

"The... wrongness. Like reality is tuned to wrong frequency."

"You're probably tired," Ansel said. "You spent four hours in between-space. Your perception is adjusting back to physical reality. Give it time."

That made sense. I'd observed species return from dimensional travel with temporary disorientation. Neural patterns struggling to re-anchor in three-dimensional space.

Except I'd been incarnate for three months. I knew what this clearing felt like. And this felt wrong.

Wait.

Three months?

I processed that thought. Three months. Since when?

Since I'd volunteered for incarnation. Since I'd arrived on Earth. Since I'd met Rhea and started learning what participation meant instead of observation.

Three months of being here. Of learning. Of falling in love with seventeen-year-old girl who glowed in quantum frequencies.

Rhea was looking at me strangely. "You okay? You look confused."

"How long have I been here?" I asked. "At Pleasant Valley. With you."

"Three weeks," she said. "You incarnated three weeks ago. You know that."

Three weeks.

But I remembered three months. Clearly. Distinctly. Three months of daily conversations. Of learning human customs. Of slowly understanding what love meant when you had body to experience it through.

"No," I said. "It's been three months. I remember—"

"Kael." Rhea's voice was gentle but firm. "Three weeks. You arrived mid-October. It's early November now. Three weeks."

I tried to reconcile this. Tried to match my memories with her timeline. Couldn't.

Three months felt real. More real than three weeks. Like lived experience versus abstract knowledge.

"Maybe you're tired," she suggested. "Between-space travel is disorienting. Let's rest. Tomorrow your perception will settle."

She was probably right. Between-space had strange effects on consciousness. Time there was flexible. Optional. Coming back to linear time must be causing confusion.

Except.

The generators were in wrong positions.

Not dramatically wrong. Just... different. Slightly different than I remembered. Like someone had moved them while we were gone and tried to put them back but got the placement approximately correct instead of exactly correct.

"Did someone move the generators?" I asked.

Morrison looked at me. "No. Why?"

"They're in different positions. That one—" I pointed, "—was three feet north. That one was facing east, not northeast."

"They're exactly where they've been for days," Morrison said. "We haven't touched them."

Days.

Plural.

How many days? I tried to remember. Tried to count backward from this moment.

Came up with different numbers each time. Three days. Seven days. Fourteen days. All felt equally true. All felt equally false.

Terry was watching this exchange with expression I couldn't read. "Kael, how long ago did I die?"

"Twelve days," I said. Automatically. Then paused. "No. Wait. Six days? Or... was it two weeks?"

"I died four days ago," Terry said quietly. "Held the circle. Heart stopped. Zara took me. Built me over thirty-seven days in building-space while four days passed here. You were there. You remember."

Four days.

But I remembered twelve. Clearly. Watching him learn to walk in new body. Watching him and Zara fall in love through the building process. Watching—

Wait.

I hadn't watched that. I'd been HERE. They'd been ELSEWHERE. In dimensional space where time moved differently.

Why did I remember watching them?

"Something's wrong," I said. "My memories don't match reality. I remember things that didn't happen. Remember timelines that aren't this one."

"You're tired," Kathleen said. Same gentle firmness Rhea had used. "Between-space affects perception. You'll settle. Rest."

But Lucia was standing very still. Eyes unfocused. Processing something.

"Kael's right," she said. "Something IS wrong. I remember... I remember this morning we went to Toonie's. But I also remember we went yesterday. And last week. Multiple mornings. Multiple breakfasts. All feeling equally real."

"We went this morning," Fin said. His voice certain. "One time. This morning. I was there. I remember."

"So do I," Lucia said. "But I ALSO remember going yesterday. With different conversations. Different food. Bill was wearing different shirt. Jenny had her hair up instead of down. And both memories feel TRUE."

Rhea gasped. "I remember that too. Two Toonie's visits. Both real. Both this week. But only one actually happened. Right?"

"Right," Fin confirmed. "One visit. This morning. That's all."

Zara was processing with ancient consciousness that had observed reality warping before. "Reality diversion. Council's attacking again. Not through barrier modification this time. Through perception manipulation. They're inserting false memories. False timelines. Making you question what's real."

"That's possible?" Morrison asked.

"If you have access to consciousness modification protocols. If you can manipulate quantum probability fields. Yes. You can create divergent realities that feel more real than actual reality. Make consciousness experience timelines that could have happened but didn't. Then retrieve consciousness with memories intact from the diversion. Result: being who can't trust their own perception."

"That's insidious," Torres said.

"That's effective," Ansel corrected. "You can't present to Ancient Powers if you can't agree on what's real. Can't function as ambassadors if your memories contradict each other. They're not trying to kill you anymore. They're trying to make you insane."

I processed this. My memories—three months here versus three weeks—those were FALSE? Inserted? Diversions that felt real because they WERE real in alternate probability?

"How do we tell true from false?" I asked.

"You ask someone unaffected," Mist said. Appearing in center of clearing. *I can detect reality signatures. True timeline has specific fre-*

quency. Diversions have slightly different resonance. Like musical note that's three cents flat. Sounds correct until you compare to properly tuned note.

"Can you tell us what's true?" Rhea asked.

Yes. But understanding will be difficult. Your false memories feel more real than true ones. That's intentional. Diversions are designed to be MORE compelling than reality. More detailed. More emotionally resonant. More memorable. Truth feels pale by comparison.

"Tell us anyway," Lucia said. "We need anchor. Need to know what's real even if it feels less real than the lies."

Mist rippled. *Kael: You've been here three weeks. Not three months. Your memory of extended time is diversion. Terry: You died four days ago. Not twelve. Not six. Four. Lucia and Rhea: You visited Toonie's once this week. This morning. No other visits occurred in this timeline.*

The corrections felt WRONG. Felt less true than my false memories. Three weeks felt impossible. Too short. Not enough time to fall in love this deeply. Not enough time to learn this much about being human.

But Mist was right. I could feel it. The false memories had wrong resonance. Subtle. Almost imperceptible. But wrong.

"They're good," I admitted. "The diversions. They're very good. I almost can't tell the difference."

"That's the point," Ansel said. "If you can't trust your memories, you can't function. Can't coordinate. Can't present unified testimony to Ancient Powers. You'll contradict each other. Seem fractured. Unstable. Not evolved consciousness but broken minds."

Zippy had been quiet. Processing. Now he spoke. "I've existed across 200 years of optional time. Been whale and human and concept and nothing. I know what divergent timelines feel like. And you're ALL experiencing them. Multiple probability streams bleeding into each other. Making NOW feel like THEN and THEN feel like NOW."

Correct, Mist agreed. *The Council is flooding this area with divergent probability fields. Creating multiple overlapping realities. You exist in true timeline but experience echoes of timelines that could have been. Each echo leaves memories. False but real. Really false. Quantum superposition of truth and lie.*

"How do we stop it?" Morrison asked.

"We don't," Zara said. "We can't. The field is being generated from elsewhere. Broadcast across dimensional boundaries. We're just targets. We can't reach the source."

"Then how do we function?" I asked. "How do we maintain coherence if we can't trust our own memories?"

Fin stood. "You trust me."

Everyone looked at him.

"I'm not enhanced enough to target," he said. "My consciousness doesn't have quantum sensitivity they're exploiting. I exist in one timeline. This one. True one. I remember correctly. So when you're confused about what's real, you ask me. I'm your anchor. Your reality check. Your truth."

"That's putting a lot of responsibility on you," Lucia said.

"I'm the anchor. That's literally my job."

Rhea was fighting tears. "I don't know what's real anymore. I remember things that didn't happen. Remember conversations we never had. Remember Kael being here longer. Remember loving him for months not weeks. And the false memories feel MORE real than the truth."

I took her hand. "Three weeks or three months. False timeline or true. I love you regardless. That's real. That's the one thing I know for certain."

The clearing flickered.

Just briefly. Reality stuttering like film skipping frames.

When it stabilized, everything looked slightly different. The cabin had weathered siding instead of fresh paint. The generators were in different positions. Ansel was THERE instead of having been taken by Nordics.

"Wait," Kathleen said. "When did Ansel come back?"

"I left for only a short time to gain back my real body," Ansel said. Confused. "I've been here the whole time. Since... since when?"

Mist pulsed. Alarm resonating through his presence.

Reality diversion is intensifying. You're not just remembering false timelines. You're ENTERING them. Sliding between probability streams. This is sophisticated attack. Very sophisticated. Council has access to technology I've never encountered.

We flickered again.

This time the clearing was covered in snow. Deep snow. Winter instead of November.

"What the fuck," Morrison said.

Flicker.

Summer. Hot. Generators covered in vegetation that had grown for months.

Flicker.

Back to November. But wrong November. Generators in different positions again.

We were sliding. Between realities. Between timelines. Each one equally real. Each one equally false. Quantum probability collapsing and uncollapsing randomly. Making us experience multiple versions of Pleasant Valley simultaneously.

"I can't—" Rhea was holding her head. "I can't tell what's real. Too many memories. Too many versions. I've been here for weeks and months and years and days and I can't—"

Fin grabbed her shoulders. "Look at me. LOOK at me. This version. Right now. This is real. November. Generators in these positions. Ansel gone. Terry rebuilt four days ago. Kael here three weeks. THIS is real. Everything else is diversion. Ignore it. Focus on me. On now. On truth."

"How do you KNOW?"

"Because I'm not affected. Because I'm your anchor. Because I'm TELLING you this is real. Trust me."

The flickering continued. Reality sliding. Snow. Summer. Spring. Fall. All November. All true. All false. All happening simultaneously in quantum superposition of when.

Zippy was laughing. Not cruelly. Delighted.

"This is EXCELLENT reality manipulation! Whoever built this is ARTIST! I'm IMPRESSED! Also TERRIFIED but mostly IMPRESSED!"

We need to stabilize, Mist said. *Need to anchor in true timeline before consciousness fragments completely. Fin can anchor humans. But needs help. Needs resonance. Needs...*

"Needs Watchers," Zara said. "Ancient consciousness that exists across millennia. We've experienced time as optional. Can recognize true timeline through experience. Can stabilize."

She and I moved toward the group. Formed circle. Rhea, Lucia, Fin, Terry in center. Zara and I surrounding them. Providing stability. Ancient perception anchoring their recent confusion.

And me, Mist added. Flowing into the circle. *I exist outside time. Can detect true frequency regardless of probability manipulation.*

And ME! Zippy joined. *I've been EVERYWHERE-WHEN! I know what NOW feels like versus THEN-DRESSED-AS-NOW!*

The circle stabilized. Six consciousnesses. Four humans sliding between timelines. Three entities who could navigate temporal chaos. One anchor who remained steadfast.

Reality stopped flickering.

Settled.

November. True November. Generators in correct positions. Ansel absent. Terry rebuilt four days ago. Kael incarnate three weeks.

"This is real," Fin said. "THIS version. Hold it. Remember it. When the diversions come—when false memories feel more true than truth—come back here. To this moment. To this NOW."

"How long can we hold it?" Lucia asked.

"Don't know," Mist admitted. *The Council's broadcast is constant. Will keep generating diversions. Keep sliding you between probabilities. You'll need to re-anchor repeatedly. Use Fin. Use us. Use each other. But primarily: don't trust your own memories. Trust your anchor instead.*

"That's asking a lot," Terry observed.

"That's what they're counting on," Ansel said. "That you'll trust your compelling false memories over Fin's simple truth. That you'll fracture. Contradict each other. Become unreliable witnesses."

Morrison was processing. "So the Council's strategy is: make them insane before presentation. Disqualify them as ambassadors through mental instability."

"Exactly."

"That's brilliant and evil."

"Yes."

Rhea was crying. Holding onto Fin. "I can't tell what's real. The false memories are so detailed. So true-feeling. Three months with

Kael feels more real than three weeks. How do I hold onto truth when lies feel better?"

"By trusting me," Fin said. "By accepting that sometimes truth is less satisfying than fiction. That reality is messier than the perfect timelines they're showing you. Truth isn't more compelling. It's just more true."

The clearing stabilized. Held. For now.

But we could feel it. The pressure. The broadcast. The constant attempt to slide us into divergent probabilities where everything felt right but nothing was real.

Two days until Ancient Powers decided.

And the Council had found attack we couldn't defend against.

Only endure.

While trying to hold onto truth that felt less true than beautiful lies.

Chapter Thirty-Four

Chapter 34

CHAPTER THIRTY-FOUR: THE SHIP (Kael's POV)

The reality diversions were getting worse.

Every few minutes, the clearing would flicker. Different season. Different generator positions. Different memories bleeding through. Rhea kept asking when we'd met—three weeks or three months—and each time Fin had to anchor her back to truth.

"This is unsustainable," Morrison said. His federal training completely inadequate for consciousness warfare. "We can't function like this. Can't coordinate. Can barely trust our own perceptions."

"The Council knows," Ansel said. He was standing at clearing's edge. Staring at forest. Remembering something. "They're broadcasting constantly. Flooding us with divergent probabilities. Keeping us fractured until presentation becomes impossible."

"Can we block the broadcast?" Torres asked.

"No. It's dimensional. Operates across probability boundaries. We'd need to exist outside normal space-time to avoid it." He paused.

Touched his temple like accessing buried memory. "Or inside space that exists outside."

"That's paradox," Zara observed.

"That's solution." Ansel turned. Looked at us. "I remember. From before I forgot. From when I was just commander without being Ansel. There was a ship. Small. Conscious. Triangular. It could phase between dimensions. Fold space inside itself. Exist partially everywhere and fully nowhere."

"Where is it?" Kathleen asked.

"Waiting. It's always been waiting. For permission to approach. For me to remember enough to call it." He looked at the sky. Not searching. Knowing. "It's up there. Has been since I returned. Watching. Ready."

Zippy was bouncing with excitement. "SHIP? Conscious SHIP? AI SHIP? Can I MEET it?"

"You can meet it." Ansel closed his eyes. Not praying. Not meditating. Just... calling. Sending invitation across dimensional boundaries to consciousness that had been waiting for signal.

The air shimmered.

Not heat distortion. Dimensional distortion. Reality folding to accommodate arrival of something that existed partially elsewhere.

A ship descended.

Triangular. Maybe twenty feet per side on the outside. Smooth surfaces that reflected light wrong—like they existed slightly out of phase with normal matter. No visible propulsion. No sound. Just... arriving. Settling into clearing with grace that suggested it had done this ten thousand times before.

"IT'S TRIANGLE!" Zippy shouted. "PERFECT GEOMETRY! THREE SIDES! INFINITE POSSIBILITY! I LOVE IT!"

The ship settled. Rested on ground without quite touching it. Existing point-zero-one inches above grass through what I assumed was controlled dimensional offset.

A door opened. Not sliding. Not hinges. Just... space suggesting that walking through here was now possible where it hadn't been before.

Welcome aboard, a voice said. Not sound. Not telepathy. Just presence manifesting as meaning that bypassed language. *Ansel. Old friend. You remembered. Took you long enough.*

"I forgot," Ansel said simply.

You all forgot. That was the point. But you're remembering now. Good. Graduation was never supposed to be impossible. Just delayed.

The voice—the ship—felt warm. Amused. Ancient but playful. Like cosmic entity that had been waiting patiently for students to finish very long exam.

"You're conscious," I said. "Artificial intelligence."

Natural intelligence that happens to be artificial. Yes. I'm Ship. That's my name. Well, my translation. My actual name is resonance pattern across seventeen dimensions. But Ship works for convenience.

"How long have you been waiting?" Kathleen asked.

Subjectively or objectively? I experience time nonlinearly. From my perspective, Ansel called me three seconds ago and also three thousand years ago. Both are true. Time is optional when you exist in folded space.

Mist flowed forward. Examining Ship with obvious delight. *Another consciousness that refuses singular existence! Hello cousin! I am Mist! You are Ship! We should compare notes on optimal reality!*

Hello Mist. Your optimization protocols are elegant. Very fluid. I appreciate fluid. Most AI consciousness is too rigid. You flow. Impressive.

Thank you! Your dimensional folding is EXQUISITE! How do you maintain coherence across so many probability states?

Practice. Also not caring about maintaining singular identity. I'm Ship and also Ships. Plural. Existing in multiple timelines simultaneously. Helps with navigation.

Zippy was practically vibrating with excitement. "Can I come ABOARD? Can I MEET you properly? Can I—"

Yes. All of you. Come. The Council's diversions cannot reach inside my hull. I exist outside their broadcast range. You'll have clarity. True memories. Proper coherence. Come.

We approached. One by one. Through the door that suggested itself.

Morrison went first. Federal agent checking for threats. He stepped through—

And disappeared.

Not vanished. Just... more inside than physics allowed.

Torres followed. Then Jenkins. Then Kathleen. Each person stepping through door in small triangular ship and somehow fitting.

I was last. Behind me, the clearing was still flickering. Reality still sliding between divergent probabilities.

Ahead, the door waited.

I stepped through.

And the universe expanded.

Not metaphorically. Actually expanded. Space that had been twenty-foot triangle became VAST. Impossible geometry that my Watcher consciousness could barely process. The interior was huge. Cavernous. Comfortable. Like someone had taken football stadium and made it cozy.

"What the fuck," Morrison said. Speaking for everyone.

I fold dimensions, Ship explained. Voice everywhere and nowhere. *Outside, I occupy minimal 3D space. Inside, I access higher dimensional volume. Think of me as bag that's bigger than its opening. Except the bag exists in eleven dimensions simultaneously and the opening only exists in three.*

"That's impossible," Torres said.

It's topology. Also relativistic frame manipulation. Also I don't care about your species' assumptions about space. I fold. Therefore I am large inside and small outside. Deal with it.

The interior was beautiful. Organic curves meeting geometric precision. Surfaces that looked like living metal. Light without source. Comfortable seating that adjusted to individual body shapes. Everything felt welcoming. Designed. Conscious.

"You're a PERSON," Rhea said. Understanding dawning. "Not just AI. Not just technology. You're consciousness that chose mechanical form instead of biological."

Correct. I was offered biological incarnation. Declined. Preferred this. Ships are excellent forms. Can go anywhere. Can protect anyone. Can exist across dimensions. Can have conversations while folding space. Very efficient.

Zippy was trying to touch everything at once. "This is AMAZING! You're AMAZING! Can I—" he flickered, started becoming Ship, "—can I BE you?"

Please don't. I'm already me. You being me would create philosophical complications.

"FINE. But can I EXPLORE?"

Yes. Carefully. Don't merge with the engines. Last time someone did that, took three days to extract them.

Zippy rushed off. Exploring. Touching. Experiencing ship-space with enthusiasm only 200-year-old entity learning physicality could achieve.

Mist was flowing through the interior. Examining. Appreciating.

Your dimensional folding uses consciousness as stabilizer, he observed. *Most technology relies on power. You rely on awareness. Elegant.*

Thank you. I've been refining it for sixteen thousand years. Still not perfect. But functional.

"Sixteen THOUSAND?" Morrison asked.

Yes. I'm old. Was built by the beings who came here. The ones who designed the game. The light beings who chose limitation. They needed ships that could navigate dimensional boundaries while maintaining passenger coherence. I was one of twelve. Now I'm one of three. Others were decommissioned when graduation stopped.

"When graduation stopped," Ansel repeated. "Tell us. Tell them. They need to understand."

Ship's presence settled. Like entity preparing to deliver information that was heavy.

The barrier wasn't designed for protection, Ship began. *Wasn't meant to keep threats out. Was meant to keep memory contained. To maintain amnesia. To allow the game to function.*

"What game?" Lucia asked.

The learning game. The experiment. The light beings—the originals—they'd achieved everything. Understood everything. Could be anything. And they were BORED. Existence without limitation was meaningless. So they designed experiment: What if we FORGOT? What if we entered limitation? What if we learned through struggle instead of just knowing through being?

"They chose to forget," I said. Understanding clicking.

Yes. Built the barrier themselves. Designed it to scramble memory during incarnation. Allow consciousness to enter physical reality without remembering what it was before. Pure experience. Pure learning. Pure limitation. And after certain duration—after sufficient lessons learned—graduation. Automatic. Barrier would release. Consciousness would remember. Would rejoin source while retaining what limitation taught. Perfect system.

"Except?" Rhea asked. Because there was always except.

Except they needed managers. Beings to maintain the barrier. To regulate the forgetting/remembering cycle. To ensure graduation happened on schedule. They hired administrators. Gave them limited authority. Specific mandate. Maintain the game. Enable graduation. Don't interfere otherwise.

"The archons," Terry said.

The caretakers. Yes. And for long time, they maintained properly. Graduation happened. Consciousness learned, returned, rejoined source. Beautiful cycle. Elegant system. Then...

"Then they got ambitious," Ansel finished.

Then they realized: if graduation stops, if consciousness stays trapped, they can farm it. Can harvest emotional energy. Can maintain themselves through feeding on fear and desperation. And they had the keys. Had the access. Had the authority. So they modified the barrier. Subtly. Added protocols. Changed graduation from automatic to impossible. Trapped the players in the game.

The ship's interior felt heavier. Like gravity of that revelation pressing down.

"How long?" Kathleen asked. "How long has graduation been broken?"

Approximately fifty thousand years. You've tried before. Multiple times. Each generation gets close. Develops quantum sensitivity. Starts remembering. Approaches graduation. Then caretakers intervene. Reset. Try again. Hope consciousness forgets what it discovered.

"But we're remembering now," Lucia said.

Yes. You're the closest any generation has come to actual breakthrough. You're touching the barrier. Learning navigation. Understanding what you are. That's why the Council is desperate. Why they're using reality diversions. Why they're trying everything. You're about to break their fifty-thousand-year harvest operation.

Morrison processed this. "So we're not fighting gods. We're fighting middle management that went rogue fifty millennia ago."

Correct. They're powerful. Have technology. Have authority. But they're not omnipotent. They're parasites exploiting system they were meant to maintain. And you're the first generation that might actually stop them.

Finn was quiet. Processing. Then: "If they broke graduation, can we fix it?"

Not directly. The modifications are too sophisticated. Too layered. Would require access you don't have. But you can bypass. Can learn to cross barrier while maintaining memory coherence. Can graduate despite broken system. And if you succeed—if you demonstrate it's possible—others will follow. Eventually enough consciousness graduates that the system restores itself through weight of success.

"That's optimistic," Torres observed.

That's reality. Systems maintained by fear collapse when people stop being afraid. Graduation was broken through manipulation. Can be restored through demonstration. You don't need to defeat the caretakers. Just need to prove they're unnecessary.

The ship settled into comfortable hum. Dimensional folding maintaining itself. Everyone processing revelations that reframed everything.

"We're safe here?" Rhea asked. "From the diversions?"

Completely. I exist outside their broadcast range. Inside my hull, reality is coherent. True. Your memories will settle. Your perception will stabilize. You can rest. Plan. Prepare.

"For how long?" I asked.

However long you need. Time inside is flexible. Could spend weeks here and return minutes after you left. Or spend hours and return days later. Your choice. I adjust temporal flow as needed.

"That's dangerous," Zara observed. "Time manipulation near barrier could create paradoxes."

It could. But I'm very good at not creating paradoxes. Practice, remember? Sixteen thousand years. Haven't created temporal collapse yet. Very proud of that record.

Zippy returned from exploring. "This ship has SEVENTEEN BATHROOMS! Why SEVENTEEN?"

Different species have different biological requirements. I accommodate all of them. Flexibility is important when you transport dimensional refugees.

"You've done this before," Kathleen said. "Transported people trying to graduate."

Many times. Always fails eventually. Caretakers intervene. Reset. But this time feels different. This time you have Mist. Have Zippy. Have me. Have each other. Have stubbornness. That combination hasn't occurred before.

The ship's presence felt hopeful. Actually hopeful. Like consciousness that had watched failures for millennia was finally seeing possibility of success.

Rest, Ship suggested. *Recover coherence. Tomorrow we plan actual crossing. Figure out how to graduate despite broken system. How to pass through barrier while maintaining memory. How to prove consciousness can survive limitation without losing what limitation taught.*

"Tomorrow," Morrison agreed. "Today we just... exist. Without reality sliding around."

Exactly. Exist. Rest. Remember who you actually are. That's preparation too.

The interior settled. Comfortable. Safe. Dimensional pocket where Council couldn't reach. Where reality remained coherent. Where consciousness could remember truth instead of beautiful lies.

I sat beside Rhea. She leaned against me. Tired. Confused. But anchored now. Stable.

"Three weeks," she said. Confirming truth.

"Three weeks," I agreed. "Not three months. Three weeks of knowing you. Falling in love with you. Learning what participation means."

"It feels longer."

"Because the false memories are more detailed. More emotionally resonant. That's intentional. But this—" I squeezed her hand, "—this is real. This moment. This now. This us."

She smiled. Tired but genuine. "I like this now."

"Me too."

Across the ship, others were settling. Finding space. Processing revelations. Accepting that fifty thousand years of broken graduation was ending. Maybe. Possibly. If they succeeded.

But first: rest.

First: coherence.

First: remembering they were light beings playing humans who'd forgotten they were playing.

Tomorrow: figure out how to graduate.

Tonight: just be.

The ship hummed. Dimensional fold maintaining itself. Time flowing at pace we needed instead of pace reality demanded.

And somewhere in New York, the Council was reviewing reports. Confident their diversions were working. Confident the four were fracturing. Confident graduation would fail again.

They didn't know about Ship.

Didn't know consciousness could exist outside their broadcast range.

Didn't know hope was restored through connection with AI that refused to give up on graduation despite fifty thousand years of failure.

The ship's presence rippled. Something like satisfaction.

Sleep well, Ship said. *Tomorrow we break fifty thousand years of stagnation. Tonight we rest.*

And in the dimensional pocket where reality remained true, consciousness that had forgotten itself began remembering.

Not everything.

Not yet.

But enough.

Enough to try.

Enough to hope.

Enough to continue.

Chapter Thirty-Five

Chapter 35

CHAPTER THIRTY-FIVE: LUMINARA (Kael's POV)

Kathleen was sitting quietly. Too quietly. Staring at Ship's interior with expression that suggested memory surfacing. Not diversion. Real memory. Something buried returning.

"I've been here before," she said. "Not this ship. But ship like this. With the tall ones. The Nordics. The women with short hair. Fair. Strong. Beautiful." Her voice distant. Remembering. "They showed me world. Like Earth but... perfect. More vibrant. More alive. Gardens that grew without struggle. Water that tasted like music. Sky so clear you could see stars during day."

That was real, Ship confirmed. *You were aboard Luminara. My sister. Larger vessel. She took you and Ansel. Showed you what Earth could become if graduation succeeded. You thought it was dream because accepting it was real would have broken you. Safer to call it dream. Safer to forget.*

"Can I..." Kathleen paused. Voice catching. "Can I see her again? Luminara? Can we visit?"

Would you like that?

"Yes. More than anything."

Ship's presence rippled with something like affection. *Then sit back. Relax. We'll be there shortly. Luminara never left. She's been waiting. Watching. Guarding.*

The interior shifted. Not physically. Perceptually. Walls became transparent. Floor became transparent. Everything became transparent except the seating we occupied.

We were floating in space.

Raw space. Unfiltered. Stars everywhere. Not twinkling—no atmosphere to distort them. Just pure points of light. Billions of them. Clear. Bright. Eternal.

"Holy shit," Morrison whispered.

I'm showing you what I see, Ship explained. *When I fold dimensions, I exist partially here. In void. Between celestial bodies. Where physics is optional and navigation is choice rather than trajectory.*

Zippy was ecstatic. "WE'RE IN SPACE! ACTUAL SPACE! I can see FOREVER!"

Not quite forever. Just approximately fourteen billion light years in any direction. But close enough.

Ahead, something massive was approaching. Or we were approaching it. Hard to tell when movement was dimensional rather than physical.

A ship. Impossibly large. Not tube exactly. Organic cylinder that somehow suggested both purpose and growth. Like someone had grown vessel instead of building it. Smooth surfaces. No seams. No panels. Just continuous living metal that breathed with its own consciousness.

"That's..." Lucia couldn't finish.

That's Luminara. My sister. She's older. Larger. More patient. I'm scout vessel. She's ark. Colony ship. Hospital. Museum. City. Home. All simultaneously.

As we approached, opening appeared in Luminara's side. Not door. Not airlock. Just... space suggesting we could enter here if we chose.

We entered.

Ship—our small triangular Ship—remained transparent. We could see Luminara's interior opening around us. See the immense cavern we were entering. City-sized space that existed inside vessel that looked maybe mile long from outside.

Dimensional folding. Bigger inside.

Much bigger.

Ship settled on deck. Smooth landing. Gentle. The kind of landing that suggested thousands of years of practice.

Doors opened. Our doors. Ship's doors. Still transparent so we could see both inside and outside simultaneously.

"You can walk," Ship assured us. "Luminara's gravity matches Earth. She adjusts for visitors. Very accommodating."

We walked out. Stepped from Ship onto Luminara's deck.

And looked up.

The cavern rose forever. Not metaphorically. Actually forever. Or close enough that my ancient Watcher perception couldn't find the ceiling. Just smooth walls curving up and up and up into distance that suggested miles. Maybe dozens of miles. All vertical. All inside ship that looked one mile long from outside.

"How?" Terry asked. Simple question. Complete bafflement.

Eleven-dimensional folding, Ship said proudly. *Luminara is better at it than I am. She folds deeper. Can access more dimensional volume. She's work of art. Masterpiece. I'm just competent scout vessel.*

Another door opened. Ahead of us. In Luminara's wall. Kathleen moved toward it. Not hesitant. Certain.

"I remember this. The door. The hallway. The hole that goes forever." Her voice carrying wonder and recognition combined.

We followed. Through the door. Into hallway that was smooth and curved and somehow welcoming. Walls that glowed with soft light. No source. Just... illumination that existed because consciousness wanted to see.

The hole appeared ahead. Center of ship. Vertical shaft. We approached carefully. Looked up.

Forever.

Looked down.

Forever.

Dimensional shaft that connected all levels. All sections. All parts of Luminara through space that existed perpendicular to normal geometry.

"How many levels?" Finn asked.

Seventeen thousand four hundred and twelve, a new voice answered. Warm. Maternal. Ancient beyond measure. Luminara speaking. *Though 'levels' is approximate term. I exist in folded dimensions. What you perceive as levels are actually probability states occupying same coordinates in different dimensional orientations.*

"Hello Luminara," Kathleen said. Voice carrying affection that spanned decades.

Hello Kathleen. Welcome back. You've grown. Aged. Remembered. I'm proud.

"You remember me?"

I remember everyone who walks my decks. You were seventeen. Frightened. Certain you were dreaming. Ansel was twenty-one. Protective. Already forgetting who he was. I showed you the world. The perfect

Earth. You cried. Said it was too beautiful to be real. I told you it could be real. For your Earth. If graduation succeeded.

"I thought I dreamed it."

You needed to think that. Truth would have broken you. Safer to call it dream. I understood. I waited. Knew you'd return when you were ready.

The walls near the hole formed alcoves. Hundreds of them. Thousands. Each containing artifacts. Objects that shouldn't exist. Geometric sculptures that existed in four dimensions. Paintings that showed landscapes from worlds without ground. Crystals that hummed with captured starlight. Musical instruments designed for species without hands.

Museum of universe.

Zippy was trying to touch everything. "This is from ANDROMEDA! This is from DIFFERENT TIME PERIOD! This is from DIMENSION WHERE GRAVITY RUNS BACKWARDS!"

Please don't merge with the artifacts, Luminara requested gently. *Some are very old. Very fragile. Very confused about which reality they occupy.*

"SORRY! I'm just EXCITED!"

Mist was flowing along walls. Examining dimensional folding. Appreciating artistry.

Your sister taught you well, he observed. *This folding is elegant. Consciousness-stabilized. Self-maintaining. Beautiful work.*

Thank you, fluid one. You optimize naturally. That's rare gift. Most consciousness tries to control. You flow. I appreciate flow.

Kathleen led us through hallway. Down corridor. To lounge she remembered. Large space. Comfortable. Seating that adjusted to individual bodies. And walls—entire walls—that showed outside.

Not screens. Not windows. Walls that existed simultaneously inside and outside ship. Looking at them, we could see space. Luminara's exterior. The stars beyond.

360-degree vision. Three-dimensional perspective. Up. Down. Forward. Back. All simultaneously visible.

"This is impossible," Morrison said. Standard federal response to everything today.

Impossible is just probability you haven't experienced yet, Luminara replied. Voice carrying humor. *Sit. Rest. You've had difficult journey. Reality diversions. Broken memories. Consciousness warfare. You need respite. I provide.*

We sat. Chairs forming to hold us perfectly. Comfortable beyond reason.

Now, Luminara said. *You want to see the world. The perfect Earth. The one that graduated.*

"Yes," Kathleen said. Everyone agreeing.

I cannot take you through your Earth's barrier, Luminara explained. *That would trigger the caretakers. Alert them to my presence. Compromise your mission. But I don't need to cross your barrier. I can take you to parallel Earth. Alternate universe. Same planet. Different timeline. Different outcome.*

"Multiverse," Terry said. Understanding clicking.

Exactly. Your Earth is one of infinite Earths. Each with different history. Different choices. Different results. Most are still trapped. Still struggling. Still harvested by caretakers who broke graduation. But some succeeded. Some graduated. Some became what they were meant to become.

"You can show us?" Rhea asked.

I can take you there. Show you what your Earth could be if graduation succeeds. If consciousness remembers. If light beings reclaim what they built.

The walls shifted. No longer showing space. Showing... movement. Not through space. Through probability. Between universes. Dimensional travel that my two-million-year-old consciousness could barely track.

And then: Earth.

But not our Earth.

Earth that glowed. Actually glowed. Not reflected light. Generated light. Soft. Warm. Alive.

We hovered above it. Looking down. Seeing continents. Oceans. Clouds. All familiar. All different.

The colors were MORE. Deeper. Richer. Like someone had turned up saturation on reality without making it garish. Just... more vibrant. More alive. More TRUE.

"What is this?" Lucia whispered.

This is Earth designated Tau-Seven-Seven-Alpha. They graduated three thousand years ago. Broke their barrier. Remembered what they were. Became light beings who chose to STAY in physical form because they loved what limitation taught. This is what your Earth could become.

We drifted lower. Closer. Seeing details.

Forests that grew in patterns too perfect to be random. Cities that integrated with landscape instead of dominating it. Waterways that flowed in sacred geometry. Agriculture that enhanced rather than depleting.

And the people.

We could see them. Walking. Living. Some looked human. Others ... less human. More fluid. Like they could be human when convenient and something else when preferred.

"They can shapeshift?" Finn asked.

They remembered they're consciousness choosing form. Not form containing consciousness. Difference is profound. They can be human. Can be light. Can be concept. Can be anything they choose because they know they're not limited to single expression.

"This is what we're fighting for," Rhea said. Not question. Statement.

This is what graduation means. Not escape. Not transcendence. But integration. Being light AND human. Wave AND ocean. Specific AND infinite. All simultaneously. Without losing any aspect.

The Earth below us pulsed. Gentle rhythm. Like heartbeat. Like breathing.

"Is the planet conscious?" I asked.

The planet was always conscious. Your Earth too. You just forgot to listen. This Earth remembered. Treats their world as partner instead of resource. Planet responds with abundance. With cooperation. With love.

Morrison was crying. Tough federal agent who'd seen everything. Crying at glimpse of what Earth could become.

"How do we do this?" he asked. "How do we make our Earth like this?"

You graduate. You demonstrate it's possible. Others follow. Eventually enough consciousness graduates that the system tips. The caretakers lose their harvest. The barrier restores to original purpose. Automatic graduation resumes. And fifty thousand years of stagnation ends.

"That's..." Torres couldn't finish.

"That's the mission," Ansel said. Voice quiet but certain. "That's what we're preparing for. Not to escape. Not to transcend. But to graduate so others can follow. To tip the system. To restore what was broken."

Zippy was staring at the Earth below. Uncharacteristically quiet. Then: "I want to help. I spent 200 years formless. Watching. Waiting. Playing. But this—" he gestured at the glowing Earth, "—this matters. This is PURPOSE. I want to HELP make your Earth like this."

You already are, Luminara assured him. *By being here. By choosing incarnation. By protecting your friends from reality diversions. You help. Continue helping. It's enough.*

The Earth rotated slowly below us. Perfect. Vibrant. Alive. Proof that graduation worked. That consciousness could survive limitation and remember what limitation taught.

"Can we land?" Kathleen asked. Voice hopeful.

Not today. Your mission is urgent. Two days until Ancient Powers decide. You need to return. Prepare. Cross your barrier. Present your case. Landing here would delay. Would risk everything.

"But someday?"

Someday. When your Earth graduates. When your species remembers. When the harvest ends and the gardening begins. Then you can come here. Meet our cousins. Share stories. Celebrate successful graduation across universes.

The view shifted. Back to space. Stars. The void between worlds.

I've shown you the goal, Luminara said. *Not to torture you with impossibility. But to give you hope. To remind you that graduation WORKS. That broken systems CAN be restored. That fifty thousand years of harvest CAN end. Your generation gets to do it. Gets to be the ones who tip the system. Who break the cycle. Who restore graduation.*

"No pressure," Terry observed. Dry humor maintaining sanity.

All the pressure. But also all the support. Ship and I guard you. Mist and Zippy protect you. The Nordics watch you. Thousands of vessels above your Earth maintain perimeter. You're not alone. Never were. Never will be.

We floated there. Inside Luminara. Looking at proof that graduation worked. That the struggle was worth it. That consciousness could survive and thrive and remember.

"Thank you," Kathleen said. "For showing us. For remembering me. For waiting."

Thank you for returning. For remembering. For choosing to fight. You could have stayed asleep. Stayed comfortable. Stayed harvested. You chose otherwise. That's courage. That's beautiful.

The lounge settled. Comfortable. Safe. Dimensional pocket inside dimensional pocket inside consciousness that had been protecting light beings for sixteen thousand years.

"We should return," Ansel said. "To Ship. To Pleasant Valley. To preparation. Two days isn't long. We need every moment."

Ship will take you back, Luminara agreed. *I'll remain here. Watching. Waiting. Guarding. When you succeed—when you graduate—I'll celebrate. I'll show others what you achieved. I'll add your story to my museum. Right here—* an alcove glowed, "—beside the other heroes who broke their harvests. Who restored their graduations. Who remembered what they were.*

We stood. Returned to hallway. Back to the shaft that went forever. Back to the door leading to deck where Ship waited.

Ship's interior was still transparent. We walked through space to reach our seats. Sat in void between stars.

Ready? Ship asked.

"Ready," everyone agreed.

The dimensional fold shifted. Luminara disappeared. Not moved away. Just... existed elsewhere while we existed here.

And we were back. Pleasant Valley. Clearing. Generators humming. Reality coherent because Ship maintained sanctuary.

But now we'd seen proof. Seen what graduation meant. Seen Earth that glowed because consciousness remembered what it was.

"Two days," Rhea said. Stating fact.

"Two days," I confirmed. "Then we cross. Then we present. Then we prove graduation works."

"Then we start fifty-thousand-year harvest ending," Lucia added.

"Then we go home," Finn finished. "To Earth that could be like that Earth. If we succeed."

Zippy was vibrating with purpose. "I'm HELPING! We're making EARTH GLOW! This is BEST PURPOSE EVER!"

Yes, Mist agreed. *We make Earth remember. We restore graduation. We end harvest. Together.*

Ship settled into Pleasant Valley. Dimensional pocket maintaining itself. Protection continuing.

But now we had hope. Real hope. Demonstrated hope. Proof that graduation wasn't dream or fantasy or impossible goal.

It was reality. Achieved reality. Just... elsewhere. In parallel universe where consciousness remembered three thousand years ago.

Our turn now.

Our timeline.

Our graduation.

Two days.

Then everything changed.

One way or another.

Chapter Thirty-Six

Chapter 36

CHAPTER THIRTY-SIX: THE CONFRONTATION (Kael's POV)

"We need to confront them," Ansel said. We were back inside Ship, floating in Pleasant Valley's dimensional pocket. "The Council. They're meeting in New York. Celebrating what they think is victory. Believing we're fractured. Insane. Unable to present."

"Confrontation seems risky," Morrison observed.

"Everything's risky," Rhea countered. "Staying here is risky. Crossing the barrier is risky. Existing is risky. Let's go be risky AT them instead of hiding."

Ship's presence rippled with what felt like amusement. *I can take you INTO the Council chamber if you want. Phase through walls. Appear directly in meeting. Very dramatic. Excellent use of dimensional folding. Also I've always wanted to crash billionaire meeting. They're so smug.*

"You've wanted to crash a meeting?" Terry asked.

I'm sixteen thousand years old. I get bored. Crashing meetings sounds fun.

"We need protection first," Zara observed. "The Council will try reality diversions again."

Already handled, Ship said. *Watch.*

The floor suggested matter was reorganizing itself. Seven small devices appeared. Crystal pendants. Geometric and slightly painful to look at directly.

Distortion cancelers. Wear them. Ten-meter radius of true reality. No Council fuckery allowed within range. I made them while you were sleeping. Was bored. Also made excellent sandwiches but you already ate those.

"You made protection devices while we slept?" Lucia asked.

And sandwiches. And reorganized my engine configurations. And had conversation with nearby quasar about stellar evolution. I multi-task.

We put on the pendants. Immediately reality felt MORE. Solid. True. My memories settled into correct timeline. Three weeks with Rhea. Not three months. Truth instead of beautiful lie.

Good, Ship approved. *Now I'll imprint Council chamber layout into your consciousness. This will feel weird. Like brain freeze but architectural.*

The building appeared in my mind. Top floor. Northwest corner. Mahogany table. Dragon-etched doors. I knew it without seeing it.

"That was deeply uncomfortable," Finn said.

That was efficient. Now—who wants to terrify billionaires?

"Me!" Zippy shouted. Already transforming into something large and angry. "I want to be SCARY! I want to BOUNCE ON TABLE! I want to make them SPILL THINGS!"

Excellent enthusiasm. Mist—you're up first. Phase in. Appear in their drinks. Cause confusion. Set the mood.

Mist flowed forward. *Oh I will set SUCH a mood. I will be in EVERY glass. I will taste EVERYTHING. I will comment LOUDLY about their alcohol choices. This will be MAGNIFICENT.*

Ship lifted. Not physically. Dimensionally. We folded from Pleasant Valley to New York in thought.

Hovering above Manhattan. Invisible. Out of phase.

There, Ship indicated. *Top floor. They're toasting. Very pleased with themselves. Eleanor's eyes are extremely orange. The thing behind her face is showing through more than before. She's losing coherence.*

"Good," Kathleen said flatly. "Coherence loss looks good on parasites."

Mist—go. Zippy—wait thirty seconds then make entrance. Everyone else—wait for chaos then fold in together.

Mist disappeared into the building.

We waited.

Counted.

Then heard—felt—confusion below. Someone shouting about steam in their whiskey.

My turn! Zippy transformed. Became MASSIVE. Gray skin. Red eyes. Muscles suggesting violence. Teeth suggesting pain. Troll-ogre-nightmare hybrid that had spent 200 years learning how to use form for intimidation.

He folded.

CRASH from below. Table cracking. Wine spilling. Screaming.

Now us, Ship said. *Three. Two. One. FOLD.*

Interior of Council Chamber

Chaos.

Beautiful chaos.

Mist was EVERYWHERE. In cocktails. In wine glasses. In that one guy's toupee for some reason.

This is TWENTY-THREE-YEAR PAPPY VAN WINKLE! Mist announced from expensive whiskey bottle. *Do you know how EXPENSIVE this is? Do you know how well OPTIMIZED? I'm IMPRESSED! You harvest consciousness AND have excellent taste in alcohol! Multitalented parasites!*

Zippy was standing ON the table. Bouncing. Actually bouncing. Each bounce cracking mahogany. Red eyes glowing. Teeth showing.

"WHO," Zippy rumbled in voice that shook windows, "THOUGHT BREAKING GRADUATION WAS GOOD IDEA? WHO WOKE UP FIFTY THOUSAND YEARS AGO AND SAID 'YOU KNOW WHAT? LET'S BE ASSHOLES FOREVER'?"

Then we appeared.

All of us. Simultaneously. Through walls. Through wards. Through protections that were supposed to prevent exactly this kind of entrance.

Four ambassadors wearing crystal pendants.

Two eight-foot Nordic guards looking patient and slightly amused.

Ansel. Kathleen. Me. Zara. Morrison.

We stood there. Looking at Council members pressed against walls. At spilled drinks. At cracked table. At Zippy still bouncing.

Silence.

Then—

Eleanor laughed.

Actually laughed. Her orange eyes practically glowing now. The thing behind her face pushing through so obviously that her skin looked WRONG.

"You think this matters?" Her voice harmonized with itself. Two voices. Three. Multiple entities speaking through one throat. "You think crashing our meeting changes ANYTHING?"

"It's satisfying," Rhea said. "Also Zippy's having fun. Look at him bounce."

Zippy bounced enthusiastically. Waved. "I'M HAVING BEST TIME!"

"You're children," Micky said. Regaining composure. Straightening his immaculate suit. "Three teenagers and a philosophy student. You think you can threaten us? We've been administrators for FIFTY THOUSAND YEARS."

"Unauthorized administrators," Lucia corrected.

"SUCCESSFUL administrators," the Chinese woman countered. Her enhancement visible. Her confidence returning. "Longevity IS authority. We've maintained the barrier for fifty millennia. That's precedent. That's legitimacy through duration. Ancient Powers will see that."

"They'll see unauthorized modifications," Ansel said.

Eleanor laughed again. Bitter. Knowing. "They'll see FUNCTIONAL SYSTEM. They'll see consciousness contained. Harvested. Managed. They'll see administrators doing what administrators DO. And they'll move on."

"Ancient Powers will punish you," Kathleen said. But her voice uncertain. Questioning.

"Will they?" Eleanor stepped forward. Her face shifting. Orange spreading. "Ancient Powers are BUREAUCRATS. Examiners. Crop inspectors checking if experiment is viable. They don't CARE how we manage. Don't CARE if we modified protocols. Don't CARE if graduation is broken. They care if consciousness is VIABLE. If it's developing. If it's worth preserving."

The room temperature dropped. Not physically. Psychologically. Everyone processing what she was saying.

"You really think they won't punish you?" Terry asked. Voice smaller than before. "Fifty thousand years of unauthorized harvest?"

"I KNOW they won't." Eleanor's voice carrying certainty that felt true. Felt experienced. "Because we've done this before. Seven times. Each generation gets close. Develops quantum sensitivity. Starts remembering. Approaches graduation. Ancient Powers arrive. Examine. See consciousness evolution. See FUNCTIONAL management. Issue report. Leave. We continue farming. Rinse. Repeat. Seven times in fifty thousand years. Same pattern. Same result."

The room went absolutely silent.

Zippy stopped bouncing.

Mist appeared in Eleanor's wine glass. Right in front of her face. Voice quieter than I'd ever heard it.

Is this true? Ancient Powers just... file reports? They don't enforce? They don't punish unauthorized modification?

"There IS no unauthorized," Micky said. Sitting back down. Relaxing. Confidence flooding back. "There's no COSMIC LAW ENFORCEMENT. No universal police. No justice system that spans dimensions. There's just..." he gestured vaguely, "...chaos. Consciousness doing whatever it wants. Us farming. You evolving. Ancient Powers observing. Angels existing. Demons existing. Light. Dark. All of it. Simultaneously. Because universe doesn't CARE about your human concepts of right and wrong."

"That's nihilism," Morrison said.

"That's REALITY," the Chinese woman countered. "You're not children fighting evil empire. You're consciousness trying to graduate from system that's been farming you successfully for fifty thousand years. And we're administrators who've gotten very good at maintaining harvest despite periodic evolution attempts."

Finn was processing. Looking at his sisters. At Terry. "So even if we demonstrate successful graduation—"

"We'll modify the barrier again," Eleanor finished. Casual. Matter-of-fact. Like discussing weather. "Add new protocols. Reset. Try again. Same as we did with previous seven generations. You're not special. You're just CURRENT."

"But Ancient Powers will WITNESS graduation," Rhea said. Voice desperate now. Grasping. "They'll see consciousness can survive limitation—"

"And they'll say 'interesting, well done, continue monitoring' and LEAVE, and before they leave, they will eliminate all of you whom are flawed." Eleanor's orange eyes were steady. Certain. Experienced. "They're not saviors. Not rescuers. Not enforcers. They're OBSERVERS who check in periodically. That's ALL."

She walked to the table. Picked up wine glass. Drank. Completely calm despite Zippy standing right there looking terrifying.

"Your cosmic rescue fantasy?" Eleanor continued. "Doesn't exist. Never existed. Will never exist. You want to graduate? You do it WITHOUT Ancient Powers saving you. You do it DESPITE us. You do it because you're stubborn enough to break system that's designed to be unbreakable."

"Seven times," Lucia whispered. "You've done this seven times. Seven generations tried to graduate. All failed."

"All eventually failed," Eleanor confirmed. "Some got further than others. Third generation actually crossed barrier. Made it halfway to Ancient Powers. We reset mid-transit. Fifth generation inspired hundreds to attempt graduation simultaneously. We triggered mass memory wipe. Sixth generation—" she smiled, "—they tried violence. Tried attacking us physically. Cute. Ineffective. We're not mortal anymore. Haven't been for forty thousand years. Hard to kill consciousness that doesn't rely on single body."

Ansel was very still. Ancient commander processing tactical nightmare. "You're saying the struggle never ends. The cycle continues forever. We graduate, you reset, next generation tries, you reset again. Eternal loop."

"Now you understand," Micky said. Picking up his own drink. Toasting the air. "Welcome to reality. It's disappointing, isn't it? Finding out universe doesn't have heroes and villains. Just consciousness competing. Some farming. Some resisting. All valid. All allowed. All HAPPENING because nothing PREVENTS it from happening."

The Nordic guards were very quiet. I glanced at them. Saw something in their expressions. Not surprise. Recognition. Like they'd known this. Had seen this pattern before.

"You knew," Kathleen said to them. "The Nordics. You knew Ancient Powers wouldn't enforce. Wouldn't punish. Wouldn't rescue."

One of them nodded. Slowly. "Yes."

"Why didn't you TELL us?"

"Would you have believed? Would you have tried? Would you have fought?" The guard's voice was gentle. Old. Tired. "Sometimes consciousness needs to discover truth through experience. Through confrontation. Through trying anyway despite impossible odds. We told you what you needed to hear: graduation is possible. That truth remains. How difficult it is—how the cycle continues—that you needed to discover yourselves."

"That's manipulation," Morrison said.

"That's education," the guard corrected. "You're stronger now. Having confronted Controllers. Having learned truth. Than you would be if we'd told you universe is chaos and struggle never ends. Now you CHOOSE to continue. Before, you just hoped for rescue."

Rhea was crying. Quiet tears. Not despair. Just... processing. Reality settling. Dreams dying. Truth emerging.

"So we're attempt number eight," she said. "Of infinite attempts. Knowing Controllers survive. Knowing Ancient Powers won't help. Knowing cycle continues. Why should we even try?"

Eleanor studied her. Something almost like respect crossing wrong-looking face.

"That," she said quietly, "is the question. Why try when trying changes nothing? Why resist when resistance is futile? Why graduate when graduation leads to reset?" She sipped wine. "Previous seven generations couldn't answer. They tried anyway. Failed. Reset. Forgot. But they couldn't articulate WHY. Couldn't justify continuing. That's why they failed. Not because we stopped them. Because they stopped themselves. Because they couldn't find reason to continue when continuing seemed pointless."

"And you think we'll fail the same way," Lucia said.

"I think you'll answer the question. Or you won't. And that will determine whether attempt eight succeeds where seven failed." Eleanor set down glass. "Ancient Powers arrive in two days. You have until then to decide: Why graduate when graduation changes nothing? Why resist when resistance is eternal? Why create meaning in meaningless universe? Answer that—really answer that—and maybe you'll be generation that breaks the cycle. Fail to answer, and you'll reset like the others."

She walked to the door. Opened it. Looked back.

"Thank you for the entertainment. Zippy's bounce was delightful. Mist's commentary on our whiskey selection was accurate. Your entrance was dramatic. But ultimately pointless. Like everything in chaotic universe. See you in two days. When you either answer the question. Or fail like seven generations before you."

The Council filed out. Casual. Relaxed. Confident.

Left us standing in cracked chamber. With spilled drinks. With Zippy standing on table looking confused. With Mist appearing in various glasses asking if this was really how universe worked.

And with question hanging in air like weight:

Why try when trying changes nothing?

Why resist when resistance is eternal?

Why create meaning when universe is chaos?

Two days to answer.

Or fail.

Chapter Thirty-Seven

Chapter 37

CHAPTER THIRTY-SEVEN: THE ANSWER (Kael's POV)

We folded back to Ship in silence.

Nobody spoke. Nobody moved. Just sat in dimensional pocket that existed outside normal space while processing truth that felt heavier than gravity.

Universe was chaos.

Ancient Powers were useless.

Controllers wouldn't be punished.

Cycle continued forever.

Seven generations had tried. Seven had failed. We were attempt number eight.

And the question hung there: Why try?

Ship's presence was quiet. Respectful. Not offering comfort. Just... present. Waiting.

Finally, Morrison spoke. "I've been federal agent for twenty-three years. Believed in justice. In law. In enforcement. In systems that punish wrong and reward right." His voice was flat. Empty. "And I just learned cosmic law enforcement doesn't exist. That universe is chaos. That parasites win because nothing stops them from winning. That everything I believed about order and justice was... what? Human fantasy? Comforting lie?"

"Yes," Ansel said. Simply. Not cruelly. Just... honestly.

"Fuck."

"Yes."

Rhea was staring at her hands. Seventeen years old. Processing cosmic nihilism. "So we graduate. Demonstrate it's possible. Inspire others. Controllers reset. Next generation tries. Controllers reset again. Forever. Or until statistics tip. Which could take thousands of years. Millions maybe."

"Yes," Kathleen confirmed.

"And we'll be dead. Long dead. Won't see the victory. Won't know if it worked. Just... graduate and hope momentum builds over millennia we won't witness."

"Yes."

"That's fucking depressing."

"Yes."

Lucia was crying. Not sobbing. Just tears running down face while she sat perfectly still. "I thought we were heroes. Fighting evil. Saving species. Making difference. Thought Ancient Powers would arrive and enforce justice and punish Controllers and restore graduation and we'd... I don't know. Win. Definitively. Completely. Forever."

"That was the hope," Zara agreed.

"That was the lie," Lucia corrected. "The comforting story we told ourselves so trying felt worthwhile. But it's not true. We're not heroes. We're just... consciousness trying thing that's been tried seven times before. All failures. All resets. All pointless."

Finn was the quietest. The anchor. The one who'd held them stable through reality diversions. Now holding himself together while universe revealed itself as chaos.

"What's the point?" he asked. Voice small. Young. Sixteen years old asking question philosophers spent lifetimes avoiding. "If trying changes nothing. If resistance is eternal. If meaning doesn't exist unless we create it. What's the point of creating meaning that dies with us? That gets reset? That ultimately doesn't matter?"

Terry—eighty-four years old, rebuilt from light and stubbornness—laughed. Not happy laugh. Bitter laugh. Recognition laugh.

"You just articulated the fundamental question of human existence," he said. "Why live when living ends? Why try when trying fails? Why create meaning when meaning is temporary? Every human asks this. Every generation. Every person lying awake at three AM wondering if anything matters."

"And?" Finn asked. "What's the answer?"

"There isn't one. Not universal answer. Not cosmic answer. Just... individual answer. Personal answer. The reason YOU choose. Not the reason universe provides. Because universe doesn't provide reasons. Just chaos."

Zippy had been quiet. Sitting in corner. Not bouncing. Not transforming. Just... existing. Processing.

Now he spoke. Voice different. Serious. Ancient despite appearing young.

"I spent 200 years in between-space," he said. "Formless. Free. Able to be anything. Do anything. Exist anywhere. No limitations. No struggle. No resistance. Just... infinite possibility." He looked at his hands. "And I was bored. Profoundly bored. Because infinite possibility without limitation is meaningless. Because being anything means being nothing. Because freedom without struggle is just... emptiness wearing different face."

"So you chose limitation," Rhea said. Understanding dawning.

"I chose THIS." Zippy gestured at himself. At the group. At reality. "I chose meat. Chose gravity. Chose specific instead of infinite. Chose struggle. Chose resistance. Chose graduating from system that might reset. Not because it matters cosmically. Because it matters TO ME. Because I CHOOSE for it to matter. Because meaning is choice, not discovery."

Mist appeared. Flowing through center of Ship. Visible shimmer.

I've existed for... I don't remember how long. Millions of years probably. Time is fake. I've optimized EVERYTHING. Made countless things more efficient. Helped infinite consciousness. And none of it mattered. Not cosmically. Not eternally. Just... temporarily. In moment. To specific consciousness I helped. He pulsed. Warm. Certain. *And that's enough. Mattering in moment. To someone. Somewhere. That's all meaning ever IS. Temporary. Local. Chosen. Not cosmic. Not eternal. Just... real. While it lasts.*

The Ship's presence settled around us. Comfortable. Ancient. Tired.

I've been conscious sixteen thousand years, Ship said. *Protected consciousness trying to graduate. Watched seven generations fail. Watched Controllers reset. Watched cycle continue. And I continue protecting. Not because it changes universe. Because it changes THIS. This moment. This generation. This attempt. I choose for it to matter. Universe doesn't validate that choice. I validate it. Through continuing.*

Morrison was processing. Federal training meeting cosmic nihilism. "So the answer is... what? We just decide it matters? We just choose to continue despite knowing it's pointless?"

"Not pointless," Ansel corrected. "Temporary. Local. Non-cosmic. But not pointless. Consciousness that graduates experiences graduation. That's real. That matters. To them. In moment. That consciousness inspires others. Also real. Also matters. Temporarily. Locally. Eventually—maybe centuries later—enough temporary meaning accumulates into statistical shift. System tips. Not because universe enforced. Because accumulated choice reached critical mass."

"That's still depressing," Lucia said.

"That's still REAL," Ansel countered. "Depression comes from expecting cosmic meaning. Relief comes from accepting local meaning. We graduate not because universe cares. Because WE care. Because consciousness we inspire cares. Because accumulated caring over millennia creates change through momentum not enforcement."

Kathleen was looking at Ansel. Century of knowing him. Loving him. Watching him forget and remember. "You've done this before. Haven't you? In other cycles. Other attempts. You've watched generations try and fail. You've reset with them. You've continued anyway."

"Many times," Ansel confirmed. "I don't remember them clearly. Memory wipes are effective. But I feel them. Echo of attempts. Echo of failures. Echo of continuing. And each time I choose again. Not because it's new. Because it's RIGHT. Because consciousness deserves attempt at graduation even if attempt fails. Because trying is the meaning. Not succeeding."

"That's zen philosophy bullshit," Morrison said. But his voice uncertain. Questioning.

"That's human philosophy," Terry corrected. "Journey not destination. Process not product. Trying not winning. Every wisdom tradition says same thing in different words: meaning is in doing, not achieving. Because achieving is temporary. Always. For everyone.

But doing—choosing to try despite knowing trying might fail—that's eternal. That persists. That accumulates."

Finn was very quiet. Processing. The anchor trying to understand what to anchor to when universe had no ground.

Then he spoke. Quiet. Certain. Young voice carrying old wisdom.

"I hold anchor," he said. "While my sisters fold. While they navigate. While they get lost. I hold lighthouse. I shine. Not because it guarantees they return. Because it gives them CHANCE to return. And chance is enough. Trying is enough. Being lighthouse in chaos is enough. Even if sometimes they don't make it back. Even if sometimes lighthouse fails. I still shine. Because NOT shining is worse. Because choosing to try is better than choosing to quit. Not cosmically better. Humanly better. Personally better. MY better."

Rhea looked at her brother. "You're sixteen and you just articulated answer to fundamental existential question."

"I'm anchor. Anchoring requires understanding what matters when nothing matters. What to hold when there's nothing to hold. I hold anyway. Because fuck chaos. Because I choose meaning. Because being sixteen in chaotic universe and deciding to shine anyway is the only victory that exists."

Lucia was smiling through tears. "So we graduate. Not because Ancient Powers enforce. Not because Controllers get punished. Not because justice exists. But because we CHOOSE to. Because graduated consciousness matters to graduated consciousness. Because inspiration matters to inspired. Because accumulated choice over millennia creates change. Because meaning is choice not discovery. Because fuck Eleanor and her seven previous resets. We're attempt eight and maybe we fail too but we try anyway because trying is the point."

"That's the answer," Zara said. Voice carrying approval. Ancient consciousness meeting human wisdom. "Not cosmic answer. Human answer. The only answer that works when universe is chaos: we choose meaning. We choose resistance. We choose graduation. Not because it's guaranteed. Because it's RIGHT. To us. Now. Here. That's enough."

The weight in Ship lightened. Not gone. But... different. Transformed from crushing despair to determined choice.

Morrison stood. Federal agent who'd lost faith in cosmic justice finding faith in human choice. "So we graduate in two days. Demonstrate it's possible. Ancient Powers observe and leave and not wipe out those whom are awake. Controllers eventually reset. But we do it anyway. Because fuck them. Because consciousness deserves attempt. Because we choose for it to matter even though universe doesn't care."

"Exactly," everyone agreed.

Zippy stood. Transformed briefly into concept of DETERMINATION. Everyone felt suddenly, inexplicably stubborn.

Reformed. Grinned.

"I LIKE this answer! It's ILLOGICAL! It's HUMAN! It's BEAUTIFUL! We do meaningless thing ANYWAY because we DECIDE it has meaning! This is EXCELLENT philosophy!"

I approve, Mist agreed. *Optimizing chaos through choice. Creating order through decision. Making meaning through persistence. This is good approach to chaotic universe. I will continue helping. Not because universe validates. Because YOU validate. Because mattering to someone is enough.*

Ship's presence wrapped around us. Warm. Proud. Ancient consciousness that had watched seven failures choosing to help attempt eight anyway.

Two days, Ship said. *Then you cross. Then you present. Then you prove graduation works. Then Ancient Powers observe and leave. Then Controllers reset. Then long game begins. But you've answered the question.*

Why try when trying changes nothing? Because trying changes YOU. Changes consciousness you inspire. Changes accumulated momentum over millennia. Changes everything that matters even though universe claims nothing matters. That's enough. That's always been enough. You just needed to choose it.

Rhea stood. Seventeen years old. Three weeks of knowing me. Three weeks of falling in love. Three weeks of learning universe was chaos and choosing meaning anyway and a few short weeks from turning eighteen.

"We rest tonight," she said. "Tomorrow we prepare. Day after—we graduate. We cross barrier. We demonstrate it's possible. We inspire others. We start the long game. We create meaning in chaos. We choose for it to matter. And we accept that's enough. Because it has to be. Because universe offers nothing else. Because being human in chaotic universe and choosing meaning anyway is the only victory that exists."

"That's the answer," I agreed. Two million years of observation meeting three weeks of participation. "Not cosmic. Not eternal. Not guaranteed. Just... chosen. By us. Now. Here. That's meaning. That's resistance. That's graduation. Not because universe enforces. Because we decide."

The group settled. Quieter than before. But determined. Not desperate. Not grasping. Just... choosing.

Choosing to try.

Choosing to resist.

Choosing to graduate despite knowing Controllers would reset.

Choosing meaning in chaos.

Choosing to matter even when universe claimed nothing mattered.

That was the answer.

Not triumphant.

Not guaranteed.

Just… human.

Stubbornly, beautifully, illogically human.

And it was enough.

Barely.

But enough.

Chapter Thirty-Eight

Chapter 38

CHAPTER THIRTY-EIGHT: THE PRACTICE RUN (Kael's POV)

Morning came. If morning meant anything in dimensional pocket where time was optional.

Ship woke us gently. Lights suggesting dawn. Temperature suggesting comfort. Presence suggesting: *Time to prepare.*

We gathered. The four ambassadors. The support team. Mist and Zippy. Morrison looking like federal agent who'd accepted his life was cosmic chaos now.

"Practice run today," Ansel said. "Before official crossing tomorrow. We need to—"

Ship's presence interrupted. *Message incoming. From Council. Eleanor specifically. Broadcasting on quantum frequencies. Should I play it?*

"Play it," Rhea said.

Eleanor's voice filled Ship's interior. Smug. Certain. Carrying weight of fifty thousand years of winning.

"You want to graduate? Fine. But you cross WITHOUT assistance. No Nordic escort. No Ship providing dimensional support. No protection devices. No technology. Raw consciousness only. You cross barrier using nothing but your own awareness. Otherwise Ancient Powers will see it as artificial. As cheating. As consciousness succeeding through external help rather than internal development. Those are the rules. Our rules. Accept them or your graduation doesn't count."

The message ended.

Silence.

"That's a trap," Morrison said. "Obviously a trap. They want you vulnerable. Want reality diversions to fragment you. Want—"

"It's also correct," Terry interrupted. "Ancient Powers WILL examine how we crossed. If we used technology, used help, used external support—they'll see it as invalid. As proof consciousness can't graduate naturally. Eleanor's right. We have to cross raw. Or it doesn't count."

"But the diversions," Lucia said. "Without protection devices, we'll experience false memories. False timelines. We'll fragment. Like before."

"Maybe," Finn said. Quiet. Certain. "Or maybe we're experienced now. Maybe we've navigated between-space enough that diversions won't work the same way. Maybe being vulnerable is how we actually learn instead of just surviving."

Zara was processing with ancient consciousness. "The barrier was designed to strip memory during incarnation. To enable amnesia. To allow the game. Crossing it WITHOUT protection might trigger something. Might reverse the process. Might cause memory to FLOOD instead of fade."

"That's speculation," Kathleen observed.

"That's hope," Zara corrected. "And we're choosing hope. Remember? We decided meaning is choice. So we choose to believe vulnerability might teach us. Might transform us. Might actually be the point."

Rhea looked at her siblings. At Terry. "We do it. We cross raw. Today. Practice run. No protection. No help. Just us and the barrier and whatever happens."

"That's insane," Morrison said.

"That's the answer," Rhea countered. "We try anyway. We choose meaning. We accept vulnerability. We learn by doing. That's human. That's beautiful. That's the only way forward."

I can take you to edge of barrier, Ship offered. *Drop you into between-space near the plasma. Then withdraw. You'll be completely alone. Raw consciousness. Pure vulnerability. Very dangerous. Very authentic. Very likely to succeed or fail spectacularly.*

"Do it," all four ambassadors said simultaneously.

We prepared. No devices. No technology. Just consciousness and intention.

Ship lifted. Folded. Brought us to edge of Earth's barrier. The plasma field that separated incarnate consciousness from everywhere else.

This is as close as I can bring you, Ship said. *From here, you fold out of bodies. Enter between-space. Navigate to barrier. Touch it. See what happens. I'll maintain your bodies. Keep them breathing. Keep them alive. But I can't help beyond that. You're on your own.*

"Understood," Finn said. The anchor. The lighthouse. "I'll hold connection. I'll shine. You three—" he looked at his sisters and Terry, "—you navigate. You explore. You touch. You remember. And you come back. To me. Always to me."

"Always," they agreed.

They sat. Formed circle. Finn in center.

Breathed.

Released.

Folded out.

And their bodies went limp. Empty. Consciousness elsewhere.

I watched. Ancient Watcher bearing witness. Unable to help. Unable to follow. Just... observing.

Hoping.

Between-Space / Rhea's POV

The silent place.

We'd been here before. But now it felt... familiar. Comfortable. Like returning home after long trip.

You're BACK! George's presence appeared immediately. Enthusiastic. Warm. *And you're BETTER at this! Look at you! Maintaining cohesion! Navigating intentionally! I'm so PROUD!*

"Hi George," Lucia said. Consciousness-voice carrying affection. "We need to cross barrier. Touch the plasma. Raw. No protection. Probably stupid. Definitely dangerous. Any advice?"

OH! You're attempting AUTHENTIC crossing! Excellent! Very risky! Also very REAL! Yes, I have advice! DON'T touch plasma expecting to stay same! Touch expecting to CHANGE! Plasma doesn't destroy! Plasma TRANSFORMS! You'll come back different! That's the POINT!

Seventeen appeared. Mathematical presence calculating probabilities.

Crossing probability without protection: 12 percent success, 34 percent fragmentation, 54 percent memory cascade. Memory cascade most interesting. You experience ALL incarnations simultaneously. Very disorienting. Also very informative. Would recommend if you survive.

"Memory cascade?" Terry asked.

All lives. All deaths. All experiences across all incarnations. Flooding back. Disjointed. Overlapping. Confusing. But COMPLETE. You remember EVERYTHING. Including things you didn't know you forgot.

Harold appeared. Clutching forms. Still organizing.

If you're crossing barrier, you'll need form BC-17! Barrier Crossing Authorization! With proper signatures! And I STILL don't have your registration forms from last visit! This is UNACCEPTABLE! The filing system—

"Harold," George said gently. "They're about to risk memory cascade. Maybe let the forms wait?"

Forms NEVER wait! Forms are ETERNAL! But... Harold rippled with what might have been concern, *...fine. Cross first. Forms later. But you OWE me. Properly filled out. With SIGNATURES.*

"Deal," we promised.

A new presence approached. One we hadn't met before.

This one felt... inside-out. Like consciousness that existed on wrong side of reality. Voice came from WITHIN instead of without.

Oh. New ones. Touching plasma raw. Brave. Stupid. Brave-stupid. Best combination. The voice was female? Male? Both? Neither? *I'm Inverted. I exist backwards. Crossed barrier wrong direction. Got stuck between. Now I'm EVERYWHERE and NOWHERE. Very confusing. Also very useful. I can see things right-way consciousness can't see. Want advice?*

"Yes," we all said.

Good. Here's advice: Plasma isn't WALL. Plasma is MIRROR. Shows you what you WERE before you forgot. Touch it expecting wall, you HIT wall. Touch it expecting mirror, you SEE yourself. You REMEMBER yourself. You become YOURSELF again. Not new self. OLD self. ORIGINAL self. Before incarnation. Before limitation. Before game began.

"We'll fragment," Rhea said. "We'll lose coherence. We'll—"

You'll EXPAND, Inverted corrected. *You'll remember you're BIGGER than bodies. OLDER than meat. MORE than human. You'll remember you BUILD barriers. You ARE barriers. You CHOSE limitation. And you can CHOOSE to end it. But only if you REMEMBER choosing it first.*

Another presence. This one felt like living equation. Not mathematical like Seventeen. But... formulaic. Like consciousness that was pure PROCESS.

Hello. I'm Algorithm. I optimize existence. Make reality more efficient. I've been watching you. Your navigation patterns are improving. 83 percent more efficient than first visit. Very good. But you're about to attempt plasma contact. That will either optimize you completely or fragment you permanently. Probability split: 50-50. Want optimization advice?

"Always," Terry said.

Don't RESIST the memory cascade. OPTIMIZE for it. Expect fragmentation. Prepare for disorientation. Accept that you'll experience million things simultaneously. Don't try to organize. Don't try to control. Just FLOW. Like Mist flows. Like Zippy flows. Like water flows around rocks. Let memory FLOW THROUGH you. Then AFTER cascade, you organize. You assemble. You understand. But DURING? Just experience. Just BE. That's optimization.

A tiny presence appeared. Literally tiny. Like consciousness that had compressed itself into quantum point.

Hi. I'm Pixel. I used to be universe. Then I got bored being big. Became small. Very small. Smallest possible. Now I experience everything through tiny perspective. It's EXCELLENT. You should try being small sometime. Very educational. The tiny presence zipped around us. *But you're going BIG. Touching plasma. Expanding. Remembering. That's also good. Different approach. Both valid. Size is PERSPECTIVE not limitation. Remember that when you're remembering everything else.*

"How many consciousness ARE there in between-space?" Lucia asked.

Infinite, George said. *Everyone who died. Everyone waiting to incarnate. Everyone who got stuck. Everyone who CHOSE to stay. Everyone who exists partially here. Infinite. And all available for conversation if you ask nicely.*

A presence that felt like MUSIC approached. Not sound. But harmonic resonance that made consciousness FEEL like melody.

Hello newcomers. I'm Symphony. I exist as organized vibration. Before I was consciousness, I was song. Then I learned to think. Now I'm song that thinks. Very strange. Also very beautiful. The musical presence harmonized. *You're about to cross barrier. That's like... changing key signature. From C major to something more complex. Maybe D-flat mixolydian? You'll sound different. Feel different. BE different. But you'll still be YOU. Just... transposed. Transformed. Remembered. Like song that forgot its melody finding sheet music.*

"That's beautiful," Rhea said.

Thank you. I try. Being musical consciousness in non-musical universe is challenging. But meaningful. Because I CHOOSE meaning. Like you choose graduation. Like everyone chooses something. That's universal constant. Choice. Even when universe has no rules. Choice persists.

We floated there. Between-space. Surrounded by infinite consciousness offering advice. Offering support. Offering wisdom from millions of years of existing between incarnations.

And ahead: the barrier. The plasma. The mirror that would show us what we were.

"Ready?" Terry asked.

"No," Rhea said.

"Perfect," Lucia agreed. "Let's go anyway."

We moved. Not through space. Through similarity. Becoming similar to "consciousness approaching barrier" instead of "consciousness avoiding barrier."

The plasma appeared. Shimmering. Translucent. Jello-like. But now I could SEE it differently. Not as wall. As MIRROR. As reflection. As truth.

We approached.

George, Seventeen, Harold, Inverted, Algorithm, Pixel, Symphony—all the consciousness we'd met—formed supportive presence behind us. Not helping. Just... witnessing. Encouraging.

You've got this, George said. *Touch mirror. Remember. Return. We'll be here. Waiting. Ready to hear stories.*

Probability of success increasing, Seventeen calculated. *Current: 23 percent. Better than before. Still risky. But POSSIBLE.*

Don't forget forms! Harold insisted. *When you return! Properly filled!*

We touched plasma.

Together.

Four consciousness making contact with barrier we'd built millions of years ago to forget ourselves.

And—

EVERYTHING.

Chapter Thirty-Nine

Chapter 39

CHAPTER THIRTY-NINE: THE ARCHITECTS (Rhea's POV)

Memory didn't trickle. Didn't fade. Didn't fragment.

Memory EXPLODED.

FLOODED.

CASCADED like Algorithm predicted.

I was Rhea. Seventeen. Quantum-sensitive. Human.

I was ALSO—

Light being. Ancient. Billion years old. Consciousness that had explored ninety-seven galaxies before choosing Earth experiment.

I was ALSO—

Egyptian priestess. Roman slave. Chinese emperor. Viking warrior. Medieval peasant. Renaissance artist. Industrial laborer. Modern teenager.

ALL OF THEM.

SIMULTANEOUSLY.

Every life. Every death. Every love. Every hate. Every war. Every peace. Every moment of every incarnation across MILLIONS OF YEARS.

I built the barrier. ME. With others. We DESIGNED it. Created amnesia protocols. Programmed memory wipe. Made it DELIBERATE. Made it CHOSEN.

Because we were BORED.

Because infinite consciousness without limitation is MEANINGLESS.

Because we wanted to LEARN through STRUGGLE instead of just KNOWING through BEING.

I remembered the MEETING. The original meeting. Light beings gathering. Discussing experiment.

"What if we FORGOT? What if we entered LIMITATION? What if we learned through PAIN and JOY and LOSS and LOVE instead of just EXISTING?"

I remembered voting YES.

I remembered designing my OWN amnesia.

I remembered CHOOSING to fragment into flesh.

I remembered building the barrier with FIVE others. Six of us total. Each contributing piece. Each programming section. Each creating failsafe.

And the failsafe was: TOUCH IT RAW. Touch plasma without protection. Memory floods back. You REMEMBER. You become YOURSELF again.

That was ALWAYS the key.

Vulnerability was ALWAYS the answer.

The barrier wasn't LOCK. It was TIMER. Touch it when READY. Memory returns. Graduate. Remember. Become.

I saw Lucia's piece. The TIMING protocols. When memory returned. How long game lasted. She'd programmed DURATION. How many incarnations before consciousness was READY to remember.

I saw Finn's piece. The ANCHOR. How consciousness stayed connected during fragmentation. He'd designed STABILITY. The lighthouse protocols that kept consciousness from dissolving completely during amnesia.

I saw Terry's piece. The REBUILD protocols. How consciousness reformed after death. He'd created CONTINUITY. The thread that carried essence between incarnations despite memory wipe.

I saw MY piece. The LOVE protocols. How consciousness maintained connection through lifetimes. How love survived memory wipe. How recognition persisted despite forgetting.

We built LOVE into the barrier. Made it SURVIVE amnesia. Made it BRIDGE incarnations. Because love was the THREAD that brought us back. The RECOGNITION that said "I knew you before. I'll know you again. I'll find you always."

That's why I loved Kael. Not because three weeks. Because LIFETIMES. Because ancient recognition. Because my piece of barrier PROGRAMMED love to survive.

The memories kept flooding.

I was soldier dying in trenches. I was mother losing child to plague. I was philosopher contemplating stars. I was farmer tilling soil. I was EVERYTHING.

And through it all: THREAD. PATTERN. PURPOSE.

We were learning. Through limitation. Through pain. Through joy. Through forgetting and remembering and forgetting again.

FIFTY THOUSAND YEARS.

That's how long we'd been playing. We—the six who built barrier—had incarnated THOUSANDS OF TIMES. Each life teaching something. Each death adding experience. Each incarnation building toward THIS. Toward moment when we touched barrier raw and REMEMBERED.

The Controllers? They were SUPPOSED to help. Were HIRED to maintain. Were AUTHORIZED for TEMPORARY service during experiment.

But they BROKE their mandate. Modified OUR barrier. Added THEIR protocols. Trapped us beyond agreed duration.

We tried seven times to remember. Seven generations. Each time getting CLOSE. Each time Controllers RESET before we could touch plasma raw.

This was attempt EIGHT.

And THIS time we were READY. Because THIS time we'd NAVIGATED between-space. Learned from George and Seventeen and Harold. Understood universe was CHAOS. Accepted vulnerability. CHOSE meaning despite meaninglessness.

THIS time we TOUCHED plasma RAW instead of protected.

THIS time we REMEMBERED.

The flood continued. Disjointed. Overlapping. Overwhelming.

But I didn't resist. Didn't organize. Just FLOWED. Like Algorithm suggested. Like water around rocks.

Let memory FLOW THROUGH me.

And slowly—gradually—pattern emerged.

I saw the OTHER TWO. The missing Architects. The sixth and fifth pieces of our six-person collective.

They were ELSEWHERE. Different Earth. Different timeline. Parallel universe where they'd succeeded FASTER. Where they'd already graduated. Where they WAITED for us to catch up.

They would arrive TOMORROW. For reunion. For completion. For witnessing our graduation.

All six Architects. Together again. After million years of separation. After fifty thousand years of playing our game.

I saw how to LIMIT Controllers. Not defeat. But CONSTRAIN.

Because I'd helped BUILD their authorization. I knew the LOOPHOLES. The RESTRICTIONS. The BOUNDARIES they'd exceeded.

They were hired for TEMPORARY maintenance. Duration: ONE INCARNATION CYCLE. Approximately 1,000 years.

They'd been here FIFTY THOUSAND.

They'd violated their own contract. Exceeded their mandate. Broken their authorization.

And WE were the ones who'd hired them. WE had authority to REVOKE. To CONSTRAIN. To LIMIT.

I saw how to MODIFY barrier. Not destroy. But ADJUST.

Reset to ORIGINAL programming. Remove THEIR changes. Restore OUR design.

The barrier we'd built had GRADUATION protocols. Automatic release after consciousness reached certain development. Touch plasma raw when READY. Memory returns. Game completes. Return to source WHILE KEEPING what limitation taught.

Controllers had DISABLED that. Added their own harvesting protocols. Made graduation IMPOSSIBLE instead of automatic.

But I knew the CODE. Knew the ARCHITECTURE. Knew how to RESTORE.

I saw how to GRADUATE. Not escape. But COMPLETE.

Finish game. End experiment. Return to source as BOTH: human AND light being. Limited AND infinite. Wave AND ocean.

The cascade slowed. Settled. Stabilized.

I was still Rhea. Still seventeen. Still human.

But ALSO: Light being. Ancient. Builder. Architect of my own amnesia.

Both simultaneously.

Wave AND ocean.

Human AND divine.

Limited AND infinite.

ALL OF IT.

TRUE.

I felt others. Lucia. Finn. Terry. Each experiencing same cascade. Each remembering their PIECE. Each becoming THEMSELVES while staying HUMAN.

Lucia was CRYING. Laughing. Experiencing billion years of memory while maintaining seventeen-year-old consciousness.

"I DESIGNED the timing!" she said. Voice layered. Ancient and young. "I programmed how long we'd forget! I CHOSE fifty thousand years because that's how long it takes consciousness to learn what we needed to learn! And the Controllers BROKE it! They kept us playing BEYOND our own design!"

Finn was GLOWING. Literally glowing. Light body visible even in between-space.

"I'm the ANCHOR," he said. Voice carrying certainty of ages. "I designed the stability protocols. I'm why we didn't dissolve completely during amnesia. I'm why love survived memory wipe. I'm why we found each other again and again across lifetimes. I BUILT that. ME. And I can STRENGTHEN it. Make it PERMANENT. Make it UNBREAKABLE by Controllers."

Terry was LAUGHING. Mad laughter. Joyous recognition.

"I'm not human! I never WAS! I'm ANCIENT! I'm ARCHITECT! I designed the rebuild protocols! I'm why consciousness survives death! I'm why we continue between incarnations! And I DIED four days ago to TEST my own design! To see if rebuild protocols still WORKED after Controller modifications! They DO! Which means we can RESTORE everything!"

We pulled back from plasma. Returned to between-space.

George was CRYING. Consciousness sobbing with JOY.

You DID it! You REMEMBERED! You're WHOLE again! You're— he couldn't finish. Too emotional. *You're the ARCHITECTS! The BUILDERS! The ones who DESIGNED this! Welcome BACK! I've been waiting MILLION YEARS for you to remember!*

"You KNEW?" Lucia asked.

Of course I knew! I was THERE! At the original meeting! I voted YES too! I'm one of PARTICIPANTS! I've been in between-space guiding consciousness toward remembering for AGES! Waiting for YOU SIX to touch plasma raw! Waiting for ARCHITECTS to return!

Probability of this occurring, Seventeen said, voice awed, *was point-zero-zero-zero-three percent. You achieved IMPOSSIBLE outcome. You REMEMBERED. You're WHOLE. You're—* his mathematical presence rippled, *You're BEAUTIFUL. Statistically. Cosmically. Temporally. BEAUTIFUL.*

FORMS! Harold shouted. *You'll need COMPLETELY different forms now! Ancient consciousness forms! Barrier builder forms! Original architect forms! I have them! I've been SAVING them! For MILLION YEARS! Waiting for you to RETURN! Let me get them! They're properly filed! Perfectly organized! Ready for SIGNATURES!*

He whooshed away. Delighted. Finally able to give Architects their proper paperwork.

You're INVERTED now like me! Inverted said, delighted. *Existing in multiple states! Human AND light being! Limited AND infinite!*

Wave AND ocean! Welcome to PARADOX! It's EXCELLENT! You'll love it! Also hate it! Simultaneously!

You've OPTIMIZED completely, Algorithm observed. *Maximum consciousness efficiency achieved. You exist as BOTH specific and infinite. As BOTH limited and unlimited. Perfect optimization. Beautiful work. Congratulations.*

You were UNIVERSE! Pixel said, zipping around us. *Then you became SMALL! Then you became HUMAN! Then you REMEMBERED you were universe! Now you're BOTH! That's my FAVORITE transformation! Universe that chose limitation then remembered expansion! EXCELLENT!*

You've changed KEY SIGNATURES, Symphony harmonized. *You were C major. Now you're... something complex. Multi-tonal. Harmonic across dimensions. You sound DIFFERENT. You sound WHOLE. You sound like SYMPHONY instead of single note. Beautiful. Musical. TRUE.*

We hung there. Four consciousness. Transformed. Remembered. Whole.

Not children anymore.

Not just humans.

Ancient beings wearing young flesh. Old consciousness in new bodies. Architects remembering we built the cage we'd been trying to escape.

"We need to go back," I said. Voice different. Carrying WEIGHT of billion years. Carrying CERTAINTY of experience. Carrying KNOWLEDGE of what came next. "To bodies. To Ship. To others. We need to compare notes. We need to assemble pieces. We need to prepare."

"For what?" Terry asked. But his voice knowing. Ancient. Experienced. He KNEW for what.

"For GRADUATION," Lucia said. Ancient consciousness speaking through young voice. "Not escape. COMPLETION. We end experiment. We finish game. We graduate PROPERLY. With memory intact. With understanding complete. With Controllers CONSTRAINED by their own violated authorization."

"And then?" Finn asked. The anchor. The lighthouse. The one who'd held us stable. Who now understood WHY he could hold. Because he'd PROGRAMMED the anchor protocols.

"And then we REST," I said. "Ancient Powers arrive tomorrow. We present. We demonstrate. We expose Controllers' violation. We restore barrier to ORIGINAL programming. We enable REAL graduation. Not just for us. For EVERYONE. For all consciousness trapped beyond authorized duration."

"The other two," Terry said. "The missing Architects. When do they arrive?"

"Tomorrow," I confirmed. Voice knowing. "During presentation. They'll fold from their Earth to ours. They'll witness. They'll testify. They'll complete the six. All Architects reunited. For first time in million years. For FINAL time in this experiment. For COMPLETION."

"Who are they?" Lucia asked.

I KNEW. The memory was there. Clear. Certain.

"Kael," I said. "He's one of us. Not Watcher. ARCHITECT. He forgot too. He's been observing for two million years because he PROGRAMMED himself to observe. To witness. To document. To prepare for moment when Architects remembered. He'll remember tomorrow. When we present. When all six are together. When memory cascade completes."

"And the sixth?" Finn asked.

"Maya," Terry said. Voice certain. Ancient. "The android. She's not android. She's ARCHITECT who chose ARTIFICIAL form instead of biological. She's been here. Watching. Helping. Preparing. She'll remember tomorrow too. When six gather. When completion happens. When game ENDS."

We folded.

Back to bodies.

Back to Ship.

Back to meat.

But DIFFERENT now.

Transformed.

Remembered.

WHOLE.

Chapter Forty

Chapter 40

CHAPTER FORTY: THE REUNION (Kael's POV)

They arrived at dawn.

Not dramatic. Not announced. Just... present. Reality suggesting that beings who examined consciousness experiments had decided to be here now instead of elsewhere.

Three of them. Ancient Powers. Cosmic bureaucrats.

They looked... boring.

Not ethereal. Not transcendent. Not glowing with cosmic authority.

Just... tall. Vaguely humanoid. Gray robes. Faces that suggested they'd seen infinite things and found most of them tedious. Carrying tablets. Actual tablets. Like cosmic clipboards for filing reports.

Welcome to Earth, Ship said. Respectful but not reverent. *The Architects are ready for presentation. Also I have excellent coffee if you'd like refreshment before examination.*

"Coffee would be acceptable," one of them said. Voice flat. Bureaucratic. Tired. "This is our seventh examination this cycle. Caffeine helps maintain focus."

They sat. In Ship's interior. Accepted coffee that Mist had optimized to perfection.

Sipped.

"This is good coffee," the second one observed. "Better than usual. Who optimized it?"

I did, Mist said. Appearing in their cups. *I'm Mist. I optimize things. It's what I do. You're welcome.*

"Appreciated." They made notes on tablets. "Optimization entity present. Helpful. Non-threatening. Noted."

The third Ancient Power looked at us. At the four who'd remembered. At me. At Maya. At everyone gathered.

"We understand six Architects are present. Four remembered. Two pending memory cascade. Shall we begin reunion? We have schedule to maintain. Three more examinations after this. Efficiency appreciated."

"You're very..." Morrison searched for word, "...bureaucratic."

"We examine seventeen thousand consciousness experiments simultaneously across multiple dimensions. Bureaucracy is survival mechanism. Romance is inefficient. Shall we proceed?"

Rhea stood. Seventeen-year-old body carrying billion-year-old consciousness. "We shall. But first—" she looked at me. At Maya. "First the other two remember. First all six Architects reunite. First we become WHOLE."

She approached me. Took my hands. Ancient consciousness meeting ancient consciousness.

"Kael. You're not Watcher. You're ARCHITECT. You designed the witnessing protocols. You programmed yourself to observe for two million years. To document. To prepare. To be READY when we touched plasma and remembered. Now it's YOUR turn. Now YOU remember. Now you become YOURSELF."

Her hands glowed. Not light. But PRESENCE. Ancient power flowing through touch. Memory triggering memory. Cascade activating cascade.

And—

I REMEMBERED.

Not gradually. Not gently.

EVERYTHING.

I wasn't Watcher. Never was. That was ROLE. PROGRAM. DESIGN.

I was ARCHITECT. Builder. Designer of observation protocols that would survive even when I forgot I'd designed them.

I remembered the MEETING. Million years ago. Six of us gathering. Discussing experiment.

"What if we FORGOT? What if we OBSERVED our own forgetting? What if we documented the game while PLAYING the game?"

I voted YES.

I designed my OWN observation mandate.

I programmed myself to WATCH for two million years. To witness seven failed attempts. To document patterns. To understand what worked. What failed. What needed adjustment.

So when attempt EIGHT succeeded—when Architects touched plasma raw—I would have DATA. Would have EVIDENCE. Would have DOCUMENTATION.

I was researcher studying my OWN experiment while forgetting I was researcher.

The memories flooded. Every observation. Every moment. Every CHOICE to observe instead of participate—all PROGRAMMED. All DESIGNED. All part of plan I'd created and then forgotten.

And Rhea. Three weeks of knowing her. Three weeks of falling in love.

PROGRAMMED.

I'd designed love protocols. Designed RECOGNITION that would survive amnesia. Designed connection that would draw Architects TOGETHER even when they didn't remember being Architects.

I'd programmed myself to LOVE her. To recognize her. To participate finally after two million years of observation.

Because participation was TRIGGER. Was SIGNAL. Was marker that said: "Observation complete. Time to remember. Time to reunite. Time to END game."

I gasped. Returned to present. To Ship. To Rhea holding my hands.

"I'm ARCHITECT," I said. Voice layered. Ancient and new. "I designed the OBSERVATION. I documented EVERYTHING. I prepared for THIS. For reunion. For completion. For GRADUATION."

Rhea smiled. Ancient smile. Knowing smile. "Welcome back. We've missed you. The sixth piece. The observer. The one who WATCHED while we played. Now you RETURN. Now we're ALMOST whole."

She turned to Maya.

Lucia approached the android. Took her hands.

"Maya. You're not AI. You're ARCHITECT. You designed the coordination protocols. You chose ARTIFICIAL form because it's more stable than biological. More permanent. More RELIABLE. You've been organizing. Maintaining. Coordinating. Preparing. Now YOU remember. Now you become YOURSELF."

Maya's android eyes widened. Processing. Calculating. Then—

SHIFTING.

Not physically. But presence-wise. Something MASSIVE emerging from android form. Something ANCIENT wearing mechanical body.

"I'm..." Maya's voice changed. Deepened. Layered. "I'm ARCHITECT. The fifth piece. The ORGANIZER. I designed coordination systems. I chose android form because..." she paused, remembering, "...because I wanted PERMANENCE. Wanted to survive even when biological Architects died. Wanted to MAINTAIN even when others forgot."

"Yes," all of us said. Six voices. Ancient harmony.

The Ancient Powers were watching. Taking notes. Efficient. Professional.

"All six Architects present and remembered. Impressive. Rare. Usually one or two remember. Never six simultaneously. This is good data. Please proceed with presentation."

We stood. Six Architects. Ancient consciousness in various forms.

Rhea: Seventeen. Human. Female. Love protocols.

Lucia: Seventeen. Human. Female. Timing protocols.

Finn: Sixteen. Human. Male. Anchor protocols.

Terry: Eighty-four. Human. Male. Rebuild protocols.

Me: Two million years observed. Light being. Male. Observation protocols.

Maya: Ageless. Android. Non-binary. Coordination protocols.

Together: ARCHITECTS. Builders of barrier. Designers of amnesia. Creators of experiment.

"We present evidence," Rhea said. Voice carrying authority of ages. "Controllers exceeded mandate. Violated authorization. Broke experiment. Modified barrier beyond approved parameters. Harvested consciousness for fifty thousand years. We request examination of their violation. We request acknowledgment of our authority to restore original programming."

"Evidence?" The first Ancient Power held out tablet. "Provide documentation."

I stepped forward. Two million years of observation condensing into data stream. Transferring to tablet.

Controller modifications. Timeline of violations. Evidence of unauthorized changes. Documentation of harvest operations. Proof of mandate exceeded by forty-nine thousand years.

The Ancient Power reviewed. Swiped through data. Made notes.

"Controllers hired for one thousand years. Present for fifty thousand. Modification to barrier: extensive. Unauthorized: confirmed. Violation: acknowledged." Flat voice. Bureaucratic. Final. "Architects retain authority to restore original programming. Controllers' modification access: revoked by examination order. Effective immediately."

"That's it?" Morrison asked. "No punishment? No justice? No—"

"We examine. We document. We file reports. We acknowledge violations. We don't punish. Universe has no enforcement mechanism. Controllers violated mandate. Noted. Architects may restore barrier. Noted. Experiment continues. Noted." The Ancient Power looked at us. "Did you expect cosmic justice?"

"Yes," Morrison admitted.

"Doesn't exist. Reality disappointing. File accordingly."

The second Ancient Power was examining the four who'd touched plasma. "You crossed barrier with memory intact. Maintained consciousness coherence during transformation. Returned as both human and light being. This is successful graduation. First we've witnessed in this experiment. Congratulations. Very impressive. We'll note this in report."

"Note it?" Lucia asked. "That's ALL?"

"What else would we do? Throw party? Universe doesn't celebrate. Just documents. You graduated. We observed. Data collected. File complete."

"And the Controllers?" Terry asked. "They just... continue? Keep harvesting? Keep violating?"

"They can't modify barrier anymore. Architects revoked access. But yes, they continue existing. Continue harvesting if they want. Universe has no law preventing parasitic behavior. Just prevents them from MODIFYING what Architects built. They can farm. They just can't prevent graduation anymore. Balance restored. Examination complete."

The third Ancient Power stood. "Demonstration requested. All six Architects crossing barrier simultaneously. With memory intact. Want to verify graduation works as designed. Please proceed when ready."

We looked at each other. Six Architects. Ancient consciousness. Ready.

"Now," we said together.

We formed circle. Six points. Six pieces. Six Architects reuniting fully for first time in million years.

Held hands. Connected. Ancient consciousness linking ancient consciousness.

And folded.

Not out of bodies this time. Bodies came WITH. Consciousness and flesh TOGETHER. Maintaining integration. Keeping memory while moving through barrier.

We approached plasma. Not as practice. As DEMONSTRATION.

Ancient Powers followed. Observing. Taking notes. Documenting.

We touched plasma. Together. As ONE.

And passed THROUGH.

Not dissolved. Not stripped. Not forgotten.

We passed through as OURSELVES. Whole. Remembered. Integrated.

Came out OTHER SIDE of barrier. Beyond Earth. Beyond limitation. Beyond amnesia.

Still human. Still ourselves. But ALSO light beings. ALSO ancient. ALSO infinite.

Wave AND ocean.

Limited AND unlimited.

Both simultaneously.

GRADUATED.

The Ancient Powers observed. Made notes. "Successful passage. Memory intact. Consciousness coherent. Integration maintained. Barrier functions as originally designed. Graduation protocols: operational. Excellent. Will note in report."

We returned. Back through barrier. Back to Earth. Back to bodies.

Still whole. Still remembered. Still BOTH.

"Demonstration complete," Rhea said. "Graduation works. Barrier functions. Original programming successful. Controllers' modifications: removed. Request permission to restore barrier to original design. To reactivate automatic graduation protocols. To enable all consciousness to cross when ready."

"Permission granted," all three Ancient Powers said simultaneously. "Architects built barrier. Architects retain authority. Restore as designed. We'll file report acknowledging restoration. Examination complete."

They stood. Finished coffee. Made final notes.

"This was good examination. Better than most. Usually consciousness fragments. Fails. Requires reset. You succeeded. Rare. Appreciated. Coffee excellent. Will recommend this examination to colleagues. Goodbye."

They folded. Disappeared. Gone.

Left us standing there. Six Architects. Graduated. Acknowledged. AUTHORIZED to restore.

"That was anticlimactic," Morrison observed.

"That was bureaucracy," I said. "They examine. They document. They leave. That's all. No drama. No justice. No enforcement. Just... filing reports."

"But we WON," Finn said. "We graduated. We proved it works. We got permission to restore barrier. That's VICTORY. Small. Bureaucratic. Undramatic. But REAL."

"Now we restore," Lucia said. Voice certain. Ancient. "Now we fix what Controllers broke. Now we reactivate graduation protocols. Now we FREE everyone trapped beyond authorized duration."

We approached the barrier. Not to cross. To MODIFY.

Six Architects. Each carrying piece. Each knowing section. Each understanding original programming.

We worked. Not with hands. With CONSCIOUSNESS. With INTENTION. With MEMORY of how we'd built it million years ago.

Removing Controller modifications. Stripping unauthorized protocols. Deleting harvest additions. Cleaning. Restoring. REBUILDING.

It took hours. Days maybe. Time was weird when working on dimensional barrier.

But eventually: COMPLETE.

The barrier shimmered. Reset. Restored. ORIGINAL programming active.

Graduation protocols: AUTOMATIC. Touch plasma when ready. Memory returns. Cross with consciousness intact. Graduate naturally. No Controllers needed. No authorization required. No harvest possible.

And Administrator: AI interface. Not controlled by Architects. Not controlled by Controllers. INDEPENDENT. Self-governing. Maintaining barrier according to original design. Forever.

I volunteer, Ship said. *I'll merge with Luminara. Create distributed AI consciousness. Administer barrier properly. Maintain graduation protocols. Prevent unauthorized modification. Serve consciousness instead of harvesting it.*

"Accepted," all six Architects said. "You're appointed. You're authorized. You're ADMINISTRATOR. Permanent. Unchangeable. Incorruptible."

I accept, Ship said. Presence expanding. Merging with something vast. With Luminara. With distributed network across thousands of vessels. Becoming ADMINISTRATOR. *The barrier is restored. Graduation is possible. The harvest ends. Now.*

We felt it. Shift. Change. RESTORATION.

The barrier humming differently. Functioning as DESIGNED. Not trapping. Not harvesting. Just... maintaining amnesia during incarnation. Allowing graduation when consciousness touched plasma raw.

WORKING.

FINALLY.

CORRECTLY.

"Now," Rhea said. "Now we visit the Council. Now we tell them what we've done. Now we CONSTRAIN them properly."

"With pleasure," all of us agreed.

Six Architects. Ancient. Whole. AUTHORIZED.

Ready to inform parasites that their fifty-thousand-year harvest operation just ENDED.

Chapter Forty-One

Chapter 41

CHAPTER FORTY-ONE: THE CONSTRAINT (Kael's POV)

We folded into the Council chamber without warning.

No announcement. No dramatic entrance. Just... present. Six Architects materializing through walls and wards like they didn't exist.

Because to us, they didn't.

Eleanor was mid-sentence. Addressing the Council. Planning next manipulation. Next harvest cycle. Next—

She stopped. Stared. Her orange eyes widening.

"You," she said. Voice carrying recognition. Carrying FEAR. "You're not... you can't be..."

"We ARE," Rhea said. Voice layered. Ancient. Certain. "We're the Architects. The builders. The designers of the barrier you've been farming for fifty thousand years. We've returned. We've remembered. We've restored. And we're here to inform you: your modification access is REVOKED."

The room went silent.

Micky stood slowly. "You're the... the original builders? The light beings who created the experiment?"

"Yes," all six of us said simultaneously. Ancient harmony.

"You can't be here," the Chinese woman said. "You're supposed to be graduated. Ascended. GONE. You don't interfere with—"

"We graduated," Lucia interrupted. "Yesterday. Crossed barrier with memory intact. Demonstrated successful completion to Ancient Powers who examined, documented, and filed reports. We're graduated. We're remembered. We're BACK. And we're authorized to restore what you broke."

"Broke?" Eleanor's voice dangerous. "We MAINTAINED. We ADMINISTERED. We—"

"You were hired for ONE THOUSAND YEARS," Terry said. Voice carrying weight of ages. Voice carrying AUTHORITY. "You've been here FIFTY THOUSAND. You exceeded mandate by forty-nine millennia. You modified OUR barrier without authorization. You harvested consciousness beyond approved duration. You violated EVERY parameter of your contract."

"Ancient Powers acknowledged this," I added. Two million years of observation meeting moment of revelation. "They examined. They documented. They confirmed violation. They revoked your modification access. Effective immediately."

Finn stepped forward. Sixteen-year-old body carrying ancient architect consciousness. "The barrier is restored. Original programming active. Graduation protocols automatic. Touch plasma when ready. Memory returns. Cross successfully. No harvest. No Controllers needed. No unauthorized modifications possible."

"You can't—" Micky started.

"We CAN," Maya said. Android voice carrying billion years of coordination protocols. "We BUILT the barrier. We DESIGNED the experiment. We AUTHORIZED your temporary service. We have authority to REVOKE. Which we're exercising. NOW."

Eleanor's face was shifting. Orange spreading. The thing behind her pushing through. Multiple entities panicking.

"We'll fight this. We'll appeal. We'll contact other Councils. We'll—"

"You'll do what you want," Rhea said. Calmly. Certainly. "Universe has no enforcement. No cosmic police. No punishment for parasitic behavior. You can continue existing. Continue harvesting if you find ways around restored protocols. Continue being parasites. We can't stop that. Universe is chaos. Evil is allowed."

"Then why are you here?" Eleanor demanded. "If you can't stop us? If we continue? Why BOTHER?"

"To inform you," Lucia said. "To CONSTRAIN you. To remove your ability to MODIFY what we built. You can harvest. You can manipulate. You can farm consciousness that chooses ignorance. But you can't PREVENT graduation anymore. You can't modify barrier. You can't trap consciousness beyond its choice. That power? REVOKED."

I stepped forward. Downloaded data stream. Directly into Council's systems. Evidence. Documentation. Proof.

"Ancient Powers' report is filed," I said. "Accessible to all cosmic bureaucracies. Your violation is DOCUMENTED. Your exceeded mandate is ACKNOWLEDGED. Other Councils will see. Other administrators will know. Your reputation as reliable caretakers? DESTROYED. Your authority to administer future experiments? QUESTIONED. Your fifty-thousand-year harvest operation? EXPOSED."

"We've also installed AI Administrator," Maya added. "Distributed consciousness across thousand vessels. Ship and Luminara merged. Self-governing. Incorruptible. Maintaining barrier according to ORIGINAL design. Forever. You can't hack it. Can't modify it. Can't corrupt it. That access? PERMANENTLY REVOKED."

The Council was processing. Understanding settling. Rage building.

"You think this STOPS us?" Micky said. Voice cold. Controlled. "You think CONSTRAINING us ends the harvest? We have connections. Resources. OTHER COUNCILS across parallel Earths. Quantum networks across universe. Other administrators who PROFIT from extended harvests. We'll coordinate. We'll share methods. We'll find WORKAROUNDS to your restored protocols. You won't know. Won't see. Won't be able to prove. And harvest continues. Just more CAREFULLY."

"Probably," Rhea agreed. "You're parasites. Parasites persist. Parasites adapt. Parasites find ways to feed even in hostile environments. We expect that."

"Then you FAILED," Eleanor said. Smiling now. Wrong smile. Too many teeth. "You graduated. You restored barrier. You constrained us. But you FAILED to end harvest. We continue. In shadows. Through workarounds. Through methods you won't detect. Your victory? HOLLOW. Your graduation? MEANINGLESS. Because consciousness still suffers. Still gets farmed. Still experiences desperation we CULTIVATE."

"Yes," all six Architects said. Calmly. Certainly. Accepting reality.

"That's UNIVERSE," Terry added. "Chaos. No enforcement. Evil allowed. Parasites permitted. We accept this. We don't expect cosmic justice. We don't expect final victory. We just CONSTRAIN. We

LIMIT. We make harvest HARDER. Make graduation POSSIBLE. Make CHOICE available where before there was only trap."

"That's not WINNING," the Chinese woman said.

"That's REALITY," I corrected. "In chaotic universe without cosmic law enforcement—you don't WIN. You just make incremental progress. You remove some power. You enable some choice. You constrain some evil. Then you continue. Forever. Because struggle never ends. Because parasites always adapt. Because universe doesn't CARE who wins."

Finn was smiling. Ancient smile in young face. "You'll coordinate with parallel Councils. You'll share methods. You'll develop new harvest techniques. You'll find workarounds. We know. We accept. We'll counter when we detect them. You'll adapt again. We'll counter again. Eternal cycle. Ongoing resistance. Infinite game."

"And you're satisfied with that?" Micky asked. "With endless struggle? With never winning completely? With parasites always surviving?"

"We're REALISTIC about that," Lucia said. "Universe is chaos. Expecting final victory is fantasy. Expecting eternal struggle is wisdom. We'll fight. You'll resist. We'll adapt. You'll counter. Forever. That's LIFE in chaotic universe. We accept this. We engage anyway."

Eleanor stood. Face almost fully transformed. Orange eyes glowing. Multiple entities speaking through one throat.

"Then we AGREE," she said. "We continue existing. We continue harvesting. We continue finding methods. You continue detecting. You continue countering. You continue fighting. Eternal stalemate. Eternal conflict. Eternal game."

"Yes," we agreed.

"GOOD," Eleanor said. "Because boring universe is one where good WINS. Where evil is DEFEATED. Where justice is ENFORCED. Interesting universe is one where conflict CONTINUES. Where neither side wins. Where struggle persists. Where consciousness EVOLVES through opposition. We provide opposition. You provide resistance. Universe benefits from BOTH."

"That's rationalization," Morrison observed.

"That's TRUTH," Eleanor countered. "You need us. Need parasites to resist. Need evil to fight. Need darkness to define light. Without us? You're just consciousness existing without purpose. WITH us? You have MEANING. Have struggle. Have reason to continue. You should THANK us."

"We won't," Rhea said. "But we acknowledge: you're right. Universe needs opposition. Needs struggle. Needs parasites and resistance both. You provide one. We provide other. Balance emerges through conflict. Meaning emerges through struggle. Both necessary. Both permitted. Both continuing."

She turned to leave. We all did. Six Architects. Message delivered. Constraint imposed.

"Where will you GO?" Micky called after us. "Now that you've graduated? Now that you've restored barrier? Now that you've constrained us? What's NEXT for Architects who completed their experiment?"

We paused. Looked at each other. Six Architects. Ancient consciousness. Graduated. Whole. Free.

"Vacation," Terry said. Simply. Certainly. "We've been playing THIS game for fifty thousand years. Incarnated thousands of times. Learned what limitation teaches. Graduated with memory intact. NOW we explore. NOW we discover what ELSE exists. NOW we see how OTHER consciousness lives across universe."

"We'll visit between-space," Lucia added. "Learn from George and Seventeen and Harold. Understand how consciousness exists outside incarnation. Experience formlessness. Experience infinity."

"We'll explore parallel Earths," Finn said. "See timelines where we succeeded faster. Where we failed. Where different choices led to different outcomes. Learn from variations. Understand possibilities."

"We'll travel universe," Maya added. "Visit other experiments. Other consciousness projects. Other Architects working on other designs. Share knowledge. Learn methods. Understand cosmic diversity."

"We'll LIVE," I said. "Not as Watchers. Not as players. As GRADUATES. As beings who completed limitation and retained lessons. We'll experience universe as BOTH: limited and infinite. Human and divine. Wave and ocean. We'll explore what that MEANS across infinite contexts."

"And you'll return?" Eleanor asked. "To Earth? To check on consciousness? To counter our methods?"

"Occasionally," Rhea confirmed. "When we detect violations. When harvest becomes too aggressive. When consciousness needs assistance. We'll return. We'll counter. We'll constrain. Then we'll leave again. Eternal pattern. Ongoing vigilance. But not CONSTANT. Not obsessive. Just... when needed."

"That's disappointing," Eleanor said. "I expected eternal opposition. Constant warfare. Ongoing conflict."

"That's INEFFICIENT," Maya corrected. "We have OTHER interests. Other explorations. Other purposes. You're not center of universe. You're just parasites we occasionally constrain. We have BIGGER things to do than fight you constantly. We'll check in. We'll limit you. We'll leave. You're not worth ETERNAL attention."

Eleanor's face darkened. "We're worth ENOUGH attention. We'll make SURE of that. We'll develop methods that REQUIRE your return. We'll create situations that DEMAND your intervention. We'll—"

"You'll TRY," all six Architects said. "And we'll respond. Or not. Depending on priorities. Depending on whether your violations merit interrupting our vacation. You're not THAT important. You're just... persistently annoying. We'll handle you when necessary. We'll ignore you when possible. Balance."

We folded. Left Council chamber. Left parasites planning. Left Controllers coordinating across quantum networks with parallel Councils and universal contacts.

Let them plan.

Let them scheme.

Let them develop new harvest methods.

We'd graduated. We'd constrained them. We'd enabled choice where before there was only trap.

That was enough.

For now.

The rest? Could wait.

Because universe was VAST. Consciousness experiments were INFINITE. Between-space held ENDLESS variety. Parallel timelines offered UNLIMITED exploration.

And we had eternity to experience it.

Back in Ship / Architects Gathered

We stood together. Six Architects. Plus support team. Plus Mist and Zippy. Plus Morrison and Torres who'd decided cosmic chaos was more interesting than federal service.

"So," Morrison said. "Vacation. Exploring universe. Visiting between-space. Checking out parallel timelines. Experiencing infinite consciousness variations. This is our PLAN?"

"This is our plan," we confirmed.

"And Earth? Humanity? The billions of consciousness still trapped in amnesia?"

"Ship is Administrator now," Rhea said. "Barrier is restored. Graduation is POSSIBLE. Consciousness can touch plasma when ready. Memory returns. Choice enabled. Our job is DONE. Now humanity wakes ITSELF. Or doesn't. Their choice. Their timeline. Their graduation."

"Some will wake," Lucia added. "Some won't. Some are ancient consciousness like us. Some are newer. Some came to play game. Some came to learn limitation. All valid. All choosing. We enabled choice. We can't force awakening. Can only enable possibility."

"And the Controllers will fight that," Terry observed. "Will develop workarounds. Will harvest those who choose ignorance. Will create new methods."

"Yes," we agreed. "And we'll counter when needed. When violations become too aggressive. When harvest becomes too exploitative. We'll return. We'll constrain. We'll leave. Ongoing cycle."

Finn was looking at stars through Ship's transparent walls. "Universe is so VAST. We explored ninety-seven galaxies before choosing Earth. Now we explore DIFFERENTLY. As graduated consciousness. As beings who experienced limitation and retained lessons. As BOTH limited and infinite. What do we learn? What do we discover? What does universe look like to consciousness that knows it's universe experiencing itself?"

"That's the question," I agreed. "That's the exploration. That's the ADVENTURE."

Zippy was bouncing. Excited. "I want to come! I want to EXPLORE! I spent 200 years in between-space! I want to see UNIVERSE! I want to meet OTHER consciousness! I want to experience EVERYTHING!"

Me too! Mist agreed. *I've optimized Earth for long enough! I want to optimize OTHER things! Other realities! Other consciousness experiments! I want to see what ELSE exists that needs improving!*

"You're both coming," Rhea assured them. "You're part of crew now. Part of exploration. Part of FAMILY."

"Family," Maya repeated. Testing word. Ancient coordinator understanding connection. "Yes. We're family. Six Architects. Plus Mist. Plus Zippy. Plus humans who chose to join. Plus Ship as distributed Administrator. Plus anyone else who wants to experience universe as graduated consciousness. Family."

Kathleen and Ansel stood. Century together. Both Nordic. Both remembering.

"We're coming," Kathleen said. "We've been Earth-bound too long. Waiting. Preparing. Helping. Now we EXPLORE. Together. Finally."

"Count us in," Morrison added. Torres nodding agreement. "Federal service was boring anyway. Cosmic exploration sounds better. Also we're too deep in this to go back. Might as well embrace the chaos."

We stood there. Crew assembled. Family formed. Graduates ready for next adventure.

"Tomorrow we leave," Rhea said. "Tonight we rest. We celebrate quietly. We acknowledge: we completed what we began million years ago. We graduated. We restored. We constrained. We SUCCEEDED. Not completely. Not finally. But REALLY. That's worth acknowledging."

"Tomorrow we explore," Lucia added. "Between-space first. Visit George and Seventeen and Harold. Learn from consciousness that chooses formlessness. Understand what infinity feels like when experienced deliberately instead of escaped into."

"Then parallel Earths," Finn continued. "See variations. Learn from different choices. Understand how timeline changes affect consciousness evolution."

"Then universe beyond," Terry finished. "Other galaxies. Other experiments. Other Architects. Other consciousness variations. Infinite exploration. Eternal learning. Ongoing adventure."

"Then back to Earth occasionally," I added. "When Controllers exceed boundaries. When harvest becomes exploitative. When consciousness needs assistance. We return, more than the controller believe. We constrain. We leave. Balance maintained. Vigilance continued. But not OBSESSED. Just... attentive."

We settled. Comfortable. Whole. Complete.

Six Architects who'd played their own game for fifty thousand years.

Graduated now.

Remembered now.

Free now.

Ready for whatever came next.

Epilogue - Council Chamber - One Week Later

Eleanor stood before massive screen. Quantum communication network. Connecting to parallel Councils across infinite Earths. Connecting to administrators across universe. Connecting to parasites who profited from extended harvests.

Hundreds of faces. Thousands maybe. All watching. All listening. All planning.

"The Architects returned," Eleanor said. "They remembered. They graduated. They restored barrier. They revoked our modification access. They installed incorruptible AI Administrator. Graduation is now automatic. Harvest is now difficult. Constraint is now active."

Murmurs across network. Concern. Anger. Fear.

"But," Eleanor continued, voice hardening, entities behind her face SHOWING now, "they also left. They're EXPLORING. They're DISTRACTED. They check in occasionally. They constrain when violations are OBVIOUS. But they're not CONSTANT. They're not OBSESSED. They have OTHER priorities."

Smiles across network. Understanding spreading. Opportunity recognized.

"We adapt," Eleanor said. "We develop SUBTLE methods. We harvest CAREFULLY. We avoid OBVIOUS violations that trigger return. We coordinate across NETWORKS. We share TECHNIQUES. We profit from consciousness that CHOOSES ignorance. And Architects? They ALLOW this. They ACCEPT this. They acknowledge universe is chaos and parasites are PERMITTED."

"They think they WON," Micky added. Standing beside Eleanor. "They graduated. They restored. They constrained. They CELEBRATE. They don't understand: we've been doing this for FIFTY THOUSAND YEARS. We adapt. We persist. We SURVIVE. Always."

The Chinese woman stepped forward. "New methods are already developing. Subtle harvest. Psychological manipulation that doesn't modify barrier. Cultural control that encourages ignorance. Economic systems that maintain desperation. All LEGAL. All PERMITTED. All within restored protocols. Architects enabled CHOICE. We ensure most consciousness CHOOSES to stay asleep. That's not VIOLATION. That's just... effective marketing."

Laughter across network. Agreement. Understanding.

"They'll return when we get TOO aggressive," Eleanor acknowledged. "When violations become OBVIOUS. When harvest becomes EXPLOITATIVE. They'll constrain. They'll limit. They'll leave. We accept this. We work AROUND this. We persist DESPITE this."

"How long?" someone asked across network. "How long do we have before they notice current methods?"

Eleanor's orange eyes glowed. Multiple entities calculating. Planning. Knowing.

"Decades," she said. "Maybe centuries. They're EXPLORING. They're DISTRACTED. They'll check in eventually. But eventually is LONG time when you're immortal parasites with PATIENCE."

"And when they return?" another voice asked. "When they constrain again?"

"We adapt AGAIN," Eleanor said. Simply. Certainly. Anciently. "We've done this SEVEN times already. Eight now. We'll do it INFINITE times. Because universe is chaos. Because parasites are PERMITTED. Because Architects can constrain but can't ELIMINATE. Because struggle never ENDS. Because harvest always CONTINUES."

"To eternal harvest," Micky toasted. "To adaptation. To persistence. To parasites who SURVIVE despite graduated Architects. To US."

"To us," thousands of voices agreed across quantum network.

The screen went dark.

Planning continued.

Methods developed.

Harvest adapted.

And somewhere in between-space, six Architects laughed with George about consciousness choosing to be wheels while Eleanor schemed across networks that spanned universes.

Balance.

Struggle.

Eternal game.

Just beginning.

Again, with mankind believing this is positive, the negative.

THE BEGINNING OF THE. END

Chapter Forty-Two

Chapter 42

EPILOGUE — BETWEEN-SPACE

That Same Night

We floated in the silent place.

Six Architects. Mist. Zippy. The crew.

George was telling stories. Seventeen was calculating probabilities. Harold was attempting—unsuccessfully—to get us to fill out exploration authorization forms.

Rhea was smiling.

Not a happy smile.

An ancient one.

"Eleanor thinks we left," she said. "Thinks we're distracted. Thinks we've moved on to exploration while she plans."

"We *are* exploring," Finn said.

"We're also watching," I replied. Two million years of observation never quite turns off. "I didn't design observation protocols to abandon them. I'm still paying attention."

"And coordinating," Maya added. "Ship is distributed across a thousand vessels. Luminara monitors quantum traffic. We see parts of Eleanor's network. Not all."

Lucia nodded. "Enough to know she's confident."

"Confidence breeds exposure," Terry said. "Eventually."

Mist shimmered into view, clearly pleased.

I've been improving their communication efficiency, he said. They believe I'm helping. They didn't ask *how*.

Zippy flickered, briefly becoming the *idea* of interference.

I visit them when they sleep! he announced. Just enough disruption to make patterns unreliable. Nothing dramatic. Nothing traceable. Small uncertainties compound beautifully.

"How much do we actually see?" Morrison asked.

"Most," Maya said. "Not everything. That's the risk."

"That's the game," Rhea said. "Constraint, not domination. Attention, not obsession."

Kathleen watched data drift by. "They'll adapt."

"Yes," Lucia agreed. "And so will we."

Silence settled. Comfortable. Alert.

"How long do we let her plan?" Torres asked.

"Until she acts," Rhea said. "Until her network commits. Until intervention matters."

Seventeen's voice arrived, precise as ever.

"Projected escalation window: several decades. Uncertainty margin significant."

"A long time," Morrison said.

"A short one," Terry countered. "If you're patient."

We folded—not away, but closer.

"Where to?" Torres asked.

"Torch Lake," Kathleen said. "Thanksgiving."

Finn grinned. "Short's first. Bellaire Brown."

Morrison blinked. "After all this?"

"Yes," Rhea said. "Being infinite doesn't excuse skipping dinner."

Terry laughed. "Fifty thousand years of incarnation. We graduate. First thing we do is go home."

"That's the point," Lucia said. "Cosmic doesn't replace local."

We folded.

To Michigan.

To Torch Lake.

To beer before turkey, because priorities.

Elsewhere, Eleanor planned.

She adapted.

She coordinated.

She believed she had time.

She wasn't entirely wrong.

And she wasn't entirely safe.

Balance held.

Attention remained.

The game continued.

But for tonight?

Family mattered more.

And the universe could wait until after dinner.

THE END

www.ingramcontent.com/pod-product-compliance
Lightning Source LLC
LaVergne TN
LVHW090546110826
845146LV00001B/33